The Poseidon Adventure

Paul Gallico

T0314369

The Poseidon Adventure
Copyright © 1969, 2014 by Paul Gallico

All rights reserved. No part of this book may be used or reproduced in any form or by any electronic or mechanical means, including information storage and retrieval systems, without permission in writing from the publisher, except by a reviewer who may quote brief passages in a review.

ISBN: 978-0-7953-0071-4

FOR JOHN TUCKER HAYWARD
YANKEE BAT-BOY;
ADMIRAL U.S.N.;
FRIEND

CHAPTER I

Rehearsal for Disaster

At seven o'clock, the morning of the 26th day of December, the S.S. *Poseidon*, 81,000 tons, homeward bound for Lisbon after a month-long Christmas cruise to African and South American ports, suddenly found herself in the midst of an unaccountable swell, 400 miles south-west of the Azores, and began to roll like a pig.

The *Poseidon*, formerly the R.M.S. *Atlantis*, the first of the giant transatlantic liners to become outmoded, sold and converted to a combination of cargo and cruise trade, entered the area with her fuel tanks two-thirds empty and no water ballast replacement. The curiously long, low waves she was encountering came at intervals just too far apart to be caught by the lagging synchronization of her out-of-date and partially damaged stabilizers. Thus, she reeled drunkenly from side to side with the result that the motion combined with the hangover from the practically all-night, gala Christmas party and dance made the bulk of her five hundred odd, one-class Travel Consortium Limited passengers miserably and uncompromisingly ill.

The big switchboard serving the cabin telephones began to light up like the Christmas tree decorating the grand dining-saloon. Calls for help swamped the office of the ship's medico, Dr Caravello, a seventy-five-year-old Italian dragged from retirement by the International Syndicate operating the trip, and his assistant Marco, an intern just out of medical school. There were also a head nurse and two sisters. The telephone in the surgery never stopped ringing. Unable to cope personally, the Doctor simply sent around pills and instructions to remain in bed. All this took place in bright tropical sunlight on a sea which, except for the interminable swells, was barely ruffled.

To add to the unhappiness of the retching passengers, things in the cabins came alive. Everything unattached—trunks, hand luggage, bottles—slid from side to side; clothing hung upon pegs took on animation, swaying outwards and back again. Nerves were further jangled by the protesting creaks and groans of the old ship's joints and the distant crashes of breaking crockery. Seasick remedies eventually lost both their potency and psychological magic. By mid-morning as far as the travellers were concerned, their happy home throughout an otherwise gay and uneventful voyage had become a hell.

As always, however, there were a few hardy exceptions, that small percentage of good sailors to be found on every liner which says, 'I never get sick' and don't.

Thus, shortly before noon Mr James Martin, proprietor of a men's haberdashery shop in Evanston, Illinois, travelling alone and unaffected by the movement, telephoned to Mrs Wilma Lewis, a widow from Chicago. Mrs Lewis was not amongst the fortunate and said, 'For God's sake don't bother me! Just let me die quietly.' And when he asked, 'Mayn't I come and see you?' groaned, 'No!' and hung up.

In another cabin Mrs Linda Rogo was abusing her husband, between bouts of being sick, with every obscenity of an experienced vocabulary. Mrs Rogo was an ex-Hollywood starlet and briefly a Broadway actress, convinced that she had lowered herself and sacrificed her career when she married Mike Rogo, plain-clothes detective of the Broadway Strong Arm squad. Between calling him every gutter name she could muster, she developed the theme that he had made her come upon this voyage of which she had hated every minute and now had not even the grace to be ill. Mike Rogo, unable to placate his wife, eventually fled the cabin followed by her curses.

Dr Frank Scott—the Doctor was not an M.D. but a Doctor of Divinity—telephoned Mr Richard Shelby of Detroit and said, 'Hi, Dick!' and got back, 'Hi, Frank!'

'How's the family standing up?'

'Okay, up to now.'

Scott said, 'There goes our squash game.'

'I'll say!'

'If this stops, we might have a try this afternoon.'

'Right!'

'See you at lunch.'

'Okay, Buzz.'

The two men had been drawn together during the cruise by common interest in football and athletics. The Reverend Doctor Scott no more than five years ago had been Frank 'Buzz' Scott, Princeton's All-America full back, all-around athlete, two-time Olympic decathlon champion and mountain climber.

Richard Shelby, Scott's senior by some twenty years, travelling with his family, Vice-President of Cranborne Motors of Detroit, in charge of commercial vehicle design, had been a useful end at Michigan in his day.

Mrs Timker, director of the Gresham Girls, the dancing troupe connected with the floating cabaret which had been entertaining thrice weekly throughout the voyage, though considering herself in the last throes, still had the strength to send around a message to the members of her company, 'No show tonight.' One of the dancers, a thin girl from Bristol, Nona Parry, with red hair and a pale, somewhat too-small face who should have been sick but was not, said, 'Oh goody! I can wash my hair.'

At eleven-thirty the only three passengers visible in the smoke-room were an English alcoholic called Tony Bates, his girl friend Pamela Reid and Hubie Muller, a lone American from San Francisco.

The Englishman, who had been nicknamed The Beamer, and Pamela had their legs coiled around bar stools which had been firmly screwed to the floor, while the batman served them their double martinis in deep whisky tumblers to keep them from slopping over as the ship canted. Neither of them were suffering from hangovers or *mal de mer*, as they were both amiably and hazily drunk and had been since the night before and on through the morning, not having been to bed at all.

Muller, a wealthy bachelor of no occupation, in his early forties, man about Europe and darling of every Mama with an eligible daughter on two continents, had wedged himself, feet up, into one of the leather corners of the smoke-room with a book and a half bottle of champagne. He was not ill but the book was bad, the champagne would not stay in the glass, the cruise had not been particularly successful for him and he was bored stiff. The ceaseless swooning of the ship he took as a personal affront.

In his cabin Mr Rosen, a retired delicatessen owner, queried his wife, 'Are you all right, Mamma? You feeling all right?'

Belle Rosen replied, 'Certainly. Why shouldn't I be feeling all right?'

Mr Rosen, who in his striped pyjamas and hair mussed managed to look like a small, plump child, said, 'I hear everybody is pretty sick.'

'Well, I'm not sick,' said Belle. She was a fat woman whose bulk almost filled her bed and she had so managed to plug the remaining space with pillows and a suitcase that she was fairly well immobilized against the motion.

Down in the ladies' hairdressing saloon on 'D' deck the hairdresser struggled to work on a blonde, shoulder-length wig that had been sent down to her by Mrs Gleeson of cabin M. 119, to be washed and set, with instructions that it be delivered to her no later than nine o'clock that evening. Marie, the hairdresser, was wondering when and where Mrs Gleeson was going to wear it if this kept up. In cabin M. 119 five decks up, Mrs Gleeson was beyond caring about anything.

Another widow, Mrs Reid, was not only desperately sick but suffering mental anguish as well over the disastrous turn the voyage had taken for her. In part its purpose had been in the hopes of finding a husband for her rather dowdy daughter. Pamela had had the bad taste to become appallingly infatuated with the most unsuitable man on the ship and with whom she was now no doubt drinking at one of the too many available bars.

Completely unaffected by the nauseating motion was Miss Mary Kinsale, spinster, head book-keeper of the branch of Browne's Bank in Camberley, near London, a reticent, tidy little woman whose outstanding feature was a huge length of glossy brown hair which she wore drawn tightly back from her face and coiled into a tremendous bun at the back of her head and descending to the nape of her neck. She had a small prim mouth but her eyes were alert and ingenuously interested.

An attempt at having breakfast served to her in bed had been unsuccessful since the movement of the vessel had made it necessary to suspend all tray service and she was hungry. She had picked up her telephone, asked for the dining-room and inquired, 'Will there be any lunch today?' to which the rather horrified voice of the assistant chief steward had repeated, 'Lunch!'

Miss Kinsale at once said apologetically, 'Oh dear, I don't mean to be any trouble to anyone.'

The voice at the other end also apologized, 'No, no, madam, not at all. It's just that we hadn't been expecting many. We'll be only too delighted to have someone to serve. But I'm afraid it will be only cold food. We shan't be cooking in the kitchens.'

'Oh, that will be quite all right,' Miss Kinsale replied. 'Thank you so much. Anything will do.' Not even in the twenty-seven or so days of the cruise that far had she been able to accustom herself to luxury treatment or overcome her shyness at being served.

When at one o'clock in the afternoon the dining-room page, whose duty it was to signal that they were open for business, came staggering along the slanting corridors striking 'Bim, bom, bum, bim' on his portable xylophone gong, the sound hitherto only too welcome to the ears of the for ever hungry, he collected this time only a meagre pied-piped train of followers. They came from their various quarters on Main and 'A' decks, lurching, slipping, sliding, clinging on to the guide-ropes that had been put up, shouting warnings to one another, negotiating the stairs a step at a time since the lifts were not running. It was actually dangerous going but these people of lusty constitutions and unaffected semicircular canals of the inner ear were seized by a certain camaraderie of hazard and the novelty of the careening platform beneath their feet which caused them either at one moment a laborious uphill climb and at the next to be launched like something out of a catapult. Thus half a hundred or so hardy souls gathered in the dining-saloon below on 'R' for Restaurant Deck.

The Shelby family: Richard, Jane his wife, Susan their seventeen-year-old daughter and Robin aged ten, made their slightly raucous way inching down the grand staircase.

For the fifth time tubby little Manny Rosen struggled to his feet with an attempted bow to say, 'Welcome to The Strong Stomach Club!'

His wife Belle said, 'Oh stop it, Manny! Ain't it bad enough without you making a joke?'

The Rosens had a table for two on the extreme port side of the dining-saloon by one of the big square, brass-bound windows giving out on to the sea that slid by no more than a few yards below. Next to them Hubie Muller occupied another table for two by himself. He also had had a standing reservation for a tête-à-tête table in the Observation Grill topside, in case an intimate friendship should occur during the voyage. An inveterate traveller he had made half a dozen crossings New York–Cherbourg, Southampton–New York in the days when the *Poseidon* had been the *Atlantis* and he knew all the ropes. The hoped-for situation however had never developed.

All the tables along the windows were twosomes but the others seated up to eight diners to promote get-togetherness. Close by the Rosens and near one of the entrances to the serving pantries, from which the stewards emerged with their heaped-up trays was the one named the grab-bag table by Susan Shelby for its mixture of persons. Its full complement numbered the Reverend Doctor Scott, Miss Kinsale, James Martin, the Rogos and Mr Kyrenos the Third Engineer Officer.

Miss Kinsale and James Martin the Evanston haberdasher, were already there when Mike Rogo arrived alone to receive his induction speech from Manny who added, 'Where's Linda? She quittin' on us?'

Rogo said, 'Linda ain't speakin' to me. She thinks it's me rockin' the boat.'

As the Shelby family staggered to the adjoining table, the ship heeled over again, catching young Robin Shelby without a handhold and yelling, 'Yay-yay-yay-yay-yay!' all the way, he shot down the side of the saloon to collide violently with Mike Rogo and bounce off him on to the floor. 'Wow!' he said.

Robin was a sturdy boy who was going to be as athletic as his father. But Mike Rogo picked him up off the floor as though he had been an infant and set him on his feet with, 'You could'a hurt yourself, sonny. You better hold on to somethin'.' Rogo, a hundred-and-fifty-pounder was himself as strong as a little bull.

Martin asked of the steward Peters, 'Say, what's going on here, anyway? We're in a calm sea and the old tub is falling all over herself.'

Peters said, 'I can't exactly say, sir. There's probably been a storm somewhere ahead of us. You often get swells like that then.'

The Shelbys had got themselves seated when Tony Bates and Pamela Reid somehow made a perfectly normal, straightforward descent down the centre of the wide staircase and as steadfastly marched across the saloon to his table for two on the fat starboard side. In some mysterious fashion the alcohol in which they were soaked contrived to counteract the gyrations of the liner.

'Oh look, Mom!' Susan cried, 'The Beamer's made it with his girl. Aren't they wonderful? How does she do it? If I take just a sip of sherry it makes me feel funny.'

Richard Shelby said, 'Hollow leg.' He and his wife were a handsome couple and their daughter a fresh, gay creature. She had her father's somewhat square jawline and dark hair and her mother's refinement and vivacity combined with the American schoolgirl's sexless figure.

The new arrivals were too far even for shouting, so Manny Rosen could only stand up and wave a welcome, for he liked them. The Beamer beamed back.

A further scattering of passengers made their precarious way into the dining-saloon: Greeks, Belgians, a family of eight from Düsseldorf by the extraordinary name of Augenblick and a dozen or so others including British, Americans and some hardy Scandinavians. Rosen did not attempt to include them in the fold of The Strong Stomach Club since they were distributed at tables far removed over the vast area of the room. This honour he reserved for the little group who through the neighbourliness of the seating arrangements had come to acknowledge one another during the voyage.

Lunch, at least to Robin Shelby, was threatening to develop into something exciting. Fiddles or racks were up on the tables to keep plates and cutlery from sliding to the floor and Peters with Acre his partner, the two stewards who served the four tables, performed ballets of equilibrium as they balanced trays.

The six-foot-four of the Reverend Frank Scott came striding to his table rather giving the impression that he was impelling the ship with his legs than that the rolling vessel was moving him.

Manny Rosen started to say, 'Welcome to...' but when Belle put her hand firmly on his arm, changed it to, 'Hi, Frank! We knew you'd make it.'

Throughout the voyage it had been difficult to think of Scott as 'The Reverend'. Nearly everyone called him Frank or Buzz with the exception of Miss Kinsale who, with her more British respect for the American cloth, insisted upon addressing him as Dr Scott, and Rogo who referred to him as either Parson or Padre and managed to make both sound faintly mocking. The Europeans on board were quite baffled by him. He was so young and his sports achievements still so recent that the American contingent was unable to see him as anything but Buzz Scott, Princeton's star full-back, two-time Olympic decathlon champion, skier, conqueror of Andes Mountain peaks and perpetual winner in the athletic lists.

Rarely off the sports pages during his college years he continued to make news during his studies at Union Theological Seminary as one of the party to climb the never before subdued San Jacinto peak in the Andes. At twenty-nine Scott was still a hustler and a bustler, an overpowering person, crew-cut, glowing with health and just saved from All-American-boy beauty by the wavering line of a broken nose. He had a direct, frank look-you-right-in-the-eye gaze that was both attractive and compelling and yet in a way also vaguely disconcerting, something undefinable and slightly disturbing behind the frankness. When he was at his games the glare of combat that came into his eyes was more suggestive of a heavyweight prize-fighter than a Minister of the Gospel.

It was certainly true that he was all over the ship during the cruise, slashing bullet shots into unbeatable corners on the squash court; pounding out five miles around the promenade deck with a train of admiring youngsters in his wake, shattering clay pigeons without a miss at the sun deck skeet shoots; overwhelming opponents at deck tennis.

His bronze torso had been on exhibition at the pool side. He daily violated the pulleys and exercise apparatus in the ship's gymnasium or put on gloves and toyed with the instructor there, a British ex-middleweight champion.

Jane Shelby once remarked to her husband that, for her liking, he took up just slightly too much space. Her thoughts about his eyes she kept to herself for it seemed too absurd to suggest that so famous a public sports figure might harbour a touch of the fanatic except when he seemed to have carried the aura of the football field over into his own peculiar brand of evangelism.

On this score he had managed to create a considerable impression by a sermon he had delivered one Sunday, when he had been asked to take Divine Service and from which one had gathered that he was keeping himself fit and would continue to do so to score victories for God.

Indeed, he had said outright during his discourse, 'God wants winners! God loves triers. He did not create you in His image to run second. He has no use for quitters, whiners or beggars. Every trial you're called upon to endure is an act of worship. Respect and stand up for yourselves and you will be respecting and standing up for Him. Let Him know that if He can't help you, you've got the guts and the will to go it alone. Fight for yourselves and He will be fighting at your side uninvited. When you succeed, it is because you've accepted Him, and He is in you. When you dog it, you've denied Him.'

It had not been exactly Sunday church to which the various communicants had been accustomed but for the moment they had found themselves succumbing to the sincerity and fervour of his beliefs and they all had to admit in the end that at least it had been an experience and had given them something to talk about.

Jane Shelby, upon emerging from the main lounge where the service had taken place, had said, 'Phew! I feel as though I ought to go out and beat someone at something.' And then she said, 'Do you know, that young man talks as though he believes he's signed on as head coach for God's team.'

Her husband had replied irrelevantly and yet almost with a kind of reverence, 'He was the greatest football player ever turned out at Princeton.'

Jane Shelby said, 'God should be pleased with that,' and he looked at her sharply to see whether she was joking but saw that she was keeping a perfectly straight face. Sometimes there were things about his wry, clear-eyed wife that eluded Richard Shelby. She had then asked suddenly, 'What do you suppose he's doing on this cruise?'

'Oh,' her husband had replied, 'he told me. Taking a vocation between jobs.'

'Between what jobs?'

'I don't know,' Shelby had replied. 'I didn't ask him.'

She then queried, 'Whatever do you suppose made a man like that go into the Church?' Then she added, 'You like him, don't you?' Jane Shelby was quite well aware that her husband practically hero-worshipped the younger Scott. She was quite prepared to look with her dry-humoured understanding on little boys who never grew up but there were unanswered questions about Scott that worried her and she wished that her husband were not quite so enchanted with his virtues.

Shelby replied, 'Yes. He's quite a boy.'

Actually, secretly Scott's choice of profession worried Dick Shelby, too. What made it all the more difficult for Shelby to understand was that Scott had come from a wealthy family. A spectacularly successful boy, what *had* led him into the ministry?

Shelby himself was neither religious nor irreligious; he was simply a lifelong social and intellectual conformer. He believed that most men went into the Church because they were not fit for anything else. The breed was completely foreign to him but because it was incumbent to his position as a Motors Vice President, he alternated Sundays between the exclusive Bloomfield Hills Country Club and the equally exclusive Grosse Point Episcopal Church.

Upon the latter occasions he sat in his pew as befitted the head of the All-American family; his eyes properly lowered, his mind tightly shut to the abstractions produced by Dr Goodall from the pulpit. He considered the Rector to be a thundering bore, but conceded that he had a place in the social pattern and so was doing his job with the minimum of interference in the life of Dick Shelby. Religious feeling or emotion in no way entered the arrangement.

Jane had then asked suddenly. 'He wouldn't be running away from something, would he? Or having a last fling?'

Shelby's consciousness of things as they ought to be brought forth the reply, 'Ministers don't have flings,' and then quickly added in defence, 'Not that Frank is stuffy and he must have had plenty of passes made at him during the trip, but I'm sure he hasn't responded to any of them.'

Jane had said, 'How do we know?' and then teased, 'He's probably too exhausted by nightfall.' Her husband hadn't thought it was funny.

The *Poseidon* now heeled over again and Robin Shelby shouted, 'Whoa-a-a-a there!' Scott loomed over the table, his huge frame following the angle of the ship. On the counter roll he slipped gracefully into his chair.

Martin, a thin-lipped, wispy, greyish bantam cock of a man who never seemed to have a great deal to say, observed, 'You're just in time to join Manny's little organization—The Strong Stomach Club.'

Scott grinned, showing fine even teeth, except for one in front that had been chipped in his last game. His smile faded as he saw Rogo alone and he said, 'Is Mrs Rogo ill?' Even though the voyage was drawing to a close they were not on first-name terms. His voice had a fine timbre and was pleasant to the ear.

'Yeah,' said Rogo.

Scott said, 'I'm sorry.'

Rogo said, 'Thanks,' and did not bother to keep the sarcasm out of his voice. He did not like Scott. In spite of his formidable physical attributes and reputation, Scott was a rah-rah boy to Rogo. All college-bred men, but in particular football players, were rah-rah boys to Rogo. The Columbia campus was a canker to him on the heart line of his beloved Broadway. He bristled with the age-old enmity between town and gown.

Muller called over from his near-by table, 'Where's Mr Kyrenos?'

Shelby replied, 'None of the officers seem to be here. I hope everything's all right.'

Muller speared an olive and went at it in two bites with it held between thumb and forefinger. He said, 'All I know is it's devilishly uncomfortable. Why the deuce doesn't the Captain do something about it?'

Rogo turned about in his chair to stare at Muller for a moment, his flat face showing unconcealed disgust. His contempt for Muller was almost as great as his dislike for Scott. If Scott was a rah-rah boy to Rogo, Muller was a sissy or a la-di-da. The San Franciscan was soft-spoken, soft-muscled, with too-white too-soft hands, slow moving and indolent and who, affecting the broad 'a' in speech, talked like what Rogo termed a half-ass Limey. He was further irritated by the cut of Muller's tailormade clothes.

Rogo himself actually was proud of his own carefully manicured fingernails, but his hands were lumpy and battered where he had broken every knuckle upon the jaws or skulls of characters who had 'argued' with him. Arguing with him was Rogo's euphemism for resisting arrest. He was also something of a dude in dress, except that his clothes were unmistakably Broadway. He also always spoke in the slightly too-loud voice of the policeman who has become a successful plain-clothes detective. In his own way Rogo was something of a celebrity, particularly to New Yorkers, and held the Police Honour Medal for going in singlehanded to break up a prison riot at Westchester Plains, in which convicts had already killed two hostages.

He had a bland, smooth-skinned face in which was set a pair of little piggy eyes, lids drawn down at the corners and which were never quite free from suspicion. To this was added a bashed-in nose acquired as a Golden Gloves welterweight champion. He hardly parted the whole of his mouth for speaking. He rarely smiled. His beat was the Broadway theatrical district between 38th and 50th, 6th to 9th Avenues, embracing some of New York's most unsavoury characters: rich gangsters, junkies, stick-up men, homos—they were all alike to Rogo when he belted them.

Belle Rosen said, 'Poor Linda, can I do anything for her?'

The detective said, 'Nah, thanks, Belle. I guess she just wants to be left alone.'

The Rosens and Rogo had known one another slightly in New York before they met again on the Christmas cruise of the *Poseidon*. The late-night crowd often patronized what Rosen referred to as his Pastrami Palace at Amsterdam Avenue and 74th Street before going home and Rogo sometimes used to drop in and look them over. This was sufficient to guarantee peace and quiet in Manny Rosen's delicatessen.

Rogo's presence aboard the ship, despite his assurances that he was on his first holiday from his beat for five years, was never wholly accepted by the passengers. They preferred the fillip of mystery at having a real detective on board and produced a spate of gags such as: 'You look as though that dick had caught you in somebody else's cabin,' or: 'Why don't you give yourself up?' or, 'I saw the fuzz had his eye on you in the bar all last night.'

Also the *Poseidon* rumour factory never gave up on the theory that Rogo was there for business, not pleasure. He was 'after' someone on the ship. The idea of a tough, Broadway cop dressing for dinner every night and going on sightseeing shore trips in Senegal, Liberia, the Ivory Coast or entering in the ping-pong tournament, simply did not wash with the gossipers and a number of attempts were made to pump him.

Rogo's slightly vacant eyes of the professional destroyer would narrow into a squint of amusement, the closest he ever came to humour, when he was queried as to what was his real mission aboard and he would say, 'Ain't a cop got a right to have a vacation? Could be I wanted to see where all them jigaboos we got back home come from. Maybe I could get 'em to take some back.'

The motion of the ship had become regularly spaced though the angle of inclination was not always the same. Her old bones protested each roll.

Richard Shelby leaned over towards the grab-bag table and said, 'No game today, Frank.'

Scott grinned at him and said, 'Like to try anyway? I'll bet it would be interesting. Spot you five points.'

Shelby's wife, horrified, said, 'Oh no, Dick!'

Shelby looked uncomfortable for a moment, uncertain whether Scott was serious or not to risk breaking an arm or a leg in a canting court. But Jane had no doubts that the Minister was prepared to try. He seemed to be a lunatic where games were concerned.

Shelby decided that Scott was kidding and said, 'Mother says no.'

On the other side of the dining-saloon The Beamer, who was a partner in a stockbroking firm in the City of London, said, 'I'll have a double dry martini.'

Pamela added, 'I'll have the same.' She was a plain, rather lumpy English girl with the thick legs attributed to games mistresses, dun-coloured hair cropped close and short and a high-flush complexion. But she had clear, friendly blue eyes and her expression, particularly when regarding The Beamer was one of almost perpetual wonder. Travelling with her mother she had attached herself to him during the voyage, or perhaps it was the other way around. She was innocently and captivatingly in love with him.

The Beamer asked, 'How's your dear old Mum?'

'Sick,' the girl replied.

'Pity,' said The Beamer and beamed at her. 'Then maybe we can have dinner together as well tonight.'

She smiled back at him. Bates was far from handsome; fortyish with a round, red, innocent face, he arranged thinning hairs neatly across the top of his skull, was addicted to coloured waistcoats by day and was to be found in a silent, constant alcoholic haze which began at ten o'clock in the morning, perched upon a stool in the veranda, midships or smoke-room bar, beaming at everyone. At first he had been alone. When he made the accidental discovery that the girl could match him drink for drink and never show it, they were from then on inseparable.

The martinis arrived. The Beamer toasted, 'Cheers!'

Pamela said, 'Cheers!'

The Beamer added, 'We'd better have another.'

Robin Shelby was playing a game. He poised his bread roll and when the ship began to lean to port, he released it so that it went tumbling end-over-end until stopped by the fiddles at the edge of the table.

The *Poseidon*, which had been sailing level for a moment, now canted over to port in a slow, continuing roll that for the first time seemed as though it would never end. Robin's bread leaped on to the floor. Everything began to go. To the musical sound of plates, knives, forks and glasses colliding with the wooden racks at the ends of the tables, was added the gentle jingling of the ornaments as the fifteen-foot Christmas tree, planted in a tub of sand affixed to the floor of the dining-room, leaned over alarmingly. Far over on her side, farther it seemed than she had ever been before, the ship appeared to hang there as though she were never coming back.

Belle Rosen gasped, 'Manny, look!' For outside their window that blue and innocent, sun-gilded sea seemed to be directly beneath them as they were tilted over in their chairs. Her plump white hands gripped the table so hard that her rings cut into the flesh of her stubby fingers.

It was no longer a game to young Robin. He was frightened and did not shout, 'Yay!' or 'Wow!', but held on tightly and looked anxiously across the table at his father. A silence gripped them all and Muller, pale, half rose, bracing himself against the glass pane. He was convinced that they were going over.

The two stewards had both been serving at the time, and Peters, the taller, balancing hard against the tilt of the ship said, 'That's all right, sir,' while Acre, forced to cling to the back of one of the chairs, added, 'She'll be all right. She always comes back.'

It appeared that the big ship had never creaked or groaned or agonized so as she laboured to right herself and slowly pulled out of the roll. The sea which had come so menacingly close receded from the port windows and now showed blue sky, striated with cirrus clouds, as the vessel leant over on her starboard oscillation. She continued to oscillate diminishingly; plates and cutlery slid back into place again.

A steward appeared with a dustpan and brush and swept up the gold and silver shards of some of the tree decorations that had broken.

'Christ!' said Rogo, and then, 'That was a stinker.'

Plump Mr Rosen and his fat wife looked up at Peters in alarm.

'Listen,' continued Rosen, 'That was dangerous, wasn't it?'

The steward replied, 'Not really, sir. I've seen her do worse than this in the North Atlantic.'

Acre added, 'She can't go over sir, not the way she's built,' and he removed a dish of cold tongue that he had just put down before Mr Rosen who said, 'Hey! Wait, I haven't had it to eat yet.'

James Martin, whose eyes were quite bright behind his rimmed spectacles, noted the incident and saw as well that in that moment where the ship had seemed to hang fire for an eternity, both stewards had gone white. 'My God,' he said to himself, 'they're rattled.' He asked dryly, 'Were you praying, Frank?'

Scott replied, 'Actually I was too busy trying to hold her up with my stomach muscles.'

The general laughter relieved the tension. Shelby leaned over and said, 'If anybody can do it, you can.'

Miss Kinsale looked faintly disapproving at the Minister's remark.

Hubie Muller said irritably to Peters, 'Who are you kidding? You may have seen her lay over like that before, but I never have. What the hell is going on here? Why doesn't the Skipper slow down or change course, or something?' He was a spoiled man unused to any kind of enduring discomfort and rich enough not to be compelled to put up with it. Whenever he found himself in a situation that was not to his liking, either in the line of accommodation or company, he simply departed and went elsewhere. However, there was no getting away from the antics of the *Poseidon*.

Martin said, 'I think he's in a hurry. We're a day late now.'

Robin Shelby piped up, 'I bet the Captain was scared too.'

Scott answered, 'Captains are never scared.'

But Miss Kinsale murmured half to herself, 'Out of the mouths of babes.'

The Beamer said to his waiter, 'Phew! I'll have another double dry... No, hold on! Make it a whisky.'

'I'll have the same,' said Pamela.

The Beamer turned his seraphic glance upon her, 'That's my girl!'

The luncheon group on the port side began to break up. Manny Rosen helped his wife and said, 'Hold on to me, Mamma,' and then said to Rogo, 'You dressing for dinner tonight?'

Rogo split half of his thin mouth to reply, 'Rawthaw', in direct mockery of the two men he did not like.

Rosen said, 'Maybe Linda will come. We missed her.'

'Yeah,' said Rogo, 'maybe she will.'

The members of the grab-bag table got up. The *Poseidon* heeled again. 'Oh dear!' cried Miss Kinsale.

'Here, take my arm,' Scott offered.

Miss Kinsale fluttered, 'Oh, thank you!' but he took hers instead. They were a grotesque-looking pair, the huge man and the tiny, doll-like figure of the spinster, he practically lifting her off the floor to climb the slope of inclination and then holding her tightly against the anti-roll.

Muller said, watching them go, 'Funny guy,' and then, 'What would have happened if we hadn't snapped back, and gone right over that time?'

Martin dabbed his lips with his napkin and said, 'I reckon we'd all be dead by now. Be seeing you.'

The Shelbys arose *en masse* and clung to one another for the march to the grand staircase.

CHAPTER II

Disaster

But Robin Shelby had been right. The Greek Captain was not only a badly frightened man but when during lunchtime his ship had heeled over and it seemed as though her normal righting mechanism would never come into operation, he had been close to panic.

For in addition to a number of other sins of omission and commission, he had known that ever since they had crossed the bar of the Tagus upon leaving Lisbon, through inexperience in handling such a vast ship he had misused the stabilizers in the shallow flurry and had to all intents and purposes impaired their usefulness and efficiency. That he had been so fortunate as not to need them throughout a good weather voyage did not alter the fact that now when he did, they were functioning inadequately.

The S.S. *Poseidon* was as high as an apartment building, and as wide as a football field. Set down in New York she would have stretched from 42nd Street to 46th Street—four city blocks—or in London from Charing Cross station to the Savoy. A third of her 81,000 gross tonnage was below the waterline, crammed with propulsion and refrigeration machinery, boilers, pumps, reduction gear, dynamos, oil, ballast tanks and cargo space.

At this particular time the *Poseidon* was light, riding too high out of the water, improperly ballasted and technically unseaworthy. The Captain had been led into this trap through a series of strokes of ill luck and timing and a bad decision on his part based upon strictly commercial considerations.

The International Consortium that had purchased the liner had converted her for a freight-cruise combination, sailing out of Lisbon, visiting some fifteen countries in Africa and South America in a period of thirty days. They had tripled her cargo space by knocking out the tourist and cabin classes fore and aft, along with much of the crew quarters, limiting passenger space to first-class while retaining her original speed of thirty-one knots. The amount of freight carried enabled them to bring the cruise price of these accommodations within the reach of those who had never before been able to afford such a holiday.

When she had steamed into La Guaira, Venezuela, the next to last leg of her highly successful maiden voyage, Christmas cruise, her cargo holds were all but empty having discharged at Georgetown, British Guiana, and her oil bunkers only a third full. She was due to replenish these with Venezuelan oil and take on a full shipment of freight.

Unfortunately at La Guaira they ran into a wildcat dock strike. After waiting thirty-six hours, the *Poseidon* was compelled by her tight schedule—she was due to leave again from Lisbon on December 30th on a New Year's cruise—to sail with her cargo holds empty and no replacement of fuel.

She had sufficient to reach Lisbon but it was the Captain's decision not to compensate for the missing oil from her double bottom tanks with water ballast that made his ship dangerously tender and landed him in his fix.

To have filled this space with salt water as he should have done, meant that the time required to flush and clean them in Lisbon would have wrecked the turn-around schedule already tightened by the delay.

For the record the Consortium sent him a cable, 'Use your own judgement.' For his private information they bombarded him with coded messages that he was inviting financial catastrophe for them. Five hundred arriving passengers would be living at company expense in Lisbon hotels, not to mention the ill will that would be engendered when they missed their promised New Year's Eve party at sea. The cables pointedly referred to a high pressure area over the Middle Atlantic with forecasts of continuing fair weather. It was the Captain's first big command: he gambled.

At Curaçao, the last port of call, collected reports from all weather stations along his route indicated high pressure area holding firm. It confirmed his decision to sail with his ship as she was.

Once at sea and encountering the mysterious swells, the jaws of the trap closed. To have tried to flood the tanks of a ship of low stability while she was rolling would have been to court immediate disaster.

He did what he could to secure his vessel: battened down, strung lifelines, emptied the swimming-pools, placed his crew on double watch alert and kept his radio room crackling, looking for the storm that he was certain lay in his path, in spite of the reassuring weather forecasts. For in his experience, limited to the Eastern Mediterranean, swells indicated the passage of a great disturbance or one to be encountered. Since up to then he had sailed through nothing but smooth water the trouble must lie ahead. The Captain's mind was centred upon locating that missing storm and avoiding it if he could.

At two o'clock that afternoon he was let off the hook. Sparks brought him a message broadcast from the seismo-graphic station on the Azores to the effect that there had been a mild, rolling, sub-sea earthquake of no great duration registered both there and in the Canaries, resulting in the build-up of the swell affecting vessels to the south. This dismissed the fears of unreported storm centres. Almost simultaneously came a radio message from a Spanish freighter, the *Santo Domingo* out of Barcelona, to whom they had spoken earlier in the day. She was now a hundred and twenty miles north-east of the *Poseidon*, had steamed out of the shock area and reported an end to the disturbance, of the sea. By six o'clock that evening, even at reduced speed, the *Poseidon* could be expected to sail out of the range of the swells.

The Captain thereupon ordered an unalarming, watered-down version of the reason for the ship's behaviour to be broadcast to the passengers with a promise that before nightfall it would have abated.

Shortly after six o'clock the swells abruptly ceased and the *Poseidon*, after overcoming the inertia set up by her rolling, sailed level on a flat, glassy, breathless sea. The relieved Captain lifted restrictions on the kitchens and cabin service, directed a few junior officers to appear at dinner to provide a sprinkling of white uniforms and gold braid, while still holding the rest of his crew and staff on alert. For he was not wholly happy nor his mind entirely at ease. But when the perfect conditions continued to prevail, he ordered maximum possible speed ahead.

The frame of the old liner began to shudder and shake as her four turbines, each propelling a thirty-two-ton screw, thrust her onwards into the gathering dark at some thirty-one knots. Glasses and drinking-water bottles rattled in their racks, things loose vibrated. The great effort the old giantess was making was only too apparent.

To the majority of those who had been miserably ill the pardon came too late. The relief arriving so close to the evening meal inspired very few to come to dinner. At half-past eight there were only a few more than had been present for lunch scattered about the huge dining-saloon. Manny Rosen's Strong Stomach Club was present, augmented by a full complement at the grab-bag table with the appearance of Mr Kyrenos the Third Engineer and Mrs Rogo.

Linda Rogo was as usual overdressed in a long, white, silk sheath gown so tight that it showed the indentation of her buttocks and the line of her underpants. From the tremendous cleavage it was probably an inheritance from the wardrobe of her starlet days, which caused Manny Rosen to whisper to his wife, 'What's holdin' them in?'

Linda was a pretty, girlie-doll blonde with a small mouth which she exaggerated into a bee-stung pout. She somewhat resembled Marilyn Monroe except for the bite of personality. She affected a blue-eyed, baby stare but the eyes were ice cold. She had let everyone know that she had been a Hollywood starlet, appeared in a Broadway play and had given up a theatrical career to marry Rogo. She never let her husband forget it either.

Frank Scott said to her, 'So glad you were able to come tonight, Mrs Rogo. The table wasn't the same without you.'

Linda flirted her head and cooed, 'Oh, Reverend, do you really mean it?' Then dropping her voice, but still sufficiently audible, she said to her husband, 'You, you bastard, you didn't want me to come.'

Rogo looked innocently aggrieved as he always did when Linda abused him and answered, 'Aw now, baby, I just didn't want you to be sick.'

The shivering of the ship was more noticeable in the restaurant and Muller's glass, touching a carafe, rang like a tuning fork. He clutched at the rim so quickly that Rosen, who was facing him at his neighbouring table for two, was startled and said, 'What happened?'

Muller said, 'Old seagoing superstition. You let a sailor die if you don't stop a glass from ringing.' He added, 'I'm irreligious but superstitious.' In a moment he had them all clutching at their glasses to stop the tinkling.

This the last night but one had brought out the third best evening frocks of the women. Miss Kinsale was in her short, grey taffeta—she had brought three for the voyage: black for best, a green and a grey which she wore alternately. Belle Rosen was in a black lace, short dress with high-heeled shoes and the inevitable diamond clips and mink cape. Jane Shelby and Susan appeared in a knee-length mother and daughter set of chiffon in contrasting shades of lilac. The men, with the exception of Scott, wore dinner jackets. The Minister was in a dark-blue suit and the flamboyant Princeton orange and black tie. Martin's dinner-jacket was tartan plaid in blue and green. In spite of the perfect fit of Rogo's clothes, his stocky body made him look like a bouncer in a night club. The two stewards Acre and Peters as usual were in their stiff shirts and white mess-jackets. Across the room The Beamer and his girl were at his table, beginning to drink their evening meal. Pamela's mother was still ill.

Robin Shelby ordered, 'I'll have the Lobster Newburg.'

'No you won't!' said his mother. 'Not at night.'

Her husband said, 'Turkey hash is practically obligatory the day after Christmas.'

Miss Kinsale asked for Salmon Timbales, and hoped they would be like the fishcakes she was used to at home. The Rosens opted for the Devilled Chicken; the Rogos never ate anything but steak or hamburgers.

Stewards with their food trays made their way through the aisles of deserted tables of the nearly empty dining-room and in between the shaking of the ship as she drove through the early evening, one could hear the occasional clink of fork and plate. It was rather a silent meal, for denied the covering hum and clatter of a full restaurant, the diners kept their voices and laughter down.

In the engine room the temporary double watch, their voices drowned out by the thunder of their machinery revolving at top speed, hovered over bearings, dials and gauges and wondered how long the Skipper intended to keep her driving at that pace. One of the oilers was sent to fetch a couple of dozen cokes. The boiler-room crew kept an equally anxious eye on temperature gauges and fuel consumption.

Topside in the radio room on the sun deck, the night wireless operator was getting off a backlog of messages.

On the bridge the Captain, thanking his stars that he had got off so lightly, nevertheless was still apprehensive. He had discarded as unnecessary as well as dangerous the idea of taking on water ballast under way, even in a calm ocean through which his ship was sailing normally again. Should there be a hurricane warning, there would still be ample time to do so to enable his ship to ride out a storm. But from all reports, high-pressure zones were holding. Once again he made the decision not to ballast. If he pushed his engines to their capacity, he would be able to make up some of the lost time and bring her in no more than a day late already provided for. Yet no skipper is ever truly comfortable when his vessel is going all out. He operated therefore with the sixth sense of the veteran seaman: weather good, forecast holding, sea track clear, nerve ends uncomfortable.

With nightfall the sky had become overcast and the surface of the flattened sea had an oily quality which was distasteful to the Master as though a leaden-coloured skin had formed over it. When his ship entered the zone of total darkness he sent a second man up into the crow's nest and posted two young officers permanently at the radar screen whose revolving arm lit up not a single blip on a fifty-mile range.

The executive, who was second-in-command and a more stolid person, could not imagine what was bugging the Skipper or keeping him striding nervously. Thrice he had asked whether the second lookout had been posted. Each time he passed the radar screen he glanced into it. He was like a man driving a car who, checking his rear vision mirror before making a turn, does not quite believe it when he sees there is no one behind him.

From time to time he went out on to the port bridge wing which projected out over the water and looked down upon the oily sea reflecting the speeding string of lights of his ship keeping pace with him on its surface. The news of the minor quake had made him conscious of what lay below. His charts showed that the submerged mountain peaks of the Mid Atlantic Ridge, extending in a gigantic letter 'S' ten thousand miles from Iceland to the edge of the Antarctic, at that point were a mile and a half beneath his keel.

The charts, however, were not specific seismic maps and hence indicated neither the three volcanoes believed to be active pointing in line towards the top of South America, nor reflected the huge fault known to exist in the Ridge in that area.

At exactly eight minutes past nine, this fault already weakened by the preliminary tremor, now without warning shifted violently and slipped a hundred or so feet, sucking down with it some billions of tons of water.

If the *Poseidon* had not been shuddering so from the power she was generating, the bridge might have felt the sudden jolt of earthquake shock echoing upwards, though its force was downwards. Indeed, the Captain and his executive did glance at one another sharply for an instant, because of something they thought they felt in the soles of their feet. But when the *Poseidon* continued to surge forward, they relaxed and by then it was too late.

For a moment they experienced that sickening feeling at the pit of the stomach when an elevator lift drops too quickly, as the ship, sucked into the trough of the sea's sudden depression, lurched downward and began to heel. At the same time there was some babbling from the telephone to the crow's-nest and the Third Officer at the radar screen gave an unbelieving shout of 'Sir!' as, eyes popping from his head, he pointed to the blips which showed them about to run into a solid obstacle that had not been there a minute before.

The Captain tried to run in from the end of the bridge wing, but it was already going uphill. He heard the clang of the engine-room telegraph as the executive reached the levers and the order, 'Right full rudder! All engines full astern!' the almost automatic reaction to an obstacle dead ahead.

And so when the S.S. *Poseidon* met the gigantic, upcurling, seismic wave created by the rock slip, she was more than three-quarters broadside, heeling farther from the turn. Top heavy and out of trim, she did not even hang for an instant at the point of no return, but was rolled over, bottom up, as swiftly and easily as an eight-hundred ton trawler in a North Atlantic storm.

The first intimation the scattering of passengers in the dining-saloon had of impending catastrophe was the sudden drop of the thick carpeted floor from beneath their feet. Chairs and tables tilted them forward or sideways, revealing a dizzying abyss before they were catapulted downwards into it.

Simultaneously the ship screamed.

The scream, long-drawn-out and high-pitched, was compounded of the agony of humans in mortal fear and pain, the shattering of glass and breaking crockery, the clashing, cymbal sound of metal trays and pots and pans mingled with the crashing of dishes, cups, knives, forks and spoons hurled, some with deadly missile effect, from the dining-room tables.

The scream mounted to a crescendo as every object in the ship not fastened was carried away in that sickening whip that laid her over on her side.

Service doors from the kitchens and pantries swung open and the metallic protest of copper cauldrons, steamers, Dutch ovens and cooking utensils bounding and rebounding down the canting floor, added to the deafening chaos of sound through which penetrated one high, animal cry of anguish which preceded a cook's dying from scalding.

The Beamer and his girl came tumbling down the 118-foot width of the two-storey dining-saloon, turning over and over in slow motion like clowns in a contortionist act, breaking their descent clutching at chairs and tables that had suddenly assumed the vertical. They fell from starboard down to port and then, as the ship completed its revolution, slid another twenty feet, the height of the room, to land dazed, bruised but uninjured in a tangle of arms and legs with the Rosens, Muller, and Mike and Linda Rogo.

It was that first drop varying from fifty to over a hundred feet, the full breadth of the ship, that either crippled or killed those passengers and serving stewards who had the misfortune to be near the centre or the far starboard side of the ship as she careened over to port.

The more fortunate ones were those at the side tables to port. Muller, Belle and Manny Rosen were simply spilled out of their chairs. The Shelbys and the occupants of the grab-bag table had not much farther to go and were able to break their descent by holding on for a moment to their seats. Manny Rosen landed upon the rectangle of the window with nothing between him and the green sea but the thick glass.

But so swift and continuous was the capsizing that before the pressure of the water could fracture it, the *Poseidon*'s entire superstructure came thundering down, burying itself in the sea. The port windows now starboard were raised up and cleared themselves. Manny, clutching wildly at Belle, found himself sliding head-first along with the Rogos, the Shelbys and the others, down the slanting side of the vessel to land on the glass-covered ceiling amidst a mass of broken china, trays, cutlery and food. The topmost branches of the Christmas tree which had come tumbling out of its tub, the ornamental star affixed to its peak unbroken, fell upon them.

The moment of sealed-in quiet that followed the death cry of the ship contained more of horror and menace than the nerve-shattering clamour, for it uncovered the small, helpless noises of the injured and dying: murmurs, moans, pleadings, the occasional tinkling drop of some errant utensil that had lagged behind and the rolling about in the pantries of pots that had not yet managed to come to rest.

During the instant just as it appeared that the ship was about to blow herself apart before the final plunge, Mike Rogo was heard to say, 'Jesus Christ! Someone get off my leg, will you?'

Thereupon there occurred an appalling explosion initiating a series of detonations as three of her boilers blew up.

If the first outcry of the stricken vessel had been a shriek, her second following the explosions was a shattering, earrending roar as her innards broke away.

The remaining boilers came loose first. Their pathway to the sea lay through two of the three giant stacks of the liner and they went down with the noise of a thousand men hammering upon sheet iron.

The engine room came apart more slowly, as the heavy turbines, dynamos, generators and pumps hanging downwards, imposed an intolerable strain upon the steel that clamped them to the floor. With the grinding outcry of tortured metal they began to crash down the ship-high rectangular shaft over the engine room and through the glass roof to join the boilers at the bottom of the sea.

Some of these, instead of dislodging completely, fractured to slide sideways and tangle with yet other break-away parts to jam together in a mass of tangled steel, torn piping and uncovered armatures. The S.S. *Poseidon* seemed to be retching up her bowels in mortal agony.

She did this to such an awful continuity of sounds: splintering wood, a whine of tearing metal, thunderclaps, surgings, hissings, great boomings accompanied by suckings and bubblings that the survivors still crumpled in heaps upon the ceiling-floor, could descend no further down the paths of terror.

They could only lie there stunned and deafened by the grinding, rumbling and thunderous poom-boom as of some great war drum, clangour of metal striking upon metal and the shouting of steam loosed as though from the anteroom of hell.

Once a great muddy cascade of water shot into the dining-saloon as though expelled from a cannon. But it ceased as abruptly as it had come, ran off into the opening made by the top of the grand staircase and which now, upside-down, had become a watery pit.

Then all the lights went out.

CHAPTER III

Reprieve

Yet, by some mystery of buoyancy connected with air trapped in the spaces now emptied of cargo, boilers and heavy machinery, the *Poseidon* still remained afloat with her new waterline lapping against the hull just below where the former ceiling of the dining-saloon had become the floor. The clouds overhead parted, letting through enough tropical night light to cast a faint glow through the reversed sidelights, now high above like clerestory windows in a chapel, upon the desolation of the saloon and the people therein waiting to die.

The convulsions of the ship diminished, except for isolated thuds, bumps and clankings, sudden roars that were stilled as quickly as they had commenced, the bursting of the hatchcovers, the rushing sound of water entering some compartment, until again there was that almost intolerable quiet through which now once more moans of pain and cries for help became audible.

Those on the bridge and topsides quarters died immediately. The Captain, his officers, helmsman, quartermaster and the watch were either slung into the port wing, or jammed up against the side of the enclosure, wedged and pinned there by centrifugal force, or crippled by the fall. None of them had been able even to get close or reach for emergency switches to close all watertight doors. They were drowning before they knew what was happening to them.

In the radio room, the Sparks on duty was thrown from his chair while transmitting and, striking his head upon a piece of equipment, lay momentarily stunned. When he tried to rise and reach for his radio key, he found himself confused and disorientated. It was not where it should have been. And thereafter it was too late. His two fellow officers in their cabins had been hurled into their bunks, unable to extricate themselves in time. Then the water crashed in and killed them.

Death visited every portion of the ship. The engine and boiler-room crews were wiped out in a body: crushed, scalded, or obliterated pitilessly in those oily lakes where once the openings of funnels and skylights had been. The unfortunate passengers in the luxury cabins of Main, 'A' and 'B' decks died more slowly.

There were four decks above the first of the cabins—promenade, boat, sun and sports —now under sixty feet of water. Their doors and windows had never been built to withstand such pressure and were blown inwards to admit the sea which came rushing or seeping, rising, exploring into the accommodation deck to drown those who had kept to their cabins that night, or caught them in the flooded corridors trying to escape by stairs that had become un-climbable.

In the dining-saloon, lights flickered on again as the sets of batteries for main power failure, somehow undamaged, came into action on a separate local circuit, dimly illuminating one out of every six bulbs on low voltage.

These bulbs concealed in the glass of the ceiling now reversed, threw up pale illumination from beneath the new floor reversing too, the shadows of stunned or injured passengers who were beginning to move like wraiths in some underworld.

In the eerie emergency lighting that waxed and waned first at intervals, dimming and glowing as though connected to a pulse that might at any moment falter and stop, the inverted room presented a nightmare to the dazed and bewildered creatures grovelling on the ceiling surface slippery with water, blood and glass. The smell of food arose from the debris.

Tables and chairs now were suspended upside-down from above like giant fungi. Tablecloths still affixed by the clamps of the fiddles hung in ghostly tatters.

There had been some fifty-odd passengers in the saloon of which a third were either dead, dying or seriously injured. Those who were able to were beginning to bestir themselves. They climbed to their feet, groped blindly and agonizingly, heads shaking as though with tic, fell down again, struggled to hands and knees, gaped about them unseeing, unable to grasp what had happened or where they were.

The ones that had been dashed the entire width of the ship, with the exception of The Beamer and his girl, were the worst off. Practically uninjured was the group that Manny Rosen had characterized as The Strong Stomach Club, whose fall had been the gentlest and the shortest: the Shelbys, Muller, the grab-bag table, the Rogos and the Rosens now began to extricate themselves.

Mike Rogo, tossed aside the slender top of the Christmas tree, its crowning star broken in half and with the effort gasped, 'Jesus Christ! What's happened?'

His wife Linda screamed over and over again, 'Oh, my God! Oh, my God! Oh, my God! Jesus, Mary, come to our aid!'

It was Jane Shelby who called the roll for her family, 'Dick? Susan? Robin? Are you all right? Dick, what's happened?'

Shelby answered, 'I don't know, I think we've turned over. Stay by me all of you. Watch out for broken glass.'

Manny Rosen picked himself up to a tinkling of shards that had all but covered him and which now fell from his shoulders. He said, 'Are you all right, Mamma?'

Belle replied, 'Manny are *you* all right? You ain't hurt or anything, are you?'

Manny said, 'I'm asking you.'

His wife said, 'If I can ask you, I'm okay, ain't I?'

'Can you stand up?' He assisted her to her feet and they stood there, holding on to one another, two grotesque figures in the wrong-way lighting. He short and stocky; she taller than him, enormously obese, trembling in spite of her words.

Hubie Muller helped Miss Kinsale to arise. The lapels of his dinner-jacket were soiled by some sauce that had come spurting out of a dish flying through the air. She was bleeding from a cut on her lip. He took out his pocket handkerchief and staunched it, saying in his soft and extraordinarily gentle voice, 'Are you all right? I think something awful has happened to us.'

She made no reply but went away from him and wading through the ankle-deep debris knelt alongside the Reverend Scott and bowed her head. Blood from her mouth fell in diminishing drops on to her folded hands.

No one had been aware that the young Minister had untangled himself from all those at his table and near by who had been thrown into a heap and climbing to his knees some little distance away from them, hands unclasped, arms spread wide apart, his gaze turned upwards to the monstrous aspect of the things hanging from the ceiling, he was addressing his God. The fighting glare was in his eyes.

He prayed, 'Lord, we are in deep trouble. You have seen fit to try us. We shall not fail you.'

Miss Kinsale sighed, 'Amen! Help us, Father!'

Scott did not so much as glance at her, but continued, 'Lord, we ask nothing but that we shall be strong to meet the challenge You have set us, and that we shall not be found wanting. We shall fight to live for You.'

Miss Kinsale added, 'Father, we will abide by Thy will.'

The Reverend Frank Buzz Scott said, 'We ask You, Lord, for nothing but what You have given us, the chance to prove ourselves. We will not fail. Trust in us.'

The Rosens, the Shelby family, the Rogos and Hubie Muller were drawn into an embarrassed group about the kneeling figure of Scott.

To Muller came the thought: *What an extraordinary kind of prayer!* And then an even more absurd one: *My God, he's wearing his college colours and telling God he's going out to win the big game. Has he gone out of his mind?*

He looked almost with relief upon the wispy person of Miss Kinsale kneeling next to him in her short, grey taffeta evening frock. The material at her shoulder was barely touching the cloth of the clergyman's outstretched sleeve. The simplicity of the words she was murmuring were almost a comforting counterpoint to the clergyman's strange perversions of the usual litany of prayers.

Still dazed and hardly aware of what Scott was saying, Shelby yet was ashamed of him somehow. He was used to the preacher clad in surplice in the pulpit with his big Bible open, talking down to him from his elevation and sometimes when he listened to him even saying things which made him think a little. It was all right in its proper setting, which included stained-glass windows, organ music and the echoes of coughing rebounding from the church roof. It was ritual with which he was willing to put up every so often for the sake of standing in the community. But here there was something dreadfully embarrassing in this big man oblivious of all else, kneeling, arms upraised, conversing directly with God.

He did not know where to look. He stole a glance at his wife and saw that she was staring at Scott with fascination but her lips were moving. She was one of those thin, fine-boned, American women who from sensational girlish beauty had developed into an even lovelier middle-age; ash blonde hair turned a shade darker, but the eyes still the same blue, lively and young and the faint lines appearing about the mouth recording the humour, the courage and the goodwill with which she had coped with the struggles of producing and raising a family, and keeping a husband.

He saw splinters of glass shining in her hair, reached over and plucked them out. She smiled a little tremulously and said, 'I've prayed, too.' But in her mind she was wondering to whom Scott had been speaking—one of those bearded figures of God on a billowing cloud from the Sistine Chapel, or the overcoated, slouch-hatted figure of the football coach pacing the sidelines?

Belle Rosen, clutching her husband's arm said, 'Manny, what's happened to us? Maybe we should say a prayer, like, ourselves.'

Manny answered, 'It's years since we've been to temple. Now we should be asking?' But automatically his hand reached inside his shirt-front for the *mezuzah* that should have been hanging from a chain about his neck, but wasn't. The Rosens were of a generation which had long since given up orthodoxy.

The weird, static moments continued. The capsized ship should long since have given a final lurch and plunged to the bottom. Instead she ceased all movement and seemed as solidly planted there in the still ocean as a rock, a long dark, whale-back beneath the emerging starlight.

The complete relaxation, the result of their alcoholism, had saved The Beamer and Pam, his girl, from nothing worse than a shaking up. It was she, with a strong arm, who lifted him up and held him to his feet, both now stone-cold sober. But though he knew he was no longer drunk the horrors around him made him uncertain that he was not under hallucination; Scott and Miss Kinsale kneeling, lights going on and off up from the floor, the stink and the noise frightened him badly. He said, 'Pam, am I all right?'

She held fast to him and whispered, 'Don't worry, I'm here. I'll look after you.'

James Martin, owner of The Elite Haberdashery Shop in Evanston, Illinois, got to his feet unaided and made for where the grand staircase had been, and then wished he had not. He was a dry little man with the smooth skin and thin lips of the Midwesterner. The eyes behind his gold-rimmed spectacles were alert but he would have been easy to lose in a crowd. He looked like no one and everyone who was in the business of selling. When he reached the area it was no longer there, but instead at a depth of six feet below the new floor line, was a large pool of water and black oil. One of the emergency lights still functioning on the upside-down stairs gave the surface an iridescence of many colours.

With a great blobbing sound a bubble burst upwards from it and inside the bubble he caught momentary sight of the head and shoulders of a human figure, but could not tell whether it was man, woman or child, for it was covered in oil. A hand reached forth and grasped at nothing then the apparition vanished. Martin crouched down at the edge of the pool and was sick and then threw himself backwards and away from it, so that it could not claim him.

Mike Rogo had got his wife up off the floor; she was still on the verge of hysteria with her teeth chattering. The bunch of false curls attached to the back of her head had been knocked askew and the tight sheath dress stained with gravy. Her state of terror had rendered her grotesque.

Rogo wished that Father Haggerty were there. He was uncertain of prayers conducted by any but a priest of his own faith. He compromised by crossing himself.

They became aware of Mr Kyrenos, the Third Engineer, who too, had managed to rise. He was a short, undistinguished man except for a scrubby moustache and dark, plaintive Greek eyes. He had been eating lobster. It was now all down his stiff, white shirt-front, the shell caught up absurdly on one of his studs.

He said, 'Excuse me, please, I must go down to my engine room. Stay here. You will be perfectly safe. Someone will come. I must go down, they will be needing me there.' He got up, ran over to the black pool where the grand staircase had been and fell in, where he thrashed and splashed and shouted for help.

Mike Rogo tried to go to his assistance saying, 'Where the hell did he think he was going?' But his wife clung to him screaming, 'No, no! Don't leave me!' He tried to free himself but she slid down his body and clutched his leg with both arms.

By the time he had extricated himself, Mr Kyrenos had stopped calling. The handrails rising out of the water were too slippery to give him a grip. The oil he swallowed probably had as much to do with killing him as drowning. He sank and did not come up again.

Martin crawled away from the edge of the pit on his hands and knees until he had reached the others. He then lay prone amidst the debris of the ceiling-floor and buried his head in his arms.

Muller, standing slightly apart still holding the handkerchief on which were the red spots from Miss Kinsale's lip, made the effort to bend his mind to accept what he was seeing and hearing. It was not made easier by the incongruity of dinner-jackets and evening frocks. He was able to accept the enormity of the disaster: *We have turned over.* And then, *But what the hell am I going to do?* The fact that he thought in terms of 'I' rather than 'we' was characteristic; the turning of his smooth, comfortable, easy-going world upside-down was deeply resented by Hubert Muller.

His thoughts were broken into by the powerful voice of Scott concluding his strange orisons: 'Don't worry, Lord, we've got the guts. We'll do our best.' He arose and taking Miss Kinsale's elbow helped her to do the same.

A voice from above their heads said, 'Mr Scott, sir! Mrs Shelby! Mrs Rosen, are you all right?'

They all looked up and for one ridiculous moment The Beamer, in his unaccustomed sobriety, wondered whether the American Minister was being answered from on high. But it was only Acre the steward talking to them from the service entry which led out from the various pantries and wine rooms *en route* to the kitchens, but which was now a full storey above their heads. He seemed to be lying on the floor, his partner Peters kneeling at his side.

'Acre!' Rosen called out, 'What are you doing up there? What's it all about?'

Acre replied, 'She's capsized, sir. Turned right over.'

'I thought you said it couldn't.'

The implications were still not clear. Shelby said, 'What do you mean, turned over?'

Acre replied, 'I don't know, sir. Something rolled her right over.'

Some note in the steward's voice must have reached Jane Shelby's ear, for she called up, 'Are you all right, Acre?'

He replied, 'I've broken a leg, madam.'

'Oh, Acre!' cried Jane, 'Can't anyone do anything?'

'I imagine someone will come along in a minute or so, ma'am.'

'And you, Peters?' Scott queried.

'I'm all right, sir,' the second steward replied. Then he asked, 'What's become of Mr Kyrenos?'

Mike Rogo said, 'He flipped! He said he had to go down to the engine room. He fell in there,' and nodded his head in the direction of the grand staircase.

As if to punctuate, with a gurgling rumble another foul-smelling bubble burst like a geyser from the centre of the pool, heaving a mass of oil and water upwards in which they caught a momentary glimpse of arms and legs before it fell back and the surface glazed again. But it was now some two feet higher and closer to the surface of the dining-room level than it had been before.

None of them were exactly certain what they had seen. What Acre then said came as even more of a shock to them, 'Mr Kyrenos ought to have known. The engine room isn't down any more. It's up.'

Scott put his hand on Shelby's arm and looked about for a moment. The fixed, half-fanatic, half-supremely concentrated glaze the older man had so often noticed in his eyes had faded and he looked utterly composed. He said, 'Hold them all together here, Dick. Try to keep them quiet for a minute, while I see if there's anything I can do for some of those people over there.' He gave Shelby's arm a squeeze of encouragement and strode off, his feet propelled by his powerful legs pushed aside the glass shards littering the floor with the clinking sound as of Christmas sleigh bells.

CHAPTER IV

The Adventurers

The ceiling of the dining-saloon of the S.S. *Poseidon* had consisted of squares of frosted glass inset into alternating steel and copper bands, the lights located behind the squares. Now reversed to become the floor, it resembled a battlefield with the bodies of the dead or unconscious scattered about in pathetic heaps of clothing that looked as though there was no one in them. They were dead of broken necks and broken backs; unconscious from concussion or skull fracture. Some of the heaps moved feebly, protesting against the pain of shattered limbs and internal injuries. Only those few who, like the group towards the stern had been close to the port side of the vessel, were on their feet.

The ship's surgeon, old Dr Caravello, had lost his thick-lensed spectacles, without which he could not see two feet in front of his face. Half in shock himself, he had begun to function by instinct but for the moment was unable to do little more than grope about and peer muzzily at the nearest injured. He still had his napkin in his hand and reached over to a man with a head injury from contact with the arm of a chair as he fell, trying to staunch the bleeding, the while crying out for his assistant, 'Marco! Marco! Where the devil are you? Can't you see I need help?'

A figure loomed up at his side. Dr Caravello asked, 'Is that you, Marco? Get me some more dressings.'

Scott said, 'No, Marco isn't here. But I'll do what I can,' and he began picking up napkins and tearing them into strips for bandages. 'Is there much we can do?' he asked.

Dr Caravello said, 'I can't see without my glasses. God knows. If the ship has turned over, in a minute we may all be dead.'

Scott said, 'If God knows and we don't behave like cowards, He'll see us through.'

'I can't see without my glasses!' Dr Caravello repeated, and began to grope amongst the debris.

'There they are,' Scott said and picked them up for him.

A young Fourth Officer, who was a Yugoslav just out of training school, had managed to regain his feet, bracing himself and shaking his head to try to clear it. He said and then kept repeating, 'Kip carm, everyboody, plis. Everysing going to be ollright.' Nobody paid any attention to him.

Of the five waiters who had been serving in the dining-room at the time, one was dead, two were unconscious and two others in shock like the rest, responded to the automatism of their jobs by picking up napkins and pieces of broken crockery and trying to clear a path through the debris by pushing it with their feet.

Scattered in helpless groups were some twenty uninjured passengers which included Greeks, French, Belgians, the German Augenblick family and an American couple in their seventies.

A woman suddenly began to scream hysterically, her voice piercing to an unbelievable pitch and simultaneously the children of the Germans began to cry. Then the woman's screams stopped abruptly as though someone had struck her but the crying of the children continued.

One of the two British junior pursers was unconscious. When the Doctor and Scott came over to examine him, the other attempted to soothe the passengers. He said, 'You must keep calm and be quiet. There is no danger at the moment. Officers will come and lead you to safety. I ask you to stay where you are.'

The sight of his uniform and the actual belief in his voice that these things would happen, had their effect. The two waiters who were unhurt had joined the Doctor in helping with the injured.

Dr Caravello said to Scott, 'The boy doesn't know what he's talking about. Nobody will come. She'll sink in a minute. There's nothing any of us can do.'

Scott said sharply to the old man, 'Don't talk like that. Get on with your work and I'll get on with mine.' He went about checking the sodden heaps, looking into dead or unconscious faces, signalling the stewards the location of one of two of the lesser injured for treatment, then went over to the groups of unhurt survivors and said to them, 'All of you who are fit and able ought to try to get out of here at once. If you'll come with me, I'll try to help you.' He transfixed them with his staring eyes and for a moment they appeared to waver.

Then the German Augenblick shook his head and said, 'No, it is besser we should stay here like the officer said. We don't know anything of where to go. Officers will come.' He looked around and found agreement with the others.

Scott's whole body expressed a sudden truculence. 'They will, will they? What if they don't?'

The German reiterated, 'If there's been an accident it is besser we wait.' Scott turned away.

Robin Shelby said, 'Daddy, what are we going to do?'

The Beamer added, 'Yes, I say, what's going to happen?'

Shelby watching Scott from a distance suddenly felt deserted and wished he would come back. He replied, 'I don't know. We'll have to wait and see when Scott comes back. He's checking.'

Jane Shelby made as though to speak and then thought better of it. She had hoped somehow that her husband would take an initiative without waiting for the return of the Minister.

Peters called down from above, 'You'd better come up here, Mr Rosen.'

Rosen said, 'Do you know any more jokes?' The doorway through which the two stewards were peering, with a third man looking over their shoulders, was now ten feet above their heads. The last flight of the grand staircase leading from 'C' deck down to the dining-saloon, now curled upwards to the ceiling, with the railing too far from the doorway to be of any use. The steps were upside-down. 'Anyway,' Rosen concluded, 'what good would that do?'

'It's higher from the waterline,' Peters said.

Rogo grunted, 'You're telling us!'

Jane Shelby made her way closer to the high-up opening and said, 'Acre, are you in pain?'

'No, Ma'am, thank you. It's not too bad.'

Peters said, 'We've got him fairly comfortable.'

Rogo added, 'The Doc is down here. Want me to tell him?'

Acre said, 'No, sir. I shouldn't bother yet. He's got the passengers to look after.'

Susan, Jane, Miss Kinsale and the Rosens all felt Acre's plight more than whatever theirs might be. Over the long cruise of almost a month's duration they had, as passengers will, formed a warm and friendly relationship with the dining-room stewards who fed them three times a day, looked after them, learned their favourite dishes, joked with them and cared about them. During the voyage the members of those particular tables had made other friendships: bridge, drinking and smoke-room partners, deck-chair neighbours, shore excursion companions, but at mealtimes they were a group under the aegis of Peters and Acre. Shelby once said it was rather like a club run by the two stewards.

They heard the jingle and crunch of glass and saw Scott striding across to them. As he came he pulled down the knot of his necktie, loosened his collar and shed his coat. They all watched him curiously.

Martin the haberdasher had conquered his nerves and was on his feet. Muller thought to himself: *The All-American boy has made up his mind about something.* Jane Shelby: *That look is back in his eyes again.*

It was there, the cast that changed his features from friendly composure to aggressiveness. He said abruptly, 'There's nothing more I can do for any of them,' and he jerked his head backwards. But there was no way of telling whether he was indicating the living or the dead. 'The Doc is coping. There isn't much he can do either. We've capsized; right over. We're floating bottom up. From now on it's up to us to get ourselves out of this trap.'

Shelby asked, 'What about the officer?'

Scott replied, 'He's confused. He's just a kid. He keeps telling them that everything's going to be all right.'

The Beamer said, 'That's a comfort.'

Rosen asked, 'What about the others—those purser fellows? Don't they know anything?'

Scott said, 'One of them is unconscious; the other is just a clerk.'

Rogo said, 'What about an S.O.S.? They'd be sending out an S.O.S., wouldn't they?'

Scott said, 'No, they wouldn't,' and then left Rogo to figure it out.

The detective began argumentatively, 'What do ya mean, they wouldn't? They always do when there's a...' His mouth closed suddenly and his little eyes went shifty. He looked discomfited and angry.

Muller picked up the thought: *Christ! If we're floating bottom up, they're dead. The Captain must be dead too, and officers on the bridge. But how many others as well? If the ship is upside-down, how can she remain afloat?*

The boy Robin spoke up for the first time since it had happened. He said, 'Maybe they didn't get the position report away, either.' The light from beneath his feet showed him up as the image of his father; the same grey eyes and square chin but the features more tenderly arranged and not yet fully developed, the mouth still soft and more like that of his mother. 'It's for the shipping computer centre. They send it out every four hours. But if it didn't go...'

His father said, 'Why shouldn't it have gone, Robin?'

The boy replied, 'They didn't always send it out on time. They let me watch. I'm learning morse code. Every astronaut has to know morse. One afternoon he was sending a long message from a passenger about...' he giggled, 'Someone sending a telegram to his girl, because the operator was laughing. He didn't send out the position report until ten minutes past five. Maybe that happened again tonight.'

'What difference would that make?' Rosen queried.

'Hell,' said The Beamer, 'a lot.' The brain behind the round, red face, when not fogged by alcohol was a sharp one and mathematical. 'Don't you see? If it went out at sharp nine, it will be four hours or more before anyone takes any interest in us. But if he was clicking off another love letter, or maybe an overnight buy or sell radiogram and it was broken off before it was finished and after that the position report never went out, pretty soon somebody would be wondering why and asking questions. When they get no answers, they might begin to do something about it.'

Muller said, 'The trouble is, if they're dead we'll never know. And that four hours can mean the difference between...' His calling upon the word 'dead' startled the others so that they did not follow him. They looked at one another in sudden confusion.

But Scott pinioned them by the power building up behind his gaze. He said, 'Exactly! That's why we've got to get going at once.'

'Going?' Rosen asked, 'Where?'

Scott raised his head, 'Up,' he said simply.

Almost as though controlled by one string, they all looked automatically to the ceiling whence hung the festoons of tablecloths, now no longer moving, and the eerie shapes of the tables and chairs.

Muller asked, 'Are you talking metaphysically, Frank? What are you driving at?'

Rogo's thin lips curled with contempt. That softie and his long words!

Scott rapped out, 'Physical! Us; our bodies; our persons. All of us here. We've got to get up to the bottom where the keel is. The skin of the ship.'

Rosen shook his head. 'I don't get it—up to the bottom? The skin?'

The boy was quicker. 'I know,' he said, 'like in submarines, to hammer on it if anyone comes, to let them know we're here.'

The Beamer smiled his round, red-faced smile and said, 'Got it in one, sonny. But have we got time? We don't know how long she can remain floating this way.'

Scott said evenly. 'What difference does that make?'

Linda Rogo screamed at her husband, 'You bastard! You mean we can sink suddenly? You took me on a boat that could sink?' She then startled them all by calling her husband an obscenity that fell most incongruously from the pouting, cupid's bow lips in the doll face.

All Rogo's features seemed to droop, the corners of his little eyes, his mouth, his chin, as he tried to placate her, 'Aw, now honey! Don't talk like that in front of nice people.'

Linda stated where the nice people could go and what they could do there.

'Aw, now baby! How was anyone to know this could happen? She must have hit something.' To the others he said, 'You mustn't mind her, she's worked up. I guess she's got a right to be. She never did want to come, did you honeybun?'

Muller asked, 'How long can she stay afloat like this? An hour? Two? Twelve hours?'

'Or five minutes?' put in Manny Rosen.

Muller ignored him. 'Can we make it? Have we got time? How do we get out of here? We can't even get up to where Acre and Peters are. How many decks are there? Five? Six? We'd never make it!'

Buzz Scott said, 'It's the trying that's important.'

Under her breath, yet sufficiently audibly, Linda Rogo said, 'Balls!'

Rogo tried to cover her up, 'Don't be like that, honey.' But to Scott he said witheringly, 'The old college try, eh? Christ, we can't even get off this floor! What about the women?' His glance went over the fat Belle Rosen. 'Use your nut! They must know we're down here. If we stick around, someone's bound to come and get us out.'

Scott turned his glare full upon Rogo and said, 'That's not what you either said or did when they were holding two wardens hostage at Westchester Plains.'

Rogo's smooth face went flat and expressionless. He said, 'Wasn't it? I knew what was there and where I was going. You don't.'

Muller wondered whether Scott would react. He was well aware of the antagonism of Rogo for the Minister and himself, only slightly masked during the trip by exaggerated politeness. To his surprise Scott did not. He merely regarded Rogo quizzically for a moment and then said, 'You may be right.'

Manny Rosen asked, 'Exactly what is it you're suggesting we should do, Frank?'

'Behave like human beings, instead of like sheep,' Scott replied.

'So?'

Muller, remembering the odd nature of the Minister's prayer, or rather deal with God, by which he seemed already to have committed them to some kind of action, wondered whether they were about to be harangued in this man's curious theological dialectic.

Instead he queried them quietly, almost in an undertone. 'Have any of you men ever taken a survival course?'

Robin said, 'You mean like astronauts, who are put down some place where there's no food or water, or help of any kind and have to know what to do?'

'That's it, Robin.'

The men shook their heads.

Scott said, 'I have. Do you know the cause of death of most people who are either lost, shipwrecked or drowned in inhospitable country?'

'Panic,' Muller volunteered.

'No,' said Scott, 'apathy. Doing nothing, just plain quitting—giving up. The statistics show it. The records indicate that the mere action of keeping busy, trying to do something keeps people alive.'

Then he went on, 'As I see it if we remain here waiting for help to come, it may or it may not. We don't know anything about how long we can remain afloat this way; how near to death we may be. But here we are, all of us, still alive, thinking and rational people with the gift of life which has been taken away from so many. I suggest that we go forward to meet whatever help there may be for us.'

No one said anything.

Scott concluded mildly, 'You know, an animal will try to fight its way clear of a trap, even if it has to leave a leg behind it.'

Rosen said, 'I still don't get what you're proposing we should do, Frank.'

'Climb,' Scott replied, 'and keep climbing.'

Rosen said, 'And if she goes down while we're doing this climbing?'

Muller surprised himself for the thought that flashed through his head was: *My God, he's right! At least it will catch us in a moment of nobility.*

Scott put it differently. He said, 'We'll have been trying. But I don't believe it will sink.'

The Beamer added, 'Aren't you being a little optimistic, old...' and then caught himself in time. One did not call the vicar, or whatever was his American equivalent, 'old boy'. He said, 'How do you know?'

'Because,' Scott said, 'I've made a promise for us. It cannot be ignored.'

The statement was ambiguous, ridiculous and yet contained force and persuasion. Through Muller's mind went all the jokes about the value of having a clergyman during a trip on an aircraft or as a golfing partner. Himself a thorough agnostic who never in his self-centred life had been on his knees, he was not immune to superstition or the atavistic allure of the tribal magician or medicine man.

Scott said, 'Robin there, knows what I'm driving at. If we stay afloat till morning, we may be spotted from the air. Ships and aircraft will be searching for us. There will be only one way to get us out and that's by cutting through the hull at the top. Our chances of being rescued are that much more if we can manage to be there when they do.

'However,' Scott continued, 'it will be up to you to decide whether you remain here or make the effort.'

Muller was struck by the incongruity of the debate when they were all poised on the brink of extinction. None of them had the faintest idea of the ship's buoyancy reserves in her capsized position, to what extent air had replaced the spaces emptied by disaster. Yet they were not behaving like people close to death. There had been screams and panic and outcries for help enough during the moment of catastrophe. But now perhaps only seconds away from the final plunge of the ship, they were calmly discussing means and chances of escape. Was it the confidence of Scott, or the fact that turned turtle the *Poseidon* now offered as steady a platform, except for the grotesqueries overhead, as she had when she was right side up? She was there beneath their feet, rigid, solid, negating panic. Yet Muller was well aware that it was an illusion that could be dispelled for ever any moment.

Shelby asked, 'What about the others?' and glanced over in the direction of the people huddled at the side of the ship at the far end of the dining-saloon and the figures on the floor, some now beginning to stir.

'The dead are out of it,' Scott said and Jane Shelby looked up, startled at the brutality of the words, the sudden indifference that showed through what up to then had been gentle persuasiveness. Miss Kinsale came into her view and Jane noticed that she did not seem to share in her astonishment. On the contrary, her expression was one of reflective repose.

Scott said, 'Seven died from the fall here. There is no possibility for the injured to make it. We can't burden ourselves with cripples. The old Doctor's doing the best he can.'

Jane thought: *But that's selfish and cruel—to abandon them.* But then her common sense said to her, *What on earth is there to be done with people who cannot be moved?* The word 'selfish' turned to 'self-preservation'. Scott was right and she was wrong and she did not like it.

Rosen said, 'Some shipping line! Imagine signing on a man who is half blind as a ship's doctor.'

The Beamer said, 'Imagine signing on a Captain who lets his ship turn upside-down!'

Shelby repeated his question, 'What about the others?' and then added, 'I mean, those over there who haven't been hurt?'

Scott said, 'I talked to them. That young purser told them to stay where they are and someone would come for them. He's wearing a uniform. They believed him.'

'So that leaves us,' said Shelby.

The pulsating lights from below the floor went dimmer than they had been for a moment, before coming on again. The Beamer said, 'There's a happy thought! How long will those last? I suppose they're on emergency storage batteries.'

'I asked that Fourth Officer,' Scott said, 'but the boy didn't know. An hour or two; maybe more, maybe less.'

'Christ!' said Rogo in an injured tone, 'What does the son-of-a-bitch know—for our dough?'

Linda closed her eyes and shook her fists like a child in temper and let out a squeal, 'I don't want to die! We're all going to die and all you do is yackety, yackety, yackety! Oh Mary, Mother of God, save us!'

Scott ignored her and replied to her husband, 'Nothing. He only saw this ship for the first time when he joined her twenty-four hours before she sailed. If I thought he knew anything, I'd have made him come along and show us the way. That's why the sooner we start the better.'

Martin spoke up suddenly. He was so small, greying and unobtrusive even in the plaid dinner-jacket he affected, that the middle-western twang of his voice surprised them all.

He said, 'I don't know about you people, but I've got to be back before the tenth. We're putting in a new line. You know, for kids. We've got a lot of youngsters out there in Evanston and you've got to give 'em young stuff. Maybe it's crazy, all those "with-it" shirts, and those ties, but that's what you've got to give 'em.' And then he added almost as an afterthought, 'I've got a crippled wife at home—arthritis.' He looked at them almost defiantly for a moment. 'But she wanted me to go on this trip. She's a good sport, Ellen.'

Scott asked, 'You'll come?'

'Might as well.'

'And you, Dick?' Scott had turned to the Shelbys.

Richard Shelby hesitated before replying for his family whom he did not consult. He said, 'Yes, if you say there's a chance.'

Jane Shelby added, 'Or even if there isn't.' A slight hint of sharpness had tinged her words, but it was impossible to tell whether it was a query or a statement.

Scott turned his open gaze upon her, but his look was more inward than outward and Jane felt it. He said, 'At least we'll have valued ourselves, won't we?'

Jane wished that her husband had not hesitated. He was the older man and ought to have been the most capable of them. His momentary hesitation before he surrendered up leadership was only a confirmation of what she had known for a long time. Yet wife-like, lover-like, she always kept on hoping.

Shelby had wanted to lead; had wanted to look good in the eyes of his family. He had kept his nerve and his self-possession during the catastrophe but he had no better suggestion as to how they might extricate themselves. Scott seemed to know what he was about. But he had caught the slight note of asperity in his wife's voice and as an afterthought said, 'Is that all right with you, Jane? Susan? What about you, Robin?'

Robin said, 'Sure! The computer centre on Governor's Island would know where every ship is that was near us. I think we ought to go, Mom.'

Jane felt more comforted. Her son had a mind.

Scott continued his canvass, 'Mr Bates?'

The Beamer said, 'It's worth a try. I don't fancy being drowned like a rat in a trap.'

'...Miss Reid?'

The Beamer answered for her, 'Oh, she'll come along with me. Right, Pam?'

The English girl nodded, 'If you want me to, Tony.'

'...Miss Kinsale?'

Directly addressed, the spinster awoke as though from a reverie and smiled a gentle acquiescence, 'But of course, Dr Scott.'

'Mr and Mrs Rogo?'

The little eyes of the detective shifted back and forth from Scott to the other members of the group. He was used to taking command in situations and if necessary even overpowering them. But he was out of his element here—there was no enemy, no one to subdue. The thought of submitting to a rah-rah boy and a preacher at that, went against all his grain. But he did not want to die either. He subscribed to the Broadway creed: shorten the odds anytime you can. He said, 'If you ain't talking through your hat about figuring a way out of here.'

Linda turned on him suddenly, her face red and puffy, 'I'm not going! I'm scared. I think he's a phony!' she bawled at her husband 'And you're not going either!'

'Aw, now baby!' Rogo soothed.

The last of the pseudo refinement she affected was torn away as she released a stream of filthy abuse upon her husband who eyed her dejectedly and said, 'Aw sweetie, don't talk like that!'

But there was no stopping her or the obscenities that erupted from her in such an endless and varied stream that the others could only stare aghast and wholly unprepared for what happened next.

Without so much as a change in his pleading and unhappy expression, faster than the eye could follow, Rogo whipped the back of his hand across her face but with his other arm he caught her before she could fall and held her up.

'Ooooow!' she wailed and then began to howl. Blood dripped from her nose.

Rogo gathered her into his arms, 'Aw, now honeybun—I didn't mean it, baby doll, look what you made me do to your little nose!' He took out a white silk handkerchief from the breast pocket of his dinner-jacket and held it to her face. 'Sweetie, you know I don't like to hurt you. Come now, there's my girl!' She subsided into sobs.

Jane Shelby and her husband, too, felt that this was a not unusual scene between them when she had pushed him to the point where the awe in which he stood of her vanished in the sudden flashpoint of the truculence that made him what he was.

The Beamer was staring with his eyes popping from his head. He made no pretence of understanding Americans. But Manny Rosen never turned a hair. He had seen Rogo in action in his own delicatessen shop, with three toughs who had taken the liberty of what Rogo called, 'passing a remark.'

Rogo said to Scott, 'She'll go.'

'Mr Muller?'

Hubie replied, 'I think it's a very good idea.' He was not liking where he was and was ready to move on.

Scott queried, 'Mr and Mrs Rosen?'

Belle Rosen appealed to her husband, 'I don't understand. What is it he wants us to do?'

'I don't know. He says climb up something to get out of here. He wants to go to the top of the ship. He says he'll show us.'

'Manny, a fat woman like me can't climb. You go. I'll stay here and wait.'

'Are you crazy, Mamma? Go away and leave you? You could try, couldn't you? What else is there we can do? Stay here and wait for the ship to go down, and drown?'

Belle Rosen said, 'What difference does it make where we drown?'

The tubby little man suddenly looked undecided at his wife's logic. He had not yet come to grips with the full extent of what had happened to them. Scott went to Mrs Rosen and took her pudgy hand in his, where it quite disappeared. He said, 'We'll all help you, Mrs Rosen. It may not be as difficult as you think.'

She looked up into his face. He and everything he was and represented was as alien to her as though he had stepped off another planet. But something she saw there fired her natural courage which had borne her through life to where she now found herself. She said, 'If you say so,' and then added, 'but I'm a fat old woman. I'll only be in your way.'

Scott smiled, 'Not if you're willing to try. Then it's decided.'

The Beamer's girl gave a little exclamation, 'Oh!' and then facing them firmly and coolly said, 'I'm sorry, of course I can't go with you.'

They were startled. None of them knew her except for exchanging a few words, or very much concerning her, apart from the gossip and this about-face in view of her prior eager consent took them by surprise.

'Mother, of course,' she said, 'I couldn't go without Mummy. She's in her cabin resting. I'd have to...' Her speech ran down and she stopped. Fear distorted her plain face as she glanced about her, taking in the nightmare ceiling above and the dark oily water where the staircase had been. 'Tony!' she cried, 'Where is she? We've got to go to her! Which way?'

The Beamer was suddenly helpless. 'Look here, old girl, you must get hold of yourself. You see—I'm afraid...' He looked over to Scott for assistance.

The girl cried, 'Don't just stand there staring at me that way! Why don't you tell me? How do I get to her?'

But by then she already knew the answer and buried her face in The Beamer's shoulder as Scott said, 'I'm sorry, but you must all surely know by now. Everyone who was above this dining-room is now below the waterline. None of them can be alive any longer.'

James Martin felt nausea swimming up and managed to turn himself away from the group before he fell to his knees once more and was violently sick again. For the first time he had thought of Mrs Lewis who had said she would not be coming down to dinner.

'God,' said The Beamer, 'I could do with a drink!'

Rogo had one more violent outburst, 'Jesus Christ!' he yelled at Scott. 'You mean everybody's dead except us? But it's all crazy, this upside-down! It's all crazy! You're crazy! You don't even know how to get us off this floor.'

'Oh yes, I do,' said the Reverend Dr Frank Scott.

CHAPTER V

The Christmas Tree

'The tree there!' Scott said, 'Give me a hand.' He called up to Peters, 'We want to get to you. If we push the tree up, can you hold it?'

Peters replied, 'I was going to suggest that, sir. We've a deckhand and a couple of kitchen staff here. If you can swing the tip up to us, we can manage.'

They had all but forgotten the incongruity of the big Christmas tree. It lay now almost at the feet of Scott's group, the bottom at an angle partly screening the space where the top of the grand staircase had been.

'What do you want to do?' Shelby asked.

'Use it to get up there,' Scott said. 'You fellows had better make yourselves more comfortable. It's going to be heavy.'

Shelby pulled at his black bow tie and opened the collar of his shirt. The others followed with the exception of Martin who was still on his knees, holding his head and retching. Somewhere below that stink of oil and water that he had seen, Mrs Lewis with her big, pneumatic bosom and her scented hair which had given him both such excitement and comfort, was floating suspended in her water-filled, luxury cabin or lying wedged and drowned in the bed that they had shared.

'We'll swing the heavy end around first,' Scott said and the six men went to dispose themselves for the job. They were joined by Susan and Robin.

Jane Shelby wanted to help too, but her husband murmured to her, 'Save your strength. God only knows what we're going to find when we get up there, if we do, or how it's going to be.'

Unbroken ornaments and bits of tinsel tinkled musically as they worked the butt around until it lay parallel to the ship's side, with the tip just beneath the opening above.

Scott ranged his crew along its length; himself with his great height and strength in the middle, then Rogo, Muller and The Beamer at intervals, with Shelby, Rosen and the two youngsters at the back to push.

'Now, walk it up,' he said. 'When I lift, get it on to your shoulders. Dick, you heave.' He lifted the trunk of the tree, some four inches thick at that point, on to his shoulders and said, 'Now walk! Push, Dick!'

The top of the tree began to rise and slide up the wall of the dining-saloon, towards the opening above from which Peters, lying on his stomach, was waiting to grasp it.

At the far end of the hall the other passengers watched them dumbly and offered no help. They were paralysed by their own indecision and looked upon what was going on as a kind of madness.

'I ain't got any more breath!' Rosen gasped.

'Manny, you'll hurt yourself!' Belle cried.

'Come on, fellow, push!' said Shelby and wondered how his fifty-year-old back muscles, unused to anything more strenuous than swinging a mashie, would stand up under the strain.

Scott turned his head over his shoulder to the three behind him and ordered, 'Now lift!' and raised the trunk high above his head.

'Got it!' cried Peters and seized the tip which had risen to the top of the opening.

'Attaboy!' said Scott. 'You pull, we'll push.' The cooperation now worked smoothly; those above hauling, those below shoving until Scott cried, 'That's got it!' He and the others came out from under the branches panting. Susan's chiffon frock had a tear at the sleeve.

The tree had come to rest at an angle of forty-five degrees and for a moment they stood there regarding it with pride, having shared in a team effort that had succeeded.

Martin stood up and said, 'I'm sorry I was sick. I'll help now.'

Belle Rosen said, 'You want we should go up that?'

Scott replied, 'It won't be too difficult. You've got the branches to hang on to. Wait 'til I see.' For all of his great bulk he went up the tree as agile as a monkey, his feet testing it. 'Great!' he called down, and dropped back on to the floor.

The tree had some of the aspects of a ladder with sturdy branches emerging from either side to give foot and handhold.

Scott turned to Martin. 'Are you all right? Do you think you could get up there now?'

'Yep.' He wanted his mind and the pictures it was screening for him to be taken forcibly away from Mrs Lewis. Paid had been put to their affair. He would never have to risk the visits to her in Chicago that he had promised. He was safe. Ellen could not possibly ever find out. If he thought of Wilma any more he might cry in front of them.

'Okay, skin up there,' Scott said. 'Then you can reach down and lend a hand to the women.'

Martin went at it effectively, thrusting the branches away from his face as he went and at the same time using them as steadying holds. But he paused in the middle.

Scott coached, 'Don't look down. Just keep going. You're doing fine!'

Martin was not looking down; he was thinking down to what that cabin, now below, must be like. Action had not succeeded in erasing the images. Why had not he insisted that Wilma come to dinner? Why had not he gone to her room?

The next moment Peters had him by the hand and was hauling him through the upside-down doorway. 'There you are, sir. We'll have you all up here in a minute.'

Scott looked from Linda Rogo to Pamela Reid. 'I'm afraid those long gowns will have to come off. The short frocks are all right, but you'll never make it hobbled like that. And take off your shoes. The men can put them in their pockets; you'll be wanting them later.'

Linda said, 'What does he want?'

Rogo answered, 'The dress! The dress! Take it off. How are you going to get up there with your can in that sausage skin?'

'What do you want me to do?' Linda spat out at Rogo, 'Strip? In front of everybody?' Indecencies rose to her lips like air escaping from water.

'Honeybun,' Rogo began, when she cut him off.

Her lip and nose were swollen where he had struck her and her doll face was suddenly all askew with venom. 'That bum, there, just wants to see me with my clothes off. I know his kind: preach on Sunday and screw all week. He's had his eye on me the whole trip.'

Rogo said, 'Aw, baby doll, you shouldn't say things like that. Here, lemme help you with your zipper.'

Linda said, 'Take your filthy hooks off me,' and raked the backs of his hands with her fingernails. Blood seeped from the marks. The others tensed for the explosion to come.

But it was milder this time, for Rogo only shook his head sorrowfully, 'They always ask for it,' and then with another of his lightning-like movements, ripped her gown from her body. She stood there in bra and pants, holding her arms over her bosom as he said, 'Baby, sweetie, you always make me do things I don' wanna do.'

Linda began to cry again, 'Oh, I'm so ashamed with everybody looking'!' She only took her arms from her breasts when she noticed that no one was interested.

'Miss Reid?' said Scott.

The English girl had been standing at The Beamer's side in her ice blue, rumpled satin dress which fitted neither her personality nor her person. She had not spoken since she had learned of the fate of her mother, but she had been thinking hard. She was a sensible girl; there was nothing she could do. Mourning could come later. She turned to The Beamer and asked, 'Is it true about Mummy?'

He said, 'Yes, I'm afraid so, Pam.'

'Is she really dead?'

The Beamer looked helpless and his eyes went to that pool where the central staircase had been and whose oily surface was now unbroken. What could he say further to the poor kid? But she had followed his glance and, accepting it as final, asked no further. She did something to the shoulder straps of her frock so that it simply fell down about her legs and she stepped out of it unembarrassed. She was wearing a short, white nylon slip. The shedding of the dress was some kind of farewell to someone or something that she had been. She said nothing but simply slid her hand into that of The Beamer.

He thought to himself: *Oh, my God! What will I do now?* For the gesture had been like a wedding. She had not a pretty body and looked no more graceful in the slip than she had in the dress. She had been a great drinking companion but he was not in love with her; did not want to be; did not want her; did not want anything ever but just to be allowed to live in alcoholic peace. The brakes on his drinking had been taken off when his wife had died a few years ago and he had found himself free to dwell in the perpetual, never-never land of whisky haze, where he could feel secure and unassailed. What was he to do with this motherless girl, who had just given herself over to him? He gave her arm little pats without realizing he was doing it.

Scott said, 'Now then, Susan, how about it, will you go next?'

'Okay!' She kicked off her shoes and handed them to her father. She was young, fresh and strong. She had found her limbs trembling after the ship had capsized but at no time had the thought of death, or that she might be going to die, entered her head. Now she understood what Scott had meant by apathy versus action. When you were doing something you stopped being frightened. She was pleased that he had selected her to go as an example to the others and hoped she would do a good job of it.

Indeed as Scott had predicted, it proved less difficult than anticipated. For with the tall Minister to reach up a hand, Susan was held firmly half-way up the climb and had only two more branches to negotiate before Martin, leaning down, secured and pulled her up triumphantly.

Unexpectedly Belle Rosen said, 'Should I go next?'

Her husband said, 'You want to, Mamma?'

'If I don't go now, I never will. I'm so nervous.'

'Good for you, Mrs Rosen!' Scott encouraged. 'You saw how easily Susan made it.'

'She don't weigh what I do. Will it hold me?'

'It held me. Here, give me your hand.'

'Must I take my dress off?' she asked.

'No,' said Scott, 'it's short. It won't get in your way.'

'You hold my shoes, Manny.'

'Take it easy, Mamma,' said her husband and helped her.

With Scott steadying her, she made her way painfully up through the branches but was stopped momentarily by the gap where there was no one to hold her. Shelby was reminded of a black bear cub he had once seen like that, caught half-way up a tree, unable to get up or down and wondered whether she was going to fall.

Manny Rosen called out, 'Belle, keep going! It ain't much farther.'

But Scott distracted her more successfully with his quiet, 'Just take Mr Martin's hand and you'll be all right.' Almost without thinking and in obedience, she climbed the next two branches and was hauled up to safety to a cheer from below. She was as delighted with herself as a child and gave them a wave and a smile.

'A regular Peter Pan,' she said.

A few minutes later they were all at the top. Scott standing at the edge called down, his deep voice carrying to the farthest end of the saloon, 'Anybody else? We're going to try to reach the ship's hull in case there's an attempt to rescue us.'

There was an unusual stir amongst the remaining passengers. A man called back and said, 'We've decided to wait here.'

A steward came shuffling forward through the debris, a bloodstained napkin in his right hand. His left arm hung queerly from his shoulder. When he reached the bottom of the tree he called up to Scott, 'I'd like to get up to my mates, if I could, sir. I've done all I can.'

'Well then, come up man. Hello! What's happened to your arm?'

'I don't know, sir. I can't seem to move it.'

'Is the other one hurt, too?'

'No, sir,' the steward replied. 'It's just that I've been looking after some of those who were bleeding.'

In an instant Scott was down the tree, gripping the man's good hand and gently hauling him up after him.

A steward said, 'Okay, Jock, you're better off with us up here.'

Peters asked, 'Need we hang on to the tree any longer, sir?' The tip was still resting on the ledge.

Scott looked down into the chaos of the dining-saloon once more—the dead, the dying and the living huddled like sheep. His expression was pitiless. 'No,' he said and kicked it away. It fell to the floor with a crackling of branches and a last tinkling of breaking ornaments.

Jane Shelby cried, 'Why did you do that? They might have changed their minds.'

Scott glanced at her briefly but she was aware that he was not there with her, was hardly seeing her.

He said curtly, 'If they do, they know how to go about it.'

Jane thought that this man's utter contempt for the weak could not have been more bitterly expressed. Was this what leaders were like? Would she have wished her husband to be like this? She wondered what would happen if Scott were to be really crossed and how much of a heart beat within that massive frame. And yet how quickly and with that resolution combined almost with tenderness he had fetched up the injured steward. She both admired and despised him.

They now found themselves in the corridor leading to the kitchens. On one side in sequence were the serving pantry, the *sommellerie* where wines for which there might be an immediate call were kept and a restaurant bar. These were the last stops of the waiters on their way out from the kitchens, where they picked up cutlery, extra glasses, serving spoons and drinks.

'Mind the pipes,' Peters warned. 'You're walking on the ceiling.'

This caused them to look up quickly and to see what had become of the floor. Its polished vinyl surface was now over their heads. Underfoot were lines of metal pipes, some asbestos-covered, of various widths and colours serving as conduits for electrical wiring, plumbing, telephone lines, steam for heating, water under pressure for the thousands of fire prevention sprinkler system heads scattered through the ship, and even pipes to bring up beer directly from the tuns to the bars; variously spaced and slippery, the members of the party found it difficult to stand.

Rogo said to Scott, 'You didn't think of that one, did you?'

The Minister replied, 'There'll probably be a lot of other surprises awaiting us. I expect the higher we go, the worse it will be.' He looked at Rogo almost with amusement and concluded, 'I never said it would be easy.'

Acre, the other steward, lay full length where he had been hurled during the roll-over. Close by were the remains of the laden tray he had just been about to carry out. Salmon timbales, chicken, steaks with potatoes, vegetables and rice grains were scattered about. When the ship had begun to heel, he had put out his leg to try to counterbalance. It had snapped between knee and ankle.

There was a strong smell of spirits, wine and beer and the head of The Beamer came up like a fire horse. But there was not a whole bottle left in either the bar or the *sommellerie*, though the floor was aslosh with the stuff mingled with soup and blood. There were broken glasses and dishes underfoot, serving trays, dishcovers, sauce-boats, ladles, soup tureens and vegetable servers, filling the spaces between the parallel lines of piping.

Peters was standing by Acre. He had managed to straighten out the fractured leg and wedge it between two of the conduits, thus immobilizing it almost in the manner of a splint. A bearded seaman in dungaree trousers and white, half-sleeved cotton shirt with S.S. *Poseidon* in blue letters across the chest, stood leaning against the wall, braced with his palms flattened against it. His eyes were mirrors of terror.

Two young chefs in white stood half-way down the passage to the kitchen. They still wore their tall hats which they must have recaptured and automatically put on again when they were knocked from their heads. Their faces were as pale as their neckcloths and their limbs were shaking.

The corridor extended on down past the kitchens which were located in the middle of the ship and not immediately visible. There were a dozen or so dining-room stewards there from other tables; several of them were injured and had already been bandaged with strips torn from tablecloths or napkins. Those who were unhurt were still dazed and the presence of the group of passengers in their domain confused them further. Passengers did not belong there. There was that uneasy air of unreality that prevails immediately following upon or during a disaster when the first terrors have abated and the victims are trying to adjust to catastrophic changes in their surroundings and their lives. Only Peters and Acre seemed to have retained a special relationship as servers of Scott and his party.

Miss Kinsale asked, with what appeared to be more interest than concern, 'Are we all going to be drowned?'

Acre replied, 'I hope not, miss.'

The smooth, unlined face of Miss Kinsale gave no indication of any fears if she had them and Susan thought how little any of them knew about her, or for that matter, about any of the others who were following the lead of the Reverend Scott. And even he was something of a mystery.

The casual query of Miss Kinsale: 'Are we all going to be drowned?' had sent a sudden chill of realization through Susan and she hoped it did not show as it did on Linda Rogo whose husband had removed his dinner-jacket and hung it about her shoulders. She stood next to the seaman against the wall, the upper part of her body encased by the black cloth and shiny lapels. She had drawn the ends together over her breasts. Her silly curls were falling over one eye. The swelling from the blow she had been struck gave her a slightly porcine look. Her teeth were chattering and she was moaning.

The Rosens were clinging on to one another to keep their feet from slipping through the pipes and into the muck from which issued sharp splinters of glass. All the women had resumed their shoes.

The Beamer came climbing out from the wine room where he had scrambled to try and find a drink. He was not looking well. He made for Pamela and stood with his shoulder, touching hers and she felt that he was shivering. She asked, 'What happened, Tony?'

He replied, 'The barman. I think he must have bled to death. There was nothing I could do. I need a drink, Pam.'

She slipped an arm about his waist and held him tightly to her. He repeated, 'I need a drink,' and did not notice her comforting.

Scott said, 'We want to get up to the very bottom of this ship.'

'You mean the keel, don't you, sir?' Peters said.

'That's right. If there is any rescue attempt that's where we ought to be.'

Acre said, 'You'll never get through, sir. She's got a double bottom.'

'I know,' said Robin Shelby, 'that's where the oil tanks are.'

'The Skipper didn't ballast at La Guaira,' Peters said. 'I wondered why. But anyway, the fumes wouldn't let you through.'

'Do they run the whole length of the ship?'

'Except for the bow and the stern, sir.'

'Could we reach either?'

Peters looked the party over: fat Mrs Rosen, her black lace dress already shredded in places from her climb up the tree; the terrified Linda Rogo; Miss Kinsale. The young girls might make it and Mr Shelby and the boy, but not the fat woman. Some of the other gentlemen did not look too fit. Besides, he could only guess at the obstacles that would face them with the ship in the condition she was. He said, 'I couldn't say, sir. You could try.'

'Which way would you go, Peters? Towards the bow or the stern?'

Peters reflected. 'I'd say the stern. The anchors may have broken away and fallen out. That's what might be keeping her steady. In that case the chain lockers would be full of water. Even if they weren't, you'd never get past the anchor chains. I'd say you'd have a better chance in the stern. Maybe somewhere towards the end of the propeller shaft.'

Shelby asked, 'Why are we still floating, Peters?' It was a question none of them had dared voice.

Peters replied, 'I couldn't say, sir. It's mathematics, I suppose. Something to do with air spaces and buoyancy. I was told the cargo holds were nearly empty. There'd be air in them, then, wouldn't there? I wouldn't know, I'm only a steward.'

'But you've sailed in this ship for a long time, haven't you?'

'Twenty-five years to be exact,' Peters said, 'but I only know my own part of her, the kitchens and below decks.' Then he added, 'But we did notice that she had settled somewhat, sir,' and he gestured towards the pool of the grand staircase. 'That's why we suggested you come up here.'

Rogo said, 'So we're here, but where the hell are we? Where's it getting us, all this yackety yack?'

He stirred the group to uneasiness. They had been led up from the dining-room floor to exchange one shambles for another. The corridor was confined.

Scott refused to be ruffled. He said, 'You don't make a decision on a play without going for the weak spot. And when you make it, that's it.' Then to Peters, 'What's your opinion of our chances?'

He dropped his voice and said to Scott and Shelby, 'She could be settling gradually; she could take a lurch and go all at once.' He shrugged his shoulders. 'Or she might float for hours before going down, unless the weather changed. An aircraft might spot us in the morning.'

Shelby said, 'Morning could be too late.'

Robin Shelby heard. He said. 'They could see us at night, too, if they knew we were missing. There's an aerospace rescue and recovery centre in the Azores. They fly Hercules HC-130s. If an astronaut came down, they'd fly over the area and drop flares. If we're sticking up out of the water, we'd show up on radar screens, even in the dark, wouldn't we?'

Peters said, 'See, he knows. He's a smart lad. I've had many a chat with him.'

Robin was wound up: 'They'd telephone to the Miami Marine Information Centre who relay it to the Shipping Computer Centre in Washington. That's why ships send in position reports. If an astronaut has to come down suddenly where he's not expected, they have to know where every ship on the sea is all the time, so they can send the nearest one.'

The Beamer said, 'I say, laddie, you're pretty sharp on all that, aren't you? So it all boils down to that damned time element again; whether or not that position report went out.'

Susan Shelby whispered admiringly to her brother, 'How do you know all that, Robin?'

The boy replied, 'Aw anyone today knows that, Sis. It's all in my astronauts magazine that Daddy gave me for Christmas.'

Scott asked, 'Do you know how long the emergency lighting will last?'

Acre replied to this question, 'About four hours, sir. One of the electricians is a pal of mine. If it hasn't been damaged. It's on two banks of storage batteries.'

Scott consulted his watch. It was half-past ten. He said, 'We ought to be able to make it inside of three hours.'

The thought of the lights suddenly going out and rendering them helpless rattled Rogo. Words spilled out of the side of his mouth, 'Then why don't we get up off our asses and get cracking? You wanna get caught stumbling around in the dark with a lot of women?'

The Beamer added, 'I say, yes. Oughtn't we to be off?'

Scott replied with a curt, 'No!' and when The Beamer looked startled, added, 'You've given me the ball, but before I run with it I like to know where the hole is going to be.'

The Beamer looked at Muller in bewilderment. The latter said simply, 'Football. American. But he's right. He's just saying he wants to know where he's going.' Then to Peters, 'By the way, what's directly below us—or rather, I suppose, overhead now?'

He drew a look from Rogo, firing his dislike again, with his soft voice and cultured way of speaking.

'The swimming-pool,' Peters replied.

Rosen cried, 'What? With water?'

Martin moaned, 'Oh no!' and involuntarily pulled his head down closer to his collar. They all looked up uneasily.

One of the other waiters smiled crookedly and said sardonically, 'Duck!'

Peters said, 'It's all right. The Skipper always orders it emptied when there's any movement. If he hadn't, none of us would be here now.'

Scott asked, 'How far does it extend?'

Peters replied, 'Just about to the end of the pantry. There's a door leading to the passage just beyond the kitchens. If you go along there, you'll come to a companion-way and can go down... I mean, up two decks which will bring you to the working alleyway.'

'Broadway,' put in Acre with a grimace.

Peters said, 'We call it Broadway. It's a wide corridor that runs the length of the first-class. From it you've got access to any part of the ship. It enables crew or hotel staff like us, or cabin stewards, electricians and all that lot, to get from one part of the ship to another without going up on deck, or into the cabin section.'

'...and scaring the passengers,' added the steward who had advised Martin to duck.

'Oh, cut it out, Williams,' Acre said.

'Pappas can show you the way,' Peters said, and then clapped his hands. 'Oi! Pappas!

Wake up! Stop dreaming of home and mother. You speak Englis'? Show these people how to get to the alleyway.'

The Greek sailor turned his bearded face but it was still expressionless, as though he had neither seen nor heard anything.

'From there on,' Peters continued, 'you'll have to work your own way. Keep going aft. At some point you'll have to get up through the engine room to get to the propeller shaft.' Here he and Acre exchanged glances and Peters said, 'We don't know what's happened there.'

Acre added, 'It's five decks high.'

Muller's courage waned again. The 'five decks high' had clouded over his mind with a picture not wholly realized except to tell him that they were embarked upon an impossibility.

But Scott was imperturbable. He asked of Peters, 'Would there be any rope about?'

'Yes. There's a locker just at the end of the pantry. When it's rough we put up hand lines here to get us through into the saloon.'

'Would you get it for me?'

Williams said, 'Let him get it for himself. Nobody's working here any more. We're all in the same bloody fix.'

Scott said, 'That's true. I don't mind, tell me where it is, Peters.'

The steward said, 'Come, I'll show you, sir,' and the two went off together.

Martin still natty in his tartan dinner-jacket with tie to match, the eyes behind the gold-rimmed glasses alert, whispered to Muller, 'What do you think?'

Muller replied, 'He's been a winner, hasn't he? Maybe that's his formula.' Scott's firmness and unconcern had restored his courage and further aroused his curiosity.

The Minister and the steward returned. Scott had a coil of light, nylon rope over his shoulder and carried a heavy, long-hafted red fire axe. The axe had a sharp spike at the opposite end to the blade.

Martin asked, 'What's that for?'

Scott said, 'If we're going to have to climb, we might as well be prepared for it.'

Muller's mind conjured up a silly picture for him; Scott, in a Tyrolean hat, leather pants and cleated boots, roped to an Alpine ledge, wielding a climber's pick. But Rogo was driven to sudden intemperate fury.

'Climb! For Christ's sake, are you off your nut? And the lights go out? And women? What about the stairs—there's got to be stairs, don't there?'

Scott said, 'The stairs may surprise you, Rogo.' The sudden glare was back in his eyes again, that straight unseeing stare. 'You're the one who wanted to get cracking. We're wasting time.'

And this brought back the urgency upon all of them again, and the horror of their situation—upside-down in the biggest transatlantic liner ever built, 81,000 tons of metal hanging between heaven and the bottom of the sea.

Muller felt sickened again because Scott had brought to his mind something that had worried him and that he had been trying to remember ever since they had agreed to follow him. It was the dining-room staircase. He struggled against the implacable clarity of the picture and wondered how long he could stand being battered back and forth between doubt and death, cowardice and courage.

Scott looked his party over and asked, 'Are you still willing to trust me?'

Shelby settled any doubts by answering for them, 'We're with you, Frank.' But Mrs Rosen clutched at her husband's arm and whispered something to him. She had evidently been alarmed by the paraphernalia with which the Minister had reappeared.

Rosen said, 'Look, we don't want to be any trouble. Belle doesn't think she would be able to climb so good. Maybe we ought to stay here and not get in your way.'

Miss Kinsale said at once, 'Oh no, Mr Rosen, you mustn't think of such a thing. I'm sure it won't be too difficult with Dr Scott to help us.'

Rosen looked uncertain and unhappy. Scott said, 'Come along as far as you are able to, keep going as long as you can.'

It rallied them again. None of them wanted to die. He had the gift of liberating the human soul from its fears, to touch upon that nerve that charged the will to survive in the face of all obstacles.

Scott said, 'I think we should have some order of proceeding and stick to it, so we know where we all are. It's going to be difficult walking on these pipes. We ought to go in twos, with the men helping the women. I'll lead with...' and he looked about for a moment, 'Miss Kinsale. Then I think Mr and Mrs Shelby and the Rosens; then the young people, Mr Bates and Miss Reid, Martin and Mr Muller, and I suggest the Rogos bring up the rear together.'

Linda Rogo said, 'Why should we go last?'

Rogo added, 'Yeah, what makes you think I'm gonna be tail-end-Charlie?'

'Because you've got a head on you and I expect you may be called upon to use it.'

The detective said no more and when his wife started to protest again, gave her arm a sharp squeeze and said, 'Shut up!'

Jane Shelby again felt a small pang of anger. If bringing up the rear in Scott's mind was a place of importance, why had not he chosen her husband over this horrid, violent man who so obviously despised him?

Even as he made his last disposals of his party, something had caught Scott's eye, an upside-down locker hanging from the ceiling from which extra tablecloths and napkins had tumbled. He retrieved eight of each that had not been immersed in the muck sloshing about the floor and distributed them to the men saying, 'Put the tablecloths over your shoulder and the napkins in your pockets.'

It was The Beamer who asked, 'Now what on earth for, old...?' and shut himself up again.

Scott said, 'The cloths may come in handy, if they don't we can discard them. As for the napkins, they'll be useful if one of us should suffer a bad cut. We can't afford injuries.'

Jane thought: *God help any of us should we become crippled! He'd leave us.*

Scott shook the shoulder of the still dazed Greek seaman and said, 'Okay, Pappas, get moving! Show us the way.'

Williams suddenly rasped, 'Sure! Okay! Get going! And what about us, here?'

The Minister turned back, 'Will you come along? I'll take anyone who wants to come —or can; Peters, you boys from the kitchen, any of you or all of you.'

Peters said, 'I don't know, sir. Our orders in case of emergency are to remain at our posts until further instructions, or by signal or voice we're sent to our lifeboat stations.'

Williams said, 'Well, there ain't been no signal and there ain't been no voice and what good are lifeboats when you're ass over tea kettle?'

Scott said, 'I should think you might consider yourself relieved of your orders by now. Very well, Williams, you and who else?'

Scott's quiet acquiescence suddenly threw Williams into an almost childish tantrum, 'Not me!' he shouted. 'You'll never make it! You got any idea what's between you and the bottom of the ship? You'll get yourself and everybody with you killed.'

Scott simply ignored the outburst and said, 'Peters?'

Peters said, 'I wouldn't be leaving Acre, here. We've been together too long. Things may still turn out all right, if we don't lose our heads.' Then he added, 'As you go past, don't look into the kitchens.'

'Why?' Rosen asked without thinking. 'Somebody get hurt?'

'The stoves came away as well as everything else,' Peters answered, 'These two boys here,' indicated the shaking chefs, 'got out. The others didn't.' Then almost as an afterthought added, 'The stoves were in use.'

It was Hubie Muller, the dilettante, whose mind was able to form the most vivid and scarifying picture, perhaps because like so many of his set he was an amateur cook and knew his way about the kitchen. All the plates of the electric stoves would have been glowing hot and overturned, would have broken loose and with the scalding contents of their pots and pans, come crashing down amongst the chefs, the second cooks, the salad and pastry specialists, dishwashers and pantrymen, crushing, burning or hammering them to death. It was probably from there that the awful animal scream he had heard had emanated as the ship had gone over.

'We'll go,' Scott ordered, but first turned and said, 'Thank you, Peters. Thank you, Acre, and good luck to you.'

Shelby wondered whether he was going to add, 'I'll pray for you,' but he did not.

The stewards said, 'And good luck to you, too, sir.'

As they moved off they heard Linda say, 'I don't need any help. It's all your fault we're in this mess.' And Rogo's plaintive, almost perpetually placating voice when addressing his wife, 'Aw, now honeybun, lemme take your arm before you bust one of them pretty gams of yours.'

Scott called out, 'Miss Kinsale.'

She said, 'Oh, thank you, Dr Scott,' and slipped her tiny hand through the proffered arm. He manoeuvred it so that she would be on his left side and away from the kitchen. The other men followed suit. No one said anything more and there was only the sound of their feet reaching for purchase between the slippery pipes.

They picked their way past the open kitchens on their right, their heads averted. They breathed a heavy mixture of acrid odours, food and behind it something sinister and sick-making. The picture in Muller's imagination supplied him with what it was: burned flesh. Most of the ceiling lights had been smashed but two were intact and the flickering rays of the emergency bulbs showed only the outline of heaped-up steel or glinted off the wreckage of overturned copper cauldrons, stoves, ovens and equipment. Except for the sounds of antiphonal ticking of metal still cooling, the place was silent.

Muller, on the near side, felt a compulsion to know. He could not help himself. He turned and was half-way inside before his foot slipped and he almost fell. He caught himself on a piece of projecting metal but not before he saw something close by on the floor that was red and might have been meat, except that it was not. He said, 'Oh, my God!'

Martin, who had gone on, his head turned resolutely away, said, 'Come on. What do you want to look in there for? I couldn't take any more, after what I saw downstairs. I'd upchuck again.'

'Oh, my God!' Hubie Muller repeated, even while he was wondering at what kind of a person he might be to have wanted to take that look.

He was shivering as he went on after Martin, his feet slipping and a piece of glass sheared his trouser leg open but only grazed the skin. He never even noticed.

Rogo snatched a glimpse as he went by and said morosely, 'I wouldn't want to die like that.'

His wife added, 'I wish you would!'

The party, with the seaman Pappas and Scott leading, came to a door. The Greek stopped and stared at it dully. The polished steel knob was at a curious level, just above their heads. Scott reached up and swung it open. They were all accustomed to the slightly raised, brass-bound thresholds of the doorways aboard ship, over which on the first day landlubbers were for ever stumbling until they got used to them. But here there was one some two feet in height.

Scott warned, 'Careful!' and helped Miss Kinsale climb over it.

'What kind of a door is this?' asked Rosen.

Shelby answered him as he assisted his wife, 'It's upside-down.'

Belle Rosen said, 'I don't understand. Is everything going to be upside-down?'

Scott replied, 'I'm afraid so, Mrs Rosen. But we'll manage somehow.'

They were in a long, narrow corridor, a wall on one side and cabins opposite. The pipes that had run along the ceiling and were now underfoot were of a smaller size and spacing than those in the pantry.

'Where are we?' Martin asked.

'Still on "R" deck, I think,' Scott said. '"D" deck is just above us and "E" would be where Peters said Broadway was. We'd better go slowly. We don't want any turned ankles.'

Jane Shelby took a firmer grasp upon the arm of her husband as the thought flashed through her mind of what a sprained or broken ankle, or any kind of serious injury would mean, since Scott would leave such a person behind. They needed to make all haste but could not afford to do so.

They were helped however, by the emergency illumination spaced at intervals in the flooring, lamps projecting from between the pipelines and lighting up their footing. But they had progressed only some ten yards before these lights went out so suddenly that it left them stunned, in darkness darker than dark shot through with pyrotechnics at the back of their eyeballs from staring down at the now extinct lamps.

From behind them they heard Rogo's voice, 'Jesus Christ!' and then the hysterical scream of his wife, 'Mike, hold on to me! Don't let me go!'

There was another sound then, a rushing and a slapping of heavy footsteps against the steel piping and some of them were struck and bumped in the dark by a heavy body. They smelled the stink of sweat and garlic.

And then as suddenly as they had gone out, the lights came on again. But this time brighter and without the fluctuation that had characterized them before.

Robin whispered to his sister, 'I'll bet the other set of batteries has taken over.'

When their eyes had got used to the brightness, they noticed that Pappas the sailor detailed to lead them was no longer there.

Rogo said succinctly, 'Why, the dirty, yellow, son-of-a-bitch! He's taken a powder!'

CHAPTER VI

Nonnie Joins Up

The implication of that brief darkness came as an after shock and for a moment the party huddled together. It was muggy in the corridor and the men removed their coats and tied them around their waists by the sleeves.

The front of Hubie Muller's shirt was frilled and pleated. His braces were black with violet flowers. Rogo wanted to say, 'Oh dearie, how lovely you look!' but refrained. He himself was trim and muscular with the thick neck of a steer rising from his open collar. His wife's artificial curls had begun to part from her own. She clawed them off the back of her head and threw them to the floor where they nestled coiled between two sides of pipes like some small, furry animal.

Susan Shelby thought that Scott with his open collar and sleeves rolled up, axe and rope at his belt, looked like an old-fashioned movie hero. Her father found it hard to remember that he had been embarrassed by seeing the Minister on his knees. He was all man.

Jane Shelby's soft, wavy hair had come down about her face like a cloud through her exertions, to give her an extremely youthful aspect. But not a strand of Miss Kinsale's tight, glossy bun was out of place, nor had her frock been greatly disarranged. She glanced at her feet and remarked, 'Oh dear, I'm afraid I've spoilt my shoes.'

The Beamer's highly-coloured face rising from his neckband, and his braces gave him rather the look of somebody's gardener. Pam, in her slip, her long frock carried over o n e arm, looked even more incongruous with her naive blue eyes and English complexion.

Manny Rosen said, 'You all right, Mamma?' With his coat removed one saw the waistband of his trousers was not pulled quite over his belly. What was left of his hair was greying. He had worried brown eyes and a baby's mouth.

She replied, 'Look, my dress is all torn.'

He said, 'You shouldn't have worse worries.'

She hauled it up to assess the damage and showed fat knees and thick legs descending seemingly without ankles to attach to tiny feet wedged into low-heeled black satin slippers. She had rather a motherly face above her several chins. Behind horn-rimmed spectacles the dark eyes were still youthful, although she had passed sixty, and gave her an expression that was slightly roguish at times. Her hair, of which she was very proud, was blue-black and still unchanged—she was always saying, 'Everybody thinks I'm touching it up, but I don't. My grandmother's hair was like this when she was seventy'—and she wore it in two braids across the top of her head. She had an expensive diamond flower brooch clipped at her left shoulder. It caught her attention now and she took it off quickly, saying, 'Oh my goodness, Manny! You'd better put this in your pocket. I wouldn't want to lose it.'

James Martin asked, 'What was with the lights?'

Shelby said, 'They were probably on two banks of batteries. When one went out there was an automatic switch-over.'

Robin Shelby whispered to his sister, 'See? What did I tell you?'

Susan said, 'Okay, Spaceman! What would we do without you?'

Muller asked, 'What happened to our guide fellow?' and Martin replied, 'He blew.'

But Scott added, 'We don't need him. The staircase ought to be along here on the left. Let's go.'

They had just begun to move off behind Scott and Miss Kinsale, when they heard the distant sound of scrabbling uncertain footsteps.

The Beamer cried, 'Hold it! I think the blighter's coming back.'

They stopped and turned to look. It was not the Greek, however, but a girl.

As she approached they saw that she was clad in a pink dressing-gown with swansdown lapels, collar and trim. Trying to run, she was slipping and sliding on the uneven surface yet miraculously keeping her feet which were encased in soft, black leather dancing pumps. As she came on she was crying in a curiously monotone cadence, like a whipped child that cannot stop, one wavering note of grief repeating itself over and over. And whenever her feet went between two conduits, it would emphasize her sobbing wail, as did each fresh breath she managed to draw. She held her dressing-gown pulled together over her breasts with her left hand and balanced herself with her right. Her hair, tumbling to her shoulders, was a true lightish red. She had not discovered the group as yet, for she was running in blind panic with her head down.

Rogo brought her up short a few yards away from them with a sharp cry of, 'Hey, there, Nonnie! Where the hell do you think you're going?'

Her sobbing turned into a scream of fright as she stood stock still, staring at them, both hands now clutching the dressing-gown about her throat. She had paused directly above one of the inset lights and they saw that the face beneath the hair, even with its dead white skin and pale green eyes swollen from crying, yet managed to be attractive.

It was an extraordinary one in that the fluffy aureole of fox-coloured hair emphasized that it was just too small and its features that much too tiny, as though everything— nose, mouth, teeth and oval chin—were in miniature. If they had been proper size, she would have been beautiful.

She was a grown person and yet everything about her appeared to be infantile and it was with a guileless ingenuous innocence, like a hurt child going to its father, that she stumbled to Hubie Muller, and into his arms, where she clung crying, 'Oh my God, I'm so frightened! I'm so frightened! Hold me, hold me! Don't let me go! Please don't let me go! Oh, I'm so scared!'

Hubie Muller held the slight body close to him as she had begged, for she was shivering. He smelled the under-arm body odour of fear mingled with some kind of cheap scent, but the hair on which his face now rested was clean and soft.

'Please let me stay!' she cried. 'Somefink awful has happened. I don' know what. I'm just so frightened I don't know where I am!'

'All right,' said Hubie in his soft voice, 'you're all right now.'

Miss Kinsale said, 'Why it's Miss Parry! The poor thing. She's terrified.'

Only Miss Kinsale and Rogo actually recognized her, the former because she had chatted with her several times and the latter because as a Broadway cop, he liked to have his nose in anything connected with show business. During the voyage he had got to know not only her but the entire company.

She danced in the chorus line of the cabaret that accompanied the cruise. The others had probably looked at her on an average of three times a week when performances were given and she high-kicked in unison with eleven other girls, but had never really seen her.

Rogo did not like that she was sheltering with a fellow who, if he was not a flit, was the next worse page in his book, a cream puff. He said, 'Pull yourself together, kid. You're amongst white people.'

The girl continued to cling to Muller, pressing the side of her face hard against his chest as though trying to hide. She was still trembling uncontrollably.

Then she cried, 'Where's Sybil? Have you seen Sybil? I can't find anyone. I'm frightened! I don't know what's happened.'

Muller held the bony shoulders more tightly to try to stop the shaking that was racking her. He said, 'There, you're all right now. There's been an accident, but we'll look after you.' Then he added, 'Who's Sybil?'

'M-my roomie. She's my chum.' She gasped, 'Oh, my God, an accident?' And then looking up and seeing for the first time where she was, she held Muller off from her and cried, 'Oh dear, I'm sorry! I've done something awful. I don't know you, do I? We're not supposed to be with the gentlemen passengers. I've been having a regular cuddle, haven't I? Timmy said if she ever caught us, she'd...'

Muller said, 'Never mind.' He regarded the flower-like features in the small, anguished face. He had already recognized the commonness of her speech which to the ears of The Beamer was a lower class mixture of Welsh and English. 'It's quite okay,' he repeated, 'none of us are really passengers any longer. We're all sort of sticking together here.'

The others now surrounded the strange little figure, the colour of whose hair clashed horribly with the pink of her négligée with its absurd fluffy white trimming. A piece of it had come loose from the collar and floated momentarily in the air like a thistledown, to settle by the black dancing slippers on her feet. She had retreated from Muller's arms and now she clutched the wrap more tightly about her, 'Oh, my God, I've got nothing on underneath!'

The Beamer said, 'Don't let that worry you, love, none of us are exactly overdressed.'

Muller explained, 'We've come from the dining-room. I'm Hubert Muller and this is Dr Scott who is trying to lead us up to where...'

More than anything it was Muller's soothing voice and his literalness that had brought the girl out of her panic. She blinked up at the big man saying, 'Oh, I know, the Minister gentleman. All the girls are crazy about him... Oh, I'm sorry! I mean...'

Manny Rosen said, 'That's all right, he's used to it.'

The girl eyed them warily for an instant, to see whether fun was being made of her. Then she said finally, 'I'm Nona Parry, but everybody calls me Nonnie. I'm a Gresham.'

Muller fumbled with the phrase. He took in the chalk-white skin, the red-gold hair and the pale eyes. What was a Gresham? Then his mind snapped the word into the proper context. Of course, one of the dancers from the show! But he could not even remember her. Perhaps make-up changed her.

Nonnie looked to Scott and said, 'Can you help me? Have you seen any of the others?' But she remained standing close by Muller as though ready to retreat once more into his arms. 'I mean from our company. Nicky—he's the funny one, Heather and Moira, the one that sings. And Timmy—Mrs Timker. She looks after us.'

The members of the party looked at each other uneasily and Miss Kinsale put her thin hand to her face and said, 'Oh dear, they were all together on "C" deck. My cabin was close to theirs. They were such nice people.'

'But "C" deck was above the dining-room.' It slipped out before Jane Shelby could help herself.

Manny Rosen said, 'Don't. The kid ain't in any shape...'

Scott asked, 'When did you leave your cabin, Nonnie? Where were you going? Can you tell us exactly what happened?'

Nonnie shook her head slightly with the effort to recollect, so that her hair shimmered in the half light. She said, 'It was just before nine o'clock, I suppose. Timmy said there wouldn't be any show tonight and we didn't have to do anything if we didn't want to. I had a tray in our cabin and washed my hair. Sybil was still sick and didn't want anything. I was going to the hairdresser's to borrow some rollers and buy some hair spray.'

Muller thought. *How are we going to tell her? How will she take it?*

Scott asked, 'On which deck is the hairdresser?'

Nonnie counted on her fingers and said, '"D" deck. That's one—no, two down, because of the dining-room. I get so confused.'

Involuntarily several of the party looked up towards the ceiling. Nonnie caught their glances. 'Not up,' she said, 'down. You go down from "C" to "D", but you have to come this way because of the dining-room.'

Nobody said anything.

Nonnie continued, 'It was so late I didn't think anybody would be about at that time. But the hairdresser sometimes is still working, so I just slipped on...' she hesitated, 'this, and went down the first flight of stairs and was walking along to get to the next one, when I got thrown down like somebody pushed me. I don't know what was happening. I was on my side like somebody was holding me down and I couldn't get up. I was scared. My head felt dizzy. Then I fell.'

She stopped suddenly and a puzzled look came into her eyes. 'But I couldn't have fallen, could I? Because I'd already been thrown down in the passageway. But why would I be falling? But I did. I fell on my back, but I didn't hit my head. I was so dizzy everything seemed to be swimming around me. And then there was this terrible noise. Did you hear it? Screams and banging and crashing. I don't know where I was or what happened. I suppose I fainted. I'm not the kind that faints, but I must have. When I woke up it was all dim-like. There was something funny about the lights and they weren't on the ceiling any more. I must've fallen down to some funny place in the ship.'

Linda muttered, 'So we all faw down! For Chrice sakes can't someone shut this little bum up?'

If the girl heard her, she paid no attention. She was wound up. 'I got up and didn't know which way to go. I wanted to get up the stairs and get back to Sybil. I went the way I thought they ought to be—where I come from. But maybe because I was so dizzy I got turned around. I couldn't find them and it was dark. I came to one place where I thought the stairs was, but there was only a hole there and I looked down and there was some water. When I saw the water, I got frightened again and I thought maybe something had happened to the ship and I'd got to get back to my cabin. So I started to run and then when the lights went out, I thought I was going to die and began to cry like a baby. I'm afraid I made a fool of myself. I'm sorry,' she stopped. She had run down like a clock.

'No, you haven't,' Hubie comforted, 'it was enough to frighten anyone.'

Scott said, 'She'll have to know. Will you tell her, Hubie?'

'Oh Christ!' said Muller. 'Must I?'

Nonnie was looking from one to the other of the party, still confused but slightly more at ease by those whom she had recognized from having met or seen in the audience. 'Tell me what?'

Half under her breath Jane Shelby said, 'No! Don't.' She wanted to spare her and at the same time knew that it was impossible. Everything that the Minister did or suggested was right, yet at the same time seemed cruel as well.

Scott went on, 'Yes, you'd better. We've got to get going while there's light.'

Muller took her hand in his and said, 'Nonnie, I'm afraid you're in for another shock.' Then he told her quietly and simply while the others watched her uneasily, wondering how she would take it. That class of people always went to pieces and kicked up a terrible fuss.

But Nonnie did not. If anything she went yet another shade whiter and her face seemed even smaller. She only murmured, 'May I sit down for a second?' and did. They waited for the tears, but she had none of those either. Her fight was to get a grip upon herself in front of them all. She put her hands before her face for only an instant and then climbed back to her feet.

Pamela Reid said, 'My mother is... was in a cabin on "B" deck.'

Nonnie went to her and put her arms about her, 'Oh lovey,' she said, 'you poor thing! If it was my Mum and Dad, I couldn't bear it.' Then she looked at Scott, indicating Hubie Muller and said, 'Can I go with him?'

'Yes, of course,' the Minister replied, 'he'll help you. We're all very, very sorry.'

Belle Rosen said with some satisfaction, 'So now we're fifteen.'

Her husband asked, 'What's that got to do with anything?'

'So we aren't thirteen.'

'You and your superstitions,' Rosen said. 'We were fourteen before.'

'So fifteen is still better.'

Linda Rogo remarked, quite audibly, 'That's all we needed; this little bum.'

Rogo pleaded, 'Don't be like that, honey. She's only a kid and scared stiff.'

Nona Parry's child's mouth went thin suddenly. 'Who's she calling a bum?' she snapped.

'Nobody,' said Muller. 'She's a bitch. Nobody pays any attention to her except that doormat she married.'

Mike Rogo, without turning his head, threatened loudly, 'I wouldn't like anyone around here to be passing remarks. Someone could get his jaw broken.'

They moved off. 'Mind,' said Muller, 'some of those pipes are slippery and you can give yourself a nasty wrench. Hold on tight.'

She did, clutching his arm and pressing her shoulder which felt thin and bony through the dressing-gown, against his. Her contact moved him in an extraordinary way, bringing an unusual constriction to his throat. There had been something touching in her flight and panic and gallant in her recovery of herself and acceptance of the tragedy that had left her the sole survivor of her troupe. It was as though the pressure was a communication, a need and a defiance at one and the same time.

Mike Rogo was wrong about Hubert Muller, though probably justified in disliking him as a type. He was neither a queer nor a cream puff, but only a rich man's son who had turned into a gentleman of no profession with cosmopolitan tastes and an international reputation as the hostess's delight. He was that extra man with unimpeachable manners who never got drunk, played a first-class game of Bridge and refrained from impregnating their daughters.

Instead, with fastidious discrimination, he preferred his bedmates married and from his own set. Hubie's contribution was that he kissed often and well, but never told. A snob, it never occurred to him to tumble the maid who brought in his breakfast tray, or any of the nubile little tramps always around on the make for a wealthy man.

He had acquired his soft-spoken, languid manner and Bostonian, semi-English accent during an otherwise useless career at Harvard. On the other hand he had survived two years in the army, eight months in Korea, and was tougher than Rogo suspected. This experience had confirmed his determination never again to allow himself to be placed in any situation where either unpleasantness or discomfort prevailed, or for that matter, work. His bachelorhood stemmed purely from selfishness. He had not yet found a woman who could supplant Hubie Muller in his affections.

Thus, at forty he still parted his hair in the middle, wore his handkerchief up his sleeve and was engagingly charming. He carried his binoculars to Ascot, Auteuil and Saratoga and was seen with the set of Palm Beach, Biarritz, Deauville, St Moritz and Monte Carlo.

Bored with the prospect of Christmas in the houses of other people's families, he had booked for the cruise upon impulse coupled with a sentimental attachment to the old *Atlantis*, now the *Poseidon*. Several of his crossings on her had yielded some highly interesting, temporary involvements.

Sexually, however, the cruise had been arid. The married women were too old and the ship's beauty after whom all the men went baying was obviously nothing but a tease.

The one attractive, blonde widow, Mrs Wilma Lewis, had run up the 'No thank you' flag in reply to his discreetly coded signals.

He stole a glance at the tiny figure next to him and thought how ridiculous they must both look, arm-in-arm. He in his flowered braces and frilled shirt, with a slit, flapping trouser leg, and she in the shockingly vulgar, pink peignoir beneath which she said she had nothing on.

And yet in this strange and dangerous situation he felt oddly possessed of her. Somehow she had become his, or at least temporarily his responsibility. In that company thrown together by disaster, every Jack had his Jill, so to speak or at least were paired off, except for himself and that drab little haberdasher. Then this creature had come tumbling out of the darkness into his arms like a storm-battered bird out of the night.

He gripped her tightly to maintain this contact that was providing him with the most unusual emotion of pity. He said, 'Hang on, Nonnie. You're safe now,' and then had to smile to himself at the ridiculousness of his use of the word 'safe' under the circumstances.

She looked up at him and whispered confidentially, 'You're nice.'

Some twenty yards farther along, Scott said, 'Hold it!' and put up his hand. They came to a halt. 'Here's the staircase.'

It was Mike Rogo, however, who expressed their feelings. 'Great!' he said, 'What do we do now, coach?'

CHAPTER VII

The Adventure of the First Staircase

None of them had ever seen or stood at the bottom of a reversed flight of steps.

In the chaos of the dining-saloon they had not even been aware of the nature of what remained of the grand staircase, emerging at its widest point from the pool of oily water, its golden handrails and carpeted steps curving upwards to the ceiling where it looked so utterly different that none of them any longer recognized it for what it was. It had become simply a part of that nightmare in which chairs and tables hung from the roof and lights were thrown up from the glass floor. Thus, they were wholly unprepared for what faced them now.

The steps now hung upside-down from the ceiling and the complete uselessness of their former functional capacity was almost as appalling a shock to their minds as the catastrophe itself. In one moment a concept utterly familiar to them, a part of their daily lives, had been destroyed.

The handrails of polished mahogany and the brassbound vinyl-covered steps, instead of providing an easy rise to which they were accustomed, jutted out in an overhang above their heads. The ceiling of the companion-way which had paralleled the angle of descent now presented the only means of ascent, a slippery and precipitous slope of painted steel with lighting panels inset and flush, an unmanageable surface offering no grip or handhold of any kind. While the ends of the handrails at the bottom were within reach of a tall man, only a trained athlete could hope to make use of them.

Manny Rosen waddled over and looked up the tunnel of the stairway. 'How do you expect us to get up there? This is crazy!'

The Beamer laughed, 'I guess that puts paid to this idea.'

'I don't get it,' said Martin. 'Are they all like that?'

Shelby was whispering something to his wife and glancing at Belle Rosen. He turned to Scott and said, 'I don't see how we can work it, Frank.' And in a curious way which he would never have admitted to himself, he was almost pleased to have come upon an insurmountable obstacle so quickly. The younger man had gone sailing off with too much confidence. They ought to have thought the situation over more carefully.

Scott said, 'It oughtn't to be too difficult.'

Rosen snapped, 'Are you kidding? What kind of talk is this? Don't you know you've got women here?' He included them all but everyone knew that he was referring to the hopelessness of ever getting either himself or his wife up such an incline.

The Beamer said, 'Are you sure you know what you're doing? I think we ought to go back to Acre and Peters.'

'Yeah!' Martin agreed, 'at least they're from the ship.'

From the movement and rustle of the party and the looks between them it was obvious that the idea of the return was popular. Because hope had been stirred in them coupled with the survival instinct they had set out upon an improbable journey and because it was only the beginning they were ready to give up at the first obstacle.

Nonnie whispered to Muller, 'What is it? Where does he want to take us?'

Muller told her. Nonnie glanced up the staircase and whispering again said, 'Don't you think we ought to have a go?'

Muller looked at her in astonishment. A few moments before she had been in a state of panic. He remembered her flare up at Linda's insult and thought to himself: *Why, she's a little fighter!*

From the vantage point of his height, taller than any of them, Scott looked his group over wordlessly.

Jane Shelby searched for so much as a shadow of contempt upon his face to set her off again in mindless fury against him. But saw none and instead thought that what she saw was a compassionate weighing of them, of their values and in herself suddenly felt small, inadequate, found wanting and a quitter. She cried aloud, 'I think we ought to go on,' and saw that her husband looked shocked.

But Scott smiled at her gratefully as though it had been the break for which he had been waiting and said simply, 'It's a piece of cake.'

The silly, boyish remark intrigued them, revitalized them and brought back their courage. Muller who was given to introspection was well aware that he had been quite prepared to give up and turn back. Now he was not.

Martin covered his own feeling of shame with a misquotation, 'Okay, lead on Macduff!'

The Beamer asked Pam, 'Shall we have a bash, old girl?'

Robin Shelby cried, 'I'll bet I could get up there!'

Only Linda Rogo whined, 'I want to go back.'

Scott ignored her. He said, 'You know all that's left of the world to us has been turned upside-down. If we would just stop expecting everything to behave as though it were still rightside up, things wouldn't seem quite so difficult any more.'

Rosen said, 'All my life I've been walking on my feet, I should suddenly have to think of walking on my head?'

Scott said, 'You're not standing on your head, are you? But you are on the ceiling and the floor is above you. Once you begin to get used to something, it's not so bad any more.'

Robin Shelby put in, 'You mean like the astronauts having to get used to weightlessness?'

'Something like that, Robin,' the Minister agreed. 'Try to think what it would be like if your own house were suddenly to be turned upside-down while you were upstairs and you wanted to get something from the cellar. You'd have to find some way to climb up to get it and because you'd know your own house so well, you'd manage.'

Susan gave a little startled cry, 'Oh! Now I remember what I thought in the dining-room, but it was so silly. Last summer I went with some friends to Bannerman's Amusement Park. There was a sort of a crazy house there. You went in and it turned upside-down, or at least it seemed to, and you suddenly found yourself walking on the ceiling. And when you looked up, all the chairs and tables and wardrobes and pictures and things were up there. I suppose they had them attached, but it gave you the weirdest feeling.'

Belle Rosen said, 'Talk, talk, talk! Everybody can talk as long as you don't expect me to go up.'

Little Rosen suddenly looked alarmed and said, 'Mamma, if we got to, well...'

Richard Shelby felt called upon if nothing else to lend him some kind of moral aid. He said, 'Look here, everyone. We've come this far. We've left the others and in a way we've committed ourselves. I've committed my family and myself. By all accounts of what happens to ships when they capsize, she ought to have gone then and there. But she didn't.'

As he spoke he had a momentary memory flash of Scott on his knees and through his mind coursed advertisements for books he had seen, THE POWER OF PRAYER. Was Scott working on a direct telephone line to the Deity and getting immediate action on the petition of a Princeton All-America turned prelate? He continued, 'We're floating upside-down with the keel up and half of her sticking out of the water.'

Jane was aware of irritation again. Scott was paying not the slightest attention to what her husband was saying, but was busying himself with preparations. Removing his shoes and socks he stuffed them into the side pockets of his jacket and laid the axe on the floor. He took the coil of rope from his shoulder, tied one end to his belt and handed the other to Rogo saying, 'Here, hang on to this a minute, will you?'

The detective's violent temper threatened to flare again. He shouted at Scott, 'I think you're a nut!' and then at the others, 'What the hell's the matter with all of you? A minute ago you were ready to go back to the others that stayed in the dining-room with the officers. Now you want to follow this crackpot again. Count me out!' But he still held fast to the rope's end.

Shelby went on, 'My boy was right. In the morning anyone searching from the air would see us like a big fish floating belly up. We're a thousand feet long. Where would they have to break into see if anybody was left alive? Through the hull, wouldn't they? As long as her buoyancy lasts, we've got a chance.'

Jane's annoyance was transferred to her husband. He was only parroting Scott; why hadn't he thought of it first?

The Beamer turned his now sober gaze upon Rogo and said earnestly, 'Do you know, old boy, come to think of it if she does go, I'd much prefer to be caught trying to get out.'

'I would, too!' said Mary Kinsale, 'It's more dignified, isn't it?' They all stared at her in astonishment.

'Oh yes, you're right, Miss Kinsale, above all, human dignity,' said the Reverend Dr Scott and leapt for the handrail above his head.

Muller understood perhaps for the first time why he personally was prepared to go on. God and the Saints were waning myths but the Minister had unfurled a banner he could follow.

He watched in silent admiration as Scott caught the rail and with the same movement swung upwards so that his feet rested ahead of him upon the steep slope. Then hand-over-hand he pulled himself up the incline via the slanting railing and in a few seconds had reached the top. Standing on the flooring which had formerly been the ceiling he fastened his end of the rope to a rail stanchion and called down, 'Okay, Rogo, you can let go now.'

The detective was shaken. A rah-rah boy had made it look so easy. Then he said sarcastically, 'I can't wait to see Belle try that.'

Scott said, 'Don't be a chowderhead, Rogo! Send Martin up next,' and to Martin, 'Use the rope instead of the handrail. Brace your feet against the slope and pull yourself up. Take it easy, don't try to do it all in one rush. Good man, that's the way.' A few moments later he was up and standing rather proudly next to him.

'Robin, you're next.'

The boy had succeeded in climbing only half-way up when his strength failed him. He cried, 'I can't any more!'

Scott called down, 'Okay, son, just hang on. Let your feet slide out from under you.' He gripped the rope and signalled Martin to do the same. They heaved back and the youngster was hauled up sliding on his stomach to wriggle to safety on the landing.

'Gee,' he said, 'I'm sorry! I thought I was stronger than I am.'

Scott said, 'Never mind, you did all right, Robin. You kept your head and what's more, you've been helping others to keep theirs.'

'Me?' the boy said in surprise, 'How?'

Scott grinned at him, 'By putting that picture into their minds of all those ships and aircraft, marine radio stations and computer centres on the lookout for us. Some people call it hope. I'd call it Pie-in-the Sky. If it's there and you can see it, you keep on trying to reach for it.'

Martin said, 'I can't afford to sink. I've got to get back to...' He had been about to say his shop, but under the circumstances to couple their survival with his spring line of with-it accessories again suddenly struck him as ridiculous, so he concluded, '...to my wife.' And immediately the thought of Mrs Lewis came up to haunt him once more.

Scott said, 'You just keep thinking that.'

Martin wondered why he did not add, 'and pray', the way most preachers would have done. Some of these modern ones were funny fellows.

Scott said, 'Okay, Rogo, you're next.'

Linda screeched, 'No you don't! You're not leaving me alone down here, like you wanted to in the cabin. I'd be dead by now, like all the rest if I'd listened to you. We're not taking any orders from him. Let somebody else go.'

Scott said, 'You needn't be afraid, Mrs Rogo. We're going to pull you up.'

Linda cursed him.

Whitefaced with anger, Jane Shelby turned upon her, 'Why don't you behave yourself, you little idiot? Can't you see we're all trying to keep control of ourselves? That we may all be drowned any minute? That he's the only one trying to do anything for us?'

Richard Shelby looked at her in surprise; satisfaction mixed with a certain chagrin. What hurt was the, 'Can't you see he's the only one trying to do anything for us?' because it was true. He had submitted so easily to Scott's leadership, even though he was only half convinced that anything would come of it.

Rogo said, 'You'll be all right, baby doll. See, Mrs Shelby here says she'll look after you.' When he wanted to, he had a wonderful capacity for neither seeing nor hearing. He slung the tablecloth around his shoulders, seized the rope and without a break in the movement of his powerful arms and shoulders, pulled himself to the top.

The Beamer went next. It was a struggle, but he made it to the edge and Scott pulled him to safety.

From below Pamela called, 'May I come up the rope? We had to climb them in gym.'

'So did we,' said Susan.

'Race you!' Pam challenged.

'You're on!' Susan replied.

Pam seized the rope, and shouted up, 'Time me!' In a moment her strong shoulders were pumping, her stocky legs bracing as she hauled herself aloft.

Robin called off, 'Sixteen seconds! Come on, Sis!'

Susan was more graceful but not as strong. When she reached the top she laughed, 'You've won!'

The Beamer cried, 'Up Britannia!' reached over and felt Pamela's arm muscles and muttered, 'Crikey!'

The little contest had cheered everyone.

Muller was standing at the bottom, looking at his hands. Rogo muttered, 'We'll never get this guy up. He's soft. Let's pull him and get it over with.'

The Beamer said, 'Shouldn't he at least be allowed to have a go?'

Rogo looked at him with contempt, 'Oh, I say! Pip pip, sporting what?' He did not like Englishmen any more than he liked queers or cream puffs.

Muller started but weakened a third of the way. He broke into a sweat, his face turned beet red and he pulled desperately at the rope. Half-way up, his feet went out from under him.

Rogo said, 'Let's get that panty-waist out of there before he hurts himself.'

The Beamer said, 'He'll hurt himself more if he lets go.'

Scott watched the struggle dispassionately for a moment and then suggested, 'Turn around and push up with your feet and rump.'

Muller managed to scramble around on to his back and find sufficient purchase to take some of the strain off his arms and began to gain on the slope. Laboriously he heaved himself to the top where Scott was able to seize his wrists and haul him in. He collapsed on to his knees gasping for breath and gazing at his hands, which had come up in blisters.

Rogo looked over his shoulder and said, 'Boy, those are some blisters! You want to watch out with them things.' But there was no sympathy in his voice.

During the struggle Rosen had been holding a whispered conference with Shelby. The latter called up to Scott, 'Frank, Mr Rosen doesn't think he will be able to make it. What's your idea for the girls?'

Scott replied, 'Sling. Haul them up.'

'With the rope?'

'No, the tablecloths. It won't hurt them. All right, leave Rosen down and we'll pull him up after the women. Come up here yourself, then, and bring his tablecloth. Rosen can help them as well as you.'

Shelby wondered if like Muller he would make a half botch of getting to the top. He had heard Rogo's contemptuous 'soft', and thought how ill prepared one was to face any kind of emergency that called for physical strength. Just before he gripped the rope he was struck with the utter absurdity, in danger of immediate death, worrying whether he was going to look good or bad before Scott, his family and a New York police detective.

He went up in fair enough style to be approved by his son, 'Attaboy, Dad!' The others were already rolling and knotting the tablecloths together. Scott attached rope to the ends of these so that they formed a curved loop which they let down to the bottom of the incline.

Rosen asked, 'What do you want they should do?'

'Ride it,' Scott directed, 'one leg over. Hold on at each side. Mrs Rogo, will you be the first to come up?'

Linda with her hands resting on her hips said insolently, 'Not on your life! Get another guinea-pig to see if it works.'

Nonnie said, 'I'll go.' She had an overwhelming sense of loneliness and wanted to reach the safety of the man whose arms had first sheltered her and who had been kind to her. She tucked up the pink dressing-gown to pad herself and thrust one bare, dancer's leg over the curve of the cloth.

'That's it,' Scott coached. 'Now hang on and turn your back to the slope. All right, boys, pull! Slowly, until we see whether everything is holding.'

With even the girls taking a hand on the ropes, she came up easily and smoothly to the landing where she was helped to her feet. Her gown fell open and showed one small, pointed breast such as one might expect to find on a fifteen-year-old child. Rogo, The Beamer and Martin all tried to look elsewhere. Scott did not bother.

At the bottom of the slope Linda said to Miss Kinsale, 'Did you see that? Preacher boy had a good look.'

She replied evenly, 'I don't know what you're talking about,' and prepared herself for the cloth loop descending again.

Miss Kinsale managed to endow her ascent with the curious kind of restrained dignity that always seemed to envelop her, as though she were quite used to doing that sort of thing. Linda on the other hand called as much attention to herself as possible in settling the loop between her legs. Before giving the signal she donned Rogo's jacket which had been about her shoulders and buttoned it saying, 'He isn't getting any look at my tits.'

After Jane Shelby had followed without incident, there were only the Rosens left at the bottom. Manny said to his wife, 'Mamma, I'm so ashamed.'

She replied, 'For what?'

'That I couldn't go up the rope like them other guys.'

His wife said, 'So what are you, Manny Rosen? An acrobat or a retired delicatessen store owner? You shouldn't have to go up ropes. Let 'em pull you.'

Rosen held the cloth steady while his wife thrust a leg through it, settled herself, and took a grip upon the two pieces that came up fore and aft. She said, 'Diapers, at my age I should be needing yet!'

Rosen said, 'Mamma, how can you joke?'

'What else is there to do?' she replied. He was aware of a wave of admiration and affection for her. He himself was sick at heart and frightened.

He said, 'Mamma, you're great,' then called up, 'Okay!'

'I bet I break the elevator,' Belle Rosen said.

'I'll bet you don't!' replied Scott, but whispered, 'Slow, and not too much strain. She's a load.'

She came up majestically, swaying from side to side. The eyes behind the thick spectacles were mischievous again, almost as though she were enjoying the ride. They reached for her and pulled her in and a small cheer went up from the group as they crowded around her to make sure that she had suffered no harm.

She said, 'Thank you, thank you! If I didn't do it, I wouldn't have believed it.'

From below came Manny Rosen's voice, 'Hey, hey, hey, up there! Don't forget me!'

Rogo went to the edge of the platform and said, 'Keep your hair on, Manny.'

Linda said to her husband without bothering to drop her voice, 'Let him get himself up. I can't stand Jews.'

Everyone froze except Belle Rosen who kidded, 'You can't? That's out of fashion today—unless you're an Arab. I didn't know you was an Arab.'

Susan Shelby giggled and Linda turned on her and said, 'I hate all of you! I know you're snickering and sneering at me! You all think you're better than I am!'

Rogo soothed her, 'Now, baby doll,' and then to the others, 'You mustn't mind her. It's nerves. I guess she's got a right to have 'em. We're in a hell of a spot, ain't we?'

Rosen came sailing up into their midst and was aware of the stiffening and the tension in the group. 'I'm here!' he said, 'Something wrong? Why is everybody looking?'

Belle Rosen said with a straight face, 'Mrs Rogo was saying how she was glad you got here, wasn't you dear?'

Linda's pursed mouth formed for reply but Jane Shelby intervened before she could let go. She said, 'We're all glad you're here, Mr Rosen. We're glad everyone's here, thanks to Mr Scott.'

Scott seemed not to have heard or to have been aware of the exchange. His mind was already coping with the next stage of their ascent. He said, 'Let's have a look at where we have got to go now.'

CHAPTER VIII

Madam Must Have Her Postiche

Robin Shelby cried, 'I think I know where we are! The photographer works down here.'

They were in a second long, narrow, deserted corridor very much like the one from which they had just come, except less luxurious. Here were the cheapest inside, below-decks cabins, tolerable enough for a swift transatlantic passage but not sold for a sunshine, warm weather cruise in the heat of the tropics.

Here were located as well the photographer's laboratory and the print shop that produced the daily menus and shipboard newspaper, the men's barber's shop and farther along the ladies' hairdressing parlour.

The corridor appeared to run the full length of the midships first-class section of the *Poseidon*. Astern the lights were not functioning and it vanished into darkness. The going underfoot was more difficult; more pipes and conduits lined what had been the ceiling. They became aware of noises and scuffling and trampling and the ring of shoes on metal from overhead.

The Beamer said, 'Hello! There are chaps alive up there.'

Shelby added, 'That must be the alley for the crew Peters called Broadway.'

Rogo gave Scott a look out of his small eyes with their curiously turned-down-at-the-corner lids and said 'Okay, coach, which way?'

Martin whispered to Rosen, 'What is this coach stuff?'

Rosen replied, 'He's a tough cop. He don't like college boys.'

Martin's thin lips parted in what was half a gag, half a grin. He said, 'Seems to me he don't like nobody, except that bitch of his who keeps rubbing his nose in the dirt.' It was unusual for him to make such a remark. He did it only as a distraction from the torment he was undergoing.

They heard a noise. A few yards down the corridor a woman had appeared, climbing laboriously over the high threshold of one of the upside-down doorways. She halted blinking and half dazed when she saw the party. She was clad in a white overall tied at the waist and her arms were bare, but over her right fist held in front of her she was carrying a lady's brown shoulder-length wig which had been set and combed out. In her other hand she had a hairbrush.

The woman said, 'Excuse me, Mrs Gleeson. I'm sorry I'm late. I'll have it all right for you in just a minute. I don't know what happened, but it got knocked about somehow.' She peered from one to another in the party and they could see that her eyes were glazed and her face white with shock. She said to Jane Shelby, 'Oh, you're not Mrs Gleeson! I thought you were her, coming for her wig and would be angry with me.'

Nonnie cried, 'Why, it's the hairdresser! The one I was going to see,' and then, 'Oi, Marie, love! Where are you going? Don't you know what's happened? Nobody cares about wigs any more.'

The hairdresser was unable to bend her mind from the article. She gave it three automatic dabs with the brush so that some loose ends came back into place and curled upwards. 'It looks all right now, doesn't it? I had it all nicely finished when it fell over, the wig-stand and everything.' Surprise came into her voice, 'I must have, too. I get dizzy spells sometimes. I haven't been feeling well since we started rolling like that.' She continued to brush the postiche murmuring, 'I can't see very well. Why have all the lights gone out? Is it me?'

Nonnie whispered to Muller, 'Try to make her understand. She doesn't know.'

He said, 'Look here, you'd better stay here with us.'

The hairdresser drew back in alarm as though she expected them to try to detain her. 'Stay with you? Why?' she cried. She regarded the wig again, turning it this way and that and from the rear it looked so startlingly like the back of a woman's head that for a moment Muller found himself questioning his own sanity.

'She said nine o'clock. She won't half cut up if she doesn't get it. She's always ticking me off anyway, when she comes here. Nothing's ever right. One of them. I'd better go.'

Before anyone could move to stop her she was off, running, stumbling and tripping down the passageway towards the stern, holding the ridiculous article before her.

The absurd incongruity of her concern took them so by surprise that she had all but vanished into the darkness at the end of the corridor before Nonnie called after her, 'Wait, Marie! Come back! They say there's nobody there any more. Please, Marie, come back!'

She would have run after her, but Hubie Muller held her back. He said, 'It's no use, Nonnie, you'd never catch her.' Indeed the hairdresser had disappeared. 'You might hurt yourself. She'll come back when she sees what's happened.'

From above there resounded another trampling of feet which distracted them momentarily. But Jane Shelby clutched her husband's arm. 'Dick! I heard a scream— from down there, where that poor woman went. She was out of her mind. We should have made her stay.'

Nonnie cried, 'Oh, why didn't you let me go after her? Something's happened to her. Marie was sweet to all of us.'

Muller said, 'I'll go and have a look. Wait here. It might have been something else Mrs Shelby heard.'

He felt a responsibility towards Nonnie because he had prevented her from going.

Scott said, 'Be careful, Hubie.'

And Rogo added, 'Yeah, don't get yourself hurt.' It was difficult to tell from his tone whether or not he meant it.

But Rogo's world and his were such miles apart that Muller did not even bother to think about it. He walked down the corridor until he came to the patch where there was no longer any light. He was uneasy now, wished he had not volunteered and wondered why he had. Was it because Nonnie had entrusted herself to him? And why should he feel responsible?

He went down on to his hands and knees and inched forward clinging to the piping, aware that the floor had begun to slant downwards. When the angle suddenly took a sharper turn, he stopped.

He took the lighter from his pocket, lit it and held it above his head. He knew now why she had screamed. He turned away, crawling on his stomach and did not climb to his feet until he was within the safety of the lighted area again. Then he walked slowly back, fighting off nausea. He had been too long away from destruction, horror and sudden death. Rogo's contempt for him was probably well-founded. He had gone soft.

When he rejoined the party they waited silently for him to speak. He said, 'Well, now we know which way we're to go. The poor creature has decided for us.' He shuddered and said, 'If we'd gone there, it might have happened to some, or even all of us.'

Shelby asked, 'What might have happened?'

Muller replied, 'it's all blown to bits but you wouldn't have seen it in the dark until it was too late. She didn't either. Some machinery or something must have come down. There's nothing but a great big hole, one or maybe a couple of decks down, filled with oil and water. That damn wig was floating in the middle of it. I couldn't see anything of her.'

Nonnie said, 'She didn't know what she was doing, did she? Oh, why didn't I hold on to her!' Her little face screwed up to cry.

Her distress moved even Rogo who turned to her and put his hand on her arm and said, 'Never mind, miss, you done the best you could. None of us was any smarter.'

Linda said to her husband, 'You keep away from that little tart!'

Nonnie flicked half shed tears from her eyes and turned on her with waspish fury. 'Who are you calling a tart, you bitch!'

Curiously, at the same time that he was disgusted by the vulgarity of the brawl, Muller felt an anger matching that of Nonnie rising in him.

Belle Rosen said, 'Now, now!' to which Manny quickly interposed, 'Mamma, don't mix in.'

Mike Rogo's eyes went hard. He said to Nonnie, 'Relax, sister. No one's calling anyone anything. You didn't hear right. We got enough trouble already, ain't we?' and to his wife he let slip out of the side of his mouth, 'Ixnay! Ixnay! Cut it out!'

With the skill of a lifetime police officer breaking up a disturbance, he placed himself so that there was distance between them. Hubie Muller was standing protectively over the dancer who was still venomously angry, her mouth pinched and tight. She had a redhead's temper and had not yet finished.

'She called me a whore!'

The dressing-gown that she held tightly to her and the flying hair made unruly by having been washed, did not lend dignity to her tantrum. Yet to his surprise, Muller found himself half amused. Actually she could not have looked more like one if she had tried.

'Never mind,' he said to her, 'it's probably just a case of transference.'

Nonnie's anger cooled as quickly as it had exploded and she looked at Muller curiously. 'I don't understand what you're trying to say. I s'pose I'm stupid.'

Rogo's piggy eyes were querying Muller. He had not understood either and wondered whether something had been said for which there ought to be reprisals.

'No,' Hubie said, 'you're not stupid.'

The girl looked up into his face saying, 'I'm not a whore,' and then added, 'I work bloody hard for my living.'

Again Muller felt that curious constriction of the throat and the wave of protectiveness, as though he wanted to gather her up and shield her. He remembered suddenly that underneath this silly pink thing she had nothing on and it seemed to make her all the more vulnerable. He compromised by moving closer to her and comforted, 'Yes, you do, Nonnie, jolly hard.' She responded with a grateful smile and edged closer to him too as though accepting and sealing their partnership.

Scott observed, 'If that's the service alley above us, there'll be a staircase at both ends. We'll have to use the forward one, then. Sometimes you give a little ground to gain more. We'd better get on.'

Belle Rosen complained, 'Oh, my feet, walking on these pipes!'

Scott reacted immediately. 'I think the girls ought to take off their shoes. It's too dangerous with heels.'

When they moved off Jane Shelby found herself in the van with Miss Kinsale who was carrying her shoes meticulously, saying, 'Isn't Dr Scott wonderful? So authoritative,' and then adding almost as if in apology, 'so many of our vicars aren't, you know.'

Jane replied, 'Yes,' but she was thinking how quickly Scott had managed to wipe the episode of the unfortunate hairdresser from his mind. Had he given her so much as a further thought, a prayer, now that she was gone? She found herself worried by such tremendous drive. Somewhere, she felt, there was something that was not normal.

James Martin had fallen in line with Scott and the two men, looking carefully down at their feet, made their way together silently. Martin was wondering whether he ought to confess to the Minister what was so fearfully upon his mind, whether this might not be the moment to rid himself of some of his torment by talking about it. Scott was head and shoulders taller than he and Martin looking up noted the concentration of the brow, the handsome head and the truculent jawline. He hesitated; the man was so unlike any preacher he had ever known. He could not reconcile the All-American boy of the face and figure of Scott with one of God's appointed—the Buzz and the Reverend.

James Martin's conscience was hurting him badly. If the ship stayed afloat; if they succeeded in reaching the outer skin of the vessel; if the world heard of their plight; if rescue ships or helicopters or whatever arrived in time to get them out, he was being let off too easily.

He had sinned. He had formed a liaison in adultery with a lusty, enthusiastic woman and ought to be punished. As a moral man although a backslid Baptist, and a merchant, he was aware that there was always a bill to be paid. The manner in which Martin differed from most men was that he was always willing to pay without bellyaching.

Mrs Wilma Lewis was not the kind of woman who could be dismissed with a present and a pat on the fanny as one of those shipboard things at voyage end. A widow of forty-eight, she had embarked on the cruise in search of nothing more than sexual satisfaction. She was willing to give as good as she got but once she had found it, she was not prepared to let go. Of Swedish origin she was a handsome, ample, big-breasted woman of good figure and fine skin with light blue eyes that were slightly prominent. She had thick, heavy, naturally golden hair which she did not mind touching up with a rinse to give it additional lustre. And when she stepped out of her clothes allowing them to tumble to her feet, she was a pink Venus, an alluring, pneumatic, sexual figure into which a man could sink with both bliss and comfort.

All this she concealed beneath a ladylike and demure demeanour with a reserve that was misleading. She was tall, almost six feet, but her grace and charming smile had a softening effect. Her clothes were conservative and expensive. She presented an almost unapproachable exterior. It called for a real man to divine the gusto and complete discarding of inhibitions with which she was prepared to co-operate in sexual play.

One such had been Hubie Muller who had gone so far as to deposit a respectful and gentlemanly but unmistakable innuendo at her doorstep. The reason it had not been picked up was that Mrs Lewis was not looking for a gentleman.

With unerring feminine instinct, she had settled upon the character who would have collected all votes as the one most unlikely to succeed. This was the little, banty rooster with the short-cropped, slightly greying hair, alert eyes behind gold-rimmed spectacles, thin Middle Western mouth with the just a little too flashy clothes. Mr James Martin, haberdasher of Evanston, Illinois dressed out of his own stock.

It needed only a hint or two picked up here and there during the early part of the voyage to put the seal on his credentials. Travelling alone, the small-town, midwestern merchant with a wife crippled by arthritis had been allowed off the leash to take his first holiday in years by himself. His taciturnity indicated that he could keep his mouth shut. And as for his bland, colourless exterior, it promised an absolute volcano of inhibited eroticism once released. Mrs Lewis, seven days out, had organized a simple experiment. Would Mr Martin join her and the So-and-Sos for cocktails in her cabin suite at eight, black tie. When he arrived it seemed the So-and-Sos had had to beg off. After two drinks, Mrs Lewis pretended to adjust a barette holding the coils of her hair. Loosened, they came cascading down, lustrous and fragrant over one bare shoulder, in an instant transforming what had been a somewhat formidable and unassailable lady into a moist-eyed, willing woman.

No further notice was necessary. Martin had been sex-starved for a decade. For the rest of the trip they had a roaring time.

It was also one of the best kept secrets of the voyage. They had not associated during the day, only when the merry-making had shut down for the night did Martin discreetly slip into her cabin.

As for the inevitable, irrevocable bill—paradise paid for—he soon found out. Like so many insignificant little men too often overlooked by women, Martin was a sexual marvel. He became a victim to his own prowess. She was not going to let him go. And since the affair had never been complicated by love and it was just sheer fun, Mrs Lewis could not see why it should not be continued on dry land. She had an elegantly furnished apartment on the Lake Shore Drive, Chicago. Martin's establishment in near-by Evanston provided the perfect excuse for a weekly business visit. She had enthusiastically discussed plans for such with him.

And there it was, payment in weekly instalments and all the trouble that would go with it—lies, subterfuges, narrow escapes and the inevitable discovery. Ethically upright, Martin cared about his wife and did not want to hurt her. But also having gradually accustomed himself to a sexless existence, now that he had begun again, he did not want to quit. He particularly did not want to quit with Mrs Lewis. Yet he really did not crave a mistress and above all he did not want trouble.

And now there was not going to be any. He could half envision the inverted room in his mind, with the furniture suspended from the ceiling. He knew so intimately its arrangements and decor; the pink and white chenille covering on the three-quarter bed, the modern two-toned chest of drawers, the stylized mural print of a formal garden, the thick carpeting, the sofa and easy-chairs. They had played in and about and around them naked, grotesque fauns. Now it would be filled with water like an aquarium in which floating, her long tresses outflowing like a mermaid's, those prominent eyes wide open and staring, would be Wilma Lewis.

The night watchman who would probably have seen him emerge in the mornings would be dead, too. Nobody would ever know and there were not going to be any consequences. And this involved him in a struggle that was threatening to tear him apart. He ought to be mourning the woman who had so generously given him pleasure and fulfilment and he was not. He should have gone to her that night in spite of her remonstrances. He should be dead with her and he was glad that he was alive. He had sinned. Sin called for punishment and he was free and clear, always provided they managed to escape from the capsized ship. Or perhaps his punishment was to be teased with a little more of life and then to be extinguished like the rest below. But as a practical man who had made his way in the world, he could not swallow a Deity who to get even with him for indulging his libido extra-maritally, would drown a thousand lives as well.

What was he to say to Scott? How bring up the subject? And would he care? What was there he could do or even say beyond the stereotypes to which his own church had accustomed him: repent, go and sin no more and he would be forgiven. It was not forgiveness he wanted but punishment for the injustice that Mrs Lewis was dead and he was alive.

He came suddenly to the overwhelming feeling that Buzz Scott would not be greatly interested in his sexual shenanigans and the consequences to his conscience. The young man had other things on his mind. He was back on the field again playing a game. Martin pressed his thin lips more tightly together again lest any foolish words that he might later regret were to escape them. Besides, he was embarrassed, the Minister was so much younger than he.

Scott almost terrifyingly corroborated his feelings when he turned to him, winked and said, 'If you can't go through the middle, go 'round the end.'

Martin asked, 'Do you think we can make it?'

Scott replied curtly, 'You bet!'

Martin thought to himself: *Hell, maybe God does need guys like this!*

The Beamer's foot slipped from one of the pipes. He swore and would have fallen if Pamela had not held him up by the arm with a firm grip. This strength and her support irritated him to the point that he became even more aware of how shockingly sober he was.

He had booked for the cruise not in search of companionship so much as because it offered a month of undisturbed drinking under pleasant circumstances. He drank in London, too, but it was more difficult when he had to go to the office. A ship was a marvellous, mobile bar room, liberated from the ridiculous licensing laws of shore-based establishments. It extended the drinking day to the point where he need hardly ever be aware of that inexplicable longing and misery within him. Why miserable? Longing for what? He simply did not know. It was just that there always seemed to have been something hollow inside him and the only thing he knew to do for it was to fill it with alcohol.

He was content with this lumpy girl, whose mother had obviously taken her on this cruise on a husband hunt. Drinking with a companion was more fun than drinking alone.

Pamela, with her clear eyes in which there was never so much as a glance of reproach, short-cut, dun-coloured hair, thick body and those two marvellous, apparently hollow legs into which whisky disappeared, had been ideal.

And she demanded nothing from him; she kept others off. She sat with him, stood with him and drank. She hardly ever even talked. He knew that she had been good at games in some English school, and little more about her.

The Beamer slipped again and the girl supported him with her strong forearm. He covered his annoyance with a laugh, 'That's what happens when you get too sober, it's dangerous. Let go. I'll be all right.' She looked hurt and he said, 'No, no, you'd better hang on to me.' He was far from a heartless man. His ever-recurring loneliness that needed quenching precluded that. It was just that he did not want to be bothered. He overcame his resentment and added, 'You're a good kid.'

The trouble was that the girl was dead cold sober herself now, else she would never have dreamed of asking the question she did. While the liquor she consumed with The Beamer had little visible outward effect upon her, inwardly she was as drunk as he and immersed in a golden glow of perpetual adoration of him. But now the shock of the loss of her mother and the horror of things she had seen had eradicated every last trace of alcohol.

She asked, 'Tony, what makes you drink so?'

The Beamer looked at the girl in astonishment and suppressed an inward sigh. His wife had asked him that, too. He replied, 'Nothing,' and then he added, 'I like the feeling. I love everybody when I'm drunk.'

'And when you aren't?'

He looked at her again and this time beamed and said, 'I can't remember.'

'Oh,' cried Pamela, 'that's why they call you The Beamer! You do beam upon one.'

'Do they?' he said. 'I suppose I must look rather a silly ass, sitting up on a bar stool all day long. But everyone looks so lovely to me and I feel friendly towards them.'

'Do you love *me* when you're drunk, Tony?'

'Prodigiously!' The Beamer answered. 'You're the light of my life—the drinking man's dream girl. Right?'

'And when you're sober?'

Bates replied with a laugh, 'How can I tell? It's the first time we've been, isn't it?' It had slipped out, meant as a joke, but he realized quickly how cruel his remark was. His regret was lost in annoyance that she had asked it and put him into the position dreaded by every man who associates with a woman he does not love.

He was placated when she said, with utter simplicity, 'I don't mind.' And if anything, even a slight feeling of male chagrin came over him; why didn't she?

Her hand gripped his arm even more firmly, 'Careful!' she said, 'There's another of those silly ones with a knob on it.'

The march suddenly came to a halt and from ahead they heard Rogo's voice, 'Holy, jumping Jesus! That cooks it!'

They had come to the staircase at the end of the corridor.

CHAPTER IX

The Adventure of the Second Staircase

The party gathered in consternation and anguished silence at the bottom of the well of the second obstacle. The invention and acquisition of a new skill by means of which they had conquered the first of the reversed ascents had given them hope and confidence in the leadership of the young Minister. They had been able to dismiss upside-down staircases as a problem. Every step they had taken away from the unspeakable and unthinkable things that lay beneath them made the horrors seem less real.

There was no slope up which the women could be hauled. The staircase here was terminal to the corridor and quite different, a broad, double companionway in which the steep overhang of iron steps and polished steel handrails was suspended above their heads, out of reach. Facing them was a bulkhead some twelve feet in height, down which in parallel lines spilled the pipes from the inverted ceiling.

Muller thought to himself, *Dead end!* and gave up. His despair through the sudden slackening of his body must have communicated itself to Nonnie, for she looked at him anxiously. He tried to smile encouragingly at her but could not.

Jane Shelby said to her husband, 'It can't be done, can it?'

He replied, 'I don't see how.'

The Beamer said to Scott, 'I'm afraid we've had it, old boy.'

Rogo turned upon Scott with angry contempt and asked, 'You got any more bright ideas?'

The truculent insolence of Rogo's speech was meant to be both irritating and dangerous, a challenge so that at the merest indication of its being picked up, he could throw his hard fists into play, the only way he knew how to dominate.

Scott refused to be drawn. Instead he merely remarked, after a few moments of study, 'The next one, you know, will probably be more difficult for us than this.'

Muller could not repress a chuckle at the manner in which Scott's calm demolishing of the problem by the use of the phrase, 'the next one' had stilled the incipient panic he had experienced. Nonnie looked at him apprehensively and whispered, 'Is he crazy?'

Muller replied, 'Like a fox.'

Rogo maintained his belligerency, 'What the hell do you mean by the next one? We can't get by here.'

'Well, for one thing,' Scott replied, 'we can still see. We may not be able to much longer when the lights go out.'

They had forgotten that they were on sufferance of a set of storage batteries which were rapidly being depleted. The thought of the total darkness into which they could be plunged at any moment struck new terror into all hearts with the possible exception of Miss Kinsale who broke the silence with, 'Yes, we should count our blessings, shouldn't we?'

'Besides,' Scott continued, 'if you will think of the next as being even tougher and in the dark, it rather softens up this one, doesn't it?'

At that moment above their heads a bearded face, pale, with frightened eyes, peered down at them for a minute.

Rogo yelled, 'Hey you, Walio! Paisan! Get somebody! We want to get up there.'

The head disappeared and they heard footsteps diminishing. They waited listening. Nothing happened. Nobody came. 'Well, the dirty, lousy, bastard!' Rogo shouted.

'Didn't you see?' Scott said, 'He was frightened to death. Probably all those up there are in the same state and useless. We'll have to depend on ourselves.'

'Oh, sure!' Rogo said sarcastically. 'Go up the wall like monkeys.'

'Or like people.' Scott went over to examine it and as he did so they saw what their preoccupation with the stairs had prevented them from noticing before.

Bottom side up, the top of the seemingly unreachable bulkhead, which would be the floor to them could they gain it, was like the one upon which they had been walking— lined with pipes—except that some of these as they came down the side vertically, were not only heavier but were equipped with wheel valves of various sizes.

There was heavy asbestos packing around the joints and at intervals the pipes were fixed to the bulkhead with collars attached to flanges recessed into the wall, a matter of some three inches but sufficient to give a finger and toe-hold. Two large and several smaller wheel valves thrusting outwards offered further purchase.

Hope swelled and the repetition by Scott of what seemed to be a pet phrase, 'piece of cake,' lifted up their spirits once more. Relief and admiration overcame Jane Shelby's doubts of Scott.

Linda Rogo said, 'Not for me.'

A sad expression came over her husband's face again as he shook his head, 'You're gonna be awfully lonely down here by yourself, baby.'

She told him what he could do with himself and then added, 'I'll have company. You think old fatty is going to get up there?'

Jane Shelby wondered whether this was to be the prelude to another outburst of violence but this time Rogo merely nodded morosely to Scott, 'She'll go.'

But Mrs Rosen who in their euphoria they had forgotten had been put back into their minds and they turned to her now.

'Look,' replied Belle Rosen, 'you shouldn't even ask me such a foolish thing. I couldn't do it. Manny should go but I wouldn't even try. It makes me ashamed even you should think about it.'

'The tableclothes...' Muller suggested, but Scott vetoed them before he finished the sentence.

'Won't work here. No purchase. It will be simpler to climb.'

Manny said, 'I should go and leave you? Are you crazy, Mamma? Who says I could go up there? Everybody else should go and leave us. We don't want to make any trouble.'

In his refined and modulated voice with its pseudo English accent, Hubie Muller said, 'There's no question of leaving either of you behind, Mrs Rosen. We all started off on this thing together and we ought to keep to it.'

Linda Rogo snapped quickly, 'Why? It's their idea if they don't want to come, not ours. Let 'em stay. And the same to all of you,' she added, for she felt the shock wave of their dislike of her.

Scott said to Belle Rosen, 'Down in the dining-room would you have believed that you could have got this far?'

Belle said, 'No, I wouldn't. But pulling up is one thing, climbing is another.' And then she added, 'You're a terrible man. I suppose I should try.'

Scott grinned down upon her almost affectionately and said, 'You're my girl! As a matter of fact, we shall have you up top there before anyone else and then you can watch the rest of us struggling.' He turned again to look at the bulkhead and said, 'We'll want the axe here. Who's got it?'

A deep groan came from Manny Rosen. Belle asked, 'Manny, what's wrong with you? Are you sick?'

Rosen groaned again, 'Am I sick! I was the last man up. I forgot it.'

Linda cracked, 'That's the Yid for you.' It was as though she was determined to acerbate them all at every turn.

Rosen answered, 'So what's Yid got to do with forgetting something? I shouldn't of, but anyone can forget something when he's excited.'

Belle said, 'Sure, Manny. Why didn't somebody say to you to bring it up?' Then, with surprising mildness she added, 'Calling names don't do any good, Mrs Rogo. We are what we are, and you are what you are, and no one should blame anyone for that.'

Linda was too stupid to catch the full subtlety of Mrs Rosen's remark, but she was prepared to battle with her when Rogo quickly interposed. 'I'll go for it.' He felt he had lost face with his obstructionism to Scott's leadership and wanted to regain some.

'No you won't!' said Linda. 'He forgot it. Let him get it.'

'Now baby,' Rogo soothed, 'don't be like that. He'd never make it. Mr Rosen is a friend of mine.' And actually at that moment the detective was thinking of the number of pastrami and Rosen Special three-decker sandwiches he had consumed in the uptown delicatessen shop and always on the house with a bottle of beer thrown in. He turned to Scott, 'Gimme the rope.'

Scott handed over the coil. 'Can you manage?'

Rogo looked at him squarely and not pleasantly in the face and said with quiet and direct insolence, 'Just because cops are supposed to be dumb, don't get any ideas in your head about me.'

They watched the stocky, compact figure make his way down the corridor from whence they had come.

Scott suggested. 'We'll rest,' and disposed his length along the piping. 'Try to make yourselves as comfortable as you can.'

Nonnie whispered to Muller, 'I liked what you said about not leaving the Rosens. They're sweet. They think about each other.' As she knelt, her dressing-gown flew open and she quickly clutched it about her again saying, 'Oh dear, I'm so ashamed about not having anything on underneath.'

It was Muller's first encounter with the paradoxical modesty of some professional performers and in a curious way he found it moving. He was aware that her shyness in this instance was genuine. Whatever or whoever she was, she valued her person. He smiled at her and said, 'I've got an idea.' He unfastened his braces, handed them to her and said, 'Here, tie these around your middle.'

'Oh,' she cried, 'what about your trousies! Won't they fall down?'

Muller patted his stomach, 'Not over this gourmet's pot,' he declared. 'I wear suspenders merely as a symbol.'

Nonnie asked, 'What's a symbol?'

Muller replied, 'In this case, kidding myself that I need something to hold up my pants.'

She whispered, 'Oh, you *are* funny!' and hugged his arm, and the pressure sent a thrill of pleasure through him.

Lying uncomfortably on the pipes, out of earshot, Belle asked her husband, 'What's with that Linda woman, who does she think she is? Why does he put up with it? I thought cops were supposed to be tough.'

'She thinks she's better than he is,' Manny replied.

'Better from what?'

'She was going to be a big movie star. She gave up her career and let herself down when she married Rogo.'

'Who says so?'

'Rogo.'

'He believes this?'

Manny said, 'I remember once before he got married, he come into the store. He had a copy of *Life Magazine* and he showed me her picture. There was four or five girls and the heading was, "Starlets Today: Star Tomorrow", and they were from different companies. I think she was with Paramount. She was cute then. She didn't look spoiled. Anyway, Rogo says to me, "Manny, I'm walking on air. We're going to get married. A bum like me married to a moving picture star!" You see, for him she was a star already. He says, "I'm crazy about her. What right has a dumb cop got with a wonderful dame like that, who could have her name up in lights?" I said to him, "She must be pretty crazy about you, too," and he said, "I can't hardly believe it yet. And me, I wasn't brung up; I was yanked up on First Avenue."'

Belle snorted, 'Huh! They must have been going to chuck her from the films, or she got herself into trouble.'

Manny said, 'I think she was in some Broadway show, but it flopped. Though Rogo didn't say nothing about that.'

'And she should spit on us, or a nice kid like Nonnie?'

Manny nodded, 'Ain't that always the way?'

Belle said, 'What she needs is another good slap across the mouth.'

But after having said this she became suddenly reflective, fingered her torn lace dress, felt her aching feet and even looked for a moment at the big diamond sparkling on her finger. She said, 'What a stupid thing to say at a time like this, Manny. Who cares? We're in bad trouble, ain't we?'

'I shouldn't tell you no lies, Belle.'

'We could go down?'

'We could.'

She was silent for an instant and then said, 'You gave me a good life, Manny.'

'I wouldn't have been anything without you, Mamma.'

She sighed, 'So what's the point of all this climbing up?'

'If there's a chance, we ought to take it, oughtn't we?' Manny replied.

She did not reply to this.

Miss Kinsale was not lying down but sitting across the pipes, her unfashionably too long, grey frock pulled well down over her knees. Her hands were folded in her lap and she was staring straight ahead at nothing.

Scott opened his eyes and sat up. He took in the figure opposite. 'Are you all right, Miss Kinsale?'

She came out of her reverie with a slight shiver and then favoured him with a small, bright smile and the softening of her expression had the effect of removing a decade from her plain, unadorned countenance. 'Oh, yes, quite,' she replied, 'thank you.'

Scott said, 'What a quiet person you are.'

It was an echo of what most everyone who had encountered her on the cruise felt about her. Miss Kinsale never said very much. One had gathered that she was a book-keeper in a bank in a place called Camberley near London. She had saved up her money for a winter holiday cruise. In the morning the promenade deck resounded to the click of her sensible heels as she did her twenty laps around, which constituted a mile. She took tea in the afternoon with a group of ladies, but listened more than she talked. She attended the cinema and during the shore excursions, one was conscious of her from time to time as an eager, interested little figure carrying a notebook, pencil and camera. She also bought innumerable coloured postcards to pile up a record of all she had seen and done. But what she thought, felt, or was like, nobody knew.

Miss Kinsale had been considering the Minister's questioning. 'There isn't very much one can say, is there?' she replied finally, and then, lowering her eyes and dropping her voice, she added, 'We're in the hands of the Lord. I trust in Him. Thank you for letting me pray with you. You've given me strength.'

'Oh… yes,' Scott said, in the manner of one who has been reminded of something he has quite forgotten. Then he asked her, 'And do you trust in yourself?'

Miss Kinsale's grey eyes suddenly became luminous, 'Oh, yes,' she replied, 'when I'm with you, I have no fear. I feel you are very close to God.'

There was a noise from overhead again. This time two heads peered down upon them and they all looked up hopefully as for a moment they thought that the first man they had seen had sent aid. But there was something even more strange about these faces than the first, a curious distortion of the mouths with spittle drooling from the sides and glazed, staring eyes that were not focusing. They vanished.

Hubie Muller tried to hold them with a shout, 'Hey! You speak English? *Français? Deutsch? Parla Italiano?*'

They did not reappear. 'If you ask me,' said Martin, startling the group, 'they're plastered.'

'What?' queried The Beamer hopefully. 'Drunk?'

Mike Rogo came walking back, the axe over one shoulder, the rope coiled over the other. He was looking dishevelled and worried. His shoes and the bottoms of his trousers half-way up the calf were soaking wet.

The Beamer praised, 'Well done, old boy!'

Rogo said, 'Nuts!'

But Scott was held by the condition of Rogo's feet. He said, 'Hello! How did you get wet? Where was the axe?'

Rogo replied, 'Under a foot of water.' And then shifting his gaze to the bulkhead he said, 'We'd better get to hell on up there.'

Cold with apprehension Shelby said, 'My God, she's settling! What about all those down on "C" deck, then—Acre and Peters? And the rest of those in the dining-room?'

Rogo regarded him without expression and merely replied, 'Yeah, what about them?'

Pamela Reid blurted out, 'They'll be under water, then like the rest, wouldn't they? Our cabin was on "B" deck.'

Nonnie's teeth began to chatter. She whimpered, 'Oh, my God! All my chums—Nicky, Moira, Sybil, Heather, Jo and Timmy, are they all dead?'

'Shsh!' Muller said, 'Don't think about it.' He reached over and put his arm about her and she buried her face in his shoulder.

Scott asked, 'Was it still rising while you were there?'

'No,' Rogo replied, 'I waited a while and checked. I had the rope tied to the top of the stairs so I could get back.'

'The ship may just have been striking a buoyancy balance,' said Shelby, graveyard whistling.

Martin was more practical. He said, 'She could fill up and sink any minute.'

They looked at one another in alarm. Their momentary feeling of security evaporated. It was beginning to penetrate that any minute could be their last.

'Thanks, Rogo,' Scott said and then commanded, 'let's go!' and this time no one questioned or disputed his order. The urgency to hurry was upon them all. Scott took the axe from Rogo and wedged it firmly, pick end first, within an angle of the pipes. He tested the haft and said, 'That'll give us a nice handhold.' Turning to Pamela he said, 'Let's see you get up there.'

The British girl went to the bulkhead, the attitude of her body a study of determination and self-confidence.

She kicked off her shoes, handed them to The Beamer and began to climb. Strong toes and powerful fingers gripped every hold. When she reached the handle of the axe it gave a grip on which she could pull and thereafter she swung herself upwards steadily without a pause, until her body projected half over the top. She then wriggled the rest of the way, got to her knees, slewed around and looked down upon them. 'Not too bad,' was her verdict.

The Beamer said, 'Good God, I've been consorting with a human fly!'

There was some laughter and a notable appreciation of spirit. Muller thought that whatever else Scott might be, he was thoroughly grounded in the psychology of athleticism. He had sent up a girl. She had done it easy as wink, and thus softened it for the rest of them.

Scott called, 'Can you see anyone about, Pam?'

The girl stood up. 'There isn't too much light. Some people seem to be milling about at the far end but I can't tell how many or what they're doing. Do you want me to go and see?'

'No,' Scott replied, 'if Martin is right and they've got at some liquor and are plastered it wouldn't do any good. We'll help Mrs Rosen next.'

The Beamer's head came up and he said, 'Did I hear the word "liquor"?' Then he sang, 'If I had the wings of an angel...'

Scott ignored him and continued, 'No, wait a minute! Dick, just nip to the top, so that you can give her a hand from there.'

Shelby moved over to obey. He had no qualms this time. Scott had created almost an atmosphere of hypnosis, similar to the ones Shelby had encountered in his college years.

Scott said, 'Stay loose. Up you go!' and he gave Shelby a slap on the bottom in the manner of a quarter-back coming out of a huddle and sending his guards and tackles into the line for play.

Shelby felt excited, light and capable as he had in his football days, when, donning his helmet, he was sent out on to the field to substitute.

The euphoria lasted and under its spell he reached the top in a few seconds to join the girl.

Scott called up, 'Kneel by the edge, will you, it will give you more leverage. Okay, Mrs Rosen, right on up!'

Belle Rosen repeated bitterly, 'Right on up!' and turned to her husband, 'Must I, Manny?'

'Try, Mamma.'

She rose heavily and walked to the bulkhead and with every step that she approached closer the difficulty became more and more obvious until she stood at the foot and turned to them with humiliation in her dark eyes. 'Look! My stummick! I can't even get close. Don't make me, please!'

Scott had signalled to the men. Muller, The Beamer, Martin and Rogo joined him. 'See,' he said, 'we're all here. We won't let you fall. You're not really as stout as you think you are. Put your feet there and your hands here. Just catch hold of the edge. Now push and pull.'

Belle Rosen rose six inches above their heads, but gave a cry, 'Oh, oh, I can't! I'm falling!' and would have done so except that the four men held her body pinned against the side of the bulkhead.

'That's fine, Mrs Rosen,' Scott said and to the others he whispered, 'Okay, lads, lift!' The enormous figure rose another six inches and she began to scream, 'No! No! Let me down! Let me down! I don't wanna do it!' even while her fat fingers were scrabbling for a handhold.

Manny Rosen said, 'Mamma, Mamma, don't get so excited! You're doing fine!'

Once more Scott ordered and they heaved. She was two feet off the floor now and held there by their combined strength. Belle continued to scream, 'Let me down! Let me down! Manny, make them stop!'

Manny Rosen hovered around the semicircle of men, now anxiously crying, 'Maybe she shouldn't do it. Maybe she's hurting herself.'

They heaved again and like something in a pantomime the fat women rose with a scaly sound as the pipes tore at the front of her dress. 'Can you take hold of the axe and hold on for a moment?'

Belle was too frightened to scream any longer. She gripped frantically at the handle and it steadied her long enough for Scott to bend over and get his own back beneath her feet, while the others reached up their hands to steady her.

'Now let go,' Scott ordered her, 'and just lift up your arms. They can almost reach you at the top.' He strained and pushed, but her grip was now tenacious, something to hold on to. Sweat was pouring from her face. A loud sound emanated from her as she broke wind.

Linda Rogo let out a yell of laughter.

Jane Shelby turned upon her crying, 'Oh, you horror!'

Linda blew a raspberry at her as loud and long as the one that had just resounded. Jane's arm had been drawn back to slash her across the face, but it was halted by Rogo's cold voice, 'Cut it out, girls! Cut it out! Time for kidding around later.'

With all the power of his great back, Scott strained again.

'Oh,' wailed Belle, 'I can't hold any more. I'm falling.' She could no longer maintain her hold and now that she was half-way up, the others below, Martin, Rogo, The Beamer and Muller who were all of no more than average height, could not reach enough of her body to keep her pinned to the wall. She teetered for a moment and the edifice seemed about to crash. In desperation Shelby from the top, secured a momentary grip with his fingers in her dark hair.

'No, no!' Manny shouted, jumping up and down in anguish. 'Not by the hair! Not by the hair! Leave her alone!'

But automatic to the pressure on her head, Belle Rosen raised her arms to try to relieve it and Pamela Reid coolly leaning over seized one of her wrists. The English girl asked Shelby, 'I've got one of her wrists, can you get the other?'

He did so. He called to her, 'Just take it easy, Mrs Rosen, and don't be afraid. We'll have you up in a jiffy now.'

Their hold had taken some of the strain off Scott and he now straightened up swiftly, quickly placed Mrs Rosen's feet on either side of his shoulders and then incredibly thus burdened, began the climb himself.

The white, upturned face of the fat woman, her small polyp-like mouth moving miserably as she made mewing and whimpering sounds, rose higher, enabling the two at the top to slide their grip to her arms and drag Mrs Rosen over the top, where she lay on her back, gasping and crying, her arms and legs twitching, like a great fat baby.

Scott dropped down again and said, 'You're next, Rosen.'

Strangely the little man did not protest although his hands and knees were shaking and his head too was moving from side to side. He said, 'Yeah, let me go. I wanna get up to Mamma. I must get up to her. How do I do it?'

Muller recognized the symptoms of man under stress. Adrenalins would be pouring into his body. 'Just go,' he said. 'Don't worry. We'll boost you.'

It was so. Manny clawed his way upwards without ever turning back or wavering.

Scott grinned as his feet disappeared over the top. He said, 'I'll bet you boys don't go up like that! Okay, the little monkey next. Come on, Robin. Do we throw you, or can you make it under your own steam?'

'I can do it,' the boy said, clambered up and then called, 'Come on, Mum! Come on, Sis! It's easy.'

Jane Shelby said, 'It is, when you're ten.' Nevertheless, she made the ascent with singular grace, followed by her daughter.

Scott asked, 'Who's next?'

'Me,' Nonnie answered.

Muller said, 'Just imagine you're in a pantomime. Exit fairies upwards, laughingly.'

Nonnie went over to the wall and stood there a moment looking up. She was so diminutive that it seemed even higher than it had been before. She said, 'Oh dear, this blasted dressing-gown.'

Linda said, 'Why don't you take it off?'

Nonnie made no reply, but two tiny teeth showed over her lower lip and without further ado, she started up. Although she had tied the dressing-gown around her waist with Hubie's braces, nevertheless it still fell open.

Linda giggled. 'Old man Shelby's having himself a look this time. Not that she's got anything to look at.'

Nonnie waved to Muller, 'Sugar Plum fairy okay, waiting for Principal Boy.'

Scott said, 'Will you go next, Mrs Rogo?'

Linda said, 'Oh, I'm scared! I'll need help. Can you give me your arm?' Rogo stepped forward. She said, 'Him, not you!' She put her foot on to the first ledge and a hand through a projection on the piping.

With her white bra and panties, she had thrown her coat to her husband, the Beamer thought for an instant that she looked like a circus acrobat about to mount to her trapeze. Scott took her free arm and lifted.

'Boy!' said Linda, 'Some muscle!' She went up a few feet and hung there, looking down at him, her rump level with his face, 'Ooh!' she said, 'I'm scared to go any farther. Boost me.'

The Beamer said to himself, 'Why, the little bitch! She's teasing him.'

Without the slightest hesitation, Scott applied one huge hand to her bottom and pushed. Linda went like a cat over a wall. 'Hey!' she gasped, 'You play rough!' but kept on going.

Miss Kinsale said, 'May I try next?' The men gathered at the foot of the bulkhead all looked around startled. They had quite forgotten her.

Scott asked, 'Can you manage?'

'Oh, yes,' said Miss Kinsale, 'when I was a girl on our estate in the country, we always used to climb trees. It's really almost like a tree, isn't it? And Dr Scott has so cleverly made a branch for us. No, no, thank you, I shan't need any help, really. But one of you might bring my shoes, please.'

She stepped out of them and climbed the wall with the same quiet, introspective deliberation that marked all her behaviour.

To Rogo, Muller, The Beamer and Martin, Scott then said, 'All right, fellows, that's that. Get on up. We've lost enough time.' And when they arrived at the top, he himself made the climb half-way, then swung over and seized the gleaming rail of the overhead staircase, freed the axe, used it to gain another hold higher up and in a moment had joined the rest spread out across the upside-down floor of the long, wide, murky alley.

Belle Rosen was sitting up, her husband kneeling with arms protectively about her and she was sobbing uncontrollably.

'Na na! Mamma,' he was comforting. 'Don't take on so. It's all over. You done it.'

'I'm so ashamed,' she wailed. 'I'm so ashamed!'

'Ashamed?' Rosen said, 'Ashamed from what? You were great. What you got to be ashamed about?'

'I wet myself,' she went on, 'I couldn't help it. I couldn't look nobody in the face any more. Like a baby I couldn't hold my water. What must anybody think?'

'Nothing, Mamma! Nonsense! So what? Who cares? But you were great! I'm telling you, you were great.' And then looking around almost defiantly at the others, he challenged them, 'She was great, wasn't she? Really great!'

Astonishingly it was the dry as dust, uncommunicative little Martin who gave the response, 'Yeah,' he said, 'that's right. You were really great, Mrs Rosen.'

CHAPTER X

Broadway

Broadway, it developed, was not only the wide, subterranean connecting alley that Acre had described to them, it was as well a warren of storerooms, butcher's shops, poultry refrigerators, bakeries and stockrooms for every kind of comestible. Numerous staircases and alleyways opened off it at intervals.

On a normal visit one would have encountered storekeepers, masters-at-arms, sailors, bakers with flour-dusted arms, stewards, waiters, men from the paint and carpenter's shops, engineers, wipers, oilers and technicians when the watch in the engine and boiler rooms changed, all going about their business with the minimum of confusion. Only now it was bottom-side up. There had been catastrophe, explosion and sudden death and the survivors amongst the staff were looking for escape.

They knew one another more or less, or could identify by dress, but they did not know the passengers who now intruded into their domain, a strange group led by a huge man in a white, open-necked shirt with a most motley-looking assemblage of women with torn frocks, a girl in a pink négligée and another in bra and panties.

Nor was this group, even when identified as passengers, any concern of the denizens of this area. Their jobs were to serve them unseen, to bake bread, to turn lamb into paper-frilled French chops or garlic-stuffed gigots, to beat up eggs for soufflés and produce whisky, beer and wine in exchange for chits noting receipt of same. From the first throb of the ship's engines after casting off to the final shouts of the dockers seizing ropes and drawing cables to bollards, most of them never so much as saw a passenger or cared. The Reverend Scott and his party were in a land as alien as visited by any Gulliver.

After the solitude of 'D' deck and the strain of the climb, it seemed as though the presence of people inhabiting Broadway would come as something of a relief. Instead it turned out to be more of a nightmare. For as Scott led them astern once more and they moved away from the staircase the place took on the aspects of purgatory, with people milling about mindlessly. Some of them were drunk, weaving and staggering on the uncertain footing for the steel conduits here covered the width of the alley; they were larger and contained more valves, turns and pitfalls.

There was one officer amongst them. His face was covered with dried blood from a head wound; the shoulder where his uniform had been ripped away was likewise bleeding. He wore the three stripes of a second engineer on the remaining sleeve. But he had no answers to their questions. His eyes were vacant and when he opened his mouth to try to speak, no sounds were forthcoming. The best that Jane Shelby, Miss Kinsale and Susan could do for him was to sit him down, staunch his bleeding with the napkins they had carried and keep him from his stunned, aimless wandering.

They found momentary contact with two English stewardesses less panicked than the others who, recognizing them, returned for a moment to that British discipline instilled in them on the voyages they had made with the *Poseidon* when she had been the *Atlantis*. One of them addressed herself to Jane Shelby saying, 'Oh, madam, ain't it terrible! We don't know what's really happened, or where we are, or how many's been killed. There's an awful lot badly hurt. Are you all right, madam? Is there anything we can do for you?'

Jane felt the pathos. These frightened women so much more needed something done for them than in their state they could ever do for anyone else.

'No, thank you,' Jane Shelby said, 'look after yourselves and your friends.'

The woman was pathetically relieved. She said, 'Yes, madam, that's what we're trying to do. But there ought to be an officer along in a moment. He'll show you how to get to your lifeboat stations. There ought to be lifeboats launched by now.'

There was no use in telling them that the lifeboats, still attached to their davits, would be fifty feet below the waterline and if any had broken loose, or inflatable life-rafts had come to the surface, they would be drifting about aimlessly with at the most perhaps, a surviving sailor or two catapulted from the top deck into the sea, unable to do more than bewilderedly cling to them.

'Yes, I'm sure there will,' Jane said. Her husband marvelled at her control.

The stewardess said, 'We're supposed to go to our posts, but we can't find them,' and then moved away with the others.

Shelby himself had to pull himself together and not succumb to the sickening, almost childlike fear that he was no longer alive; that he was dead and in hell. For the men passed them by as though they were not there, sometimes brushing up against them as if they had been invisible. And indeed, in the gloom it was difficult to distinguish and had he not been so fearful, he would have noted that there was a considerable diminishing of light from the emergency bulbs.

A group of deckhands and artisans stumbled by. Hubie Muller had continued to try all the languages he knew and now hit upon two Italian artificers and talked with them.

Rogo said, 'Muller's got a hold of a couple of Ities,' and then addressing Hubie directly, 'Find out where the hell they think they're going.'

Scott queried, 'What did they say?'

'There's no use going that way,' Muller said, indicating the stern from whence the group had come, 'one said it's blocked off. *Punto di fermata. Caotico.* I gather it's chaos. One of the boilers blew up; two of the others just ripped loose and fell into the sea. It's the same in the engine room. You can't get through any more. He says the turbines and generators have torn away. He looked in there earlier and it's full of death. They're going to try to get through to the bow.'

Scott was unimpressed. He said, 'Tell them we're still going aft.'

Rogo spoke up angrily, 'Oh, are we? What about asking us? You heard what those guys said it was like. They seem to know what they're doing.' A short while before he had seemed resigned to Scott's leadership but the eerie atmosphere of the gloomy alley and the confusion there had unsettled him again.

Scott said evenly, 'If you want to join them that's up to you. But since when did you accept a situation on the say-so of somebody else without investigating?'

Linda cried, 'Don't let him talk you into it, Rogo. I want to go the other way.'

Rogo ordered, 'Aw, shut up for a minute, will you?' His truculence drained from him. He was a hard man but out of his element. He was a big shot in New York—Mike Rogo. Here he was nobody.... He hated Scott for it but he hated himself, too. For he knew that basically the Minister was right: once you were committed to a line of action you didn't go off half-cocked because of something you heard. To Scott he said, 'Okay, okay, keep your shirt on!'

Scott told Muller, 'Ask them if they want to come with us.'

It precipitated an argument. While it was going on one man quite suddenly detached himself and came over to Scott's party. He was built like a wrestler; squat, powerfully muscled, semi-bald with a short scrubby moustache, but his dark eyes were strangely mild and gentle. He was clad in a pair of dungaree overalls, shirtless but with the straps fastened over broad shoulders. He had a huge mat of black hair covering his chest.

Ranged alongside Scott who loomed over him, he said, 'Me go you.'

This set off a gesticulating harangue to which the man paid not the slightest attention. Muller queried the Italians further and told Scott, 'He's a Turk, an oiler. He seems to have survived the engine room because they had sent him to get some cokes when it happened. His name is Kemal. He speaks Turkish and Greek but only a few words of English.'

At the mention of his name the man nodded his head vigorously and smiled, showing several gold teeth.

The Italian said to Muller, 'He's crazy! I think you're all crazy! Anyway, what difference does it make? We're all going to die.'

The group turned and moved away. Linda made as if to follow them. Rogo stretched out an arm and hooked two fingers into the waistband of her panties. Had she proceeded, they would have ripped off. She burst into tears, turned and beat upon Rogo's chest with her two fists. He made no resistance and seemed hardly to feel the blows. Eventually she stopped.

The lights were now noticeably dimmer. The ghostly population of Broadway at times surrounded them, at others melted away leaving the alley all but deserted as they searched for a way to escape, popping in and out of the side aisles, most of them unable to adjust to the new situation of their domain turned upside-down. They were bound by their old habits, unable to think clearly or compensate.

Robin Shelby said, 'Mother, I've got to go.'

'Oh lord!' his father cried, 'Must you?'

Jane said, 'Mustn't one?'

Shelby said, 'Yes, but where?'

'There ought to be one or two for the crew along here,' Muller remarked. 'They'll be marked W.C. But don't forget it'll be reversed.'

Scott said, 'Yes, that's right. And I suggest that if any other of you have similar needs, that you attend to them now. I'm going aft to see what it's like. I don't know how much longer this lighting is going to last. If they should go out, there'll be panic amongst these people here. If it happens all of you press to the side of the alley. Lie down. Cover your heads with your hands and remain exactly where you are. I'll find you, then, by voice.' He turned to the new member of the party and said, 'Come with me.'

The Turk grunted unquestioningly, 'Okay.'

Scott nodded and remarked, 'We're lucky. He'll know the engine room.'

Muller thought to himself: *Lucky?* Or was it something in Scott's dynamism that had communicated itself to this Turk? What had made this animal desert his own and suddenly decide to come and cast in his lot with them? He was a primitive, a peasant. What had he smelled? Was he marked for living or dying by his decision? Whichever, up to then Scott had been winning all the way.

Jane Shelby said to her son, 'Come on, Robin, we'll look.'

The looking part of it struck Jane Shelby as an absurdity in the face of the catastrophe in which they were involved, where life and death hung in the balance completely out of their control. The sensible thing would have been to have chosen some dark corner and ordered her son to squat. And yet she knew that for all of this she, too, was the victim of that human tendency to go on doing what they had been taught to do or what they were used to doing every day of their lives.

She reflected that even in war, under fire, latrines were built where a man who in every other detail was living like an animal might retire and eliminate in privacy. And so there they were, the two of them, trapped in the corridor of a capsized ship, remaining afloat by the grace of God knows what, searching for a brass plate with 'C' reversed, 'M' on it, the old-fashioned signal for that apparatus known in Victorian days as a water closet.

They were intelligent, thinking people now, familiar with the new architecture of their environment, yet each discovery came nevertheless as a shock and a renewal of that sinking of the stomach and feeling of helpless dismay.

'Oh, Mother!' Robin cried.

They regarded the upside-down urinals, six of them thrust out from the wall, close to the ceiling, like some ridiculous modern sculptural frieze. Similarly there were the toilet bowls emptied of any water, the hinged seats swinging down. The seal of incongruity upon it all was set by the festoons of the paper rolls that hung to the floor in broad ribbons.

'Mommy!' Robin wailed, 'I can't!' and he used the name for her that he had in his younger days, before he had graduated to the more grownup 'Mother'.

It made Jane think of those times too, and she replied, 'Oh come, you're not a baby any more. You must learn to take what comes and adapt yourself. People were using the ground long before anybody ever invented all that nonsense up there on the ceiling. And it was supposed to be much healthier, too.'

'Mother, I can't,' Robin protested. 'Not in there. It's all full of...' Others had been there before him.

'Well then, do it out here,' she said. 'It isn't going to make all that difference. But hurry.'

The boy still hung back and through her mind flashed the days and years of his toilet training to pot and seat and all the wonderful blessings of plumbing, and the thought that as a city-bred boy, even on visits to the country, he had probably never once squatted down behind a bush. What a marvellously sanitary world they had created.

'Then you go away, Mother,' he said.

'Oh, Robin!' Jane said, 'If you only knew the number of times I've officiated at this rite.'

'Mother, please!' the boy begged. 'I can't, I couldn't! You said I'm not a baby any more.'

Jane reproached herself. Of course he was not. And it was she who had moulded his habits. 'Oh, all right,' she said.

'And don't hang around,' Robin begged, 'I mean really go away. Is anybody coming?'

Jane looked into the alley but at this time it was almost deserted. She said, 'No. Very well then, hurry, Robin. I'll be with the others.'

Her instincts bade her remain just around the corner but her sense of fair play countered this and she walked up towards their party.

Miss Kinsale came forward to meet her with something on her mind. She said, 'Have —have you found it? Dr Scott suggested that perhaps...'

Jane suppressed a smile and said, 'Yes, I have. But it's not fit for man nor beast. It's all gone topsy-turvy, you know.'

'Oh dear,' murmured Miss Kinsale. 'I'd forgotten.'

'Is it anything serious?' Jane asked.

'No,' Miss Kinsale replied, 'you know, just...'

'Well then,' Jane said, 'I suggest that we nip down this aisle where it's dark, lift up our skirts and dribble quietly, the way we used to do when we were little girls.'

She wished then that she had not been quite so facetious but to her astonishment Miss Kinsale was not at all put out and merely said, 'How very sensible of you,' and went with her.

***

Scott had not yet returned. Left on their own, his followers were inclined to explore.

'We trust,' The Beamer suggested, 'our noses and our ears. There is the scent of vinous spirits and the sound of raucous laughter.'

'Right-o,' Pamela said, even though she had never felt less like tippling. She was haunted now by her mother dead in some horribly obscene manner and in some grotesque position that she could not even envision. She knew why she had been taken upon this cruise. It was for her to meet new people, make new friends—eligible if possible—to broaden her circle which, as owners of a small but successful dry cleaning establishment in an outlying district of London, was limited.

She did not even know how to mourn her mother. The city dweller knows death in hospital or home, the unaccustomed silences, the tiptoeing about and 'that room' into which one went in and out with unadmitted irony as noiselessly as possible. But here she was lost and confused.

She was further miserable because of the man at her side. She would have stayed with her mother that evening if The Beamer had not come tapping at her door. Her unsuspected capacity for holding drink had developed early on in the voyage, when she had outlasted an entire party invited by The Beamer late one night in the smoke-room. Tony Bates, it seemed, was fastidious and did not like lady drunks but this girl who could match him whisky for whisky had been a find. In this manner had begun their curious friendship. But it was no time for drinking now.

And yet against her very nature she wished The Beamer drunk again so that once more he would be wholly hers. Sober he saw too clearly and there was a hint of mockery in his attitude towards her which was painful. She remembered those two brief sentences which had pierced and wounded her: 'We've only just met!' and 'My

God, I've been consorting with a human fly!' Drunk he would lean towards her and rest a warm, moist hand upon her arm in almost an affectionate gesture and say, 'Old girl, I'm afraid I'm beginning to hear what people are saying. We'd better have another one, what?' And thus she was his accepted associate.

She said, 'I think it comes from there,' and indicated the direction forward on the port side, which formerly had been starboard, where were located most of the storerooms with gangways connecting with interior staircases giving access to the kitchens above. There were service lifts for the speedy transfer of supplies and in one room were enormous tuns of draught beers and ales that were piped foaming directly to the half-dozen bars serving the passengers.

The Beamer took her by the arm, saying, 'Let's go, my girl!'

Pamela's heart warmed. Already at the mere thought of finding drink, his behaviour towards her was changing. She was his companion again; he was relying upon her.

They proceeded down the corridor in the direction Pam had indicated and explored an aisle. On one side of it were what had been right-side up of a series of steel half doors, the tops of which consisted of heavy wire mesh. Now, upside-down, the grill part was on the bottom and the wooden cases of wines had come tumbling from their racks and displayed their stencilled labels tantalizingly: Vin de Bourgogne, Bordeaux, Rosé, Côte du Rhône. The doors were heavily padlocked. The display was at eye-level and the two stood hand-in-hand like children looking into the cages of a zoo.

'God,' breathed The Beamer, 'what a sight! What we want now is the Reverend's axe. A wine drunk is a lovely one. You can understand why the Bacchi wove vine leaves in their hair.' He then pounded upon the iron with his fists and cried aloud, 'Chinese torturers!'

'Oh, Tony!' the girl said and bled for him.

The opposite side was the champagne room. Here the cases, tightly stocked to the ceiling, had not been dislodged by the whip of the capsized vessel and simply advertised their contents upside down: Roederer, Lanson, the yellow-labelled Veuve Cliquot, Mumm, Pommerey, Dom Perignon, Cristal.

The Beamer said, 'Bubbly, phui! A woman's drink, recommended by society doctors in cases of *mal-de-mer* or in early pregnancy.' And then with a grimace he added, 'Sour grapes and no pun intended. I'd drink even that. But what about that nose of yours?'

'Farther down, I think,' said the girl. They followed the scent to the spirits room. It was open. Cases and bottles were tumbled about. The storekeeper in a blue uniform and a half naked sailor lay before the doors, each clutching a bottle, unconscious.

The Beamer cried, 'Wonderful girl! Wonderful nose! Nirvana. Whisky, rum, gin, vodka, brandy—we're home! What will you have?'

***

'I'm hungry,' Nonnie announced, 'I didn't have much din.'

Muller said, 'We ought to be able to find something to eat. Come on, let's forage.'

The long alleyway known to the crew as Broadway, not only was their thoroughfare but served as a staging area for the vast supplies of food and drink stored under deep refrigeration or semi-cold, or packed away in rodent-proof rooms below at special temperatures for preservation.

Every twenty-four hours consignments of tinned goods, cereals, jams, jellies, conserves, bacon, hams, cheeses, butter and eggs, coffee, teas and sugar, fish, meat and fowls, sausages, vegetables and fresh fruits were sent up to special rooms off the alley on their way to the kitchens, thus preserving everything fresh with less likelihood of wastage.

Not packed as tightly or as carefully racked as in the bins below, the powerful whip of the overturning ship had spilled most of the edibles into an unsavoury heap.

The floor of the breakfast storeroom was a glutinous mass of coffee, flour, milk, bacon, sausage and hundreds of smashed eggs. Nonnie made a face and gave a little shudder, 'Boy,' she said, 'what a mess! I was in a show once where they did a scene like that. Two comics with a lot of eggs and flour and water, chucking it about. We had to do six minutes in front of the drop afterwards while they cleaned it up. Is it all going to be like that, or do you suppose we'll be able to find something? I could do with a good tuck-in.'

Muller had been lost in the picture she had drawn of the famous knock-about comedy act adored of children and Nonnie, in some absurd costume, high-kicking in front of the backdrop while stage hands operated with brooms and shovels. He said, 'Come on, I think I see succour ahead.' They went past tumbled quarters of beef, lamb and veal which would have been on their way to the butcher's shop for final processing and tumbled about heaps of tins, inviolable to anyone not equipped with a tin opener.

Nonnie stumbled on ahead with a little cry of delight, 'Bikkies! Lots of them.'

The upside-down locker they had found smashed open was the one that supplied those dull and inevitable afternoon teas awaited so eagerly by the British, served on silver trays by those immaculate stewards in the main lounge promptly at four every afternoon. Here, besides the tins of Oolong, Orange Pekoe and Earl Grey China teas, was collected sandwich bread, tubes of fish paste, jellies, jams, muffins for toasting, raisin cake, petit-fours and packets of tea biscuits, in short all of the non-perishable articles necessary to the rite.

It had all been overturned and hurled from the shelves into a jumble upon the floor, not disgustingly but rather like a heaped-up Christmas pile of edible treasure trove; unopened packages of ginger nuts, sugar wafers, chocolate wholemeal, vanilla fingers, mingled with muffins and cup cakes and heaps of petit-fours covered with multicoloured icing.

The sight was entrancing to Nonnie and she cried, 'Oh, yummy!' her eyes grown large, her tiny face a mask of anticipatory greed. 'What shall we have first?'

'Wait,' said Muller, 'we might as well make ourselves comfortable and tackle this Roman fashion.'

He burrowed into the pile, pushing it into two halves to make a space in between where they could lie down side by side and had only to reach out to pluck something delectable from the mountainous heaps. He prised open several jars of preserves which he divided between Nonnie and himself.

'Sorry about no tea available,' he said, 'but there ought to be a coke machine somewhere around.'

'Never mind,' said Nonnie, only half audible due to a mouthful. She was stuffing herself with both hands. It was actually the same choice as passed around by the stewards but the very profusion of the cakes brought on a kind of frenzy of eating to the girl.

Leaning on one elbow, Muller rather fastidiously dipped half of a muffin into strawberry jam and ate it with the same delicacy he would have shown at a tea table in Claridge's.

Nonnie laughed at him. 'You're a proper gent, aren't you?' she said.

He was amused. 'How would you define a gent? I've seen a lot of them all over the world, an extraordinary number have managed to incorporate a large amount of heel.'

Nonnie's mouth was filled again. She had engulfed a square chocolate petit-four topped by a half-candied cherry, in one hand she held a cup cake and in the other a half-opened packet of cream biscuits. Compelled to keep it short, she confined herself to trying to say, 'kindness', but it came out 'kin'eff'.

When she had swallowed, she asked, 'What did you mean Roman style?'

'Oh, well,' Hubie replied, 'you know. The Romans ate their banquets lying down.'

Nonnie said, 'I've been in Rome, but nobody ever ate like that.'

'I mean the ancient ones, as in Nero's time.'

'Oh,' cried Nonnie, 'you mean when they had orgies? I went to an orgy once, but it was in London. It was frightfully dull. Everybody got drunk and said we should all take our clothes off.'

'Did you?' said Muller.

'Not everything!' Nonnie replied. 'Then we stood around with egg on our faces giggling and thought what a rum bunch the men looked without their trousies. A lot of men have such rotten legs.'

Muller asked, 'So what happened?'

'The men were too tight to do anything. They got off to one side and started playing leapfrog and kept falling down. It was winter and it was bloody cold as well. Sybil and I put our things on and went home.'

She suddenly turned her back upon him and Muller heard a slight catch of a sob and wondered what other memories this absurdity had suddenly stirred. And then he thought he knew. He touched her shoulder gently, 'Sybil?' he asked.

Nonnie turned back to him. 'Y-yes,' and he saw that tears had come. Then she asked, 'Is there any apricot jam?'

'Coming up!' Muller said. He unscrewed the top of a jar and passed it across to her.

She dipped in a finger, licked it clean, repeated it and was comforted. She said, 'You're kind. You understand things, don't you? That's my idea of a proper gent.'

Muller was experiencing a most curious kind of contentment even while he was reflecting upon what more perilous and at the same time ridiculous situation in which anyone could be plunged, to be lying here clad in the remnants of dinner clothes, as it were, on a capsized ship in the midst of a mountain of cookies, next to a common little hoofer with nothing on but a vulgar pink peignoir held together with his braces. Her face and little mouth were sticky with cakes and jam and so were her fingers. She lay on her side, leaning on one elbow, contemplating him with childlike enjoyment. He was utterly charmed by her.

CHAPTER XI

What about the Reverend Dr Scott?

Crew members had generated disturbingly again. They seemed to come out from the walls, though actually it was from the side aisles and the upside-down storerooms and workshops.

The long alley echoed with their shouts to one another, the rasping of their breathing as they floundered this way or that and some were weeping. The reversed staircases defeated them. Most of them still had the old topography of the ship so firmly implanted in their minds that they could not see her as she was now; topsides under sixty feet of water, keel up. They were still thinking in terms of stations and lifeboat muster. No one was helping or advising them. They were lost souls in a world where they no longer knew left from right or up from down.

In the half gloom they could still identify and avoid the staircases and companionways that had led originally from the alley up to 'D' deck and which now were wells. Aft a whole section of the partition had been blown away, leaving a dark, bottomless pit.

Shelby said, 'Scott's right. If the lights fail, it'll be hell here. Those people will go crazy. We'd better get out of their way.' He and the rest had remained where Scott had left them.

'Such as where?' Rogo asked.

Martin said, 'Along the side, I expect, like he told us. Up against the wall there. The big pipe will give us some protection. I could do with a rest.'

Rogo said, 'That makes sense. Lie down there, Linda, and you won't get stepped on.'

Linda cursed him as usual but no one even heard it any more. Her obscenities used like a sailor's had lost all potency and meaning.

A big pipe some nine inches in diameter gave further shelter by sprouting valve handles like giant mushrooms at intervals.

A bald old fellow in dungarees, half-seas over, carrying a square bottle of Johnnie Walker Red Label, from which he simply had knocked the neck to open it, paused by where Manny and Belle Rosen had wedged themselves. He proffered the bottle.

'No, thank you,' Manny replied, 'I don't drink,' and then so as not to hurt his feelings added, 'Doctor's orders.'

The bald-headed one did not understand a word, but he smiled, tilted his head back and took a long slug. Then he went tottering off, stumbled and fell flat on his face, smashing the bottle, keeping intact only the one side with the label of the ridiculous trademark, the man in the high top hat, cutaway coat and monocle. He glanced at his broken bottle, lay there on his stomach and began to cry.

'Oh, the poor fellow!' said Belle Rosen, 'the things that can happen to you when everything turns upside-down like, the things you find out about people that you wouldn't never know.' She was quiet for a moment and then added, 'You know something else I'd like to find out now? Just on account of my curiosity?'

'No, what?'

'What's Rogo doing on this boat? Who's he after? Did you ever find out?'

'He says no one. He says he just come on vacation like us and everybody else.'

Belle said, 'You believe this? A cop can take a month off for a cruise like this?'

'Shhhh, Mamma!' Manny whispered, 'Not so loud, he could hear you. Anyway he has his wife with him, don't he?'

'Manny, don't be so foolish. That's only so nobody should think anything. Any time you got a cop around, there's a reason.'

He reflected, 'I thought the same, but who could it be? Nobody's even suggested a game higher than a quarter of a cent a point. So card-sharpers we ain't got. Anyway, that ain't Rogo's racket.'

Belle lowered her voice conspiratorially, 'Listen, Manny, could he maybe be after the Minister?'

'Mamma, don't be foolish. Everybody knows who *he* is.'

Belle said, 'You know something? Every time Mr Scott went on the shore when we went sightseeing, the Rogos went wherever he went.'

Her husband chuckled, 'And so did a couple of hundred others, and sometimes us, too. You got to do better than that, Belle.'

Belle snorted, 'Okay, Mr Smarty. So maybe you know something else about him?'

'No, what?'

'He got fired from his job.'

'So? How do you know?'

'I read it in *The News*. I remember it because I was looking for something in the ads and it was right next to it: "The Reverend F. C. Scott has severed his connections with the Tenth Avenue Church and Boys' Club," and then something about how over the past years he coached the Boys' Club to three titles in basketball, baseball and running.'

Manny said, 'Severed his connections? He quit.'

'Manny, you got something to learn yet. In newspapers, severed means fired. Maybe he done something with a girl in the choir, like you're always reading in the paper with ministers. You know, rape maybe, or getting 'em into trouble.'

Manny laughed, 'Mamma, you got an imagination. It's for people like you we got tabloids. The Tenth Avenue Church is in a bad neighbourhood. If he was coaching them kids, he wouldn't have had time to fool around with girls. Maybe he got too good and somebody got jealous.'

'Well, one thing for sure, Rogo don't like him.'

Manny shrugged. 'Rogo's like all those tough kids brought up on the East Side, they don't like nobody that had any education. He don't like Mr Muller. Maybe he's got his eye on him.'

Belle said, 'Mr Muller's a gentleman. Rogo's wife don't like the Minister either.'

'You think so? If you ask me, Linda's got a hots for the big boy and he ain't giving. For this he should want to arrest Mr Scott?'

'Ask Rogo,' said Belle aloud, 'maybe now he'd tell you.'

'Ask me what?' said Rogo. He and Linda were wedged, resting a little farther on from the Rosens.

'Now,' whispered Belle.

Rosen crawled up a little closer and said, 'Who were you after on this ship?'

Rogo replied, 'No one.'

But Rosen was not to be put off. He said, 'Oh, come on now, Mike! It's like Belle says, since when does a big Broadway detective go cruising around Africa and South America? What's the difference? You could tell me now. Whoever he was, if it's true everybody drowned, he's dead now—unless it's one of us.'

Rogo turned his fishiest stare upon him. 'What the hell would I want with one of you?'

Rosen said, 'I don't know. You know me and I know you. But who's anybody else? Mr Muller? Mr Martin? The Shelbys are a nice family, but Belle says even maybe it could be...' and here he lowered his voice but kept the inflexion of question, '...the Minister?'

Rogo's fishy stare did not change a flicker. 'What's Belle been reading?' he asked.

'That's what I said to her,' agreed Rosen, 'but she's got an imagination. You know how women are, and she says he was fired from his job in the Tenth Avenue Church.' Rosen was watching the detective shrewdly as he dropped the information, but Rogo's blank face remained wholly expressionless.

'Was he?' he said.

'Yeah,' Rosen continued, 'she read it in *The News*, but it didn't say why.'

'I wouldn't know.'

'So maybe that's why he's taking a vacation now.'

'Maybe it is.'

'Just like you.'

'Yeah, that's right,' said Rogo. 'Just like me.' And then he added, 'Why don't you forget it, Manny?'

Rosen subsided and when he rejoined Belle and she queried, 'Did you ask him? What did he say?' He replied, 'Nothing. When a cop like Rogo don't want to talk, he can be like a sphinx.'

'Did you say about the Minister?'

'Yeah. He wanted to know what you'd been reading, like me.'

Belle said, 'So somebody can be wrong, but I ain't never seen a Minister like him before. He could have been a big gangster, maybe.'

'Belle!' her husband reproached her. 'How foolish can you talk? Everybody's heard of Buzz Scott the great athlete.'

Belle would not let go. She said, 'A big athlete couldn't get into trouble?'

'Rogo said to forget it.'

'That's an answer?' said Belle.

***

Farther along, tucked as far as possible out of harm's way and the zombie-like packs roaming through the murk of the fading light, something of the same topic was under discussion. Shelby said to Martin, 'What do you think of our Minister friend?' It seemed to be the first time he could remember having addressed a direct question to him. Although they were table neighbours, their orbits had been quite different during the voyage and he knew little or nothing about him. The truth was that he was so quiet, taciturn and almost invisible that practically no one asked his opinions. Martin proved voluble enough now.

'Well, come to tell,' he replied, 'I'd say he was quite a boy. Yessir, quite a boy! He's got something, ain't he? You wouldn't expect it of a minister, now, to take hold like that, would you? You take back home. We got a Baptist Minister who wouldn't be worth a hoot in a spot like this. Soft as a marshmallow. He can give you a tongue-lashing like Jeremiah, but he can't hardly lift the big Bible off the pulpit. The Sexton carries it up and down for him. Come to think of it, I ain't so sure he's worth much of a hoot back home, either. He's agin sin and can scare the pants off you preaching hell-fire. Hellfire Hosey, we call him, but he's got a mean streak in him a yard wide.'

Susan Shelby said, 'Oh, Mr Martin, you aren't serious, are you? A minister really couldn't be mean, could he?'

He regarded her quizzically but not unkindly and said, 'Miss Susan, when you've growed a bit more into the beautiful woman you're going to be, you'll find that meanness ain't confined or unconfined to any one kind of people. It's just sort of universal. Why you know what he done the other day? Well, not exactly the other day, but a couple of weeks before I left. We were having a baptism at the Sunday night meeting at our Baptist Centre Auditorium in Evanston. Ed Bailey who has the Ford agency was up for baptism, and Hosey dunked him and held him under 'til he damn near drowned. He claimed that Ed sold him a lemon on his last Ford and wanted to take it back. Ed said that Hosey drove it like a lunatic and near burned out the engine the first five hundred miles, so he wouldn't. When Ed came up, practically blue in the face and half choked to death, Sister Stoll, who was waiting her turn, heard Carl whisper, "You gonna take that car back? Or do I baptize you again real good this time?" Then Sister Stoll heard Ed say, "Okay, you..." and he called him a name which I'll not repeat in front of Miss Susan here, but it was what you might say a reflection upon Hosey's mother, if you know what I mean. Can you beat that? And afterwards his sermon was, "Do unto others as you would have others do unto you." And he was laying it on thick and half the time he had his eye on Ed Bailey. Now, this fella here, is something more like it. He gave us all into the hands of the Almighty and after that he's putting the rest up to us.'

'Well,' said Shelby, 'that didn't seem to be exactly the way he put it. We had an assistant football coach at Michigan once, who used to talk like that—"You fellas ought to thank the Almighty God that you're allowed to go out on to that field and carry the ball for this school."'

Martin grinned, his lips were so thin and drawn so tightly over his teeth that when he smiled it looked more as though he were gagging. He said, 'What's the difference, if it works?'

Shelby asked, 'Do you know anything at all about him? What do you suppose made a boy like that who had everything going for him—his people are Middle Atlantic Food Processing—millions—turn to the Church?'

'How can you tell?' Martin replied. 'What made a fella like Carl Hosey turn preacher? He hates everybody and everything. His wife don't dare open her mouth around the house and he treats his kids like they was living in a reform school. What's more, he's a runty little guy with a face like a baboon and yet all the biddies in the congregation go for him and think he's Jesus Christ's Uncle. Scott's got some funny idea about himself and God.'

'I'm not sure I like him,' Susan put in suddenly.

'Why, Susan!' said her father, 'That surprises me. I admire him greatly. He's always seemed most pleasant and polite to you. Robin thinks he's immense.'

Susan said, 'Oh, kids!' and then added, 'Maybe it's because he's too good-looking.'

Martin gave a dry chuckle. 'I didn't know a fella could be too good-looking for a girl. Now what kind of looks do you like, Miss Susan?'

Susan reflected. 'Well, not the All-American boy, if you know what I mean. And then he has that funny stare sometimes. You know, he looks you right straight in the eye.'

Shelby said, 'That's how an honest man looks, isn't it?'

Martin laughed again. He said, 'Brother Hosey never raises his eyes above your third shirt button. We're lucky it wasn't him along with us. We'd still all be down in the dining-room with Hosey pointing that bony finger and shouting, "Repent ye sinners, for the day of judgement is at hand."'

The smile faded and the trap mouth closed. He said no more. 'Repent ye sinners' had brought it all back to him again: sick wife; pneumatic mistress; warm, soft, exciting body; adultery; floating corpse. The secret nobody need ever know. However could he expiate his guilty conscience? Through his mind passed a picture of ancient biblical characters in torment, beating their breasts and rending their clothes and for the first time he understood them. He wished he could have got at his own entrails with his fingernails. How and before whom could he shrive himself? Surely not the baboon he had just described who would only lick his lips and ask to hear every detail. Hell fire and damnation!

***

Scott and the Turk had not yet returned from their exploration. The Rogos began to quarrel again.

It struck neither of them as extraordinary that they should continue their running domestic battle under circumstances where it might be violently terminated by the death of them both. To abuse and quarrel was Linda Rogo's nature; to love and placate her was his.

Actually neither had any real understanding of the pre-cariousness of their position. The sea and the inner topography of the *Poseidon* was as unfamiliar to them as the moon. To Linda it was nothing more than another hotel. She had hated it from the moment she had come on board.

She and Mike lived in a hotel, too, but it was one of those tatty ones, called The Westside Palace, on 8th Avenue between 48th and 49th Streets, where the lift was one of those rickety cages that rattled from side to side, the Negro elevator boy's collar was never buttoned, his uniform soiled and where the switchboard was rarely answered. There they had two rooms and a bath, the latter a centre for roving bands of cockroaches.

Over a gas ring Linda would make breakfast, but that was all. There was maid service of sorts and she had to do no work whatsoever. The location in the heart of the

Tenderloin was good for Rogo. A neglected switchboard was not a problem, since he had a direct police line into his apartment from headquarters. He was not a hankerer for home cooking and they invariably ate out in one or another of the hundreds of Broadway restaurants which were a part of Rogo's beat. The life suited them both. There were free tickets for shows and the best seats at prize fights. Mike Rogo was a personality who was frequently mentioned in columns and from time to time had his picture in the paper.

There were many Lindas on Broadway; failed, refugee actresses from the coast who were not even good enough to be call girls. When Linda had achieved a Broadway musical, one of the major flops of the season, the critics, fed up with the doxies of rich angels being presented as performers, had teed off on her. She had married Mike Rogo to cash in on the burst of fame he had achieved through his break-up of the Westchester Plains prison mutiny that had cost the lives of two warders held as hostages. Mike had walked into the prison singlehanded, killed three armed criminals and subdued the mutineers.

'WESTCHESTER MUTINY HERO WINS HOLLYWOOD BEAUTY', sang the newspaper headlines, ignoring for the sake of romantic content her recent disastrous Broadway appearance. It looked like a satisfactory publicity ploy until to her dismay, Linda found that she was only basking in the fame of the little hundred-and-fifty pound detective who feared nothing on two legs. The casting directors continued to remember that she could neither sing nor dance, speak lines, or walk across a stage without wriggling her behind like a Midway cooch grinder.

She took her bitterness out upon her husband. He was as proud of her as though she had been Doris Day or Julie Andrews. To hear him tell it, he had never got over the miracle that Linda had condescended to marry him. For three years she had been engaged in beating him down. His resilience was unassailable. When the battles were over, with one or the other or both, victims of his low threshold of truculence and violence, he nursed her and loved her with all his heart.

Somehow the cruise aboard the *Poseidon* had been for Linda the last straw. The itinerary of the ship covered first the black and then the coffee-coloured belt. To her one port had been like another and the inhabitants niggers. The elevator boy with the unbuttoned collar at the Westside Palace was one and so was the bum who was always asleep at the switchboard, or down the street for a drink or a pack of cigarettes. The janitor and the maids were niggers. Why did they have to go on a boat ride to see more of them?

She had been unable to fit into any category even with the highly diverse passenger list and had made very few friends, like Rogo who, as a police detective was himself secretive and a loner. Besides which, people tended to fight shy of Rogo. To some cop-haters he was a policeman and they retired behind the aphorism once a copper, always a copper. To others he was a famous detective and gunfighter. And while it never progressed beyond a shipboard joke, nobody really believed that he was not in pursuit or on the tail of one or more of the passengers.

Linda had even put it to him straight. 'Listen, you bastard, have you dragged me along on a job? What the hell is the idea of this lousy boat ride, anyway?' Only to see that morose, injured expression come over his flat features and the shake of his head as he said, 'Aw, now, honeybun, can't a guy take a trip? We ain't never been nowhere. Why don't you go and find somebody nice to talk to and enjoy yourself?' leaving her no wiser. Rogo never spoke about his work. When he made a pinch, roughed up a couple of hoodlums, or left a stick-up man dead on the pavement, she would read about it the next day in the papers.

She was nursing a further grievance. Stepping aboard the *Poseidon* after their charter flight from New York to Lisbon, even the slightly shabby and gone-to-seed appointments of the one-time luxury liner, was a reminder of the awful gap between the two rooms and grubby bath in the Westside Palace and the surroundings to which she felt herself entitled.

She was at Rogo now on the same subject that was occupying the other members of the party—Scott. She said, 'You're a fool, Rogo. You're supposed to be a smart cop who knows his way around and you let this big hunk of beef who says he's a minister take the play away from you.'

Rogo replied morosely, 'What do you want me to do?'

She sat up, bridled and tried to arrange her hair, 'Ack like a man,' she said. 'Can't you see he's been waiting to make a pass at me?'

'Aw, now, Linda, where do you get ideas like that? He may be a nut, but he couldn't be more respectful.'

Linda laughed, 'Huh! Didn't you see him looking down the tits of that little tart?'

Rogo protested, 'Why do you keep calling the kid a tart? She's in show business like anybody else. Anyway, what if he did take a look at her bubs, he's a guy, ain't he? What's that got to do with making a pass at you?'

Linda sniffed, 'I guess a lady knows a tart when she sees one, and I guess I know when a guy's going to make a pass at me. Of course, if you don't care...'

Rogo said, 'If he tried anything I could break him in two with one hand.'

Linda tossed her head and the stringy curls swayed about her china face, 'I wouldn't want to make a book on it. I've seen Mr Joe College act up mighty rough on a football field.'

'Kid stuff!' Rogo sneered. 'Kick 'em in the nuts and they're all down to the same size.'

He realized suddenly that he was working up that truculence which could so easily explode into attack for nothing and his voice became plaintive again as he said, 'Aw, Linda, why don't you lay off him and me, too? At least he's doing something, ain't he?'

Linda said, 'Okay, so where is he now?'

'Didn't you hear, they're having a look?'

'You know what I think? He's taken a powder. He'll never get that fat Jewess up any more places like the last, or the rest of us either. He'll save his own skin.'

Another memory suddenly rose up and she spat out, 'The way that Shelby woman looks at me, like I was dirt under her feet, and calling me names. You don't even stick up for your own wife, after all I done for you.'

Rogo said, 'Anyway, he didn't take any powder. Here he comes.'

He was so tall that they could see him above the heads of those still milling about in the corridor and they could see that he was walking slowly towards them, still accompanied by the Turk who was gesticulating with his arms and hands as though to pantomime something.

At that moment the lights flickered once and then went out, leaving them in total, unrelieved darkness.

CHAPTER XII

Broadway after Dark

The ship, still balanced on that brink of buoyancy that was keeping her afloat, never stirred, but to the crew the extinguishing of the emergency lighting was the signal that the *Poseidon* was about to go down. The blackness enshrouding them robbed them of all control. Not to be able to feel or see how they were going to die, not to be able to preserve that last shred of human dignity but to be tumbled blindly into oblivion, turned them into a nightmare of fear-crazed creatures rushing they knew not where in the dark, from or towards death.

In fleeing from death, they dealt death. In their panic they struck out at whatever or whoever they touched; each was the enemy of the other. They knocked one another down, or, stumbling upon the unfamiliar footing, fell and were trampled upon. Some died then and there.

The confines of the passage became a bedlam of shouts, screams, curses, insane bellowings, moans and weeping, the thud of blows mingling with the heavy sounds of their flight: stamping feet, rush of air, the ringing of their shoes upon the piping underfoot and grunts of pain. They stank, too, the sweat of fear oiling their bodies. Those that were not trodden upon were swept away in the torrent like packs of lemmings, rushing to their destruction. They fell into the pits of inverted staircases, to continue their flight down the corridor beneath, or met their ends as they poured over the edge of the open shaft that penetrated the centre of the vessel and were drowned.

Yet the small group of passengers wedged at the sides, in danger of being infected by the panic all about them, kept a semblance of discipline as the result of the warning they had had from Scott.

When the lights died, Scott had anticipated the stampede by a fraction of a second. He gave the Turk a violent shove over to the side and down, shouting, 'Don't move, Kemal!' and stood over him. This was his game—bodies hurtling at him and he deflected them or bumped them off their feet, or when threatened with being engulfed, struck out with huge fists and bony elbows, lashing and thrashing until the knot dissolved. He could have been the Archangel Michael battling the demons of the pit.

Rogo, too, had been caught momentarily on his feet but with his policeman's instincts he knotted the fingers of his left hand in his wife's hair to hold contact with her and struck out with his lethal right hand until he had fought himself free and managed to throw himself down and cover her with his body, while she whimpered in self-pity, 'Ow, you've hurt me! You're hurting me!'

Jane Shelby and Miss Kinsale who had been returning to Broadway from the end of the companionway where they had relieved themselves, remained unscathed, for the lights had gone before they reached the entrance to the working alley. The horrid phantasmagoria swept by them and the two women clinging to one another, felt the wind of their passage, smelled them, heard them, yet standing upon the brink of a black abyss, saw nothing.

Shelby had caught sight of the returning Scott and the fact that the man was there stifled the panic that had risen within him, too, and bid him run and run and run through that darkness until he should find himself falling into eternity.

He gasped, 'Stay down!' to Susan and Martin and shielded her at the side of the alley. Beyond having one hand trampled upon by a heavy boot, he suffered no injury. He once heard little Martin cry out in pain and then let forth a string of oaths in a high-pitched voice not at all like his own. Somehow this torment of souls and bodies struggling unseen in this confined space was far worse than that initial moment of catastrophe when they had been spilled upon their heads and in what seemed a fraction of time, their whole world turned upside down. Purgatory was a figure of speech, an outmoded concept, a swear word, a laugh and here physically it seemed they had passed through its gates and it had become a living thing.

In the storeroom, Nonnie Parry reached for Muller with a little whimpering, shuddering cry, 'We're going to die, aren't we?' she asked.

Hubie Muller was convinced of it. In one way or another it was going to be all over.

He felt her lips searching his face for his mouth and when they found it, they were soft, smelling and tasting of sugar biscuits and sticky with apricot jam. But with the hungry pleading touch with which they fastened upon his, she simultaneously gave him her life and her death. In the next moment they were joined.

And to Hubert Muller, discreet and cynical champion of a hundred bedroom encounters, countless emissions, numberless groans and cries extracted from his partners and himself, there ensued a unique experience. For the first time he made love in which mingled with passion was both tenderness and pity. Never before had he endured the richness that flowed through his being from this frightened little creature who had coupled her small self to him and with all that she was or ever could be, was sharing with him what she felt were her last moments of life, and making him a parting gift of what she was.

The enthralling sweetness of the spending that had happened to them simultaneously subsided and passed. But what remained to Muller was the overwhelming feeling of compassion and protectiveness towards this body with which he was still united, not knowing who she was, or even what she was really like.

Through Muller's mind passed the social euphemism of his class for what had happened. He had 'made love' and he knew that there, in the dark, with this unknown girl who only a little while before had slipped into his ken, for the first time it was true. Love, something he had never known before, had been made. It enveloped him, filled him, choked him and brought tears to his eyes.

They clung to one another, shivering and murmuring, touching each other's faces with their fingers and slowly came to the realization that in whatever form death was raging and howling in the corridor without, they were still alive.

The Rosens were protecting themselves as best they could, he crying over and over, 'Lie down, Mamma! Stay down like he said. Don't worry, I'm here,' and remembering what Scott had warned about covering heads, he covered hers with his hands. He was not concerned with any visions of Hades, the bottomless pit or devils rampaging through the infernal regions, since there was no place in the Jewish religion for such nonsense. He was aware only that they were in a bad jam with a lot of crazy sailors yelling and pushing and running round in the dark, and he was trying to protect Belle as best he could. When a body pressed or fell against his, he would push it away saying, 'Go on, get off! Get away!' while Belle kept reiterating, 'Manny! Manny! Don't be so foolish. Lie down so you shouldn't get hurt. Here, come behind me. Who knows what crazy kind of things are going on?'

The running and tumbling and shouting was diminishing and beginning to fade away in the distance. The commanding voice of Scott was heard over the remainder of the scuffling, 'Stay where you are! Don't move any of you. It's almost over. Are any of you hurt?'

Manny's voice came in reply, 'I wouldn't know. How could we tell in this darkness? They've been stamping all over us.'

Then the sounds were no more. There were one or two more isolated yells and then silence again and the enveloping heavy darkness.

Scott's voice was heard again, 'Has anyone got a cigarette lighter?'

'I have,' came from Shelby.

'Light it.'

There was a click and the first tiny sparklet shone out.

The flame which illuminated a portion of Shelby's face like a magician's illusion, quieted the nerves of the others and gave them back their sense of cohesion, of being members of a group, no longer isolated from one another. Lights from Martin, Rogo and Rosen snapped on and marked their various positions. There was also the sound of the scratching of book matches.

Scott's voice came through again, 'Save it! Save it! We don't know how much we'll be needing them. Just Shelby's. Dick, will you hold yours up? All of you make your way to Dick's light, until we're together again and count noses.'

Hubie Muller and Nonnie had heard and picked their way slowly and carefully, their arms about each other's waists. She pressed her head against his chest, moving ever so slightly as if trying to bore through his clothes, his skin and into his heart. It had become almost unbearable to her not to be a part of him any longer.

The Rosens were inching their way along the side of the corridor towards the beacon. Belle groaned, 'Oooh, my feet!'

Manny said, 'Take your shoes off again.'

'It feels better with them on, only them heels.'

'Wait,' said her husband, 'lemme have them.' He felt for her in the dark, took them from her and there were two sharp cracks as he broke off the points to give her a flat surface on which to walk. He said, 'I should have my head examined, I wasn't thinking of this before.'

Belle slipped them on again, 'Good enough you should have thought of it now. That feels better!'

Jane Shelby and Miss Kinsale had to cross the alleyway diagonally. They had their hands clasped firmly and braced each other further with their forearms. Jane took a particular comfort in that the tiny spark of beacon was her husband's. Her family would be intact.

Jane suddenly felt pressure upon her arm as Miss Kinsale wobbled and gave a little shriek, 'Oh!'

Jane asked, 'What is it?'

Miss Kinsale replied, 'I stepped on someone.'

'Oh dear,' said Jane.

Miss Kinsale suddenly clung more firmly to her hand and said, 'She didn't move.'

'She?' Jane asked, 'How do you know it was a woman?'

'One just knows,' Miss Kinsale replied. 'Ought we to do something?'

'In this dark?' said Jane, 'We'd better do what Dr Scott suggested first. Afterwards...'

Miss Kinsale was immediately amenable, 'Oh yes, of course. He did say he wanted us all together.' And then she added, 'The poor thing is probably dead.' They walked gingerly, touching several other bodies on the way, from one of which issued a groan of pain. Miss Kinsale merely said, 'That was a man.'

Jane marvelled at her nerve and control and felt that something extraordinary must be holding her together. She herself felt on the verge of collapse.

When he thought that they were collected, Scott said, 'Save the light, Dick.' The Minister began to call the roll. 'Mrs Rosen?'

'Speaking,' replied Belle.

'Are you okay?'

'Oh yes,' and then, 'Manny fixed my shoes. He broke of the heels.'

'Mr Rosen?'

'Okay. Somebody stepped on my hand, but it's all right now.' In the dark they could hear him working and wringing it.

Scott said, 'That was bright of you with the shoes. Any others with heels should do the same,' and then, 'Hubie? Nonnie?'

'We're here,' Muller replied. From then on he felt he would never think of themselves as anything but 'we', if they survived, and yet they had not exchanged so much as a single word of love.

'Mr Bates? Miss Reid?'

There was no reply. Out of the darkness came Rogo's flat voice, 'They must have found out where that booze was coming from. They're probably stoned.'

The Minister raised his voice and sent it booming down the corridor, 'Mr Bates! Miss Reid! Can you hear me?'

Into the empty silence that followed his call Jane Shelby's voice intruded sharply, 'Dick, is Robin with you? Robin, are you there?'

Shelby replied, 'Robin? Why no, he was with you.'

Jane's gasp was drowned out by Scott's shouting once again, 'Mr Bates! Miss Reid! Can you hear me? Where are you?'

From somewhere down and across the alley came the voice of Pamela, recognizable even though it was slightly slurred, 'We're here!'

Rogo laughed and said, 'I knew it. Stiff!'

'Jane!' said Shelby in alarm, 'Robin must be with you. You took him.'

'No, only Miss Kinsale. I left him to come back to you.'

Linda said, 'What about asking about us?'

Scott complied, 'Mr and Mrs Rogo, are you all right?'

Rogo replied for them, 'Yeah.'

Linda said, 'A lot you care! I could have been trampled to death.'

Martin reported, 'I'm here—just.'

Susan cried, 'Mummy, are you sure? Robin was with you. He isn't here.'

Jane Shelby battled against the panic rising in her breast as Shelby called out, 'Robin! Robin! Where are you?' and then to Scott, 'Frank, Robin's missing!' He snapped on his lighter and all the other lighters and some matches too, came on and were held up, but they could do nothing to drive back the heavy dark, only vaguely showing up a heap on the ground a little distance away, ominously still—the figure of a grown man.

Shelby, his voice cracking, shouted, 'Robin! Robin! Where are you? Answer me!'

As Jane joined in calling his name they were both close to panic when the professional investigator in Rogo came to the fore once more. He said, 'Excuse me Ma'am, where and when was he last seen?'

She was able to collect herself via the sensible question in spite of the terrible thoughts crowding in upon her and the memory of the soft, immovable thing that Miss Kinsale had stepped on and which had not cried out. 'By the W.C.,' she replied, 'he had to go. But he wouldn't with me there. He was shamed. It was upside-down and so horribly filthy. He wasn't used to it. Then Miss Kinsale and I... I thought he'd be back here long ago, even before the lights went out. Oh, my God! I've got to go and find him! Something has happened to him.'

She was on the verge of floundering off when Scott reached out and caught her. 'No, Jane, no!' he said, 'Not yet. We mustn't separate. Wait.'

'Let me go!' Jane shrieked, her voice rising to hysteria level, 'Let me go! Let me go! Let me go!'

'Jane, you can't!' her husband cried and too, clung to her wildly thrashing figure. 'Pull yourself together! We must do as Frank says. It will be hopeless in the dark.'

Scott said, 'We can't do anything in the dark. There's a Fire Station up the line. Kemal pointed it out to me just as the lights went out. There ought to be some lamps there. There's got to be. Let me have a couple of your lighters and I'll take Kemal with me. Give me a few minutes, Jane, and we'll have a chance of finding him. I beg of you not to do anything foolish.'

'Frank is right,' Shelby said.

With a sudden low, stinging bitterness in her voice, Jane said, 'Frank is always right,' and then giving way to pure hysterics shouted at the top of her lungs, 'I want my boy! Can't you understand? I want my boy!'

Susan took her in her arms crying, 'Mummy, Mummy! We'll find him. He'll be all right. He can't be very far away.' But within her she was badly frightened.

Shelby, his voice shaking, said, 'We'd better save the lights,' and snapped off his. Matches were blown out and they were in the darkness again, except for the two sparks of Scott and Kemal the Turk, moving off aft, lighting their way down the corridor.

Eventually the thin, gas flame glinted from a polished steel handrail and a brass plate knee-high, attached to the upside-down threshold on a door which, right-side up, read, 'FIRE STATION'. Scott paused to orient himself for a moment. The room was below the level of the ceiling on which he was walking, the Fire Station originally having been located up a short staircase leading upwards from the alley.

He made Kemal understand that he wanted him to remain there at the top. He took both the lighters, putting one in his pocket and shone the other for a moment on the railing until he had memorized its position, shape and layout. Then, extinguishing the light, he leaped and half slid, half worked his way down hand over hand.

He snapped on both his lighters and held them aloft to identify upside-down fire extinguishing gear, oxygen equipment, asbestos suits, fire axes, helmets, foam dispensers and the electronic panels which would illuminate the instant the temperature from a fire rose in any part of the ship, to reveal its location. Then, close by the door he had a momentary glimpse of a cylinder of black rubber. He snatched at it, but it would not come away until he remembered to lift it in the opposite direction from which it was hanging. He pressed the button at the side of the object and a yellow shaft of light from the waterproofed torch cut through the gloom.

At the top, the Turk peered down and shouted, 'Hoi! Good! More! More! Much more.'

Aided by the single torch, Scott located what he was looking and hoping for, a cache of treasure trove: half a dozen powerful, emergency fire-fighting lanterns for use in areas where normal lighting had been short circuited, and a further stock of waterproof hand torches, encased in rubber. The lanterns threw a beam as powerful as a small searchlight. They were heavy with their large, dry-cell batteries, but came equipped with straps in addition to the carrying handle which enabled them to be fastened to the back of a fire-fighter, leaving his hands free.

He shouted up, 'Okay, Kemal! We're home!'

There was rope in the Fire Station as well, to enable Scott to attach six of the large lanterns, one at a time and then bundles of hand torches for the Turk to draw up. The Minister had a last look round for anything which might prove useful, but beyond more of the nylon lifeline which he looped and hung around his neck, he saw nothing. He leaped for the rail, pulled himself aloft and rejoined his companion. They divided up the burden between them, extinguished all but two hand torches and started back.

Some thirty yards away, the waiting party caught sight of the glow of their torches. Shelby said, 'Thank God, they've found light!'

Miss Kinsale breathed, 'Amen!'

CHAPTER XIII

Susan

The Minister was excited, exhilarated, triumphant. He said, 'We're a cinch to make it now. If we use these sparingly they ought to last.'

The Beamer murmured, 'Bit of luck.'

Scott's voice became suddenly truculent, 'We'd have made it without these, just the same. Do you think I'd have given up?' And then he asked almost as an afterthought, 'Has the boy come back?'

Martin said, 'No.'

Jane, shivering, cried, 'Oh, hurry, hurry! Give me one of those. Give me one now.'

Scott snapped on one of the hand torches. The glow caught him under the chin and brought the handsome face into relief and Muller thought for a moment that he looked faintly irritated.

'Yes, yes,' he answered her, 'we'll find him. We'll split up; a search-party and the others to remain here as a base, in case the boy should reappear while we're looking. He might have been only momentarily knocked out.'

Linda Rogo protested, 'Count me out. I'm tired and my leg hurts.'

'Gimme a flashlight,' Rogo said, 'I'll go.'

His wife snapped, 'Boy Scout!'

Scott nodded, 'Take one of the lanterns. I trust your eyes to see things others might miss.'

'That's big of you,' Rogo said.

'Okay, then, Jane, Dick and Susan, Rogo, Martin, the Turk and myself. Hubie, Nonnie and Miss Kinsale might stay here, and Mr and Mrs Rosen—both of you need a rest.'

He distributed lanterns to Rogo, Shelby and Kemal, keeping one for himself and to Jane, Susan and Martin and Kemal he gave hand torches. The Turk, suddenly bewildered, was unable to understand what was happening and Scott had to make him understand with pantomime.

Again Muller caught the look of annoyance on Scott's face. The Minister was not pleased. Muller saw him steal a quick glance at his wrist-watch before he said, 'Come on, then, let's go. Jane, can you show us exactly where it was you left him?'

Jane said, a little uncertainly, 'It was, I think, that way—down there,' and she pointed towards the bow. 'I'm sure I could find it again. But when I left him I didn't notice how far I'd come before I met Miss Kinsale. She and I were together when the lights went out and...' Her breath came with a sudden catch, as she said, 'Oh dear, there was a woman —over there.'

Scott pointed his heavy lantern. He went over and knelt by the figure of a woman, a stewardess in white overalls, who was lying face down, her head wedged in between two pipes. He examined her briefly and then returned shaking his head.

Rogo beamed his lantern down the corridor and said, 'Jesus! Look at 'em!'

They found the body of a messman whose throat had been trampled and the remains of the drunken fat man who had fallen with his bottle of Johnnie Walker. His spine was broken. There was a man with a shattered leg and a mangled hand who lay moaning and another with his arm twisted around almost to his back, palm up. He was unconscious. There was no other living being to be seen in the long alley.

Jane said, 'I'm sorry, I can't wait,' and never remembered how she had hated the Minister for his seemingly callous abandoning of the injured.

Scott agreed, 'Yes. Time's running out. Besides, there isn't anything we can do for them.'

It took them longer than Jane ever would have expected. It was her first encounter with places one has seen that suddenly disappear until one loses all trust in one's own judgement. The trouble was her confused recollection of the distance and the fact that she forgot to play her light downwards and not upwards in search of the brass, 'W.C.' Once little Martin was heard to say, 'Oh, oh!' and the mother's heart leaped half with dread and half with hope as she cried, 'What have you found?'

His light had picked up the liquor storeroom where, amidst the jumbled cases of name brand spirits, sequestered in a kind of alcove made by the boxes, Pamela Reid sat crosslegged with the head of The Beamer in her lap. She was staring straight before her. The Beamer was unconscious. The place stank like a distillery. The girl did not even look up or speak when the lights flashed upon her. The fingers of one hand were moving, gently touching some of The Beamer's sparse hair.

'Paralysed,' Rogo said.

'It was here,' they heard Jane call, and they all went down to the alleyway where she pointed out the W.C. 'I'm certain of it.'

There was no one there. The alley where the W.C. was located was a dead end with no stairs and only storerooms for cased goods on either side: soaps, detergents, washing powders, cleaning materials.

Jane struggled to control herself, 'What could have happened to him? Where is he?'

Her husband comforted her. 'Don't worry. He can't have gone far.' He turned to Kemal and queried, 'Where are the stairs—the others? Where does this lead to? What's become of all the others? Where can the boy have got to?'

But the Turk did not understand.

'The mob was going both ways,' Rogo said. 'It's a wonder more weren't killed or hurt.'

'Didn't anybody hear anything?' Martin queried, 'Didn't the kid call out?'

Shelby said, 'In all that racket and pounding? God knows, he might have cried out, but none of us heard him.'

Martin thought: *Everybody thinks or says, or uses the word 'God' except this minister.*

Scott said to Rogo, 'This is your kind of job. You handle it.'

Jane addressed herself to Rogo, 'What ought we to do? Where ought we to look? Which way should we go?' The fact that he was a policeman in some way would make his advice more trenchant.

Rogo replied, 'Spread out. Break up. Not everybody together.' He was remembering searching parties in the parks or outskirts of New York for kidnapped or missing children, the line of men strung out a hundred yards across a field, moving slowly, their eyes cast down, half willing, half unwilling to be the first to stumble across a mutilated little body.

But this was not that kind of hunt or a place where that kind of tactic could profitably be employed. If the boy had been trampled to death, they should have found his remains near by; if he was still alive and had been swept away, caught up in the panic of that throng, well then, it called for a thorough search of every exit and entrance.

Scott said, 'We must hurry. There may not be too much time left for any of us, unless we get on.'

Jane Shelby turned on him and said, 'Are you serious? Not too much time left to find my boy?'

Scott did not reply and Shelby interposed, 'Frank didn't mean it that way, Mother. We mustn't lose our heads.'

'Will you keep yours, if we don't find our son?' She was beginning to shake again. Her face had turned into such a mask of fury that her husband was taken aback and could only say, 'Why, Jane!'

Rogo said, 'Ma'am, don't excite yourself. Maybe he got scared when all that running around happened, ducked behind something and went to sleep. You never know with kids. We'll start here at the middle and work both ways. We'll look down every alley, see? If a door is shut, I wouldn't bother. He wouldn't have been able to reach up to open it. Anywhere a door is open, he could have crawled inside. Look for staircases. Holler! The kid's got a head on his shoulders. He wouldn't be going down, would he? He knows we're trying to get up.'

Susan Shelby answered, 'Supposing he was knocked or dragged down? Where did all the others disappear in the dark?'

'Yeah, yeah,' Rogo said, 'but we needn't talk about that yet, do we?' From habit he was resorting to the policeman's heavy tact employed when there was almost a certainty that a tragedy was involved.

Susan said, 'I'm going to look down there.'

Her father asked anxiously, 'Where? By yourself? Oughtn't someone to be with you?'

The girl said, 'I don't need anyone to come with me. I know the way. Let me go, Daddy.' She wanted to be the one to find Robin.

Rogo gave her a quick glance. She was sturdy and self-possessed. He said, 'Okay, it won't hurt to take a look. She'll be all right. Work the alleys on your way back and we'll join up with you. Martin, why don't you and Shelby start checking both sides down from here? Scott, maybe you'd better go back to the other end with this monkey,' indicating Kemal, 'in case they ran the kid up in that direction.' Then he said to Jane, 'Ma'am, you and I will just have a good look around here, in case maybe we come across...' He hesitated, 'Well, say something you could identify, or anything and if one of the others should pick him up or need help, we'll be handy. Okay?'

Scott nodded and glanced at his watch again. Jane Shelby asked with chilling emphasis, 'What time is it, Dr Scott?'

He replied, 'It's a quarter to twelve.'

'And how much time have you allotted to the finding of my child?'

Scott ignored the direct question and said, 'We'll do as Rogo says.' He had accepted the detective's dispositions without argument. 'He knows his stuff. If the boy is anywhere about, we'll locate him.' He tapped Kemal on the shoulder and the two set off to explore the area aft.

***

Susan picked her way carefully, throwing the beam of her torch ahead and from side to side, to make certain that no little form lay wedged between these rows of pipes to which she had now almost become accustomed as normal flooring. From time to time as she passed one of the alleyways leading off from both the left and right of Broadway, since she had now progressed beyond both the centre shaft and the forward funnel, she would illuminate it momentarily but did not yet investigate it.

She was deeply troubled. An image had formed itself in her mind: that of her brother lying dead at the foot of the wall they had climbed from the deck below. She envisioned him spilled over with the panic-stricken rabble, trampled and lifeless. This image drew her on and it was there she felt compulsion to look first, to dispel it and see for herself that it was not true.

There were other things only half suspected that added to her distress and it had nothing to do with fear of death, because she was yet too close to birth—seventeen scant, joyous, growing up years—even to think upon death or not being there, not breathing, seeing, smelling, tasting, being a part of something very wonderful which was living. It was a curious premonition, a hint of disintegration in her family.

Her brother had disappeared which was loss sufficient. What if he were never found again, and in the end they were rescued? What did you do when someone like Robin was wiped out of your life? What would her mother do? And her father?

She said to herself and to others that she loved her brother; she loved her parents. But she did not know of what that love was compounded. Sometimes Robin was a little beast and they fought and tried to hurt each other and once he had almost broken her finger. Love of her mother was in a way an emulation of the kind of person she was and the kind of person Susan wanted to be—calm, smooth, chic, soft-spoken, desirable. She admired her father and his rugged features.

The boy with whom she had kissed and necked once or twice on the sofa in the dark and whose hand for the first time had touched her breast, stirring her simultaneously to longing and abysmal fright, had been hawk-faced and lean, a track man, a sprinter. He was nervous, temperamental and explosive and she remembered at meets when the gun cracked, how he burst off the mark with such violent expenditure of energy that he had the race won within the first five yards. It was there too, in the touch of his hand upon her breast, a breathless danger moment of impetuosity which she had dampened, controlled and escaped, for that was not the way she had wanted it. Shortly after they had quarrelled and she had broken up with him, for although he was attractive, he was unbearably egotistical. But the message had been delivered; the summons to awaken, and often afterwards she had wondered what it would be like, when it happened and with whom.

Brother, mother, father, love, liking, habit—what was an emotion? What was anything? What was more sure than the security and cohesion of her family and the pleasant life they all led together? Susan could not even remember so much as a quarrel or even an exchange of words between her father and mother.

Yet the disappearance of Robin had set something to grating in her mother other than worry and distraction, something Susan had felt rather than seen and did not understand, nor had she ever encountered it before, something curiously abrasive.

The girl left the others behind. When she turned around she could see the movement of their lights and once one of the big, emergency lanterns carried by either Rogo or one of the other men, blazed down the length of the alleyway to pick her up and throw her shadow outlined upon the bulkhead at the end of the passage, a young thing in a short frock, her hair curving away from her face on either side of her head. Then the big light was turned from her and she was again enshrouded by darkness except for the pathway she cut with her own torch. She saw that she had reached the edge of the companionway out of which they had climbed and wondered whether she would have the courage to look down.

She flashed the beam to the deck below and saw no one; no human being living or dead; nothing but an oily film of water. The implication of this did not strike her, so relieved was she at the banishment of the certainty of that image she had conceived. Wherever her brother might be he had not died there.

The next step, then, was to follow directions and carefully search each alleyway. She did not know exactly what she thought of Rogo for he and his wife were so completely alien to her. She despised Linda for her cheapness and beastliness and Rogo for his curious mixture of meekness and brutality towards her. But the very fact that they were both so far removed from her sphere made it less puzzling. Perhaps that was what those people inhabiting a world with which she never came in contact were like. On the other hand, when it came to arranging a search for someone missing, the common little man with the turned-down eyelids and strange manner of speech seemed to know what he was doing and somehow even had defined her need to go on her mission to find her brother by herself.

She moved cautiously down the first aisle to her left. Two doors were shut but a third at the far end was open and as she illuminated the room to investigate, she thought she would die of fright.

Within, overhead, an indescribable, heart-stopping 'thing' was coiled as though to pounce upon her. She thought she saw a dead white face, black insect body and not only two arms reaching for her, but tentacles waving snakelike and glittering wickedly in the torchlight. It was so unexpected, so monstrous, so unbelievable, so imminent that her limbs froze and her throat constricted choking off her scream.

Then she was seized from behind in a relentless grip, paralysing her with cold terror. Her light was knocked from her hand, but before it went out it flashed across the monstrous thing on the ceiling, still immobile, and she was aware that it was another pair of arms that had embraced her. She had not heard the soft footsteps or breathing behind her. It was this knowledge that kept her from fainting; this embrace was human. It took her, spun her about and pinioned her own. A hand was forced over her mouth.

She felt herself thrown violently upon her back and with the hand still cruelly pressing her lips to prevent outcry, a body, a something, a someone lay on top of her in such a manner that she was unable to move.

Strangely she was able to separate the two horrors now; the 'thing' from the ceiling and that other pressing her down, imprisoning her limbs and her will. She felt helplessly immobilized not only by the one holding her but by the weight of the darkness itself enveloping her. A hand tore at her underclothes and not until she felt the sharp internal pain did she understand that she had been pierced and entered—was being violated, abused, defiled and taken.

Oddly enough the word 'rape' never entered her mind. She was aware only that something was being done to her and that she was powerless to move or cry out, helpless from hurt and the awful indecency of the jostling. The smothering hand pressed so hard that she felt her teeth cutting into her lips. Darkness, evil and pain!

The agony continued. She wanted to shed tears like a child who is being beaten, but could not. Sounds reached her ears but not like any she had ever heard before; hardly human but frightening in their intensity and so, in the end, she could only lie there filled at last with knowledge and recognition, wondering when he would have done with her.

The sounds and the movements ceased and the body still lay upon her. The physical pain diminished but transferred itself to somewhere within her being at her very centre, an anguish of grief. The hand was removed from her face but she no longer cared about or even thought of calling out or giving vent to any kind of cry. She was lost; the blackness was a bottomless pit into which she was falling, falling, from which she would never rise again. She was not aware that her arms were no longer pinioned either, or that the person on top of her had relaxed. Unconsciously she moved her hand. It came into contact with the torch. Her fingers closed over it and hardly knowing what she was doing, she snapped on the light and illuminated the face above her.

It was almost that of an infant, a fair-haired young boy of no more than eighteen, and perhaps this was to her the greatest shock of all. For while during the turmoil of what was being done to her in the darkness she had not been able to form a picture at all of the doer, nothing that might have come to her mind had done so, but only an all enveloping effluence of beastliness. And here was only this flushed youth, sandy-haired with light blue eyes, a curiously touching button of a nose, pink cheeks and an almost feminine curve of mouth.

Why! She thought to herself in total surprise, *He's only a baby!*

'Oi!' said the boy, 'Don't do that. Don't look at me. Ah couldn't 'elp it.'

He lifted himself from her, knelt and fumbled for a moment, took the light from her fingers and turned it upon her. From behind the glare came his horrified whisper, 'Aw, my Gawd! Ah've done it to a passenger! My Gawd! Ah thought you was a stewardess.' He repeated, 'Ah've done it to a passenger! They'll hang me!'

Terror was in his eyes. 'Strike me dead! You're a passenger. Ah've seen you before, when Ah was up on deck on the brass. Ah didn't mean no 'arm to you. Ah thought Ah was goin' to die. There was a skirt and Ah thought Ah'd just 'ave a last bit of it. When you think you're goin' to die you don' know what you're doin'. But Ah wouldn't 'ave done it if Ah'd known.' And suddenly he laid the torch down, put both his hands to his face and began to weep, not like a man but as Susan would have wept if she could have done so.

He was so like a child that she soothed, 'Hush! Don't cry so! It's happened. You didn't mean it. I wouldn't tell. No one need ever know. Please don't cry so.'

He could not stop. He was filled with remorse, fear and horror at what he had done, the dreadful, unforgivable transgression, not so much the violation but the line he had crossed.

'There,' Susan heard herself say, 'don't take on so. Come, put your head here for a moment,' and she pulled him down and nestled his head in her arms. It was not any Susan she had ever known before. She could see the tears welling from the light blue eyes, rolling down and staining the pink cheeks and the quivering of the beautifully formed lips. He was so very young and she suddenly so very old that he touched her heart, and she held him and stroked the soft hair and hushed and soothed him until he ceased to cry and lay there nestled.

That other Susan that she did not yet know asked, 'What's your name?'

''Erbert.'

'How old are you, Herbert?'

'Eighteen.'

'What are you?'

'Deck 'and, ma'am—miss.' His replies were half muffled by his face being buried in the material of the frock covering her breast. The dialogue somehow seemed no stranger to him than it was to her. For the moment he was comforted.

'Where do you come from?' Susan had no idea why she was questioning him thus.

''Ull,' he replied.

'Hull?' she repeated, 'Where's that?'

'You know, on the 'Umber, on the north-east coast.'

'Are your parents still living?'

'Mum and Dad? 'Corse! Dad 'as a fish and chip shop. Mum 'elps him out. Me. I couldn't stand the smell of it.'

'Did you run away to sea?'

'Aw no, miss! My Dad ain't like that. I was apprenticed proper. I always go 'ome on leave. They're champion, me Mum and Dad.'

And that last thought appeared to trigger both the enormity and the absurdity of what he had done and where he now was and what was going on, for he suddenly tore himself from her arms and all the tears and childishness had gone from the blue eyes and they were filled with terror again. He sat up, looked at her and cried once more, 'Jesus!! A passenger!' and climbing to his feet, he turned and ran.

Susan called after him. 'No, no, Herbert! Don't be afraid. I'll never tell.' But she heard him slipping and stumbling amongst the pipes and then suddenly a cry and a splash and another cry, and she knew he had fallen down the open well of the staircase and must have hurt himself. She remembered then that there had been an oily film of water and wondered whether it was so deep that he would drown. But it could only have been a few inches, for then she heard more splashing as, in the grip of terror, he ran and ran in senseless and helpless panic, along the dark corridor below until she heard him no longer.

Hurting in every part of her body, within and without, Susan picked herself up off the floor, retrieved the torch and arranged her clothing. She did not bother to examine herself. It was all being done by that other Susan that had been born out of that moment of darkness and with whom she must now get acquainted. She walked painfully to the entrance of the alley and as her torch flashed across it, she was once more picked up by the beam of the big lantern.

She heard her father's voice echoing down the long alley, 'Hello there, Susan! Are you all right?'

She called back, 'Yes.'

'Was there somebody there?'

'Yes.'

'Who was it?'

'A sailor.'

'Did he say anything? Had he seen Robin?'

'No. He was frightened. He ran away.'

The big light switched off. Her father's voice said, 'Keep looking. We're working in your direction. We'll meet you.'

Susan sat upon one of the round valve handles and bent over, her hands folded together between her knees, staring into the darkness.

She knew that she was an old-fashioned person, brought up in an old-fashioned way by a family with old-fashioned ideas.

For the new American revolution, the surging unrest and upheavals of the late sixties had passed the Shelbys by. It had barely touched Grosse Point and left it an enclave of life as it had been lived twenty-five years earlier, as happened in so many communities where the old ways of living were encrusted. Growing up in this atmosphere had been smooth and painless.

Yet the new kind of world revolving just beyond her threshold had impinged upon Susan, coloured her thoughts, desires, emotions and bodily yearnings and she often wondered what she would be like in the end, caught up between changing ideas and customs.

In spite of the new permissiveness and boldness of boys, she had been sheltered during her high-school days by her own fears and fastidiousness. Girls carried contraceptives in their handbags, or took the pill but the curious obscenity that seemed to connect with these articles and their licence protected her from them. She had understood her own youth her own body and its values and had not wished anyone yet to take liberties with it.

But she had not been unaware of the higher temperature of the sexual excitement of the times in which she was living. It was her last term at Julia Chandler High School and the following year she would be eighteen and going away to college and later art school at the University of Chicago. She had often wondered whether she would fall in love with and sleep with a boy, shack up or live with him during college years and then marry. Or would she wait, old-fashioned to the end, a shy and virginal bride to be seduced by an understanding husband.

She had placed no particular value upon the concept of virginity. She did not know even if after the strenuous sports in which she had indulged whether she still was one technically. Sometimes she had an intuitive prescience of what love might be like and felt that she heard it like sweet and distant music. Because of this she was not going to have any spotty adolescent messing about with her for his own entertainment. If some day that music came so close that it would engulf and rob her of all her senses, then she would yield her person without regret and without shame. There would be the excitement of being made into a woman and at the same time beauty. This was, or had been the secret Susan.

Only then did she begin to weep softly to herself. Her dreams, wonderings and longings, the speculations upon what it would all be like had ended in a moment of pain, horror and outrage which, against all that was natural, had suddenly turned to pity. In one instant she had been destroyed and yet understood and forgiven her destroyer.

She felt chilled through and through, an icy coldness from the crown of her head to her toes and numb as well, as the delayed shock of the experience took over. Yet what seemed to affect her the most was the memory of the frightened boy in her arms and her holding him as one might hold a lover after love was spent.

She heard the others approaching, searching down the side aisles of the long corridor and saw the light from their lanterns flashing this way and that. She blinked the tears from her eyes and automatically returned to her work of looking for her brother.

Yet first she was drawn back to the scene and the first moment of terror she had endured, she had to satisfy herself as to what it had been and the courage to do so was lent her by the knowledge that nothing ever again could hurt her any more.

Once more she picked up the mysterious 'thing' lurking on the ceiling, but this time she recognized it for what it was and verified the recognition by reading the upside-down brass plate identifying the office: 'DENTAL SURGERY. CREW'. The tentacles had been no more than the dentist's drilling paraphernalia hanging from the ceiling and the white arms the dental chair reversed. How difficult it was to remember and to believe in this upside-down world. Would it be equally difficult to orient her own self? Who was she now? What was she? What was left of her old person? What would the new Susan Shelby be like, now that a poor, panicked sailor had used her body and run away?

And she said to herself, as she shone her lamp on doors open and closed and looked into storerooms and tiny offices that had belonged to chief cooks and head stewards and murmured, 'It's incredible, but one behaves in the end just as though nothing had happened.'

Her search revealed no sign of her brother and a third of the way back from the stair-well she joined up with her mother, her father, Rogo and Martin. She and her parents looked at one another, not speaking the question but only miserably and forlornly shaking their heads, while Rogo and Martin stood by in unhappy embarrassment.

CHAPTER XIV

A Rattling of Bones

The party worked its way back again, rechecking, peering behind cases, boxes and bales that had been tumbled from floor to ceiling when the ship keeled over, looking now for a young, dead hand stretched out from beneath some pile, afraid to find it, afraid not to find it, growing more and more fearful of being compelled to face the fact that he was nowhere.

They met once more near the centre of Broadway where they had left the others, the bobbing lights coming together.

'Did you find...' Manny Rosen was about to ask, when Belle poked him, 'Don't even ask. Wouldn't they have said so? This is terrible!'

Scott said, 'I'm sorry, Jane, he isn't there. He couldn't have got past us. We've been to the end.'

He said nothing about the gap in the inner wall of the alley and the dark hole at the bottom of it where the lantern had shown unspeakable things floating. Kemal had pointed down and said, 'Boiler—Boom!'

The second one aft had not exploded, but plunging downward it became wedged in the funnel shaft. There had been no chance of the boy ever reaching it.

They fell silent until Nonnie said, 'But he can't have disappeared, he was such a lively little...' and then she cried, 'oh dear!' as Muller squeezed her arm to silence her, for with one exception they were all aware that he could very well have done so.

Rosen asked, 'What about staircases?'

Rogo said, 'There are plenty of those, going both ways.'

'Mightn't he have got up one of those?'

Martin said, 'What, in the dark?'

Belle whispered to her husband, 'Shsh! Don't talk so much, Manny, don't ask so many questions. Ain't it bad enough without making it worse?'

Susan said, 'I looked down where we came from. There was nobody there. There's about six inches of water now.' She remembered that it had just covered the pipes and Herbert had run splashing away into oblivion.

'Yes,' Scott said, 'in the corridor of "D" deck below. The ship is deeper in the water than she was.'

Rogo said, 'Jesus! She could go any minute, then. What's holding her up?'

Muller said, 'Maybe the cargo holds and the ballast tanks at either end. Acre said they were empty. She could be flooding in the middle, but...'

'Then we ought to be getting the hell out of here,' snapped Linda Rogo. 'If the kid's gone, it isn't our fault. I don't want to drown. If he was anywhere around, he would have hollered, wouldn't he?'

'Yes,' Jane Shelby said, 'you must be getting on, of course.' Her speech, under this provocation was astonishingly calm. 'All of you, please. I shall stay here until I have found my son...'

Susan caught her breath and said, 'But Mother—you can't!' and realized suddenly that what she was saying was '*we* can't'. All the selfishness of youth came welling up in her. For she didn't want to be left behind in that black and forbidding alley with the memory of what had happened to her there. She wanted to escape from it by climbing, going up, rising, reaching for the light, to survive to find other dreams perhaps. She was too young to be condemned to this eternal nightmare of scrabbling about in the dark from which had emerged so swiftly the destruction of the person she had been. She did not want to die.

Scott said, 'You mustn't, Jane. Your boy will be found, I promise you...'

'*You* promise me! Why? How? How do you know...? Have you seen him? Do you know something and aren't telling me? Why do you talk like that?'

'Because,' Scott replied, 'he will not be allowed to be lost.' And only Muller realized that his voice had risen a pitch higher and he wondered were he to flash his torch into the Minister's face, whether that strange glare would be reflected back.

Scott repeated almost as a litany, 'Save the light,' and so used had they become to obeying him that there was a general snapping off of lanterns and torches, except for those carried by Jane Shelby and Scott himself, so that the uneasy party was again shrouded in deep gloom. Scott added, 'We've been spendthrift with our light. From now on we must save every second of it because without, we're finished. I don't know how long it is since these batteries have been renewed. I would think that in a first-class ocean liner, the fire authorities would keep them in proper shape. But this has become a sloppy ship and we just don't know. Therefore I suggest you don't use your torch unless you absolutely must.'

Jane said, 'I'm sorry you feel we've been wasting light. What is it you want to do now? How do you propose to find my boy without it?'

Had Scott been less engrossed in his ends, he might have taken more notice of the edge in Jane's voice and the strain showing in her face, and the disarray caused to her person by the rigours already endured coupled with her anguish.

The Minister misread her, as did all the others with the exception of Nonnie, who whispered to Muller, 'Oh dear, can't he see? She's going to blow up.'

Scott said, 'I'm afraid we'll have to go on, Jane. We can't remain here any longer if we're to have a chance. We must use every minute. You've seen that the water's rising. And there's another reason.'

Manny Rosen asked, 'What's that?'

'Air,' Scott replied. 'We're trapped inside the hull. We don't know how much oxygen there is, or how long it will last. Haven't you noticed it's hotter? We've got to go on.'

Nonnie whispered to Muller, 'But how can we? Hasn't he any heart?'

Muller said, 'Hush!' and held her more tightly in the shadows outside the circle of yellow torchlight.

Jane Shelby asked, 'And my son?'

Scott replied, 'We'll find him on the way.'

'Brother,' said Rogo, 'I wouldn't be all that sure.'

For the first time it seemed that with an innocent enough remark the detective had got under the Minister's skin, for in a voice again risen in pitch he replied, 'Where's your faith? I've told you, he'll be found.'

Jane declared, 'I'll stay here and look.'

Richard Shelby added, 'Susan and I will stay with you of course, Mother. We won't leave you…'

He did not mean it. He did not mean it at all. He did not want to, he did not want either Susan or himself to stay behind in this awful tunnel that already stank of death. Scott had promised they would find the boy. He believed him. He wanted to believe him. If there was a chance that his son was alive or in the vicinity he would not have gone on, but they had searched the alley thoroughly, aided by a police-force detective. Yet if his wife persisted in her decision on the chance that after so long a time he might suddenly reappear, it was their duty to remain by her side. But he could not help himself hating the sacrifice, or thinking of the injustice of it; three more lives for one, Jane, Susan and himself.

Jane knew it as she always had. He would inevitably do the right thing from the wrong motives, the perfect outward man, the male animal, Homo Sapiens Americanus who never put a foot wrong, a clean mind in a healthy body and a heart the size of a pickled walnut in his big chest.

He had loved his son in the same way he had loved her, by all the outward signs; had played football with him, hiked and camped with him, done everything a father should do except love him and understand him. In place of love he substituted pride: pride in his looks and talents as a little reproduction of himself.

Or, thought Jane, for pride substitute vanity. He was vain of his wife, his daughter, his son, his job, success, career, home, friends, his position in the community. Nobody could fault Dick Shelby. He was a great guy with a great family. He had it made, made, made. And she knew that within he was as hollow as that football he so passionately enjoyed throwing about with his son so that one day the boy would garner the same automated cheers that had rung in his own ears on the football field and make him feel even more proud. 'That was Robin Shelby. Dick Shelby's kid. Remember Dick Shelby '49? He had a great pair of hands. The kid's just like him.'

Jane had discovered this a year after their marriage had been celebrated in Detroit with the pomp due a daughter of a motor hierarchy. Young Dick Shelby was known as a comer and her father, Howland Cranborne, President of Cranborne Motors, was wagering Jane on his own judgement that this was so.

As for Jane, she had been in love and had married Shelby of all the young men she had known or at one time or another had cared about, all rather stamped like auto parts from the same mould, because she had felt something vaguely pathetic hidden away within Dick which had excited her compassion.

The love she received in return was compounded of the gamut of Madison Avenue advertising clichés woven around the word. In terms of the 'How To…' books, she could not fault his performance in bed. It was his pride to satisfy her, but never his need. Often, when they had done and she was flooded with warmth and tenderness she would be chilled by the intrusion of the feeling that he was lying beside her as though he expected the door to open and the coach walk in to give him a pat on the back, or Prexy to award him a diploma.

But the real shock of disillusionment had come with the discovery that the pathos she had misjudged as a need lacking in him that she could supply was something quite different. It was nothing but a fear of being found wanting in conformity. His craving to conform to the accepted standards was overwhelming.

He wanted neither more nor less out of life. He was good at whatever he did, better than good enough, but never smashingly outstanding. Thus he could associate himself with and hero worship a Scott both at the same time. He belonged. He too, had once scored the winning touchdown. World War II had seen him achieve a Captaincy of artillery with a year's service in the Pacific in which his behaviour had been exemplary. He had returned, undecorated and untarnished, popular with his company, cool enough under fire, a man who had done everything an undistinguished soldier should, because he could not have dared be anything either less, or more.

Jane was well aware that by his marriage to her he was certain he had taken the cup in the Conformity Stakes. And because she was a thoroughbred herself and a good sport, she had played the game his way and managed a not too unhappy marriage in which perhaps her greatest achievement had been to conceal from Richard Shelby for twenty years, the fact that he had been found out.

But now the suppressed resentments of those two decades were brought to bursting point by the bald production of the pattern. He was offering to remain behind, not because he had been stricken by the loss of his son, but because it was the right and proper gesture.

In her anguish, she was like a receiving set vibrating and tuning into the wavelength of every emotion. She felt the impatience of the others in the party. Her fate, her dilemma, her person or what happened to her was not really any of their concern. She had become an obstacle and a nuisance like fat Mrs Rosen, who was threatening their chances of survival. She knew her husband wanted to conform to their wishes too, and to Scott's leadership.

Belle said, 'We shouldn't go without the boy. For my part I wouldn't care if we didn't take another step. To me it all sounds crazy—up, down—down, up. When the boat sinks we'll all be going the same way.'

'I don't see what could have happened to the little feller,' said Manny Rosen. 'I didn't hear nothing in the dark when the rush came, if he called out, maybe. But if he got tramp... I mean, knocked down, maybe we would have...' He trailed off lamely, knowing that with each word he was making it worse.

It was the not knowing! Had she found him dead, Jane could have mourned him as those already crushed, lacerated and drowned beneath them would be mourned. But if he were still amongst the living, alone, terrified, blundering about in some pitch black, inverted corridor, or store space, or fallen down one of those awful wells...

Nonnie went to her, took her hand and said, 'Oh, Mrs Shelby, we don't want to leave you!'

And Muller added, 'We do understand how you must feel.'

Martin said, 'Maybe we ought to have another look.'

And Miss Kinsale put in, 'Yes I do think we should.'

Rogo said, 'I wouldn't know where, unless he got picked up by people trying to make it up to the bow. They wouldn't turn back for him and he wouldn't have been able to go it alone.'

Linda said, 'It's her own fault. Why didn't she stick with the kid?'

For all of the beastliness of the remark, Jane knew that it was true. She ought never to have listened to him, never have given in to the squeamishness that same conformity had instilled into her boy.

Racked, Jane felt the falsity behind all their protestations. The little dancing girl might be sincere; the rest of them wanted to get on. She had felt it herself, the urgency to climb up and out while there was still time, to survive where so many had died, the triumph of each little victory, the terrible suspense of the crippled ship. But her rage flooded towards her husband.

Scott was honest. 'Dick, it will have to be your decision. I have pledged myself to go on with these people. They've trusted me. We will leave you your torches and one of the big lanterns but remember, they won't last for ever. If I didn't feel that the boy was safe or that we'd find him in the end, I would never suggest...'

'Naturally,' said Shelby, 'I shall remain with my wife.'

Suddenly-grown-up Susan seemed to herself to be standing on one side, observing. Lost Robin, harrowed mother, sacrificing father! And who was asking Susan whether she wished to live or die, for which of two forlorn hopes she might care to opt? And in her nostrils was the scent of break-up, of the final explosion of the undercurrent she had divined.

It happened as Jane Shelby turned on her husband and said, 'Oh no, you won't!' in a voice shuddering with hatred and disgust.

To Susan who had been expecting it, it came almost as a relief. Richard Shelby, completely unaware of the feelings stored up in this for ever gay and graceful woman and about to be let loose, stared as though she had gone suddenly mad and stammered, 'But Jane! What do you mean—why?'

'Because I don't want you to. Because I don't want you near me. Because I loathe and detest you. Because you are nothing but an automaton programmed to walk and talk and act like the cardboard cut-out of a man.'

Shelby began to tremble. It was still unbelievable. 'Jane, do you know what you're saying?'

'I know very well what I'm saying, that you are a weak, spineless creature who has settled for anything and everything except growing into a human being. You've never once thought of or even dared to do something that wasn't done; I've hated being in your home, I've hated being in your bed.'

The outburst stunned everyone but Scott, who was a little to one side, waiting and distributing the big lanterns and the coils of rope between Kemal and himself. The others stood about trying to look away with the exception of Linda who laughed and said to Rogo, 'There's your lady for you! And you kick about me!'

In growing horror Shelby was becoming aware that what he had felt to be the safe, secure foundations of his marriage were beginning to disintegrate. And blunderingly he had recourse to the clichés of the man unexpectedly faced with an aroused female, 'But Jane... I've always loved you.'

She cried, 'You! You wouldn't know the meaning of the word. I've hated your loving when I ought to have loved you most, I've despised your cowardice and squaring up to the good husband image. You haven't even had the guts to take yourself a mistress, or crawl into bed with somebody else's wife for the sheer lark of it. I'd have respected you if you had, but you conformed even there, whoring it with tarts with the boys out of town, so that they wouldn't think you weren't a man's man.'

The edifice began to topple. How had she found out about those little escapades during meetings in New York, Chicago and Atlanta?

'You don't even know what I'm talking about,' Jane said. 'You're standing there wondering how I knew about your tarting? Do you think I cared? Did you ever think of me as a human being with understanding? Whenever I wanted to open a window on the life we were leading, you put on double locks until I stopped trying. You'll try to make me go with you for the sake of my life; Susan's and yours. You'll stay behind with me because a man doesn't desert his wife even when he thinks that she's being selfish and a fool. But your heart isn't breaking inside your ribs because you've lost your boy, because he may be trampled, smothered, drowned or just a terrified child lost in the dark.'

She sank to her knees, buried her face in her hands and cried over and over, 'I'll never know! I'll never know!'

Again Nonnie was the first to reach her, kneel by her side and throw her arms about her. 'Oh now, lovey, please!'

Miss Kinsale hovered about the two, fluttering and making little sympathetic noises.

The practical Belle Rosen said, 'Look, Mrs Shelby, you should do what you think is right and Manny and I would stay with you, too...'

The hurt that Shelby had suffered in those few appalling seconds was such that it left him rigid and paralysed and rendered him unable to go to her.

Nor was Susan able to give her mother physical comfort at that moment, but rather stood regarding them both, a spectator looking upon two strangers. She was almost as bewildered as her father. How could her mother have been such a wonderful wife all those years, masking her feelings as she did? How could her father have been so blind as to the reality of the person living in his house with him? How could she herself never have known or suspected what her mother was really like, or for that matter, her father? The fall of the House of Shelby left her sympathies divided between her anguished mother and shattered father and the ridiculous thought that came to her mind was: *Poor, conventional Dad! If he knew what had happened to me...!*

As swiftly as she had collapsed, Jane Shelby recovered and raised her face from her hands and in the light of their lanterns they saw that it was tearless.

'Oh no,' she said, in a voice that had suddenly gone flat with all tone and living timbre out of it, 'I'll come with you.' She pointed to Scott, 'That monstrous man is right. His duty is to the living and I suppose mine is too. I've held up all of you long enough. Let's go.'

That monstrous man Scott said without emotion, 'I'm sure that you have made a good decision, Jane, and a wise one.'

Of them all, Muller was perhaps the most pleased with Jane's decision. He had been too long in a situation far from his liking. He turned to Nonnie and whispered to her, 'You're a good girl.' In his heart he was wondering what Scott was made of, what it was that made him tick.

Susan went to her mother now, put her arms about her and said, 'Oh, Mother, I just don't know what to say.'

Jane was still quivering, sensitive to every minute radiation. She said to her daughter,

'I hope you'll never know what's it's like to desert your child.'

The rebuke told, but the shaft did not wound where it was directed, but elsewhere to the heart of that new Susan who thought to herself; *Oh Lord, what if I have one?*

Scott was already occupied with reorganizing. He said, 'I'll lead the way with one of the big lamps. Rogo will bring up the rear with another. That should give us enough light to save the spares. We're going through...' he hesitated for a second, 'what's left of the second boiler room. We shall need everything we've got to make it to the engine room.'

'And God's help,' put in Miss Kinsale.

Scott looked down upon her from his towering height and said, 'God is waiting on us. I don't believe in importuning, or deafening His ears. We've been given the strength to rely upon ourselves, we mustn't disappoint Him, must we?'

Miss Kinsale blinked like a child who has been reproved trying to hold back tears and answered, 'Oh yes, of course, you are so right, Dr Scott. If you put it that way...'

Muller was tempted to ask Scott about the lost boy, a staunch and courageous little fighter if ever he'd seen one and so young. Where, as the first victim of their attempt to save themselves, did his loss fit into the Minister's theology? But he refrained. There had been enough talk.

But the interruption came from another source. Rogo said, 'The Limey and his girl aren't here.'

They had each with his own worries forgotten The Beamer and his friend Pamela.

Scott looked annoyed, 'Where are they?'

Linda giggled, 'Dead drunk.'

Martin said, 'They got into the liquor stores somehow.'

'Oh, lord!' said Shelby, 'If he's drunk, he...'

Scott asked, 'Have you seen them?'

'Yeah,' said Rogo. He, Martin and Scott detached themselves from the group and led by Rogo, made their way down to the storeroom where their torches picked up the figures of The Beamer and his girl much as they had been last seen, except that she now, too, was asleep.

Scott shook them both by the shoulder, but only Pamela woke up. She had the faculty upon waking of being instantly aware of where she was and of the situation. She said, 'Oh, I just dropped off for a minute.'

Martin asked, 'What about him?'

The girl actually smiled at them and said, 'Oh, he won't wake up for hours. He had nearly a whole bottle of whisky.'

Scott looked down upon them angrily and swore. He asked Pamela, 'Why did you let him do it? Don't you realize he's finished? I'm afraid you'll have to leave him. We can't possibly handle him in this condition. We can't afford to wait, we've wasted enough time already.'

The plain girl ignored his question, glanced at The Beamer fondly for a moment and then looking up replied, 'Oh, I wouldn't leave him. I must be here when he wakes. He'll need me then.'

Martin pleaded, 'Look, miss, can't you see the jam he's got himself and all of us into? Are you going to throw yourself away for this guy?'

Pamela stared at him as though she did not understand the phrase. 'Throw myself away?' she repeated.

Scott said sharply, 'Why didn't you stop him from drinking?'

The girl replied, 'He needed it, that's why. And it made him happy again.' But she did not add, *And sweet and kind and fond of me again.*

Rogo was less tactful, he said, 'Look, miss, this guy's a whisky bum. You're a young kid. Maybe we're all gonna go down with this tub, but if we don't you've got a right to live your life. You come along with us. It's his problem.'

'But I *am* living my life,' Pamela answered with an intensity of conviction that left no room for doubt. 'You go on. We'll follow after you when he wakes up.'

The men exchanged looks and Martin said, 'She's levelling. I know that kind. Some gals just have a thing for drunks.'

Scott made his decision. 'We'll leave you this flashlight. It's all we can spare. I'm afraid we can't wait any longer.'

Pamela said, 'Thank you, Dr Scott. We'll be perfectly all right. Not to worry about us. I'll look after him.'

Scott said, 'In an hour, at the most two, this deck may be under water.'

The girl, looking up at him, merely nodded, took the torch and snapped off the switch. 'I'd better be saving it, hadn't I?' she said. 'Thank you for coming for us.'

The three men moved away. Rogo said, in disgust, 'The dumb bunny! Doesn't she know she's going to die if she stays there, the both of them?'

'Yes,' Scott replied, simply, 'she knows.'

Martin thought to himself: *Jesus! And I thought our Carl Hosey was tough.* What does this guy believe in next to himself?

When they rejoined the others, Rosen asked, 'Well so where are they? What's happening?'

Scott replied merely, 'He isn't in any condition to move. The girl is staying with him. I've left them a torch.' He marshalled his party. The expression on his face was harsh and his eyes once more reflected the lamplight.

No one wished either to question or consider the implication of what he had told them. Only Jane Shelby said, 'I envy her.'

CHAPTER XV

Belle Zimmerman of the W.S.A.

The first set of boilers, red hot, had ripped loose from their fixtures and plunging through the forward funnel into the sea, had exploded. The second farther aft only partially torn away, cracked and now cool, had created a weird lunar landscape of crumpled iron hills and valleys.

Upside-down as well as shattered, the three-storey high room had lost all semblance of its original almost aseptic aspect. The rows of burners behind the tiled façade which with their mica glass windows through which the boiler-room gang could inspect the fiery, orange glow within, now exposed their cores. The remains of the temperature gauges, oil feed and once immaculate control panels, gave the impression of one of those fake façades of compo board, papiermâché and crudely painted canvases supposed to represent the nether regions, framing the entrance to one of those amusement park spook-in-the-dark rides.

The party had reached it through a narrow entrance breached into the wall of Broadway almost at the after end to which Kemal had led them. Here Kemal on what had once been familiar territory paused and for the first time pantomimed a gesture that neither Scott nor any of the others had understood. With his right hand, the palm flattened and pointing downwards, he did a kind of scooping motion several times and then turned anxious, inquiring eyes upon Scott.

Muller asked, 'What's he trying to say? I don't get it. Those other chaps said this way was blocked. Do you suppose that's what he means?' To Kemal he queried, 'Okay? Okay?'

This time the Turk merely nodded and Muller said, 'He wants us to go this way.'

The entrance was so narrow that Belle Rosen said, 'If it gets any smaller, I can't go through.'

Scott called back, 'It's all right, it opens out again. Stay together. Rogo, throw your light towards the floor.'

For the passage was now undulating as though rippled by an earthquake and at one point fractured, so that they had to step across a gap of several feet. Liquids were still oozing from broken piping.

A sharp turn ended in a staircase which, ladder-like, seemed to ascend almost normally instead of hanging from the ceiling.

Muller, puzzled, asked, 'Why isn't it upside-down, like all the rest? We haven't righted ourselves have we?'

For a moment they used all their lighting to examine it. Shelby said, 'No, it's just been twisted around back to front. My God, what force must have been exerted!' It was the first time he had spoken since Jane's tirade and the sound of his own voice seemed to alarm him so that he looked around almost anxiously.

Martin remarked, 'That's lucky.'

Scott said, 'You make your luck.'

It had been one of those open, iron companionways with no backing to the steps, so that contrary to the others it presented no major difficulty.

Scott sent the men up to stand at intervals and pass the women along from one to the other. The top would have been level with 'F' deck except that they now found themselves in the remains of the boiler room.

The dead lay in forlorn heaps where the canting of the steamer had hurled them.

Linda screamed, 'Oh my God! They're dead! I won't go there...'

Belle said, 'What have you got to be afraid of? Maybe they're better off than we are. Sometimes being alive is worse than being dead.'

'Maybe for you, but I've got my life to live.'

Her husband said, 'They won't hurt you.' That was one thing his profession had taught him. Once a bullet had torn the breath out of a man, he worked no further evil or good.

Miss Kinsale intoned, 'Oughtn't we to pray for them?'

'Later,' said Scott and scouted the area, showing up the scarified slabs of iron and heaped up wreckage. 'I think Kemal has been here before the lights went out and knows part of the way. We'll follow him.' He indicated to the Turk that he was to lead.

They fell into file again in what had become their order of procedure; Scott and Miss Kinsale, Martin, Shelby, Susan and Jane, the Rosens, Muller and Nonnie, Linda and Mike Rogo bringing up the rear.

The rise was gradual. Underfoot it was jagged and dangerous like trying to negotiate a volcanic slope of rough, sharp points of lava. Kemal in the van with one of the heavy lanterns led up and pointed out the easiest way. It was slow, tortuous going.

Shelby wanted to offer his arm to his wife, but he did not dare. He was crushed, bitterly angry and a good deal frightened of her. After all those years of peace and harmony to have such hatred spewed out at him, to be belittled in front of strangers as an unsatisfactory lover and a failure in life.... Nevertheless, he turned around and whispered to his daughter, 'Look after your mother, Sue,' and then lamely felt he had to go on saying, 'I... I don't know what's come over her...'

If Jane had heard, she gave no sign but when at a difficult passage Susan took her hand, she held it tightly.

Belle Rosen gave a little scream, slipped and fell. Her husband was beside her at once, trying to lift her. She groaned, 'You want I should go on, Manny? How much longer do you think an old woman can stand this? I'm only a burden to these people. Think how much faster they could be getting on without us.'

Manny, aided by Rogo had raised her up. Nonnie came and put her arm about her waist. 'You mustn't feel like that, Mrs Rosen. We all like you.'

Muller heard Linda mutter, 'In a pig's ass.'

Rosen said, 'Only a little farther, Mamma. It's not much farther, is it, Frank?'

Scott replied, 'I don't know. I can't tell you yet. We've got to go on as long as we can.'

Belle said, 'I guess you're right. You make me feel ashamed, bellyaching all the time. I'm okay.'

Suddenly the pathway selected and illuminated by Kemal's lantern began to descend, first gently, then sharply.

'Hey!' Rogo shouted from the rear, 'Does this guy know what he's doing? We're going down. You know what's down. To hell with that! I thought you wanted to get up to the top.'

They had already descended somewhat more than their last climb on the reversed staircase and now must have been close to 'E' deck again.

Scott turned and stopped their line of march. He said, 'We'll get there. Why do you think this fellow left the others and joined up with us?'

No one said anything but Rogo at the far end and higher up, shone his lantern full on Scott's face like a balcony electrician spotlighting an actor.

His gaze never wavered. He did not even blink. Dramatically outlined, they were aware that he was looking at no one. He turned away and resumed the march.

They were committed again and there was nothing to do but follow on. With a sickening feeling at the pit of his stomach, Muller reckoned that they had given up at least ten feet of their hard-won height. Then the way dipped even more sharply. They were surrendering without a struggle the decks for which they had fought so bitterly. They all felt it, hated it and with each descending step felt their morale and courage drain away.

'Scott,' Rogo yelled down, for at the end of the line he was now higher than the rest, 'you dumb bastard! We're going to wind up in the drink again. This is the way the others said was blocked.'

Scott called back, 'Take it easy, Rogo, Kemal didn't seem to be convinced. Remember this is the part of the ship he knows.'

They crawled painfully down a few yards farther and found themselves at the end of the line. The flooring of the boiler room simply disappeared into one of those now all too familiar pools of dirty water with its multicoloured film of oil atop. This one was some eight feet square and extended to a shining, solid steel wall that rose up out of the far end.

Exhausted, dispirited and filled with consternation they sank down on to the slope beside the pool, Jane Shelby murmuring, 'Oh no! Oh no!' and Miss Kinsale praying, 'Oh Lord, what have we done to offend Thee?'

They hardly heard Linda's string of obscenities, but Rogo came through loud and clear, 'Okay, you stoopid son-of-a-bitch, what do we do now?'

Martin was murmuring to himself, 'Oh Christ!' for whenever he saw this black water, he also saw the rosy figure of Mrs Lewis. They must have reached some shaft connected with the boiler room into which the sea had risen.

Only Scott and Kemal were on their feet. The Minister stood there silently contemplating the scene. He seemed to be waiting.

Kemal pointed at the wall, hard, as though to extend and jab his finger through to the other side. 'Engine,' he said. And thereafter, pointing to the dark well, he again made that strange scooping, half-swimming motion with his hands.

Rogo asked, 'What's he trying to say? What the hell did he bring us here for?'

Muller said, 'The engine room must be on the other side.' He tackled Kemal, 'Look here,' he said loudly, 'what's down under that water? Is there a passage? Is it connected? How deep is it?'

The man did not understand the words, but with his eager intelligent eyes picked up their import. Now he began to pantomime again. He made a box-like shape with his hands, then spread his arms apart several times and followed it with the mime as of someone climbing a ladder or steep staircase. Then he did his explosion pantomime again with his deep 'Boom!' and shrugged.

Muller said, 'There's some kind of passage under there. Wait a minute! Turned right-side up it would connect with both the boiler and engine rooms, an entrance to them or a way up for the engineers. Now it's underwater.' He pointed down to the pool and made swimming motions at Kemal. The oiler smiled gently and shook his head in negation. Muller said, 'He's not having any. God knows what's down there, or how far or how deep. I don't blame him.'

Belle Rosen said, 'Hmm! Swimming under water I can do.' But no one paid any attention to her. They were gathered around a dark pool of despair that led down into no one knew where or what.

Rogo reverted to his favourite line, 'Okay, coach, you show us what we do next. You gonna go down that hole?'

Scott shone his light upon the patch of water, picking up the iridescence of the oil film and breaking it into primary colours. He said, 'Yes.'

The wave of relief that ran through the men was almost something tangible and Jane Shelby angrily tried to stifle the stab of admiration for Scott. Whatever else might be wrong with him, as a leader he had courage.

Rogo said, 'You can have it.' His remark expressed the feelings of the other men in the party. Kemal had refused and there was no question of Rosen. If Scott had not accepted, the dangerous task would have devolved upon Martin, Muller or Shelby to volunteer and while all of them were at home in the water, none of them had the stomach for fishing about to encounter God knows what obstacles or horrors beneath that surface.

Yet it was Muller who threw it right back into their laps again. He said, 'It won't work, Frank. We can't let you do it.'

The Minister repeated, 'Can't let me do it? Why not?'

'Because,' said Muller succinctly, 'you're the basket we've got all our eggs in,' and let the idea percolate.

Little Rosen was the first to catch on, 'My God, yes! If something should happen to Frank...'

Nonnie whispered to Muller, 'Don't you go. Oh, please don't!'

He allayed her fears, 'Don't worry, I simply wouldn't have the guts.'

Scott said, 'Nothing would happen to me.'

But Shelby said, 'Muller's right. We can't afford to take a chance. We'll have to turn back. Maybe we ought to have tried to reach the bow in the first place.' The old Shelby would have volunteered, or at least offered for the sake of his image, but the old Shelby had been destroyed.

Miss Kinsale shivered and said, 'I couldn't bear to go back through that Broadway place again.'

Martin said, 'We can't. We've got an investment going for us. We've put in all of two hours getting this far.' But he did not volunteer either.

Rogo said with heavy sarcasm, 'Nice work, Frankie boy!'

Muller wondered how long it would be before the Minister would turn upon his tormentor and slug him but the big man seemed to be unbaitable. Muller was hating Scott for his imperturbability and himself for lacking the courage to probe down into that black sink to see if it offered any way of escape, unlikely as it appeared.

Scott announced with finality, 'As I see it, there isn't any choice. It's up to me.'

Belle Rosen said, 'Such a fuss for a little water. If you leave it to me, I can find out in a minute. Like I said before, swimming under water I can do.'

They all turned to stare at her and Martin said, 'You can't be serious, Mrs Rosen.' What she was saying came so utterly incongruously from the wretched figure, her black lace dress in rags, the rouge purged from her lips and cheeks, her skin grey and sweat-stained with great dark patches showing under the tired eyes behind the thick lenses of her spectacles. She had blotches of bruises beginning to show on her arms and legs from the difficult climb up the wall of pipes and the knocking about in the working alley.

She was regarding them heavily now and said, 'Because I'm a fat old woman now, you think I couldn't have been an athlete, too, when I was young? You should ask Charlotte Epstein from the W.S.A. God rest her soul. She's dead now. For the underwater swim I was her champion three years.'

Linda Rogo whispered, 'My God, what the hell's the old bag yacking about now?'

Belle Rosen heard. She always did. She turned her melancholy gaze on the girl. 'About what you wouldn't know. Because you never heard of Eleanor Holm, either, or girls like Helen Meany, Aileen Riggin, Ethelda Bleibtrey or Gertrude Ederle. They were all W.S.A. champions. I could hold my breath under water for two minutes, and once for two minutes and thirty-seven seconds. You know what that was then? A world's record is what it was. Eppie—Charlotte Epstein, head of the Women's Swimming Association in New York, was the greatest thing that ever happened to swimming in our country. L. deB. Handley was our coach. He's the one taught Gertrude Ederle to be the first to swim the English Channel. Trudy said maybe I could have swum the English Channel under water, if I'd wanted to.'

She was running on garrulously. No one thought or cared to try to stop her, and her sudden reminiscences of people of whom they had never heard. Besides in some unbelievable way it was penetrating that she was holding out some kind of hope to them in their predicament.

'I used to be terrible,' Belle Rosen continued, 'scaring people. I could stay under so long, nobody knew when I was coming up and once I gave even Eppie nearly heart failure when I swam two-and-a-half lengths of the pool in practice when I was feeling good.'

'Look here,' said Martin suddenly, 'were you Belle Zimmerman?'

Manny Rosen spoke up proudly, 'Was she Belle Zimmerman! She's been telling you, ain't she? You should see all the cups and medals she's got, and a whole book of clippings. And once when she broke the world record, she was on the front page of *The Daily News*. If you don't believe it, we got the book home to show you.'

Belle said, 'Oh come now, Manny, he's too young to know. That was a long time ago.'

Martin said, 'I'm older than you think. Do you know how I remember? It's one of those funny things that stick with you. When I was a kid, around six or seven years old, my old man took me to a swimming meet at the old Illinois Athletic Club in Chicago. There was a girl there and the name Belle Zimmerman comes back to me, who swam under water and I got so scared that she was drowned and wasn't going to come up, I hollered and carried on so that everyone turned around and looked at me.'

'That was me,' said Belle complacently. 'We won the National championship. I broke the American record. After I quit I got married, I put on a lot of weight.'

Rogo confirmed, 'Sure that's right, Belle. I remember seeing some of your pictures up in the store now. You were a good-looking kid.'

Linda Rogo suddenly shouted, 'So what? So what? Yack, yack, yack!' and then her voice rising almost to hysteria, 'I want to get out of here!'

Belle said quietly, 'You shouldn't get so excited, Mrs Rogo. What have I been telling you for? Gimme one of those lamps and I'll go down and see what's there. None of you can hold your breath as long as I can. If it's open, we'll know. If it ain't...' She shrugged.

Her offer galvanized the men. Shelby said, 'We can't let you do it, Mrs Rosen. It's too dangerous. We don't know what's underneath. We ought to find out first how deep it is.'

Muller put in, 'Yes, one of us should have a go first.'

Martin added, 'I suppose if it comes to that...' He did not finish the sentence lest anyone should think he was volunteering, but then ashamed, continued lamely, 'I'm not much of a swimmer.'

Surprisingly it was Manny Rosen who spoke up firmly, 'Look fellas, if my wife says she can do it, she can do it.'

Belle added simply, 'It don't take much when you're used to it. Only a good pair of lungs which I still got.'

Her offer was so degrading to them that instinctively they turned to their leader hoping that somehow he would rescue them from the imminence of their humiliation.

The Reverend Dr Scott turned his powerful gaze from on high upon the diminutive, roly-poly figure and finally spoke. 'Okay. We'll let Mrs Rosen try.'

The members of the party looked at him in astonishment and with some indignation. The men had been hoping that he himself would insist after all upon the trial, over their objections.

He continued in his deep, compelling voice, 'You've all heard what she said, Mrs Rosen has been a champion. Champions are different from other people, another breed.'

Belle Rosen beamed with pride and suddenly seemed to grow inches taller.

'Yes,' Scott went on, 'from the very beginning you've been considering her a hindrance and a drag on us and what's more, in one way or another some of you have managed to let her know. She's offered to help us in good faith. Why shouldn't she be allowed her moment of dignity?'

Again Jane Shelby was racked by ambivalence, an internal cry: *How can you who made me abandon my boy, make me love you so for what you are doing for this woman?*

Scott said, 'If you'll try, Mrs Rosen, we'll take every precaution we can.'

'Precautions I'll take myself,' said Belle, 'I'm not a fool.' And then ordered, 'Put out the lights.'

In the total darkness that once more enveloped them Muller murmured half to himself, 'Buzz Scott wins again.'

Nonnie asked, 'What?'

'Never mind,' said Muller.

They heard Belle's breathing for a moment and the sound of rustling and then she said, 'Okay, you can put them on again.' It had been the actual moment of disrobing she had not wished them to see. Thereafter she did not really seem to care, except that she remarked, 'So without my clothes my figure don't look so good any more, like it used to.'

She had removed her girdle as well and stood there in a pair of black underpants and bra, with her white skin ballooning from their confinement. She looked grotesque and at the same time suddenly incredibly gallant. Her movements had taken on a certain precision and vitality. She took off her eyeglasses and handed them to her husband. 'For heaven's sake don't lose them,' she said. 'Where's the torch?' Scott handed her one. She snapped it on and proved that she was no fool by leaning over and plunging it beneath the water to make sure that it was waterproof and test the power of the illumination.

'Could you fasten it now to the back of my wrist?' and she held out her right arm. They still had a number of napkins and Muller affixed the torch firmly.

'The rope you could tie around my waist, the knot at the back.'

Scott took one of the longest lengths of the nylon rope from Kemal and attached it as she asked.

'Listen,' said Belle, 'world records we're not breaking today. I can hold my breath now maybe still for two minutes. If I get through, okay, I give a yank on the rope. If after a minute and a half on your watch there ain't no yank, you pull. Wish yourselves luck.'

Hubie Muller said, 'You mean, wish you luck.'

'No,' said Belle, 'I don't need luck. You do, that I should get there inside of a minute. Because for two minutes, you wouldn't be able to hold your breath, none of you.'

They had not thought of that.

'Dr Scott and Mike, maybe you'll take the other end of the rope, like you're the strongest. Before a minute and a half, don't worry. Mr Muller, you could time me on that fancy watch you got.'

For a moment she sat down on the edge of the pit and let her fat legs dangle in the water. 'It ain't even cold,' she said and Hubie Muller had a momentary vision of her like one of those vulgar, seaside resort postcards of fat ladies posed as bathing beauties. The others watched fascinated as she prepared.

Belle Rosen began to breathe deeply from the bottom of her stomach: two, three, four, five times, more deeply each time, until with her lungs filled to absolute capacity she pushed off. They saw her underwater light and her body sinking like a great, white sea slug and thereafter she passed from sight.

'Ten seconds,' said Hubie Muller.

The rope paid out between the fingers of Scott and Rogo. It ran for a few yards and then stopped and Rogo said, 'Jesus!'

'Don't worry! Don't worry,' said Manny Rosen. 'I'm telling you, under water Mrs Rosen is like a fish. You think I would let her do it if I didn't know?'

Hubie said, 'Twenty seconds.' The rope began to move again. It paid out and continued smoothly. Then it stopped and went first slack, then tautened.

'Oh, God!' said Hubie Muller, 'Forty-five seconds.'

'Take it easy,' said Manny.

The rope slid forward once more. 'See?' said Rosen.

Hubie Muller's wrist was shaking so he could hardly concentrate on the second hand of his watch, 'One minute!' he said.

Martin put in, 'She said if it was more than a minute, none of us could make it.'

Shelby panicked. 'For God's sake, pull her back before she drowns.'

With unbelievable calm and confidence, Manny Rosen said, 'In my advice, you should do like she said. Otherwise if something goes wrong, you've got the blame.'

Scott ordered, 'Check your time, Hubie.' He was watching the rope.

'A minute and twenty seconds,' Hubie called, his voice unsteady. He felt that above everything else in the world, he did not wish this brave, fat woman to die down there, alone in that stinking blackness because he himself had been a coward. 'I'll count down now.' He picked up the seconds, 'Ten, nine, eight, seven, six, five, four, three, two, one —Pull!'

Rogo and Scott heaved back on the rope and nearly fell in a heap for there was no tension on it.

'Pull! Pull!' shrieked Hubie and Martin and took hold as well. 'Oh, my God, if it's cut and she's down there and lost her way!'

They hauled in yards of slack and suddenly felt tension on the end like hooking into a big fish. There was a glow from the black of the pit and a white body rose and burst the surface with a tremendous whoosh of air rushing from tortured lungs and new breaths being caught at a rapid rate of respiration. The men reached down and hauled her out and sat her on the edge again.

Jane Shelby, Susan and Nonnie knelt at her side, looking anxiously into her face, 'How do you feel, Mrs Rosen?'

She said, 'Don't get so excited, everyone. I'm okay. It's for only thirty-five seconds you got to hold your breath and you come up on the other side. If there was a door there once, there ain't now. There's one place you got to look out, where something sticks out but it ain't bad.'

Hubie Muller said, 'But if it's only thirty-five seconds, why did you stay for so long and nearly give us heart failure?'

Belle replied, 'Ain't I terrible, always scaring people? But I wasn't meaning to. As long as I was there, I wanted to have a look at the other side.'

Scott asked, 'What could you see?'

'Not much,' said Belle, 'there wasn't enough light. There's a sort of platform like here, only bigger and flat. Anyway, I got a fresh lungful of air before I came back. So now let's try it out here first and you'll see. Everybody should hold their breath for forty-five seconds to be on the safe side. A minute is hard if you ain't used to it, but less you should be able, and then we ain't got any worries.'

Scott said, 'You tell us what to do, Belle.'

Belle replied, 'I'll fasten the rope on the other side and you can pull yourselves through on it. All you have to do is hang on. I wasn't even swimming fast. You hold your breath, close your eyes and in half a minute you're there.'

Manny Rosen said, 'You believe now that Mrs Rosen's got cups and medals?'

Martin said, 'By God, I do! Of all people, Belle Zimmerman!'

Richard Shelby added, 'You're magnificent, Mrs Rosen!'

Belle replied, 'Baloney! What you can do, you can do and what you can't, you can't.'

Muller asked, 'What about our clothes?'

Belle said, 'You take 'em off, like I did. Who wears clothes when they go swimming?'

Miss Kinsale asked, 'What about on the other side?'

Belle said, 'That's up to you. You can carry 'em along, or leave 'em behind. I wouldn't think you'd need 'em. It seemed like it was hotter through there. I would leave it to Dr Scott.' And thus she handed the leadership back to him again.

The Minister said, 'I think we ought to keep our shoes. With climbing to do we'll need to protect our feet. But for the rest, I think Mrs Rosen's right. The less we're weighted down and burdened with, the better. Wet suits and dresses aren't going to help anyone. Rogo, Muller, Shelby, Kemal, Martin and I will strap on the big lanterns. We can fasten all the shoes to them. Each one ties on his or her own torch and we do exactly as Belle tells us to.'

Belle asked, 'You ain't worried?'

Scott laughed, 'With you I'd swim under the Arctic ice pack.'

Manny Rosen said, 'That's a nice compliment, Mamma.'

Miss Kinsale asked, 'Do you want us to take everything off?'

Belle replied, 'You could keep on your underwear, like me. So it's like a bikini. On the beach sometimes you wear a lot less.'

Nonnie said, 'But I've got nothing on under this.'

Belle smiled, 'With your figure you should have bigger worries, dearie. But that stuff could catch on something.'

Nonnie asked, 'Would you put the lights out again?' In the dark they could hear the ripping of cloth, then, 'Okay now,' and the lantern light revealed that she had fashioned a creditable bikini set from the remnants of the dressing-gown. She looked even more childlike.

Linda regarded her figure with open contempt and said, 'I guess preacher boy didn't miss much. I can't wait to see how he strips.'

Rogo said, 'Yeah, yeah, honeybun and you'd better take off my coat.'

Linda peered into the water and asked, 'Oh, my God, what's going to happen to my hair?'

Rogo's expression never changed, 'Maybe there's a hairdresser on the other side.' Linda swore at him again.

They began to remove their outer clothing. Jane wondered whether Miss Kinsale was going to be able to manage, or ask for lights out. But the spinster's only reservation was to go off a little to one side to take off her frock and then appear in panties and bra, apparently without the least concern.

They had equipped themselves as he had suggested, strapping their lamps and securing shoes. Scott was a compelling figure in a pair of white shorts. Martin had a small snicker to himself, thinking: *Our padre ain't with it. He should see our line in stripes.*

Scott then said, 'I think you had best tell us exactly what to do, Belle.'

Belle said, 'Okay, now? The main thing is don't get scared. All of you can swim. Okay. Well, the first thing is holding your breath. Try, take a big, bellyful of air—I mean, lungful but fill up from deep down, and then hold it. Don't think about anything and don't count. Counting only makes you nervous. Mr Muller will say when it's forty-five seconds.'

Muller gazed at his watch and held up his arm at the given moment. There was a rush of exhaled breaths and Martin said in surprise, 'I could have held mine longer.'

Susan said, 'So could I.'

'So you see,' Belle said, 'thirty seconds is nothing. I go again first with the rope tied around me.'

Muller asked, 'Is there anything we've to look for?'

Belle replied, 'In the middle something busted through and sticks out. You can go either over it or under it. I go under it, because there's more room for me. When I get to the other side, I fasten the rope and give two yanks. Then you'll know it's okay. Send the ladies through one at a time when I give two yanks on the cord. You all know you can hold your breath long enough so don't panic. Don't try to swim; pull yourselves along on the rope, it's quicker and you don't use so much energy. If anything goes wrong, I'll come down and get you.'

Belle had turned professional again. She made sure the life-line was well fastened around her and her flashlamp secure. She turned to her husband, 'You ain't worried are you, Manny?'

He replied, 'Like you made it out, it's a breeze, Mamma. Be seeing you!'

She lowered her head and went plummeting down, her lamp glowing.

The rope paid out smoothly. Hubie Muller counted off thirty-five seconds when it went slack and ceased to move. Half a minute later there were two short, sharp jerks on it. 'She's done it,' he said.

CHAPTER XVI

Welcome to Hell

The women went through without a hitch, Miss Kinsale first, then Susan and Jane Shelby. Nonnie covered her fears with a joke, "'Ere goes the big underwater ballet number,' She gazed ruefully at her makeshift bikini, still with the swansdown trimming. 'I'm going to look just terrible when I come out of there.'

Two yanks signalled her safe arrival.

Linda Rogo made the most fuss and held them up the longest. She complained, 'I don't want to go into all that oily stuff. How do we know what's on the other side, or whether we can get anywhere? I think you're all crazy. My hair will be ruined.'

Her husband produced a handkerchief from his discarded dinner-jacket. 'Here. Tie this around your head.'

She made herself a scarf of it and said, 'You come right after me, Rogo, do you hear?'

He said, 'Now honey, you'll be all right. I'd better stay at this end until you've all got through.'

'Still playing Boy Scout,' Linda said. 'Some day I'm going to make you so sorry you ever got me into this.'

She climbed in gingerly and awkwardly, feet first, testing the water. 'Jesus!' she said, 'It stinks.'

'Oh, come on, baby,' Rogo pleaded, 'and don't forget to fill up with air.'

The section of the rope that Muller was holding suddenly leaped to life but not the two signal yanks that had been agreed upon, but something new and it was not until the third time that he got the rhythm: 'Dum-de-de-dum-dum, dum dum...', and he recognized it for what it was, Belle Rosen's sense of humour. She was aware that Linda was the last of the women and must be delaying them through sheer cussedness. He could not help grinning to himself. He felt a sudden warmth of affection for Mrs Rosen. His old-maid fastidiousness had made her unattractive, at first. Now she had dramatized herself into someone quite remarkable to him. He said, 'They want to know who's holding up the works.'

Linda told him what he could do, held her nose with one hand, gripped the rope with the other and finally dunked her head. She must have fairly sizzled through because the arrival signal came through much sooner than the others. Shelby said, 'Phew! What a relief. If they can do it that simply, I would imagine we can.' But they stood around for a moment in silence, not wanting to say who would be the first to go.

Scott solved it. 'Your honour,' he said to Manny Rosen, 'You've got a wonderful wife. She'll be glad to see you.'

Manny looked a forlorn figure in a pair of pink and white checked shorts, his stomach protruding. A great wedge of greyish black hair covered his chest. His knees were shaking. He said, 'I don't know if I could do it with holding on to the flashlight. And Mamma's eyeglasses. And what about mine?'

Rogo took over with a curiously affectionate expression on his usually blank face. 'Manny,' he said, 'we're going to fix you up just dandy. You got any handkerchiefs?'

With one he tied the torch to Rosen's forearm. With a second he wrapped his wife's glasses and tucked them inside Rosen's shorts. 'Keep your own on. Belle took hers off because she didn't know what she might find down there. Okay, Johnny Weissmuller, don't forget to hold your breath.'

Rosen looked around sheepishly for an instant, 'Anyone thinks I was built for a hero should have his head examined,' took his grip upon the rope and plunged.

One after the other Shelby, Kemal and Scott went through. Muller said to Rogo, 'You've got guts to be the last one.'

Rogo replied, 'Yeah,' with a rising inflection, but made no further comment. He was busying himself with strapping on his big lantern and laying out the remainder of the long coil of rope so that there would be no chance of its tangling or snagging when they went to pull it through after them.

Muller was wondering whether he would be the one to funk it and what it would be like when he was down there in the black with only one last gulp of air in his lungs to see him through. He had little faith left in himself as a man prepared to cope with danger or trouble. Even Rosen, he felt had more guts than himself and seemed better equipped by whatever kind of life he had lived to do the necessary to survive. But at the other end of that passage was Nonnie, poor frightened Nonnie, who had tried to make a joke of it. She would be wet, bedraggled, her hair streaked with oil, naked and shivering. She would be needing him.

Rogo seemed to have read his thoughts. His expression was quite blank again as he said, 'You better git goin'. The kid'll be waiting for you.' Muller felt his contempt but could not blame him. He did his best to put a face on it by saying, 'Be seeing you.'

'Yeah,' Rogo replied, this time without any inflection at all.

Forty-five seconds. The shaft descended some eight feet. His body, filled with air, did not want to go down and he had to pull on the rope hard. His torchlight did not penetrate more than a few feet to show the inevitable piping but the passage narrowed suddenly as though some gigantic force had squeezed it. He saw an outcropping in time not to hit it with his head and the rope bent upwards and along the inside.

He realized that this was a steel walk that had originally been flooring and now was reversed. How many seconds had elapsed? His chest had not yet begun to feel tight. He kept his light on his lifeline and managed to entertain the most absurd thought: *Hubie Muller, if they could see you now!* 'they' being the jet set of which he was a part.

Muller endured a thrill of fright as a dark shape ahead seemed to reach out for him. It was rounded and stretched almost to the far side of the passage and was actually a section of a hydraulic pump that had been blown apart. Muller had time to wonder further at the courage of Belle Rosen when she had encountered this obstacle for the first time and had made her decision to swim under it, not knowing what might lie ahead or whether she could ever get back.

There was room enough for him to go over it. He was feeling strain in his lungs. Forty-five seconds could not have passed that quickly. When he had been holding the watch on the others it had seemed much longer. Actually no more than twenty had passed, but he was already aware of the rise of fear that might turn into panic and kill him. Darkness, water, lurking shapes. How brave a man was he by himself? How did one combat fear when one was alone? What resources did men call upon to be men?

He could feel his heart pounding and pressure in his throat and chest to let go that precious few cubic inches of air...

The back of his hand no longer scraped the steel ridge above him. The rope rose sharply. He pulled at it and shot upwards, his head breaking the surface into a glare of lantern lights. He saw what looked like an assortment of demons straight out of the Inferno: white, half-naked bodies, oil and grime-streaked, limp straggling hair, strange faces that he no longer seemed to recognize. Hands reached for his armpits and he was dragged out of the water and on to a kind of platform. Without ever having encountered the Divine Comedy, little Martin said wryly, 'Welcome to Hell!'

Shelby handed him the rope, the end of which was fastened to a bent bar and said, 'You've made it. It's your yank. Give it two.'

But instead, Muller, like Belle, went, 'Dum de-de-dum-dum,' with it to Rogo at the other end. Thirty seconds later, the detective emerged from the well, resembling something prehistoric rising from the deep.

Muller searched for Nonnie. She had turned away from him and said, 'Oh, don't look at me! Please don't look at me.'

Belle said, 'What's the fuss? Nobody don't exactly look as though they'd been to the beaudy parlour.'

But Muller had seen her, a desperately begrimed nymph. The two pieces of cloth clung to her frail form. Her red hair, darker from the water, was stuck together and clung to her shoulders. Her face, smeared, appeared smaller than ever. Whatever delicacy she had was destroyed. She looked, indeed they all did, as though she had crawled up out of a sewer. Yet somehow the other women bore their filth and dishevelment with a certain dignity. Nonnie's was all gone and Muller longed to enfold and comfort her. For more than ever her queer little person applied that strange twist to his heart for which he could not account. Everything within him told him to take her and let her hide what she felt was her shame close to him. But he could not do it with everyone watching. He could not bring himself to go to her and open himself to her need with the eyes of Linda and all the others on him. He did not do it until later when Scott ordered a rest and the lights put out to save the batteries.

But first Rogo, having regained his breath asked, 'Where the hell are we?'

Scott replied, 'In the engine room.'

'Where do we go from here?'

Scott raised the big lantern and stabbed the heavy darkness with a ray of light that travelled some fifty feet up before it spotlighted a smooth shaft of metal that reflected its shine.

Rogo said, 'Are you kiddin'?'

Scott replied, 'No. Up there, but not directly over our heads, is the outside hull of the ship. But it's still the double bottom Acre told us about. Once we get up there we shall have to make our way still farther aft.'

'You haven't seen the worst yet,' Shelby put in. 'Martin meant it when he welcomed Muller to Hell.' A hollow shout echoed back from the cavernous roof, '...to Hell!'

Martin and Rogo sent their beams roving over the appalling scenery of wreckage, an alpine scape of lacerated steel, twisted pipes, dangling wires and girders, peeling dynamos, cliffs of turbine rotors, peaks and ravines made by shattered generators only half-torn loose from their foundations, split open and pouring forth their metal innards.

'The women won't look,' Shelby said, 'we've told them.'

Martin added, 'I'm not looking either. It's too much for my stomach. I'd be sick again.'

There were bodies crushed to death and wedged in amongst tangled remains of machinery, twisted ladders and catwalks. A detached arm was lodged in a crevice. The upper half of a man hung from the jagged rim of an electro hydraulic coupling. Something had sheared him in two at the waist. They could not see his face. His body had long since been drained of blood. And there were bits and pieces no longer with people in them, caught upon edges and these were almost worse than the bodies. One pleading hand was still thrust out from beneath what must have been tons of metal which had crashed down to the level of where the party now found themselves. There was no telling how many dead there were.

The probing lanterns revealed that there was no one alive in the vast cavern. Nor was there so much as a sound except the slight lapping of water of the black lake some twenty yards square. Things unidentified floated on its surface; objects were thrust up out of it that, caught at the sides, had failed to follow the rest of the debris to the bottom of the sea. They themselves were now on a kind of peninsula jut-ting out from the shore which must originally have been the reverse one of the supervisory platforms at the top of the engine room.

Miss Kinsale suddenly said, 'Oh dear, oh dear.'

Shelby inquired, 'What is it, Miss Kinsale?'

She was sitting close to the edge of the platform with one leg curled under her in the pose of a beach beauty in bikini at a poolside. The astonishing thing was the change made in her by her length of hair. The swim had dragged or knocked it out of its bun and the strands hung to her waist. In the gloom and the occasional passage of a torch beam over her figure she resembled a summer naiad.

She replied, 'Those two poor people, the gentleman you call The Beamer and the girl who always seems to be with him...'

'Oh Lord,' said Jane Shelby.

'Oh, Mummy!' Susan added, 'They said they'd...'

'Come after us when they could,' Muller concluded.

Miss Kinsale brushed her long hair out of her eyes and said, 'But they can't. However will they get through where we've come by themselves.'

Rogo said with finality, 'They can't, the stupid slobs.'

Linda snapped, 'Well, it was her idea to stick around. We said we'd take them... I mean her.'

Jane Shelby said, 'But you see she was a woman. She wouldn't leave him.'

Her husband shrivelled. They had not even dared to shout for Robin up into that awful black void of shattered gear from which pieces of dead men hung. And Rogo had said the boy would be climbing.

Miss Kinsale said to Linda, 'You mustn't be too hard on her.'

Shelby asked, 'Should we go back for them?'

Linda said, 'And if the guy is still dead drunk?'

There was no answer to this. They were ashamed that there was not, that Linda's toughness for once had let them off from something. No one wanted to go back through that tunnel again. Besides, how get a man in a drunken sleep to hold his breath while being towed under water. And they had their own case to consider.

'Welcome to Hell,' Martin had said, and in the sense of their surroundings, the ghostly echoes heat and the feeling of utter abandonment of having entered the domain of the damned, it was true.

While they had been making their way along the uncertain footing of the ceilings of the ship's corridors, or struggling to overcome the reversed staircases, even during the nightmare of their sojourn in the working alley they had begun to become somewhat accustomed to this new world of upside-down and there had been still some semblance of things recognizable. The topsy-turvy signs over storerooms and offices confirmed that it was yet a steamer they were inhabiting. With their subterranean entrance into the engine room they had left behind everything they had ever known, could adhere to, or compare. They might have come out on to another planet, the tortured desolation of the pitiless ruptured steel crags and pinnacles revealed by lamplight, and above all, the foul, oil covered lake on the shores of which they found themselves marooned, drained the courage out of all of them with the exception of Scott.

With the beam of his lantern he was exploring the steel mountain he meant to have them conquer, memorizing every jagged steel promontory and pinnacle.

It would be unlike any ascent he or anyone else had ever attempted. Here there could be no cutting of steps, no circumventing or bypassing. The engine room had spilled its guts down the sides when the vessel, keeling over had subjected the turbines and all their auxiliary equipment to stresses for which their anchorage had not provided.

To make things worse, everything was slippery from the oil that had leaked out of the tanks in the double bottoms, now overhead. How much of the black lake was salt water intruded into the shaft and what was oil, could not be determined. The huge airspace of the cavern must be helping to keep the ship still afloat. Yet it had been evident to them all that she had been slowly settling and the water in the lower corridors rising. They had no way of even guessing as to what air and buoyancy remained in the forward and after freight compartments.

'Do you mean to get us up to the top of that?' Shelby asked.

'Yes,' Scott replied. He moved his light along the bright, oily cylindrical shaft far above. 'That must be the propeller shaft. But do you see just behind it, that is, on top of it that long, thin flat piece. That must be the catwalk that enables them to follow the shaft down to the collar, in case of trouble.'

'But it's upside-down,' Shelby said. 'We can't cling to it like flies.'

'We've got to make it on to the other side. Then we can walk along it.'

'Where do you get your strength from?' Shelby asked suddenly and expected Scott to answer 'From faith', but instead the Minister merely replied, 'From knowing how.' Then he added, 'I think I've seen a path. We'll rope together, alternating man and woman. There's plenty of line. It will be up to both the man in front and behind the woman to see that she steps exactly in the right place. I'll put you, Dick, where you can work with Susan and Jane. Rogo can bring up the rear again. He's reliable.'

'He doesn't like you,' Shelby said.

'It's mutual,' replied Scott. 'But he's dependable. Life has given him fibre.'

And robbed me of mine. Shelby thought and felt shamed again. Nobody had mentioned Robin. If he had been anywhere about, if he had managed to climb and gain entrance from some other direction, he would have heard them and managed a hail. How could Jane have lived so serene and composed all those years hating every minute of it?

Scott said, 'If you don't mind, lights out. We'll save batteries. We've come through some difficult trials. There are others ahead. We'll rest for a little. If you are able to snatch a few minutes of sleep, do so. Keep your lights off. We shall be needing them every minute later. I'll let you know when it's time to start again. Sleep if you can...'

None of them with the exception of Shelby and possibly Rogo knew what lay ahead of them. They were aware that they had farther to go. How and when was in his hands. His voice soothed them. They separated into their own little groups and lay down upon the oily steel. It was better in the total darkness, for then they could not see. And if the darkness were to become permanent... well, then they might not even be aware of the transition.

Yet there was one more phenomenon which in one way or another affected them all and of which they had not become aware until they had reached this dark lake that Martin had named 'Hell', and in which by lantern light their reflections had been mirrored.

Each, while able to see the disarray and utter dismantling of the physical shell of the others, up to then had not thought of this as applied to himself or herself.

They had been reduced to the primitive state of near naked savages, debased to breech clout and filth, yet individually they had somehow managed to retain an image of themselves as they had been. On the way, as necessity had demanded, they had been compelled to shed the garments which differentiated them from one another and from primitives. But they had not divested themselves of the memory of these articles: trousers, jackets, frocks, slips.

As by lantern light they caught glimpses of one another they found themselves aware of the absurdity of Rosen's pot belly emerging from the waistband of his shorts; the Minister turned Tarzan; the thin body of Miss Kinsale protected almost like Lady Godiva by her long hank of hair, or the show-girl's makeshift loin and breast coverings looking like something out of a bad jungle film. But they never thought how they must look to each other.

In some way this contributed a measure of self-esteem and courage, enabling them to do what was required without thinking too much or at all how they must appear. Much of this was drained away at Hell Lake whose oily surface when illuminated showed them up for the ridiculous scarecrows, caricatures of human beings they had become.

Jane Shelby felt shamed by the utter preposterousness of the undergarments that only served to emphasize the parts they were worn to conceal. The reflection of her triangular panties and carefully engineered, cup-shaped breast supporters irritated her to the point where she felt the impulse to tear these last bits of fabric from her body, to feel herself free and mother-naked.

Of the men, only Scott in briefs amounting to track shorts, appeared to feel comfortable and unconcerned. The others had suddenly become aware of the all too flimsy protection to their genitalia afforded by their underpants. They were not only embarrassed, but hated the idea of injury or sudden extinction finding them so vulnerable.

Further to Muller, the comfort-loving Muller, who more than any of them was aware of the variety and complexity of the globe, over whose surface he wandered so restlessly, it was astonishing how his world had diminished and almost vanished from his memory. He could think of places and people and bring up images in his mind, but they no longer seemed to have any connection with reality. There was only the here; this dark, fetid gruesome cavern. They were marooned upon a lifeless planet, bumbling about like insects on a Lunar landscape, as cut off from everything familiar as though indeed they had been projected through space.

He supposed it was perhaps their constant proximity to death, their closeness to becoming one with nothingness that made the earth, and life as they had known it, seem so many aeons away. It surprised him how wholly not only his body but his mind could become confined to this narrow space, the gloom, the echoes, the cruelty and the limitations.

Then why did hope persist? Why this upward striving, this eternal climbing by himself and these ill-assorted people, castaways in a floating tomb, the odds on whose chances for rescue were astronomical?

Suddenly death was imminent. The ship's buoyancy must fail. But evidence of this that had already come to others was also all about them. This blind crawl was ridiculous; it was stupid; it was ant-like. Yet indomitably they persisted. For a moment Muller entertained what amounted to almost a flash of pride and joy in himself and his companions, before he again succumbed to what must be the utter futility of their position and surrendered to the encompassment of this prison. Nonnie was all that was left. Beyond was too far away to be any longer grasped by the mind.

He and Nonnie lay apart from the rest, nearest the spot from which they had emerged. He had taken her now as he had wanted to do, holding her—he thought of it as an enfolding—and she had crept as close to him as she could. She said, 'Squeeze me tight.'

Even as he did so he was aware of the vulgarity of the expression but was unable to react to it. She whispered, 'I love you. Do you love me a little?'

'Yes.'

'I never felt like this about anyone before. It's different. I love you terrible.'

The strange emotion that Muller felt could not bear to be translated into banalities. He did not want to hear her speak of it, or say those commonplace things to her that he had so often parroted, the senseless, meaningless phrases tumbling from his lips like formulae from a computer at a given signal.

He felt her shiver again in spite of the increasing heat. He said, 'Hush. Lie still. I'll warm you.'

Ice-cold lips once again searched for his, found them and clung. In their touch was all her childishness, her fears and her dependency; an abused little animal creeping to shelter. In the dark, her sharpness and overlay of suspicion, her self-reliant gamin person vanished.

She whispered, 'Can we do it again?'

For an instant the old Muller who never made love until he had cleared the coast, arranged the conditions and made sure the doors were locked, was scandalized. 'Here?

With everybody about?'

'They wouldn't know. I'll keep very quiet. I promise. I want you.'

'Supposing someone turns on a flashlight.'

'Then they'll see me in your arms. Maybe that's what some of the others will be doing too. Hubie please...'

When her begging mouth touched his again he forgot everything but her and the surge through him of something he could not identify; hunger for this one person and the exquisite joy in union with her.

At the climax of the all engulfing sweetness he prayed that they would never awaken, that the stricken ship would show mercy and gather them now together into oblivion.

Her whisper, her breath so close to his ear brought him back. 'I was a good girlie, wasn't I?'

'Yes you were.'

'I didn't wriggle or make a sound, did I?'

'No, you didn't.'

'I wanted to. You do something to me. I never loved anyone like this before. I don't know what's come over me.'

She fell silent and he knew that she was waiting for him to tell her that he loved her too, to join her in those meaningless post-coitus murmurings which to her, for whatever reason, guilt, practice, or limit of emotional depth were a necessity and perhaps even a habit. Would he ever be able to explain to her, or make her understand how greatly he was lost in her, that again when he had been joined to her something further had happened to him that he did not understand. It was like the turning of a page or the opening of a door; even a reversal within him of all he had ever known or thought before. Down was up and up was down and where was Hubie Muller to whom this girl had become as necessary to him as breathing.

And she was such a common little thing.

Again she whispered 'I'm crazy over you, Hubie. It's something different, really. We hardly even met. Do you love me?'

He whispered his reply almost fiercely, 'Couldn't you feel?'

'Oh that,' she replied, almost in disappointment as having too much everyday normality connected with it. And he knew that she wanted, must have... words.

'Yes, I love you.'

'A lot? More than anyone else.'

'Yes. Much more.'

'*Is* there any one else?'

'No.'

'Are you married?'

'No.'

'Gee!'

And in the breathlessness of that expression and the wonder, Hubie thought that Nonnie had told him all of her story there was to tell. But he knew that she was craving to be interrogated, that she had her confession to make and that if he truly loved her he must abide by the rules.

'And you? Have you a...' he was certain she was unaware of his split-second pause while he abolished the word 'lover' and quickly substituted 'boy friend?'

But she did hesitate and perhaps wished him to note it as she replied, 'No-no. Not now.'

'But you've had them.'

She put her lip closer to his ear and he could barely hear the confidence. 'Only two.'

He knew it to be a lie and loved her the more for the perverse and infantile stupidity of it. Her instincts were those of self-preservation. Everything she did that was wrong and against his upbringing and nature charmed him. He knew all about the professed chaperonage of the Gresham Girls, but there probably had been a succession of married men.

She was satisfied now and her mind shifted yet in a manner that was so pathetically simple to follow. She said, 'Poor Moira. She won't have to worry any more. She got herself pregnant in Rio.'

'Do the girls often get pregnant?'

'We're not supposed to. They're awful strict with us.'

Hubie asked, 'Were you ever pregnant?' and then was sorry that he had. He didn't really want to know.

There was a longer hesitation while she determined whether or not to lie again. She decided against it. Gents like Muller had a way of finding things out. Her whisper dropped into an even lower key. 'Yes. Does it matter?'

Hubie was involved now. In platitudes lay safety from the emotion she roused in him. 'Does anything matter now? Or did it ever? What did you do?' He wondered if there was a child left behind with grandparents or relatives somewhere in Bristol?

'I went to a doctor. You know, one of those who helps you. It happened in Rome. Those Eyties can soft-talk you into anything.'

'Have I soft-talked you into something?'

'No. This is different. You put your arms about me when I was scared, and it done something to me. I didn't love him. I love you.' But her mind would no longer stay on the subject. She asked, 'What's become of the others? Are they all floating around in their cabins like dead goldfish in a bowl?'

'Don't say that, Nonnie. Don't think of them.'

'I can't help it. We been together so long. Three years now. It seems like just a minute ago I was asking Sybil whether she was coming to dinner and she said, "Go away, you pig! I just want to die." See, she was still sick. So she died. And I suppose the jailer did too and all the rest who stayed in their cabins.'

'Who was the jailer?'

'Mrs Timker. She was in charge of our group, kept us up to scratch; practice; clean costumes; and snooped what time we came in. But Timmy was a good sort. She'd close an eye. She was one of us until she married Bert Timker, the Assistant Manager. Only thing she used to say was, "Have your fun, but put a bun in the oven, and out you go."'

'A bun in the...'

Nonnie gave a tiny tinkling laugh still close to his ear and whispered, 'Oh well, you know... What we was talking about before.'

Muller laughed too and pressed her nearer to his heart.

'Why are you squeezing me so?' she said.

He replied, 'Don't even ask.'

Out of the stilly darkness and its silences broken only by whisperings and an occasional snore, came a hard, cool impersonal voice and what it said was so astounding that none of them at first even identified it as coming from Scott.

'Take your hand away from there, or I'll break your arm.'

It was followed by a movement and a gasp from a woman. James Martin heard it with a shudder and thought to himself, *Holy Mackerel! Who's having a go at whom?* And then he thought of the soft, plump hand of Mrs Lewis.

To Susan Shelby came an instant vivid recollection. On the swing couch in the garden, behind the house back home and her saying sharply, 'Toby, take your hand away. That's enough!' But oddly her mind never turned to Herbert or what had happened to her.

Manny Rosen woke up and said, 'Somebody's broken an arm?'

It was Mike Rogo who turned on his torch and said, 'What the hell's goin' on here?'

Scott was lying down on his side, resting on an elbow, Linda Rogo was sitting up near by, her face flushed with fury. She pointed to Scott and said, 'That bastard was trying to give me a feel.'

Rogo said, 'What? Who was? Him?'

Scott interrupted him coolly, 'Work out the sequence for yourself, Rogo.'

What Rogo really hated Scott for at that moment was setting the minds of the others on to the same track. If it were true that the Minister had been trying to take liberties with his wife, why should he call attention to himself in that manner? Rogo knew all there was to know about guys and broads and the way they behaved and had been suspecting for some time that Linda had a yen for the preacher. Obviously in the dark she had been trying to have a go at him. And just as obviously it must be covered up.

He said in his loud copper's voice, 'Don't nobody try any funny business around here. Anybody tries to get fresh can collect a busted jaw. What are we gonna do, stick around here all night? I thought the idea was to get up to the top somewhere so they can hear us.'

Scott rose to his feet. 'Yes,' he said, 'you're right. It's time we were moving on. If three of you will throw your lights up along this side I think I can show you the way we have to go.'

CHAPTER XVII

Mount Poseidon

The engine room of a great quadruple-screw ocean liner consists of a series of platforms, some five decks high, connected by ladder-type stairs leading to open-work steel flooring or catwalks. These platforms are built around the huge central steam turbines and reduction gear housings. The auxiliary machinery, such as turbo generators, condensers, compressors, emergency compressors and a whole battery of pumps are ranged around the four sides, joined by what seems to be completely helter-skelter coils of pipes and wiring to feed steam under various degrees of pressure, oil, lubricating materials and electrical power.

All this is attached to the double-bottomed fuel and ballast tanks which constitute the floor of the vessel, planned for maximum stresses of a 45° roll. Cross beams of heavy girders support the platforms, catwalks and conduits.

When the *Poseidon* turned over, almost everything but the main propeller shafts was twisted, shaken or torn away, either plummeting directly into the sea through the open well of the engine-room shaft, or tumbling down the sides in a cascade of tangled metal. Dynamos had plunged through their housings, shearing the steel as though it had been paper, leaving wedge or spear-shaped pieces razor sharp, thrust upward in menacing pinnacles like miniature Dolomites.

Mingled with these were curling sections of the platforms, reversed ladders with a half-dozen steps smashed out of their centres and the curved surfaces of the larger pipes, some of them crumpled, others cut open lengthwise, the way one slits a sausage skin. Everything was covered with a film of oil released from the bottom tanks when the heavy turbines had ripped loose from the floor plating.

At one point a giant reduction gear and its housing had broken completely away from its turbine unit, but instead of falling through to the sea, had been slammed against the sides of the engine room by the centrifugal force of the capsizing and locked there, with the gear wheel jammed at an angle and held aloft by the crumpled housing. Scott's probing lantern showed up the square edges of the finely milled teeth curving outwards for several yards in an overhang, before receding into the general tangle of battered steel.

Fragments of this jumbled mountain reached to within a foot of the platform on which they had been resting. Their lights showed up a similar range across the stygian lake.

Scott studied the outcroppings on the far side. Had he judged it an easier climb, he would have been prepared to have got himself and his party across the water. But it was, if anything, more formidable-looking and there was an overhang of metal pushed out at a thirty-degree angle, some eight feet from the edge which made it an impossible task.

Muller asked, 'What are you looking for?'

Scott replied, 'Path!' and then removing the light beam from across the lake, added, 'Well, that leaves us no choice.' He studied the precipice of metal on their own side.

Rogo said, 'Where do you think you're going now?'

Scott replied simply, 'Up there.'

Shelby was horrified and cried, 'Frank, you must be out of your mind! It's impossible. My family could never...'

The fanatic look was back in the Minister's eyes and his voice suddenly filled the vast cavern, 'We're being tested. You believe in God; worship him by being worthy!'

The echo repeated, 'Worthy' and died away. In a quite normal tone he said, 'Don't think of it as you're seeing it, but simply as a mountain to be climbed. It's everything you find on a mountainside: crevices, projections, buttresses, pinnacles, clefts, foot and handholds. There's hardly a single peak left in the world that someone hasn't managed to climb.'

Martin muttered under his breath, 'Someone!' and Muller said, 'The Mount Poseidon Expedition.'

'Exactly,' Scott continued. 'You've all seen photographs of mountain climbers roped together. The line is so arranged that the entire weight never falls upon one person, but is distributed. Is that clear? It's actually much simpler for us. We've only an ascent of fifty feet to make. There are...' he made a quick count as though he had forgotten —'thirteen of us. We'll be double roped at say a distance of three or four feet apart.'

'My God,' Hubie Muller muttered, 'you'd think he was preparing to take an alpine tourist party up the Jungfrau for an outing.'

Scott looked the group over. 'I'll lead, followed by Miss Kinsale. Nothing seems to worry her. Then I think Martin, Susan and you, Dick, followed by Jane and Kemal. Then Mrs Rosen, Manny, Nonnie and Hubie; Mrs Rogo and her husband. Rogo, I'm afraid I'm putting you last as usual because you're not likely to lose your head if something goes wrong.'

Rogo said, 'Thanks!'

'The success or failure of any climb depends upon two things; the leader and the manner in which he is followed,' Scott explained. 'The leader maps out the route; the others follow in his footsteps. In fact it goes right back to that childhood game you've all played, "Follow My Leader", in which you must *do everything exactly as he does, or you're "out"*. Remember, if he wiggled his fingers to his ears or something else crazy, you had to do the same thing.'

'Manny, do you understand any of this talk?' Belle Rosen asked. 'All I heard is we was thirteen and thirteen I don't like. I always said we were thirteen.'

'He's telling us how we got to going next,' Manny said.

'How I'm not interested in, but where.' She was still lying down. Her triumphant underwater swim ought to have elated and stimulated her. On the contrary, oddly, it seemed to have taken everything out of her that she had left. Perhaps as much as fatigue to an unaccustomed heart and set of muscles, it was the transition mentally she had made backwards and forwards over a span of forty years.

'Each step, I take, each place I put my hand or foot, each thing I do, one at a time will be observed by the climber behind me,' Scott went on, 'and copied exactly. That will be you, Miss Kinsale. In turn, Martin will copy you, then Susan and so on. Get it, everybody?'

Martin asked, 'You really mean you think we can make it?'

Scott replied, 'Yes, or at any rate that we must try. It's simply a matter of imitating the one ahead of you. If you'll stick to that we'll reach the top safely.'

'Reach where?' asked Belle Rosen.

Manny replied, 'Look! Up there!'

Belle Rosen dragged herself to her knees and for the first time looked to where the beams of light were fingering the greasy surface of the distant propeller shaft. 'I couldn't do it,' she declared. 'Not in a thousand million years for a thousand million dollars.'

'Belle, look. Like Frank says, we'll all be tied together so...'

'So one falls, all fall. That ain't for me.'

Scott promised, 'You'll be as safe as walking upstairs in your own home.'

'When I'm going upstairs in my own home, I go in the elevator.' She looked upwards once more. 'No not in a thousand billion years. You couldn't talk me into it.'

'But, Mamma, you can't stay here. Look, I'll be right behind you.'

'Yes, I can. Go on, Manny. Go on everyone. Leave me. Can't you see I'm tired, that I ain't got any more strength?'

'But, Mamma, you'd die. We'd both die. You think I'd leave you?'

'Or that we would, Mrs Rosen?' cried Nonnie.

Belle gazed at them out of dark eyes, heavy lidded and filled with fatigue, despair and memories. 'Is living so wonderful?' she asked.

Her husband said, 'I'm surprised at you, Mamma. Do you want to die?'

'I don't want to have to climb any more. My feet are killing me from all those pipes. I'm old. I'm too heavy to lift myself up there.'

Susan Shelby bent over Belle and took her hand, suddenly filled with a tenderness she had not known that she possessed. 'Dear Mrs Rosen,' she begged, 'do please try. We...' She had been about to say, 'love you,' but suddenly felt embarrassed. 'We think you're a wonderful person. Look how you went through that awful tunnel by yourself, where nobody else really dared. We never would have got here if it hadn't been for you.'

'So where are we?' said Belle. 'I appreciate your remarks, but swimming ain't climbing. You want I should swim across there for you, okay. But up any more, never! Anyway, my heart is hurting me.' Then to her husband, 'I'm surprised at you, Manny when you know about my heart...'

'Belle, Belle, your heart always!' said Manny, and it was apparent that this had been a longtime family affair. 'Look, Mamma. You know there's nothing the matter with you. The last time we saw Dr Metzger and he listened, he said you should live so long before a heart like yours gave out.'

'Dr Metzger don't know what I'm feeling. It kills me if I climb, it kills me if I stay here. Here it's easier.'

Linda turned on her, 'Oh, for Chrice sakes stay, then!' she shouted and then to the others, 'If she chooses to sit here and die, let her. But she has no right to keep us back.'

Belle said gravely, 'Nobody chooses to die, Mrs Rogo. When it comes, it comes and then you go. I'm sixty-four years old. You're young. I understand how you feel. Nobody should stay here with me, please. I never thought anything like this could happen to us but when it does, you got to look at it from how you are.'

'Mamma,' Manny pleaded, 'how can you say such things? With sixty-four you are nothing. Look how you still can swim like a champion. Don't you want to see Irving again? And Sol and Sylvia? And Hy and Myra, your own children and grandchildren?'

Both Shelby and Muller noted a small bit of starch enter the limp, surrendered backbone of Mrs Rosen. 'Sol and Sylvia I could do without,' she said. 'All those years they been chiselling from the store. Tongue or pastrami ain't good enough for them. No, it's lox and sturgeon every time. Or like she's saying, "Belle, I am just happening to be hungry, maybe a little caviar on a piece of white bread would be good."'

Tubby little Rosen in his shorts began to look like a hurt child. 'Aw, now, Mamma. Don't go picking on my relatives again. We had that all explained. Sol has been a good brother to me, he put money in the shop when...'

'Yeah, and Sylvia ate it all up, twice over,' Belle interrupted. 'An appetite she had like a horse. So she's my sister-in-law, but she used to be worse than cops for free handouts. Every day, every day, a sandwich here, a dill pickle there, I'm all out of mustard, at home, Belle, could I borrow a jar. Mmmmmm, does that herring salad look good, you mind if I taste? Don't give me Sylvia.'

'Belle, Belle, you mustn't talk like this. Not in front of strangers.' He was worried about what Mike Rogo might do or say at the allusion to cops, or Linda. And the others standing there embarrassed, trying to pretend they weren't listening.

Rogo surprised him, however. He said, 'Let her get it out of her system, Manny. She'll feel better afterwards.'

'Like a larder they used to use our shop,' Belle went on, 'and Sol was as bad as she. The half of it you don't even know because when I was a kid in Wadleigh High, one of the things I learned was not to snitch. You know where half the stuff comes from the time their Simon went Bar Mitzvah? Our stock room. Only I covered it up you shouldn't find out such no-goods should be your family. And what did they ever do for us? You know what Sylvia gave our kids for last Christmas? Each a handkerchief with an initial on from Woolworth's. Big deal, when Sol sells out his business for half a million. If I'm not saving every penny, where do you think we would be today?'

Rosen with a sheepish and unhappy little smile looked around at the others. It was an old story to him but to have people like the Shelbys and Scott and Muller let into the privacy of family squabbles! With her expression Jane Shelby tried to message him, *It's all right, Mr Rosen, we understand.*

And Rosen's eyes almost popped from his head. Had or hadn't Scott tipped him a wink? Feeling a sudden flood of relief he said, 'Mamma, Mamma, I'm sorry. Like you say, half of it I didn't know, otherwise...'

'Sorry, sorry. Now you're sorry, when it's too late and we're retired.'

'You're right, Mamma. But we got plenty for ourselves. We got a lot yet to look forward to.' Rosen hesitated and then decided to risk it. Maybe Rogo was right. What she needed was to get it off her chest again. 'Could you come now, maybe, Mamma. See, we've been holding up Mr Scott and everybody.'

She looked up at him. Her expression had changed to something almost half humorous, but the liquid, dark eyes were affectionate, as she sighed and said, 'I suppose so, Emmanuel Rosen, like I always said, you're a terrible man. What is it I got to do now?' She rose to her feet. It was Martin who raised the cheer: 'Atta girl, Belle! To hell with Sol and Sylvia,' and sent a ripple of laughter through the party, and felt embarrassed at the attention he had drawn and apologized, 'Oh, I'm sorry, Mrs Rosen, I didn't mean...'

'Never mind,' she said, 'so I talked my head off like an old fool. So show me, and I try.'

Carefully Scott explained the roping which, because of the brevity and steepness of the climb plus the size of the party, would have to be different from ordinary alpine practice. There would be two ropes, one attaching the members of the party to one another, and the other a guide-rope which would be alternately fastened and shifted by Scott as he progressed to the top.

Muller asked, 'How do we get the Turk to capisco all this? I wouldn't care to have him down on top of me.'

'This is a bright boy,' Scott replied. 'He was smart enough to join up with us. You watch, he'll get it when I demonstrate. Miss Kinsale and Martin, you're first. Hi, Kemal, you look. You see!'

Laying out the two coils of line retrieved from the Fire Station, Scott tied one end of one of them about his own waist, looped it slantwise across the upper part of Miss Kinsale's body fastening it with a curious knot and running the second line through it.

'The body rope will hold you secure and the guide-rope you can use to help pull yourself up. Do you see how it works? Here, Kemal, how about you?'

The Turk grinned and said, 'Hokay, hokay!'

Muller asked, 'Why have you got the Rosens in the middle? I should have thought that...'

Scott replied, 'It figures, doesn't it? The most difficult part of the climb is the middle. By the time the Rosens reach there, I'll be on top. The guide-rope will be secured and I'll be able to give them a lift with the body rope. That's when they'll need it.'

He had made it sound so easy, every step thought out, every precaution taken. And curiously the manner in which he had put the challenge to them as an act of worship had stimulated them all, even the non-religious or the doubters such as Muller and Martin, who sold themselves on the idea that to bring off such a climb was near enough miraculous that it must be somehow rewarded. They were eager to begin.

'Let's go!' cried Scott, 'Let's show Him what we're made of!'

Shelby thought again of that half hysterical assistant coach giving him a wallop on his backside and saying, 'Go out there and show those bastards what Michigan men are made of.'

But Scott had one final caution. He said 'We'll make it if you remember one thing. Don't vary in a single instance from what the person above you does. I will have tested out every foothold, handhold, loophold. That will be the only way to go. Also don't ever look down. Only up to what the person above you is doing, or has done. Don't talk. Save your breath. From time to time I'll call a rest. Stay where you are then, loop your slack, use it as a bight or hitch when you need to, put your weight on your rope and work and relax your fingers. When you're breathing normally, we'll continue. Everyone got shoes or slippers on? Rogo, see that the guide-line pays out properly. Okay! We're off!'

He made his way carefully up the gradual slope of tumbled debris collected by the edge of the lake, the foothills leading to the first almost vertical rise upwards.

With curious delicacy, Miss Kinsale picked her way after him, her head down in concentration to see that she trod where he had, her long dark hair falling down on either side of her face. Muller thought how closely Scott had hit it with his description of the game—girl following boy carefully over the sharp shale of some holiday beach in carefully stylized pursuit.

'All right, Miss Kinsale?'

'Quite, Dr Scott.'

'The climb really begins now. Watch what I do and where I go.'

The body line went taut between her and Martin who moved off behind her, followed by Nonnie and Muller.

With the smaller flashlights still tied to their forearms, it left their hands free with adequate lighting directed at the gripping point, with major illumination provided by the larger lanterns.

While Scott's practised climber's eye had mapped out a possible pathway, shadows and the impossibility of seeing all sides involved some guesswork and made improvisation necessary. Yet once started with these soft and tired people behind him, relying upon his confidence, there was to be no turning back. Now with the main climb at hand, he reached up, looped the guide-rope over a piece of broken handrail, and secured his first foothold.

Miss Kinsale asked, 'Do I do anything about that guide-rope?'

'No, but use it to help you. I'll be constantly taking it higher but it will always be anchored for your next step. Are you frightened?'

'No, not with you.'

'Good. See that the arch of your foot rests on any projection if it's narrow. Then you'll be less likely to slip.' Scott went on again, finding a handhold on the tubular crosspiece of a railing that had been carried away and a secure footing on the inner surface of a ripped pipe. He called down, 'Martin, are you following?'

'Yup!'

'We're in luck. I've found a piece of ladder turned the right way around. Five steps like going upstairs and there's a piece of the platform at the top where we'll have our first rest.'

The Shelbys were now beginning to climb. The only difficulty they found in following Scott's instructions was the slipperiness of every piece of metal due to the oil. But Scott was proceeding so slowly and meticulously that there was time to secure a firm grip.

Shelby, looking down, saw Kemal and the Rosens crossing the initial slope. He called back to Belle, 'It's a breeze! Kemal's there to give you a hand-up. Scott's taking it very easy.'

They did not reply. Shelby turned back to concentrate on the next step upwards. He was filled with admiration for Scott's organization and forethought. Kemal had understood why and where he had been put in the order, for after each movement he turned around to make sure that Belle was following in the right place and reaching down with his huge hand, helped to pull her aloft.

Overhead Scott had come up against his first real obstacle. It was a solid wall of metal some six feet in height barring the way and extending across and out over the edge of the lake below. Some earlier damage from the fall had cut a 'V' into it at that point, with the outer part forming a five-foot, needle sharp spearhead pointing upwards.

Directly above his head a stanchion, some severed pipes and a downward curved piece of steel effectively blocked the path. Had Scott been alone, he would have slung a rope over one of these and been over the hurdle in a few minutes. With the others it would be impossible.

The menacing spearpoint cut off access from the right. There was no shifting the piece overhead.

He called out, 'Rest where you are,' and then studied the problem from the left side, where two lubricating pumps had ended their collapse, spilling their contents.

Miss Kinsale looked up and inquired, 'Are you in trouble, Dr Scott?'

'For the moment.'

'Surely, if you ask for the help of our Heavenly Father...'

Scott replied curtly, 'That would be an impertinence. This is a mountaineering job. There's always a way.' He had seen it already. One partially risky foothold on a foot wide strip of metal, fortunately inclined at an angle slightly upwards, around the obstacle and the broken pumps then turned themselves from there into a kind of vertical circular staircase from which a piece of broad undamaged platform could be gained. All that was necessary was for each person after having negotiated the narrow turn about the edge of the wall to pause and give his or her follower a steadying hand.

Scott smiled with satisfaction. He wanted to get on. The ugly, menacing, triangular spear had now become an arrow pointing upwards and onwards.

He said, 'I've got it.' He worked his way around the narrow ledge, flipped the loop of the guide-rope over the next overhead projection and said, 'Give me your hand, Miss Kinsale until you are around this corner. Then wait and do likewise for Martin and tell him to pass along the same instructions to the others. The next section will be a piece of cake.'

'I prayed,' said Miss Kinsale.

Scott did not reply, but steadied her around the corner. While she waited for Martin, he had started up the next part of the climb.

Scott suddenly cried, 'Hold it for a moment! Don't come any farther.'

They waited. To Miss Kinsale just below him it seemed that he was struggling with something which finally came loose and a moment later from the lake below they heard a splash. Shelby asked, 'What was that?'

Scott replied, 'Nothing.'

But Rogo's body was momentarily turned and the big lantern strapped to his back had picked up the object for an instant. It was part of a severed leg wearing a rubber boot. For a moment he felt sickened and no fonder of Scott. He thought: *What the hell is that guy made of?*

The line lengthened. Belle and Manny Rosen were already at the beginning of the vertical ascent, shepherded by Kemal; Nonnie and Muller on the slope. Only Linda and Rogo were still on the flat, awaiting their turn.

Linda said, 'Why did you let him make us suck hind tit again? If anything gets screwed up, we'll get it, or somebody falls down on top of us.'

Rogo replied, 'It's psychology.'

'Psychology, my ass!' said Linda. 'You let that randy bastard buffalo you. Fine thing not standing up for your wife when a man tries to make her right under your nose.'

'Yeah, sure,' said Rogo in his flat monotone voice, 'That's right. He gives you a feel and then yells for help. Don't give me that. What have you got in there, a set of teeth?'

'You bastard!'

Rogo said, 'I thought you had more sense than to go for a panzola. I've got Mr preacher Scott's number now. He's queer as a coot.'

'*Him?*' The accusation actually outraged her sensibilities.

'Yeah, him! This guy can't go for dames so he makes with the turn-around collar. And he sure slapped you down.'

The line about Linda's waist tautened and there was a pull on the slack in her hand. 'Get going,' Rogo ordered, 'and for Christ's sweet sake, don't try any funny business, but do like he said and let's git ahda here. You got Muller ahead of you. He's no bargain, but at least he's all there. I heard him laying that kid. I'm behind you and won't let nothing happen to you, honeybun. Just take it easy.'

They started on their way up.

'You making it okay, Belle?' Manny called. The yellow light of his flashlamp was trained on her white bottom that glistened with sweat and oil.

She replied, 'It's my breath. Every time I go up a step I can't get my breath.'

'But you're not frightened, Mamma?'

'No, I ain't frightened. I only looked down once and then I couldn't see nothing. This Turkish feller is a nice man. He helps me. How much farther is it?'

'I dunno. Not much, maybe. We just keep on going like we are 'til we're there. You're doing great.'

'Manny, if we ever get out of this, you won't get me farther than the corner of Amsterdam Avenue and 89th Street from our apartment.'

'That's right, Mamma. Think about our apartment, what a fine place we got.'

She couldn't resist it, 'With Sol with his feet up on our best chair and Sylvia sticking her nose into my closet to see what new clothes I got, if any. Okay, okay, Mr Kemal, I'm coming.'

Muller was waiting for Linda at the narrow ledge turning about the steel wall. He held out his hand to her. She took it and said, 'Oh, Mr Muller, hold me. I'm so frightened.'

'Here, take my arm.'

When she had it, the signal he received was unmistakable. Muller was an expert at overt pressures. He thought to himself: *The bitch! Poor Rogo.*

The party toiled upwards. Linda said to Rogo, 'Why do we have to go like this? I can see a better way over there, look!'

Rogo held her back, tightening his grip on the rope so that she could not try. 'For Jesus' sake, baby, don't try any funny business. The guy's got it figured out. It's working. Don't forget I'm at the other end of this rope.'

'Like always,' Linda said, 'low man on the totem pole.'

They reached the portion of the platform half-way to the top that Scott had spotted. He and the others were waiting there. There was just room enough for them.

Scott said, 'Sit if you can, and lights out. We'll rest here for a few minutes.'

CHAPTER XVIII

And Then There Were Twelve

Out of the darkness came Belle Rosen's voice, 'What are we doing here?'

No one replied; no one knew whether the question meant the return of her sense of humour, or was drawn out of despair. But she repeated it, 'I mean it. What are we all doing here? How can this happen today? A couple hours ago we are sitting down to supper and maybe afterwards looking at the show, or playing some cards, and now here we are practically naked with no clothes on, climbing up like monkeys so we shouldn't get killed.'

Richard Shelby said, 'You've got something there, Mrs Rosen.'

It was strange that all through this adventure which should have knitted them together, members of the party who had not known one another before continued to use last names. The Shelbys and the Rosens had never fraternized or exchanged more than polite greetings. Shelby found it impossible to call her Belle, particularly now that she was nearly nude. He felt that she had earned the dignity of 'Mrs Rosen'. He said, 'A modern vessel with every safety appliance, rolling over like a canoe...'

Muller added, 'Look what happened to the *Andrea Doria*. Two ships with radar steaming into a head-on collision.'

Manny Rosen put in, 'It's all so nice when you're sitting in the Captain's cabin for a cocktail party, eating caviar sandwiches on the company and drinking champagne. So where is the Captain now, when we're needing him? Or all those other officers always dancing with the passengers?'

Nobody answered the question which hung there heavily in the enshrouding blackness. Obsessed with their struggle it was so easy to forget, yet they all knew. Nonnie began to cry softly, 'All my pals...'

Jane Shelby, who was near her, groped an arm about her shoulder and said gently, 'I've lost my boy.'

Rogo said, 'Don't say that, ma'am. In an investigation of a missing person, we never give up until there is a...' He had been about to say *corpus delicti*, but checked himself in time, '...a definite indication that there's no chance. We may find him when we get to the top.'

Jane said, 'Thank you, Mr Rogo, I understand. But by now he would have heard us. He would have seen our lights.'

'It's a big ship, ma'am. He may have gone another way.'

Jane thought: *It was the way that he went that I cannot bear, amidst filth and stench. That I left him so as not to shame him... a boy being shamed of a bodily function in the presence of his mother. He was so young to be blotted out like that, and I'll never know when or where, or how, or what his last thoughts were.*

Rogo said, 'I'd do anything to find him for you, ma'am. Maybe I should have stayed back and had another look.' All his easily stirred policeman's sympathies lay with the mother of the victim.

'Thank you, Mr Rogo. No, it was useless. He wasn't there.'

Scott's voice was heard, 'He'll be found. The kid had guts. He was playing the game.' He spoke with such confidence and assertion that for an instant Jane's heart was filled with hope until she felt suddenly that he might very well be speaking not for her, but for himself.

He then said again, 'Let's go!' and snapped on the lantern strapped to his back. It threw its beam upwards into the tangled steel that yet awaited them. 'I won't kid you. The last half will be more difficult, more tiring and more dangerous.'

A little distance from the top was the overhang Scott had seen, a weird circular ladder made up of the square steel teeth of the reduction gear wheel jammed against the side when the entire unit had ripped loose. It offered hand and footholds but the climber for six or eight feet would be tilted backwards with his body angled precariously over the abyss below.

This was again the problem they had encountered before, the inverted staircase which twice they had solved by avoiding it. This one could not be bypassed. It had to be negotiated to the point where the teeth receded once more into a position where the weight would be thrown forward again, easing the pressure on arms and thighs. Neither from below or, now that they were close to it, had Scott been able to see any way around it. All he could count upon was the fact that he, Martin and Shelby would be at the top by the time the weakest members of the party reached the spot. They would be able to hold and help them via the ropes.

'Anyone know what time it is?' Martin asked. 'My watch stopped at a quarter past two.'

'Hell!' said Muller, 'So has mine. That muck we swam through.'

Shelby said, 'It's been a half-hour at least since then. It must be almost three o'clock.'

'We've been this way almost six hours,' said Martin. 'My God, what's holding the ship up?'

Miss Kinsale was arranging her ropes, 'It's you who said it, Mr. Martin... God!'

'With an assist from the Reverend Dr Scott,' Muller muttered to himself.

'What did you say, darling?' Nonnie asked.

The 'darling' grated on Muller but then he looked at her and loved her again.

Rogo said, 'She ain't gonna stay up much longer.'

'So, then, is there any use we should keep on climbing up like this?' Manny queried.

Scott was ready to leave now, but he turned back to them all for a moment and replied simply, 'Yes, because we are human beings responsible to ourselves.'

The simple statement rang through Muller like a bell and for the first time he felt he understood something of the character of this ecclesiastical athlete and his climb, as well as himself for following him; the goal they had set themselves in the face of almost insurmountable obstacles and a well nigh hopeless situation.

Up had always been good; down was bad. God and Heaven were up; Hell and the Devil were down. The road to damnation was the downward path. Resurrection was ascent. Phrases rang through his ears: 'So-and-So is rising in the world. He's on his way up... Poor old You-Know-Who is slipping they say. Losing his grip. If he doesn't watch his step, he'll be down and out. Down and out! Up and safe on top of the heap. Man's whole history had been an ascent... upwards, always upwards out of the ooze and slime of the sea, on to the land, higher and higher and now reaching out his arms to the planets. His mythology created the dwellers underground as misshapen dwarfs and monsters, the creatures of the upper air were exquisite, graceful, winged fantasies of light.

Where else, indeed, was there to go but up, as long as one had a single breath left in one's body? Even the poor, wheezy fat woman to whom every move must have been an almost unbearable torture, was not quitting. Was it really the hope of a miracle of rescue that was driving them onwards, or the curious hypnotism of the climb itself, the very upness of it. They had protested and quarrelled, balked and tried to shirk, all but given up. But always they had come back to the striving aloft.

This must be at the core of Scott's religion, or his faith to justify himself as a man. Whether or not he truly saw rescue as the end result, if he and they failed, with one's last gasp one would be maintaining the dignity his God had bestowed. And Muller wondered if from the very first Scott had not led them, would they now be dead in the grip of the dark water below; would they each on their own have made some effort to adapt themselves to this once familiar world turned upside-down and struggle in the right direction?

Aloud he said, 'Okay, let's go.'

Scott made one change in the order of their proceeding. He altered the positions of Manny Rosen and Kemal, so that Manny came before Belle and the Turk after. Then he took the latter and pointed upward to the bad patch, pantomiming.

Kemal nodded and said, 'Hokay, hokay!' with a glance from his broad hands to Belle Rosen's bottom.

'We'll make it,' Scott promised and took his first hand and foothold to start them on their last lap.

He had been right. It was more difficult and more dangerous and their unused muscles were beginning to cramp and give out. The pauses had to come at more frequent intervals, particularly for Belle who groaned, complained and lamented with every rise and yet kept going as they all did. For there was also the hypnosis of discipline and obedience that Scott had instilled, each to follow the other in exactly the same manner, and it was their concentration in obeying, in watching the one above and trying to follow, that to some extent kept their minds off their failing strength.

The overhang of the gear wheel ascent was now above the Minister's head. Slight as the angle was, he wondered however Mrs Rosen would manage it. Much depended upon Kemal. He said to Miss Kinsale, 'Let your slack go so that we have about ten feet between us. Watch how I do it, then try to do the same, except I'll be pulling you as well. Do you see? Pass the word along to Martin and on down.'

He started up, using not only his hands but his knees and elbows to brace himself. He was strong and still in condition from daily workouts on the squash courts and deck tennis. But he could feel the pains crawling up his wrists into his forearms, then his biceps. It was heave, push, pull and hang on. His thighs were aching.

'I'm praying,' said Miss Kinsale.

'Never mind that! Keep your eyes open and your wits about you,' Scott gasped almost testily. 'When you reach where I am, lean to the left, understand?'

'Yes, Dr Scott,' Miss Kinsale sounded contrite. 'I'll tell that to Mr Martin too.'

Scott pulled himself over the last overhanging piece. The next was vertical, and those above tilted backwards like steps. When he caught his breath he climbed them without any trouble. To his relief, the last lap was what he had suspected he had seen, a companionway intact, but reversed with the steps unbacked. They had only to go around behind it and use it like a ladder.

'It's a *cinch*, once you get up here,' he called down. He grasped the guide-rope and took a turn with it around his wrist. 'Okay, come up,' and pulled.

Miss Kinsale made the passage astonishingly easily, whether it was because she was slight and wiry or the example and added help of Scott on the rope, but in half the time it had taken him, she stood beside him. She said, 'Dr Scott, I'm afraid Mrs Rosen will never be able to do it.'

He replied, 'She will. If she can't, we will have to leave her behind. But she's very brave.'

Miss Kinsale stared at him with an expression on her face as close to shock and disapproval as she had ever mustered. 'You're not serious, about leaving her?'

'We've had to leave that Englishman and his girl and dozens of others who could not or would not come. How do you think we've come through this far? We're winning.'

Miss Kinsale said, 'We've lost the boy,' and was taken aback by the sudden expression of fury on the Minister's face.

'Don't ever say that!'

She apologized, 'I'm sorry, Dr Scott. I didn't mean...' Then she added, 'May I stay here and help her?'

'No. There are others to come. I have done the best I can for her. We can be of more use from the top.'

Miss Kinsale asked, 'Do you mind if I pray for her?'

Scott replied, 'If you want to. But she must already have pleased God beyond anything words of supplication could do. We'll see.'

Laboriously, step by step they made their way higher, pausing only to help Martin by hauling on him. Susan, young and athletic had enough left to negotiate it, but Jane and Richard Shelby were in agony. Shelby thought that he would fall backwards and dangle helplessly. Yet even as he felt he was giving up, he had crossed the danger line.

By now Scott, Miss Kinsale and Martin had reached the top where they could apply enough power to get Manny Rosen over the worst of it, so that he could crawl up the rest, scraping his knees and belly. But he was very proud of himself and shouted down, 'See Mamma, I made it! It ain't so terrible.'

But it was.

For Belle Rosen was indeed at the end of her strength. The higher they climbed, the hotter, more oppressive and airless it became and she could not suck oxygen into her lungs. When those above pulled on the rope it tended only to jam her more closely to the gear wheel where she clung moaning and gasping, 'I can't, I can't! Oh, let me go, let me fall! I can't, I can't!'

It was Kemal's power below her, pushing, lifting an arm and a leg at a time that was keeping her there. He was trying to force her limbs into the spaces between the teeth so that her whole weight would not be on the rope that was cutting into the bulging flesh of her side. He had her half up when he felt his own great resistance failing and he began to cry out and shout, 'Oh, oh, no can! No can!'

Muller squeezed past Nonnie, dragging Linda with him. The thoughts he had been having had charged him anew. He was obsessed with up; rising, climbing, ascending, high, higher—the road to up must not be blocked.

Linda cried, 'Stop it! You're hurting me. Look out! The old cow'll come down on top of us.'

He said, 'Keep quiet, you stupid bitch,' and ranged himself next to the Turk.

With an unexpected ally on his side, Kemal found a last reserve. The two men pushed and heaved. And now what had before been a handicap, suddenly came to their rescue; the film of oil covering all. For lifted and shoved, she suddenly slid over the slippery surface to be dragged bumping and slapping against the remainder of the pseudo staircase at the top of which she flopped, writhing and gasping.

Scott gave her no time to collapse further but nipped down the ladder, lifted her up and practically carried her. He called down, 'Good job, Hubie! Go back to your regular place before you get tangled up. Okay, Kemal, and you next, Nonnie. Use the guide-rope. It's been fastened. We can get you over the worst.'

Kemal's great chest heaved as he fought to regain his breath. Then he gave a great 'whoosh', sucked in air and crawled his way clear of the obstacle. There was so much power at the top now that both Nonnie and Muller were able to make it without too much difficulty.

It was Linda who balked, as always. She cried, 'No, no! I dont want to go that way! I'll hurt myself. Muller hurt me already. I won't do it! Let me go my own way.'

'Aw now, sweetie pie,' Rogo coaxed, 'It's only that one bit. I'm right behind you.'

Scott shouted, 'Mrs Rogo! Keep to our way. There isn't any other.'

'You keep your goddam mouth shut! I've had enough out of you. Let me, let me...' She was becoming hysterical, lurching and tugging at the rope that held her. 'Stop it, don't pull! Let me go. I'm going around the other side.'

There was a small plank of metal a foot wide that stuck out to the right and above it was a maze of tubing, pieces of stair rail and torn electric wires. She went for it.

'No, Linda!' Scott ordered. 'It's no good. It's not safe. I tested it. Rogo, hold her!'

For a moment she was rearing and plunging like a pony at the end of a tether. Then suddenly, a cunning look coming over her face, she ascended a step to get slack, loosened the body rope, threw it over her head and was back down again to where the gear tooth climb began.

'See you,' she said, stepped out on to the metal planking and reaching up, pulled on the wires, hauling herself aloft to where she could get a grip upon the tubing.

The wires came away, dropping her down again on to the plank which tipped up and broke her hold. Two of the women above screamed as she began to fall.

Rogo, his lantern illuminating her momentarily, reached for her and with a superhuman effort caught her arm as she went by. But his hand and her own flesh were slippery and she slid through his grasp.

The women screamed again. Lights were shafting down upon the body which turned over once so that when she hit the triangular steel spear point thrust out from the side, it pierced her through her back, and emerged from her chest.

She gave a long drawn out, 'ahhhhhhhhhhhhhhhh' of pain, first high pitched, then trailing off. Thereafter her voice echoing through the dark cavern, she cried out, 'Rogo, you son-of-a-bitch!'

And after that, she moved once, like a person stretching after a long sleep and then became still and neither stirred again nor made another sound.

CHAPTER XIX

'You Can't Win 'Em All'

In the light of the lanterns blood flowed blackly from the breast of the doll-like figure, curved backwards as though thrown haphazardly away. Some of the members of the party entertained the most shaming thoughts.

Nonnie whispered spitefully, 'Serves her right, always at everyone!'

Muller said, 'Hush! You mustn't say that about the poor creature.'

Nonnie was instantly contrite and cried, 'I shouldn't have. How rotten of me.'

But Muller was having a struggle of his own, for the ridiculous phrase that kept intruding itself into his own mind, *It couldn't have happened to a better person.*

Miss Kinsale was thinking, *She was stupid, stupid, stupid. She didn't obey Dr Scott.*

Martin was saying over and over to himself, 'Don't think ill of the dead...'

Belle asked, 'What happened?'

Her husband replied, 'She fell. Linda Rogo. I think she's dead.'

Belle said, 'The poor kid!' but she thought; *It's God's punishment.*

Susan was wondering whether the heart within her had turned to stone, that in the face of this swift and terrible death she could feel no emotion whatsoever.

Shelby said, 'The foolish girl. It was her own fault,' but he did not dare look at his wife whose face, staring down at the corpse was hard and unfathomable. Jane was wishing it had been herself. Linda did not deserve the peace of extinction.

Rogo was at first too stunned to shift from his hold at the foot of the overhang. Not yet suffering the shock of the full reality of what had taken place he was asking himself, 'Now what did she have to go and do that for?' But then he gave a cry, 'Linda! Jesus Christ, Linda!' and was taking a step forward on to the treacherous plank, when he was halted by Scott's voice.

'The guide-line, Rogo! Go down on the guide-line. I'll join you.'

The counsel penetrated. The detective seized the rope and slid down, bumping and bouncing off the sharp projections cutting himself and burning the palms of his hands.

He had hardly arrived at the steel wall and the narrow ledge they had used to circumvent it when Scott was beside him.

She lay, bent like a bow, legs and arms limp, her head with the curls falling away from her white forehead, the dark blood still welling forth from her torn heart. There was no glimmer of any life whatsoever in the staring blue eyes. The lips of the cupid's bow mouth were still parted from the framing of her last words.

Rogo, who had seen death in every form was weeping. He didn't touch her as though to do so might hurt her more, fix her more firmly on to the sharp point. He asked, 'Why did she call me that before she died? I caught her but I couldn't hold her. My hands were slippery with oil. Are you sure she's dead?'

'Let me see,' Scott crowded past him. He did not touch her either, for there was no need. He stood looking down at the dead form of the girl and although Rogo did not notice it, his face was suddenly distorted as with anger. 'She's beyond help.'

Rogo said, 'She called me a son-of-a-bitch! She never wanted to come on this goddam trip. I made her. That musta been what she meant, wasn't it? She couldn'a thought I let go of her on purpose?'

'No,' Scott said. 'She ought not have thought that.'

'Say a prayer for her soul, padre,' Rogo asked and suddenly self-conscious that he, a Catholic, was asking a non-Catholic, added, 'Any kind of a prayer.'

He waited for the Minister to make the sign of the cross over her, but Scott did not do so. Instead, his face even more darkly suffused, he shouted aloft, 'What did You have to do that for? Why?'

Shelby called back down, 'What's that, Frank!'

Scott bawled, 'I wasn't speaking to you! Get out of the way and let my voice through.' And then he shouted, 'You! What need You did have for that poor creature? I'd have had them all safely up if You hadn't interfered!'

Rogo said, 'What the hell kind of a prayer is that?'

'What am I supposed to pray?' cried Scott, 'God save a soul snatched from her in another senseless killing?'

Rogo stared at him. 'What are you, looney? If you can't, let me.'

'I'm sorry,' Scott replied. He seemed to be in a daze. 'We'll pray together. God rest the soul of this woman and let her come unto Thee. In the name of Jesus Christ, Amen.'

Rogo repeated it. Then he said, 'We got to get her up.'

'Where? What for?'

Rogo's nerves were beginning to crack, 'Where... where? Where the hell do you think? Up there with us.'

'How will you do it?'

'Carry her, drag her, pull her. Whatdya wanna do, leave her spitted down here like a piece of meat? How'd I ever be able to shut my eyes again without seeing her?'

'Or your ears,' said Scott.

'You bastard!' Rogo said levelly, his little eyes glaring malevolently. 'For a guy who's supposed to be a minister you're the lousiest bastard I ever...'

'I'll carry her up,' Scott said.

Rogo stared at him, '*You* will.'

'Yes, you're strong, but you're not a good enough climber.'

'How will you get her up?'

'We'll tie her on to my back.'

Rogo said half to himself, 'You'd do it, too.'

'Yes, I will, if that's what you want.'

'But you don't think we oughta.'

'Do you? All the way along we have had to abandon the dead, the crippled or the weak for the sake of the living, when there was nothing further we could do for them.'

Rogo spat out, 'Like you did that Limey and his girl. They weren't dead or crippled.'

'Would you have wanted to die for a drunk who didn't have the guts to look after himself or the kid? Every minute we stay here may be the difference between life and death.'

Rogo's voice came as near to despair as he was capable. 'What did she have to die for?'

Scott's own voice rose almost to a shout, 'Nothing! Damn all! It's all wrong.'

'So you want me to leave her down here like she is?'

'It's up to you, Rogo.'

'Christ! What have you got inside you, anything?'

Scott looked from Rogo to the dead girl and then to Rogo again, and said sharply, 'This ship won't float for ever. I've pledged myself to get us out before she goes. Godammit, man, make up your mind!'

Rogo had a sudden incongruous memory of a newsreel he had seen of Scott when he was a college boy, travelling some nine yards with four men clinging to him to butt over a fifth and cross a goal line, his forward progress never checked. Maybe that was the way to bang away at getting people to church or God, or heaven, or out of a stricken ship alive. And Rogo remembered that once this Minister had got up off his knees in the dining-saloon, his forward progress had not been stopped either. True, fat old Belle Rosen had had to come to their rescue but the fact remained that she had, almost as though ordained. There was no single thing that Mike Rogo liked about the Reverend Frank Scott, but the guy had something. He was a winner.

The detective himself was a loner in courage, action and sheer guts, but he knew a leader when he saw one. Whether or not he was a homo, this guy had the power to rally. 'Okay,' he said nodding his head in the direction of the climb that faced them both, 'Let's go.'

As he watched Scott turning and edging around the wall again, finding the now familiar foot and handholds to begin the ascent, Rogo thought that something was suddenly missing from him; some bounce, some drive. His progress was slower almost as though his back *had* been burdened with the dead girl. The detective wondered whether Scott had gone first on purpose to leave him alone for a moment with what remained of Linda, or whether he just did not care and was letting Rogo find his way back up as best he could.

He turned for a last look at his wife. He had seen too many dead to be shocked by death itself, or the violence that can be done to the human body to turn it into the technical name of corpse. The sadness in him that was causing the tears to continue to flow was something else and it found expression at last in the words he addressed to the torn doll with its extruded sawdust soiling its body, 'Honeybun, if you only had knowed what a son-of-a-bitch I *ain't* bin...'

Then he too, recommenced the arduous climb to rejoin the others.

The survivors were strung out precariously, lying face down upon the height they had conquered, a narrow reversed catwalk above the propeller shaft. Suspended in the gloom over the chasm of that bottomless lake of oil and sea water below, they were so exhausted that their limbs trembled uncontrollably and because they had all hated, despised or loathed Linda, in one way or another their nerves and emotions were further harrowed by guilt feelings.

None of them dared look at Rogo. Scott's light passing over his face for a moment showed it as blankly expressionless as ever. If he knew or suspected their feelings in connection with the death of his wife, he gave no sign. He said, 'What next? Do you know what you're doing, or where we're going?'

Scott replied, 'Across to the other side. There's a platform there on which we can get our breath.'

Shelby cried, 'We can't cross in this condition, Frank. Can't you see that we're all at the end of our strength? We've got nothing left. You'd lose the rest of us.'

To their surprise for the first time Scott answered sharply, 'Cut out feeling sorry for yourself, Dick. You've only come part of the way. You're not home yet. We can't *not* cross. You can congratulate yourself when you get there. Right now this is no place to stop.'

Whether it was Shelby's accusing, '*You*'d lose the rest of us,' or the accumulation of the missing boy and the death of Linda, a change had come over Scott. He was angry. He had lost that serenity that had characterized his decisions, his manner of tackling what seemed like insurmountable obstacles. Yet that, too, seemed to have its values. For as simultaneously he robbed them of their sense of achievement, of having made this perilous ascent and gained an objective, he whipped them up to tackle another.

He knew that they were all thinking of what lay beneath them, the pit and the fallen girl and were remembering how wickedly the surface of that lake had mirrored their lanterns and torches. He said, 'It's not strength you need but willpower. If you knew there was a floor six inches beneath you, you'd walk across that thing blindfold. Well, I'm telling you there is a floor beneath you. Think it; believe it and nothing can happen to you. I'll take each of you across in turn.'

He did it then, unwaveringly. He had the balance and total fearlessness of a professional steelworker on a girder sixty storeys above the ground. To a man who had spent a night in howling gale, sleet and snow on a six-foot rock ledge on the side of an Andean mountain, with a sheer drop of seven thousand feet below, there was nothing for him to fear. One after the other he lifted them to their feet, placed his two hands on either side of their shoulders, the beam from the lantern strapped to his back lighting up the steel of the catwalk and marched them across; the men and the women. To prevent them from slipping, he said to each one, 'Don't try to walk. Just slide your feet. Look straight ahead. Once you're on the other side, the worst is over.'

He had them hypnotized; they went like sleep walkers, unable any longer to think of what lay below. Their minds were on the beckoning haven and the words he had connected with the broad platform: 'Safe', 'rest', 'worst will be over'.

To Miss Kinsale he said, 'You're a great girl'; to Susan, 'You're going to grow into a fine woman, like your mother,' and she thought to herself: *Will I? Will what I shall never be able to forget make me a better or worse person?*

Jane Shelby said, 'I'd rather you wouldn't touch me. I can go by myself. I'm not afraid.'

Scott placed his steadying hands to her shoulders. 'Jane, Jane!' he whispered. They set off and she was glad of the strong touch though it did not assuage her bitterness. Staring straight ahead as he had bidden her, she said, 'You promised me my boy.'

He answered, 'It isn't over yet. We don't know what yet lies in store for us, except that we shall meet it like men and women.'

Into Belle Rosen's ear Scott murmured, 'The W.S.A. was never like this.'

'Oh, my God!' she cried. 'Don't make me laugh now. You're a terrible man, Dr Scott, to make me do the things I done. I never would believe it.'

Kemal went over by himself. Scott walked Manny, Nonnie and Muller across and then went back for Rogo. The detective was standing up on the narrow walk in the dark and

Scott heard the click of his lantern snap on and saw the shaft of light directed downwards. 'Don't look there again,' he said.

Rogo paid no attention to the advice. His batteries were fading. His light now could hardly illuminate where the body hung impaled upon the silvery steel sliver.

'Put your light on her,' Rogo ordered harshly.

Scott obeyed and sent the brighter shaft of his own heavy lantern cutting into the gloom. It picked up detail; the blood that showed up so dark, the drained white face and staring eyes. Rogo asked, 'What was the idea? What for? Why did she have to go?'

Scott did not reply and Rogo felt his gorge rising in anger. He wanted an answer—something. There had to be one. Even if it was something foolish and futile like 'God's will', that was always being rattled at them by Father Moloney of the Broadway Tabernacle, when things went wrong: when Linda had lost the child she was going to have, or Rogo got into trouble for stepping on the corns of a big new shot New York politician. 'God's will, my son. Have faith and pray for understanding.' A distraction, a crutch, anything! This guy was a minister, and stood staring down at the corpse of his wife with not a single thing to say?

Eventually Scott did speak and this time there was something almost mechanical in his reply, as though what he said differed from what he was thinking or feeling. He muttered first, 'I don't know,' and then added, 'It was probably mercifully swift. She didn't suffer.'

Rogo said, 'She suffered death. Violent death hurts. When you see the faces of those that get it, you know.'

'Yes,' said Scott, 'I guess perhaps you do.'

'Go ahead,' Rogo said to Scott, 'I'll follow you. I can see okay.'

The Minister lit his way across to the others. Rogo found that he could think of nothing to say, but, 'God rest her soul,' even as he wondered what had become of that tortured thing. Had it already taken flight from that Purgatory to penetrate the iron hull above them and rise through the firmament to the angels? A vision passed through his mind for a moment to be rejected: Christ with the bleeding heart, golden saints with pearly halos, God on a cloud, majestic, bearded, and chromo-coloured. Holy pictures.

Heaven, or whatever 'up' was, consisted of a belt of gas, a mixture of nitrogen and oxygen surrounding the earth and above that was space through which the stars and the planets travelled aimlessly and endlessly to some mysterious and inexplicable design.

Rogo knew that he had never been much better than a half-ass Catholic, going to Mass, kneeling, genuflecting, dipping into Holy water, giving lip service to responses while other things would come floating up in his mind, things that had no business in church such as sometimes the two men he had shot in a gun duel at the corner of 6th Avenue and 47th Street, amidst an after-theatre, home-going crowd, killers who had drawn to shoot it out with him. In church amidst the music and the incense, the carved, wooden saints and the stained-glass windows he would see again how the neon sign of a restaurant had turned the nickel-plated pistol of one of them a glowing red. Rogo had fired two shots for their one, and that had finished it with never another person or innocent bystander injured. He had looked down at the bodies sprawled on their backs upon the pavement and the clay-grey faces unstained, since he had shot them through the heart, and thought to himself: *Dead is dead.* And it could have been the other way around with curious spectators gaping at the remains of Rogo, and that would have been that and no resurrection. The hole through his natty fedora hat had been sufficient to corroborate this.

So he said, 'God rest her soul,' once more and supposed what he meant was that he hoped that whatever was left of her would not be compelled to endure the agony of what her living had seemed to be like, that if nothing else, she would be allowed oblivion. Then withdrawing the shaft of light from the depths and focusing upon the steel pathway, he coolly walked across and joined the others.

'Rest,' Scott ordered and they flopped down upon the platform where they were with the exception of Shelby and the Minister.

The former asked, 'Where are we?'

Scott trained an examining finger of light to the four quarters, then to one side where something jutted out that looked like a gigantic cup, ten feet across and at least five feet deep. He asked Shelby, 'What does that look like to you?'

The motors man replied, 'Probably the turbine housing half broken away. You can see the bolts up above where it was fastened.'

'And that?' His light now travelled along a gleaming, polished, continuous cylinder some two feet in diameter. Above it, inverted, was another catwalk.

'That must be the propeller shaft,' added Shelby.

'Leading to the propeller shaft tunnel,' Scott concluded. 'At the end of that catwalk is the bottom of the ship. That's where we've got to get to.'

Shelby groaned. It was another twelve to fourteen feet above their heads. He said, 'How?'

The others sighed. 'Well,' Scott replied, 'there must have been steps or ladders, or a companionway going down to it when she was rightside up. There ought to be one going up there now.'

'And if there isn't?'

'Climb!' Scott said in a voice so curiously grim and hard-toned and unlike him that Shelby stared in amazement. He moved off, leaving Shelby standing there watching the wavering passage of his light overhead as he beamed it first this way and then that. He came back and said merely, 'It's there. It's half cut away, but we can tackle it.'

Without a moment of warning the platform on which they were all gathered gave a lurch, tumbling Scott and Shelby off their feet. From the depths of the ship arose a grinding, metallic screech of agony accompanied by great bubbling belches and distant internal rumblings.

The floor tilted momentarily at such an angle beneath them that frantically they all scrabbled for some kind of handhold, or clutched wildly at one another trying to brace themselves with their feet on the slippery surface. Muller experienced that same gone, sickening helplessness he had known once during an earthquake in Mexico.

The platform levelled again, though not wholly but the breaking-up noises continued. A huge, hot, stinking bubble burst from the pit below and from amidships came an explosion, one great thudding boom like the striking of a single note on the bass drum, followed by metallic cymballike clashings. Something had given way and the ship began to shudder and shake as though her engines once more were driving her at full speed. The tier tilted again, this time forward. The women screamed helplessly.

'Christ!' cried Rogo. 'She's going!'

'No, no, no!' yelled Scott, his voice high pitched verging on hysteria as he ran out to the centre of the slanting catwalk.

Rogo yelled, 'What the hell d'you think you're doing?' and Shelby shouted, 'Frank! For God's sake come back here!' He spotlighted the tall figure of the Minister bracing himself, legs apart, against the incline.

'No, no!' he shouted, 'I say no!'

They saw him raise his arms above his head and for that instant were too engrossed and distracted to think that death was at hand for all of them and the *Poseidon* poised for her final plunge.

'What do you want of me, God?' their leader bellowed, shaking his fists up at the dark over his head. All but nude, the lantern strapped to his back, the fire axe still bound about his middle, caught in the yellowing shafts of light he looked like some primitive tribal priest at invocation.

'What more do you want? I made you a promise. We've kept it. We haven't quit. We've never stopped trying, have we?' His powerful voice booming through the vast chamber produced an echo, '...v'we', that made itself heard over the apparent death rattle of the liner.

Scott's voice rose to a shriek, 'Why did you let us come so far, you bastard, if you're going to take us now? It's us who invented you. If it weren't for us, you wouldn't be! Jaweh! Marduk! Baal! Moloch! You're still the same old killer with the smell of blood in your nostrils!'

Martin shouted, 'He's off his rocker!'

Shelby found himself clutching Muller who said, 'We've got to get him off there.' They managed to climb to their knees. The shuddering steamer seemed to be in her last convulsions; the distant pounding increased in volume.

Shelby, his head swimming, his guts turned to water stammered, 'I c-can't go out there.' Muller said nothing and made no move himself.

Scott had to raise his voice still higher in pitch to make himself heard, 'Eater of babies!' he shrieked. 'Butcher of women! Slaughterer of men! You've already had the boy and the girl. What is it you want—another sacrifice? More blood? Another life?'

Over all the terrifying sounds of the ship's struggle rose the cry torn from Miss Kinsale, 'Dr Scott! No, please!' For of them all she was the only one who foresaw what he was going to do.

'Spare them! Take me!' bawled the Reverend Frank 'Buzz' Scott and threw himself into the pit below.

He fell limply, his body submissive and his still burning lantern marked an arc across the cavern of the engine room. Then man and light were extinguished beneath the surface of the lake to send up a fountain of oily water.

The survivors were aware that the sound of the splash had echoed hollowly but were not yet wholly cognizant of the reason they were able to hear it, which was that the other noises had abruptly ceased.

There was no longer the thudding from amidships or the awful shuddering and quaking of the vessel. Too, the angle of tilt had diminished and the platform to which they were all clinging, returned almost level with only a slight inclination towards the bow.

Shelby found his nerve, arose and moving to the edge shone down his light.

The waters of Hell Lake had risen higher, swallowing up the slope of what had been their approach to Mount Poseidon. There was turbulence and an uneasy stirring but Scott did not surface. Rogo, Muller and Martin came over and joined Shelby. The widening rings made by his plunge lapped up at the sides of the pit. There was a rushing of water pouring from some place and then that ceased, too. The ship lapsed once more into silence.

The epicentre of the rings showed where the body of the Minister had vanished but there was no sign of him. Shelby searched the surface of the waters. The silence was broken by a cry from Rogo, 'Christ, Linda's gone!'

It was true. The body of his wife impaled upon the triangle of steel was no longer there, nor was the staircase of the reduction gear wheel.

The conformity of Mount Poseidon had changed. Much of it had fallen away. Muller saw with half an eye that it was no longer climbable.

Rogo mumbled, 'She's gone after him.'

The ship steadied.

Shelby was shaking his head from side to side in wonderment. He repeated Scott's words, '"Spare them; take me."'

James Martin said in a voice filled with surprise, 'Well, what do you know, maybe it worked! It don't look like she's going to sink.'

From Miss Kinsale arose a long-drawn-out howl, half animal, half human; a wail from a breaking heart.

CHAPTER XX

The Top Sarge Takes Over

Jane Shelby went to Miss Kinsale who was kneeling, her rump in the air, her forehead knocking against the iron of the platform. 'Miss Kinsale, you mustn't! Oh, poor dear Miss Kinsale, please, please don't! I understand, but you mustn't.'

She took the woman in her arms but could only partly muffle the awful, 'Oh, oh, oh, oh, oh!'

Looking down upon the now placid, undisturbed surface of the lake, Shelby found himself thinking, *Why didn't he come up?* And immediately as he remembered Martin's remark, he came to the terrifying thought: *The pit is satisfied; the sacrifice has been accepted.*

Hubie Muller said, 'The goddam fool! Can't we get him up out of there?'

Martin said, 'He must have got hung up on something. Anyway, we can't either get down or back.'

Shelby felt suddenly as though he would go to pieces. He cried angrily, 'Jane, for God's sakes can't you stop that woman howling?'

She did not reply to him but addressed herself to the miserable person again, 'Dear Miss Kinsale, please try to stop. I understand. But he really believed he did it for us.'

Miss Kinsale buried her face in Jane's arms and moaned, 'I loved him! I loved him!' and wept.

Somehow her mourning of him was a mourning for all and released them from the tension and horror that had held them paralysed in its grip, so that they were able once more to think and see and even query and rationalize.

Belle said, 'What did he call God—a bastard? He called God a name and killed himself?'

Susan Shelby said, 'He must have been out of his mind.'

'He shouldn't have abused God,' Mrs Rosen insisted. 'Nobody likes being abused.'

Little Martin came back from the edge of the platform shaking his head. He said, 'He didn't have to do it. She ain't going to go.'

Rosen said, 'She ain't? For me, I said goodbye.'

Muller said, 'We seem to have levelled off again. The poor goddam fool, he really thought he was holding her up.'

To everyone's surprise Nonnie spoke up sharply, 'Well, wasn't he? He kept us going.'

Rogo queried, 'What was all those names he said? I didn't get it.'

Muller replied, 'Semitic names for God, or Gods. People-eaters—Assyrian, Babylonian —before the Jewish God. They liked human sacrifice.'

Martin said, 'It sounds crazy to me.'

Miss Kinsale's moaning had stilled somewhat and she lay quieter in Jane Shelby's arms. Belle Rosen said with some indignation, 'Our God isn't like that! When we Jews are good, He gives us milk and honey. When we're bad, we get it in the neck. Okay, so He loves us only when we're good. Just now the Egyptians got it in the neck.'

Manny Rosen remarked, 'But killing himself? And saying it's for us? This is a religion?' He suddenly realized what he had said and began to splutter, 'I'm sorry, I didn't mean that like it sounds. He was a good man.'

Susan put in, 'He really did believe, didn't he?'

Muller said gently, 'Maybe too much so. He was the kind of man who always had to win and then in the end he found himself competing in the wrong kind of game.'

Thereafter for the moment no one said anything and breaking the silence there was only the sound of Miss Kinsale's sobbing and Jane Shelby hushing her.

Martin asked, 'What about friend Kemal?' He turned to the figure of the Turk kneeling on the platform, calm and quite unfrightened. Of them all he was probably the best prepared to accept whatever should come but he shocked them by tapping his forehead with a finger to show what he thought of Scott's act.

Rosen asked, 'What happened with the ship? I don't understand.'

Shelby said, 'Something must have given way; maybe a bulkhead blew and changed the balance. She's probably too big to go all at once. A smaller one would have been finished long ago. The next time will be the last.'

Muller thought to himself: *And we've lost the man on whom we have all been depending like children.* And then he incongruously framed a tabloid-type headline: 'BUZZ SCOTT QUITS IN THE STRETCH.' Aloud he murmured, 'Why on earth did he do it?'

Rogo said, 'He couldn't take it. When he thought the game was up, he dogged it.'

Miss Kinsale had come to the end of her weeping and rebuked him dryly and primly as ever, 'He did not, Mr Rogo. He did what he thought his Father wished.'

Martin's voice: 'So then you all think we're finished?'

There was a long silence, then that of Shelby was heard, 'We might as well face it. It may only be a matter of minutes.'

Rogo's flat tone: 'Suits me.'

Then Belle Rosen's long, tired sigh: 'And me. The sooner it comes now, the quicker.'

Jane Shelby said, 'It seems such a waste after so much effort.'

Her husband added, 'We're all together. We might as well wait it out here as anywhere else.'

And then Martin's dry speech came again, 'We're not there yet.'

Shelby: 'Where?'

'Where he was trying to get us to. Up there at the top, over our heads. The bottom of the ship.'

Rogo said, 'He was off his rocker. I wish I never would have listened to him. Linda would be alive now.'

'Or both of you dead,' Martin said sharply. 'He may have been a weirdie, but he had the right idea and he had guts. Without him we'd never have got this far.'

Muller kept seeing his headline again and said, 'Until he quit on us. What good will it do us now, when the ship goes...?'

'I don't know about you,' Martin interrupted, 'but when the ship goes, I'm going to be up there where we were heading for. Maybe she won't go.'

Shelby laughed bitterly and said, 'That's a maybe in a million. Can't you feel her? She's hanging by a thread.'

Martin said quietly, 'I'll take the odds. Wasn't that Scott's idea? He never said we'd be rescued. He just said that if somebody came, we ought to be where they could get to us.'

And then they heard the haberdasher's dry chuckle. He said, 'Everybody's got some motive or other for wanting to survive. You'll probably think mine's nutty but I've got a new line coming into the shop in the middle of January, real 'with-it' stuff. You've got to cater for the kids today. My wife can't handle it. Arthritis. So you see, I've got to get back to dress those windows.'

It was the first time in many hours that any of them had thought of or been reminded of Martin's occupation. Rogo's voice heavy with sarcasm cut through, 'Brother, you've really got a lot to live for, ain't you?'

Martin's reply startled them. He said, 'I don't know about you, but there's no dying in me until my time comes.'

'You going it alone?'

Martin replied, 'Oh, I expect you'll all come along.'

Manny Rosen said, 'You heard my wife say she couldn't make another step.'

Martin replied, 'She said that before.'

Belle moaned, 'My heart's hurting me.'

From habit her husband began, 'Mamma, please, not with the heart again.'

Martin urged, 'We ought to have one more try. It isn't far any more. Scott said there was a ladder that could be reached.'

Why he did it, he did not know, but Muller clicked on his lantern and with its beams picked up the thin, grey insignificant countenance of Martin, who had raised himself to his knees.

Martin snapped, 'Put that out! We'll be needing it,' and then after a pause, his chuckle again, 'I know what you're all thinking. But what's so strange about a haberdasher not wanting to drown like a rat in a trap, if he can help it?' He paused again, then, 'Harry Truman did all right, didn't he? He started off selling socks, shirts and ties.'

Muller laughed and thought to himself, *Why, you little banty rooster!*

Susan was thinking: *Oh, Daddy, why couldn't you have taken over like that? The little man is going to make us go on.* And then immediately after; *But how could father, after the way mother's beaten him down? Why do people do such things to each other?*

Nonnie reached over to Muller and placed her lips close to his ear, so that her whisper would be heard by none but him. 'Let's not go. Let's just stay here and do it until we drown and die together. It doesn't hurt very much to drown, does it? I wouldn't care then.'

But the spark of hope had been blown upon again in Muller. 'No. Martin's right. You can't waste all that effort and trying and then lie down and quit.'

Martin rose to his feet. Almost automatically the others followed his example. Through their exhaustion and shock penetrated the fact that someone again was making decisions for them and they were relieved.

Belle asked, 'What am I doing?'

It was Shelby who in a rush of shame and self-accusation replied, 'What you've always done, Mrs Rosen, been the bravest of all of us.' For once the cliché rang true. There was a murmur of approval and Belle said, 'Na, na...'

Miss Kinsale had complete control of herself now. She said, 'We owe it to Dr Scott to go on. He died to save us.'

Rogo said under his breath, 'Nuts! He died because he went off his chump.' Then,

'They're both down there together now. She always had a letch for him.' And finally, 'Christ, why did she have to die like that?'

Manny Rosen said, 'I'm... we're sorry, Mike.'

Rogo said bitterly, 'Oh no, you're not. You hated her, all of you. Well, you're even. She hated all of your guts, and so do I.'

Martin asked quietly, 'Coming, Rogo?'

All emotion was again drained out of the reply. 'Could be.'

Jane compromised, 'I'll come if only for the chance that we might find my Robin. Frank was certain we'd find him—so certain.' Puzzlement came into her voice, 'Why was he so certain when...?' They heard her catch her breath and she said, 'He was only so certain because he was so sure he couldn't fail. But he could fail, couldn't he? And the knowledge that he had, that he had lost Robin and Linda killed him, didn't it?' She checked herself on the verge of breakdown again, brought herself under control and continued, 'I won't give up. We may still find him.'

'Ma'am,' counselled Rogo, his voice and attitude changing startlingly as the policeman once more took over, 'I wouldn't be putting up too much hope there now.' He had worked on too many kidnap and missing child cases during his career. As long as there was a bare chance, he would hold it out to a parent, but when in his bones he felt that something was over, that all they would someday stumble across would be a ravished, mangled, half-buried corpse, he felt it more humane and wise to extinguish that hope, to prepare them for what he knew must be the worst.

Jane curiously understood him and what he was trying to do. She said, 'You are a kind man, Mr Rogo. And I'm truly sorry about Linda. Deeply so. I don't think any of us ever understood her, or her troubles.' And then she added, 'But I will hope until there is no more hope.'

The white beam of Martin's big lantern was imperceptibly changing colour. 'Oh, oh,' he said, 'batteries beginning to go. Only one light at a time now.'

This gave them something to think about. They were even more afraid of the dark now, every one of them. They did not want to be enveloped by its thick, oily smell. Yet each quickly checked his or her light for an instant, just to see what strength was left, whether it too was diminishing and would soon be nothing but the faded yellow glow of the burnt out flashlight, hardly enough to illuminate a watch face.

Martin said, 'Well, now you know.' Many of them were considerably dimmer. Then he went on, 'If you want to come with me, I'll do the best I can for you. Scott will be a hard man to follow. I haven't got the stuff he had, but I know what he was out to do and where he wanted to go.'

He was a modest little man and it seemed suddenly such an imposition on his part to foist himself upon them that he felt called upon to justify the leadership. He began, 'You know, there were quite a few plain guys in the war, too; shoe salesmen, accountants, wrappers, shipping clerks, floorwalkers, soda-jerkers and the like.' Then the absurdity of what he was saying struck him and he chuckled again, 'However, so that you won't get any funny ideas about my trying to say I was a hero, I was in the quartermaster corps, handing out supplies.' Then after a slight pause he added, 'But I made top sergeant.'

Muller thought: *And I'll bet you were a little stinker.*

Rogo said, 'Let's go, if we're going.'

Beneath the strongest of the lantern beams they saw that the ladder or iron staircase Scott had found leading from the next to last platform to the plating of the double bottom of the vessel had been twisted around sideways offering a not too difficult climbing angle, except that the last five steps had been sheared off, leaving a gap about level with their heads. A man could take hold of the bottom and swing himself up. Above, at the top, the light showed the gleaming silver cylinder of the propeller shaft, the entrance to the tunnel and the reversed walkway of solid piping that followed it to the stern of the ship.

Linda was dead. Linda was no longer in their midst, but Linda had left some taint of a legacy of her cruelty with them all. Belle Rosen spoke up for herself in answer to the thought in one way or another crossing all their minds: *What are we going to do about the fat Jewess?* She said, 'If somebody will give me a boost up, maybe I could go the rest by myself. It looks like a regular stairs.'

Manny said, 'Sure you can, Mamma. I said it all the time.'

She seemed suddenly to have taken on a new lease of life, to have found some unexpected reserve of strength or even determination, probably due to the fact that the simplicity of the haberdasher and the things he talked about had taken much of the drama out of the final effort. She understood Martin better than she had Scott.

Martin tapped Kemal on the shoulder, pointing first up, then to Belle. The Turk understood at once, swung himself on to the staircase, mounted four steps, then reached down with one arm free.

Martin ordered, 'Okay, fellers!' Then to Belle, 'Put your hands on our shoulders when we lift, then grab Kemal. You'll go up like in an express elevator.'

He, with Rosen, Shelby and Muller each secured a grip on Belle's legs and thighs and heaved upwards. She rose from their midst like a grotesque caricature of an adagio dancer. She even managed to struggle around the end of the reversed companionway to gain what had once been the ceiling of the propeller shaft tunnel and was now the flooring. These were the carriers that served the electro-hydraulic system controlling the 40-ton rudder. The shaft itself was higher up, at shoulder level and a few feet above it now forming a roof was the steel catwalk used by engine-room hands to patrol the length of the tunnel to check and service the bearings of the shaft. Slightly higher than this was the plating of the double bottom of the ship which when she was rightside-up formed fuel or ballast tanks.

When she had got her breath Belle called down, 'See, like I said, with a boost up anybody can do it. You got no more worries.' But then of a sudden she gave a gasp and a cry.

Rosen beamed his fading torch up the steps and cried, 'Mamma, what is it? Have you hurt yourself?'

The reply was a few moments in coming. 'It's... It's what Dr Metzger said... is nothing. So... you shouldn't worry.'

Rosen lowered his voice but it had an embarrassed note as he said to the others, 'Mamma—I mean, my wife—for thirty years has been thinking she's got a heart, on account of having been an athlete and then getting fat. You know, 'athlete's heart'. But the doctor always said...'

Muller interrupted, 'She's been through a terrible ordeal, Mr. Rosen.'

Martin simply said, 'Next!'

Nonnie begged, 'Let me go, I could look after her a little.'

They shot the dancer aloft and heard her murmuring to Belle. Jane cried, 'Is she all right?'

'She's breathing a little better,' Nonnie reported. 'I'm massaging her. She's fab, really.'

'Miss Kinsale.'

She came trotting forward, lifting her arms to facilitate their gripping her. Her body was too bony and unrounded to be feminine, her breasts small and undeveloped by love. But the long sweep of the dark hair away and down from the angular face made her so momentarily striking that Shelby found himself suddenly stirred and desirous of the excitement of awakening her. He wondered why she had never married. In the darkness he flushed at the memory of his wife's outburst against him, *You didn't even have the guts to have a mistress or crawl into bed with somebody else's wife for the sheer lark of it.*

In one vengeful movie reel that spun through the projector of his mind, he seduced Miss Kinsale to show Jane, burying his face in her hair, set her up in an apartment in Detroit and visited her there regularly as his mistress. But with the touch of her hard, fleshless hip against his hand the moment passed and he wondered at himself that he had ever considered such a thing.

They sent her flying like a woods' dryad up to Kemal. The rest followed.

Now that they were actively engaged in doing something, no one thought of the ship going down. It was as though by their decision to go on with Martin and see the journey through, they were winning her and themselves some sort of reprieve.

Jane Shelby went to the mouth of the tunnel and called into it, 'Robin—Robin, are you there?' Simultaneously Muller threw the light of his lantern into it.

There was no one to be seen. There was no reply, no human voice. From somewhere a tortured part of the ship creaked and groaned.

Martin said, 'Let me have a look,' and marched a few yards down the tunnel. He came back and said, 'I get it. If we follow the propeller shaft, we ought to come to her skin. Those stewards said the double bottom didn't extend the full length of the ship either front or back. We'll go down here until we find it. But look out, the footing's rotten.'

They paired off, Martin leading with Miss Kinsale, then Rosen with Belle, Kemal with Jane, Shelby with his daughter Muller and Nonnie and Rogo, as usual, bringing up the rear.

There were three of the large lanterns left. Martin allowed only one to be used to light the way ahead and show up the irregularities of the flooring. They moved along silently now, too tired to speak, too numbed even to think about what had happened since they had gone to lunch the day before and been welcomed to the Strong Stomach Club by Mr Rosen.

Muller, grasping Nonnie's hand and arm tightly, marvelled at the adaptability of men and women, what horrors and privations they could endure and still hope and strive and even talk almost like normal human beings. Without warning their ship had rolled over and people were killed before their eyes. A son was missing; a girl they had known was dead. Two of the party that had set out with them were probably drowned by now. A stewardess had been trampled to death. Walking on those eternally slippery pipes underfoot, they had passed men with broken backs and legs, seen fragments of humans hanging from the projections of the steel mountain they had climbed. They had looked on as the Reverend Frank Scott, cursing, blaspheming and miscalling his God, had hurled himself into eternity via the black pit they had named the Lake of Hell. And he, Hubie Muller, had fallen in love with a dancing girl and the touch of her filled him still with that strange elation compounded of passion and compassion.

Susan, as she walked by her father, sore, bruised, heavy-hearted, wondered again what he would say or think or feel if she were to tell him what had happened to her. She knew that in his lexicon rape was the most bestial and terrible of crimes. Men went to prison, were electrocuted or gassed to death for committing it. She saw once more the pink curve of the young sailor's cheek and found her eyes suddenly wet with tears. What would she have done, what would have happened to him had he not run away? She had been violated but for one moment they had been close, brought together by fear and pity.

'Martin,' her father suddenly called out sharply, 'Hold it!'

They came to a halt and the leader's voice drifted back, 'What's up?'

'The tunnel's closing in on us,' Shelby said. 'It's getting lower and narrower, too.' He had been the first to notice it because he was a head taller than Martin.

'Lord!' said Muller. 'What do we do?'

'Crawl on our hands and knees if we have to,' Martin replied savagely. He had taken over the leadership not because he wanted to, but because no one else had offered and he did not want to die. But he could not escape the feeling that already he had blundered somehow and that he was leading them into disaster.

The narrowing became more marked. Martin said, 'Let the girls wait here. Rosen, you stay with them. The rest of us will go on up ahead and see what gives.'

They crawled now, another ten yards, on their stomachs until forward progress was brought to an end once and for all by the great steel collar filling the whole of the tunnel through which the shaft passed. Over their heads the lights still showed the plating of the double bottom. They had come to the inside of the thrust block of the propeller against which it pushed to drive the ship forward.

Martin was almost childlike in his disappointment, 'It ain't like they said it would be.'

Rogo behind him said, 'Dead end again. Christ, you're as good as Scott!'

Martin's thin lips split into his mirthless grin, 'Thanks, Rogo! You've been a great help all the way. "What do we do now, coach?" What the hell am I trying to save you for? So you can go back on your beat and belt some more poor bastards.'

Rogo's truculence rose immediately, 'Look, don't start any trouble, sucker.'

Martin laughed now, 'You haven't got room to swing here copper. So Scott was wrong, and this is the end of the line. You got any better ideas?'

They started to back out of the tunnel. When there was room, Kemal tapped Martin on the shoulder and gestured. Martin shook his head. 'No good, Kemal. Napoo! Finish!'

But the Turk too, shook his head and was insistent with his gestures, so that they were compelled to watch him.

First he made a revolving motion with his index finger. Then he held up four fingers, and looked around to see whether there was comprehension. Next he showed them two and with both hands indicated the left side and repeated the pantomime for the right side.

Muller murmured, 'Four, split up into twos...'

Now Kemal, his eyes burning with concentration as he willed them to understand what he was trying to tell them, made another shift of the position of his hands. He moved one forward so that the grimy blackened nails came just to the wrist of the other.

Startlingly, Shelby cried, 'I've got it! We're in the wrong tunnel!'

Martin said, 'What do you mean? I don't get it. What difference does it make?'

'It's what he was trying to tell us.' He imitated Kemal's revolving finger and then the show of four. 'The ship has quadruple screws, two of them on a side, that is, either side of the rudder.'

Rogo was still smarting at having had the wind taken out of his sails by a shrimp of an ex-sergeant who had won the war handing out uniforms, or checking up stock in the PX. He said, 'So what does that get us? We're in the same jam in any other tunnel.'

'No,' Shelby said excitedly, 'that's the last thing he was trying to tell us by the position of his hands. The propellers aren't in a line. One is set forward of the other on each side of the hull. We're in the tunnel which doesn't go beyond the double bottom.'

Muller was catching on. 'Then Peters and Acre would be right. The second one would be set farther aft...'

'Exactly!' said Shelby. 'The other shaft tunnel ought to extend out beyond the double bottom and towards the rudder and the skin of the ship.'

Martin said briefly, 'You don't learn things like that selling socks. Let's go. Do you want to take over, Rogo?'

The detective smiled crookedly on one side of his face, 'Sorry, Sarge,' he said, 'I talked out of turn.'

Muller said, 'How do we find the other tunnel?'

Shelby indicated Kemal, 'He'd know.' He held up two fingers to the Turk who nodded, delighted that he had been understood, and beckoned them to follow him.

Rogo said, 'Why didn't the dope tell us we were in the wrong tunnel in the first place?'

Muller replied briefly, 'The ship's turned upside-down for him, too.' The light of the lantern flickered and turned a darker shade of yellow.

'Oh, lord! The batteries,' Martin said, 'we've been wasting them.'

The four crawled back until they could walk upright again. When they reached the others Manny Rosen asked excitedly, 'What happened? Some trouble? We can't go on? I heard...'

Martin came to the point, 'Sorry, I boobed. There are two tunnels like this. I picked the wrong one. We've got to get to the other, Kemal thinks he knows the way.'

Jane Shelby moaned, 'I had given up for Robin. If there's another tunnel, must I hope all over again?' She began to cry softly.

Susan put her arms around her and comforted, 'Oh, Mummy...'

Manny said with heat, 'You want my wife now to be walking all the way back again?' And then, 'God knows what else we shall have to do, like acrobats. What do you expect?'

Martin said, 'I don't expect anything. I'm just telling you what happened. There's still a double bottom between us and the outside world—if there still is any such thing. Shelby can explain it better than I. If we stay here, we might as well be back in the dining-room again, for all the good it will do us.'

Belle Rosen had slumped down on to the floor. Even in the spare use they were making now of their torchlight, they could see how grey her whitish skin had become, and the trembling of her limbs. Her voice had changed to a hoarse whisper as she asked, 'In God's name, what is it you want we should do now? Climbing any more I couldn't.'

Miss Kinsale spoke up, 'We must go on, Mrs Rosen. You wouldn't want Dr Scott to have died for us in vain.'

'Dr Scott went his way,' Belle said, 'why couldn't you let me go mine, now, in peace?'

Rogo refrained from repeating his opinion of the Minister's sacrifice. Instead he said, 'Don't forget you were Belle Zimmerman, the champ, once and the newspapers said you were the greatest. Like Shelby said, when it comes to moxie, you got us all beat, Belle. You'd feel like an awful sap if they came knocking at your door, and you were out.'

Martin said, 'There won't be any more climbing. We're at the top now, just in the wrong spot. The batteries of our lights are running down and the air here ain't any too good to breathe any more. Maybe it's our last chance.'

Nonnie said, 'Are you going to make that poor woman move again? It's cruelty! Can't you see she's had it? And I've bloody well had it too. I don't want to go any more, Hubie, hold me!'

The 'bloody' caused Muller to shudder for an instant, to be replaced by a renewed rush of affection. Whatever she was, Nonnie had been a little fighter all her life. He did not want to see her give up now. But what he did want, with a sudden desperation, was to bring her forth into the sunlight again; to keep her at his side, dress her, love her, give her things, cherish her, in some way repay for the mystery of what she had given him.

'I ain't any poor woman,' croaked Belle Rosen. 'Help me up, Manny.'

Kemal hurried on ahead with Martin following. One of the big lamps from the fire station still gave a good light. When they came out of the tunnel the Turk, flashing it about, suddenly cried, 'Hoi! Good! Hokay!'

'Oh brother,' breathed Martin fervently, 'manna from heaven.'

A gap of some twenty feet separated the two parallel, port-side propeller shafts. What they saw was that a companionway originally leading up to the next platform had been wrenched loose and had fallen, handrail and all across the chasm, bridging the two.

'Christ, a break!' Rogo said.

'Piece of cake!' Muller cried, and then wished he hadn't.

This had been Scott's rallying phrase. He didn't want to think of Scott. 'Come on, Nonnie!'

Martin said, 'Better let me test it first. Light me across, Muller. If it's okay, the rest of you can come over.'

The steps were resting solidly, the handrail was firm, the passage called only for care that one's feet should not slip down between the rows of steps. But Martin wanted to see what lay at the other end.

When he reached the second propeller shaft and saw what had happened, he laughed first and then for a moment was blindly angry at this last joke played on them by whichever God it was Scott had cursed. For the first time he had an understanding of what it could have been that had led the Minister to throw himself away. The propeller shaft leading from the shattered turbine housing entered the tunnel some twelve feet or so to his left but there was no bridge, except for the cylinder itself. The original connecting catwalk had been ripped loose from its moorings when the reduction gearing had torn away and carried with it into the pit below.

He remained there so long without summoning them that Rogo and Shelby came across to look. The detective said, 'Jesus!' between his teeth.

Martin turned on him, 'If you say "What do we do now, coach," I'll kill you!'

'I ain't saying nothin',' Rogo said. 'It's your baby. You asked for it.'

Shelby had himself a look and breathed, 'My God, what are we going to do?'

Something seemed to swell inside Martin and raise him up ten feet tall, whether it was wrath or the combat of cocky aggressiveness of little men, and he said, 'Straddle it.'

They looked at him aghast and Shelby said, 'Belle!'

'We don't tell her,' snapped Martin. 'We hustle her between you and Kemal and she'll be across before she knows it.' He raised his voice, 'Okay, everybody, come on over.'

He stood at the bridgehead, a grotesque little figure in his begrimed striped shorts and suddenly before their eyes he turned into a carnival barker reeling off his spiel. 'Hurry, hurry, hurry!' he shouted. 'Come one, come all! Martin's Rodeo Thrill Ride! They all love it! Step right up and bring the little lady. Chance to hug your sweetheart. Get your tickets for the Rodeo Ride! Everybody on! Everybody gets a chance! Here we go!!!'

It was the surprise that did it, the not having time to think, the utter absurdity and incongruity of being snatched in spirit and body from the charnel house to something remembered by all from childhood, the fun fair, the amusement park, the carnival rides. Martin had clouted Kemal on the shoulder and pushed him astraddle on to the shaft and then with Shelby seized and hustled Belle forward, eased her down so that her legs fell into position with Shelby behind her.

Belle had only time to gasp, 'What are you doing with me?' before she was being edged onwards.

'That's the girl!' crowed Martin, 'Now you're away for the big thrill ride. You're headin' for the last roundup. Grab the brass ring and get a free trip. Come on, who's next? Step up! One at a time! Miss Kinsale, that's the girl! Right here. Jane—Susan. You too, sir?' This to Manny, 'Slide down right here.' Then to Muller, 'Come on, mister, and bring your girl with you. Off you go! Keep moving, up front!'

Then, lowering his voice, he said, 'Rogo, you light us across and for Christ's sweet sake don't let them see what's below.'

'Hind tit for Rogo, again,' said the detective.

Martin laughed and said, 'You've got to be good for something,' and himself dropped on to the shaft. Then he whooped it up again, slapping the steel with the palm of his hand. 'Ride 'em, cowboys! Yippee-yi-yay! Give 'em the spurs, my buckaroos!'

Whether or not they thought that like Scott he had gone out of his mind, he had them and it was all over before they realized what was happening to them. The ballyhoo, the rhythm and movement he had initiated with someone always pressing from behind had whipped them up to make the crossing.

Martin continued to pepper them along. 'Atta-girl, Jane! How's old Belle doing up ahead? Only a dime for the next Rodeo Thrill if anybody wants to stay on. Move right along! Last one off's a sissy.'

Kemal had already reached the other side, leaped off where the shaft entered the mouth of the tunnel and swung Belle Rosen to her feet and inside. Then one after another he caught the others as they came inching along and snatched them to safety.

Rogo had remained standing on the bridge-end, keeping the light steady. Now he turned its beam downwards.

'Rogo!' Martin called, 'Come on!'

The detective seemed transfixed momentarily at the height showed by the beam and the deathbed of shattered machinery awaiting him below. He mocked Martin, saying, 'Last man across is a sissy!' and then, 'She's down there with him,' and he approached the unguarded edge of the bridgehead.

Martin called across again, but softly this time and in imitation of the voice of a queer, 'Why Miss Rogo, what the hell do you think you're going to do, dearie?' And after that he cried sharply, 'Everybody's heard of Mike Rogo, the tough cop. Do you want them saying he was nothing but a yellow bastard?'

The stocky little man wavered on the brink for another instant, then pulled himself back and gripped the railing. A moment later he said in his usual flat monotone, 'Yeah, maybe I guess you're right.' He straddled the shaft and worked his way across. Martin reached out his hand and pulled him into the tunnel. Rogo said, 'I ought to bust you one. It could have been all over.'

Martin grinned his dry grin, 'Pick on someone your size.'

Jane had already advanced a slight distance down the tunnel and was calling, 'Robin! Robin! Are you there, Robin?' Her voice echoing was the only reply.

Muller said to Nonnie, 'Did you notice anything?'

'What?'

'The echo was different than from the other tunnel.'

CHAPTER XXI

Under the Skin

None of them would have been able to tell what each had expected the goal would be like when attained. They only knew that collectively and individually, they were bitterly disappointed when the roof which formerly had been the floor of the tunnel suddenly opened and they found themselves looking upwards above the propeller shaft at a cavern crisscrossed by flat steel bracing and square baulks.

The top of this space showed steel plates, but the rivets that held them together were of another kind than those in the double bottom; twice the size and the spacing was not the same.

With a grunt of satisfaction, Kemal had pointed at this ugly conglomeration and then had sat down crosslegged. They were there.

They sat or kneeled, or collapsed upon the inevitable rows of piping, drained of everything but frustration at what had been almost childish dreams of reward that would await them at the end of the journey.

Seduced by their sufferings during the long climb, even the most realistic amongst them had succumbed to the illusion that courage, pain, endurance and refusal to give up no matter what the obstacles encountered must invariably and immediately be rewarded. In Scott they had followed each a kind of image of the hero who crashes through to victory to deafening cheers and is carried off on the shoulders of his comrades. Even Rogo had cynically accepted Scott's leadership because he was a winner.

They had deserved, they felt, to find the hull of the vessel already pierced and some kind of reception committee awaiting to congratulate them upon their feat and carry them to safety. Their ultimate destination as phrased by Scott and then oft repeated, 'the skin of the ship', had made them think of something smooth and regular, enamelled and white, or even a special room or enclosure dedicated to the separation of their floating hotel from the encroachment of the sea.

But this awkward confused and confusing space numbed and defeated them, sapping their hopes and spirits. The steel girders were rusty, the pipes were painted terracotta, the baulks seemed to have been flung helter-skelter and to no particular purpose. The cavity was no more than five or six yards in length. Thereafter, the tunnel narrowed again, as had the other, until the propeller shaft met the internal collar of the thrust block. Beyond that would be the thirty-two ton screw and the gigantic blade of the rudder.

Now that at last they were there, the disappointment was deep and they felt filled with grief and tears.

Martin, with the sinking sensation at the pit of his stomach that he had failed again, that this ugly arrangement of space could not possibly be their final destination, shone his torch upon Kemal and asked, 'Are you sure?'

The Turk nodded affirmatively with vigour, pointed into the cavity, then gave the thumbs-up sign and said, 'Hokay! Hokay! Hokay!' and further pantomimed by first holding hands apart, as he had to signal the double bottom to them, and then bringing the palms pressed close together and holding up a single finger again.

Muller nodded, 'He's saying that's it, all right. We've made it.'

Nobody said anything until Manny Rosen broke the silence with, 'Maybe they been and gone away already.'

Martin groaned, 'Oh Lord, don't say that!'

Susan asked, 'What time is it?' She was remembering that Robin had told her of aircraft flying overhead and what would happen if they sighted an unidentified object in the sea below. But if it were still dark outside...

Their watches had all stopped at differing times. The latest, Rogo's, said five minutes to four.

'Hell!' said Muller, looking at his own dead disc. 'How will we ever know what time it was and where we were the last time we looked, when they were working?'

Shelby said, 'It was half-way up Mount Poseidon. Martin said it was a quarter to three.'

Rosen asked, 'How long could we have been?'

Muller said, 'I don't know, I've lost track. One hour—two? Maybe less, maybe more.'

Rosen said, 'Then somebody *could* have already come and gone away.'

Shelby said, 'I don't believe it. I think it's probably still dark. The sun was just coming up the time we stayed 'til morning, after the costume ball.'

Muller said, 'We'd have heard something even in the other tunnel.'

'That's right,' Martin agreed. 'Don't scare me like that, Rosen. We may have a long wait ahead of us. Lights out, everybody.'

Rogo asked, 'Why, what difference does it make now? We won't be needing them any more.' He had once without hesitation gone into a pitch black cellar after a gunman, hunted him down and shot him by his breathing. But he did not want to be in the dark now.

'We might,' Martin replied. 'You never know. Besides which, maybe some of us could get a little sleep.'

Sleep! The word startled them into forgotten thoughts and ideas as had Shelby's mention of the costume ball, that long-ago rout of makeshift get-ups, second-rate dance jazz, champagne at excise-free prices, paper hats, false moustaches and noses, noise-makers, confetti and cotton balls to throw at one another. Not once had the thought of sleep crossed their minds since they had been sent flying into the world of upside-down. Sleep was something one did tucked up in a bed with a pillow under one's head and a book in hand to make one drowsy. For sleep one retired to one's cabin when there was no more fun, excitement or ecstasy to be squeezed out of the night or the early morning.

Rosen asked, 'Supposing somebody comes while we're all sleeping?'

Martin replied, 'We'll divide up into watches. I'll take the first, 'til I get tired. If we can get some rest we'll be in better shape for whatever happens.'

The darkness enveloped them again and the stifling heat and airlessness, the feeling of having already entered the tomb, of being buried alive with no one to hear their cries for help.

Shelby whispered to Muller, 'What do you think of our chances?'

Muller replied, 'Rotten!'

'Why?'

'It's two to one against. Sink, or smother to death? She's already given one lurch that nearly finished her off. Scott was convinced that she was going. The next time she will. There's no fresh air circulating. We're using up oxygen. That's why Martin doesn't want us moving about. He's right. We're above water, but to all intents and purposes it's like being trapped in a sunken submarine. The chances of being spotted from the air depend upon whether we are floating in an air-lane and at what hour a plane might fly over us. A sea search is more likely to find us if they have an approximate idea of our position and the nature of the catastrophe that turned us over. But it takes hours for ships to divert from course and reach the scene of a disaster.' He added, 'You know, actually, I was never wholly comfortable with the name they gave this tub when they converted her from the R.M.S. *Atlantis*. I've crossed seven times in her in the old days, on the Atlantic run. Do you know who Poseidon was?'

'Some kind of God.'

'He was the Greek God of earthquakes and water and only secondarily of the sea. One of his most significant titles in Greek was "Earthshaker". He was one of the Gods Scott forgot to curse before he did himself in.'

'Then you think that all we've gone through to get here was for nothing?'

'I've always thought so. Haven't you?'

Shelby reflected. He said, 'I don't know. Perhaps. Then what did we do it for? Why put ourselves through all that struggle and anguish? My... Robin might still be with us if we hadn't.'

Muller said, 'Because even an animal will fight to get out of a trap. Whether we live or die, we haven't taken it lying down.'

Shelby asked, 'What about those that remained behind in the dining-saloon, waiting for officers to come and tell them what to do? Or just waiting, doing nothing?'

Shelby could not see, but he felt Muller's shrug. 'They didn't believe Scott. We did. We're human, but there's a lot of sheep left in all of us.'

'What was your opinion of Scott?'

'A looney,' Muller replied, 'crazy as a bedbug.'

'Are you serious?'

'What else? A young fellow from a rich family whose name is a household word in the world of sport, throws it all over, signs on as a parson and goes to his death calling God dirty names because this was one he thought he wasn't going to win? What was he doing on this cruise all by himself, anyway?'

Shelby said, 'I think you've got it all wrong, Muller. As an ex-football player myself, I have always been a great admirer of Scott. I got to know him rather well on this voyage. He was deeply earnest about his profession. He had felt the call.'

'In this day and age?' Muller scoffed, 'Oh, come on, Dick! By the way, did you know that he had been in some kind of trouble in New York?'

Shelby was glad that the darkness hid the fact that the question had disconcerted him. 'No, I didn't. What kind of trouble?'

Muller said, 'I don't know, it's not my home town either. But there was some kind of gossip going around the ship that he was fired or forced to resign or something.'

Nonnie said, 'What are you two whispering about? I thought we were supposed to sleep.'

'About life and death and the Reverend Scott. I'll whisper to you now.' He crept closer to her so that the others would not hear. 'Do you know what I would ask him to do if he were here with us now?'

'No, what?'

'Marry us.'

He heard her quick catch of breath. 'Marry us? Marry *me*?'

'If you had no serious objections.'

'Hubie!' Although she was whispering too, he heard agony. 'Don't pull me leg. I don't want to be hurt.'

'I wouldn't want to hurt you, Nonnie.'

'Do you know what you're saying? Do you know what marry means—always staying together—putting up? You're a man of the world.' She was struggling, 'And it's not *my* world. I'm not anybody; I haven't had...' She was so desperately trying to show him the gap between them that her shrewdness and experience warned her would never be bridged, 'I don't know anything. You'd be ashamed.'

Muller thought to himself: *You are right, my dear love, I would and I will.* But aloud he said, 'I'll let you in on a secret, Nonnie. I'm nobody either, only less so than you who work hard for your living and fight for everything you have or get. I'm just an educated bum. You would be lowering yourself, as Mrs Rogo always kept reminding her husband she had done. But you wouldn't remind me, would you?'

He had to tell it to her with banter that he loved her and never again wanted to be without her, else the new found emotions struggling against his intellect and his old habits would have overwhelmed him. But his lightness frayed her nerves, because neither had she ever truly loved before, or understood its sweetness, its longing, its anguish and its terrors.

She said with sudden bitterness, 'You can talk. Scott isn't with us. And besides, you think we're going to die. I heard something of what you and Shelby were saying. You don't have to be kind to me. I never ast you.'

There was that shattering commonness of speech again. Negating it was his overwhelming tenderness and need for this one strange, indeed, out of his world, person.

He said, 'No, Nonnie. Perhaps we're to die, perhaps we're to be let out of here just to spite the idiocy of Scott's end or, as Miss Kinsale devoutly believes, because of it. Well, then there's a globe full of Licence Bureaux and Scotts of every known faith. You can choose, Catholic, Protestant, Jew, Moslem, Hindu, Parsee, Shinto, Buddhist, Medicine Man; I'll stand before any of them with you and make my vows to cherish you into eternity, or as long as I have breath to carry them out.'

And now that he had said it, now that it was certain he was making the biggest mistake of his life, now that he had made a promise from which he would as a gentleman never withdraw, the anxiety within him subsided and he felt happy and at peace.

If she did not understand the full import of his words, his sincerity penetrated, 'Do you really mean it, Hubie!'

'Really, Nonnie.'

In the darkness she moved nearer to him and put her cheek to his chest. She said only, 'Let me cry close to you.'

There were more whisperings and movement in the area of the shaft the survivors of the party had pre-empted. The tube of the tunnel acted like a sounding board to conduct every noise of the ship, for since her last shift and disposition she had never again been wholly silent, grumbling and muttering to herself. There were distant thumps and rumblings, some of them curiously repetitive as though something loose was sliding or rolling back and forth. Occasionally there would be a different and louder noise, metallic or aqueous, a ringing, or a running of water.

Weary as they were, these noises had them sitting up, or leaning on an elbow to listen with alarm. Along with the heat, the fetid air and the beds of torture on which they lay, they made sleep impossible.

Martin's voice came to them out of the darkness, 'I guess that was a screwy idea of mine. We won't be able to sleep. Well then, we might as well talk.'

But none of them seemed disposed to talk either, at least no one replied to his invitation. The little man, however, was aware from his own feelings of the disappointment and let down that something was needed, if not to bolster their spirits, to keep their minds occupied, lest life, or the desire to live it should ebb. As their oxygen would diminish the struggle to survive was far from over.

During a momentary hiatus in the ever alarming bubbling and clankings of the distant parts of the stricken vessel, Martin said, 'Do you know what will be funny about all this if we get out?'

Rogo said, heavily sarcastic, '*Funny!*'

'We're nobody.'

From Muller's section, 'What do you mean we're nobody?'

'Who is nobody?' This was Manny Rosen.

'Us. All of us. Nobody important. Who are we, any of us? What would it matter if we didn't get out? What difference will it make?'

Miss Kinsale's voice was a sibilant and slightly outraged whisper. 'How can you, Mr Martin? Aren't we all God's children?'

'What about all His children down below, already knocked off wholesale?' Muller contributed.

'We aren't even a cross section of anything to stock a survival ark with,' Martin said, 'you know, "Rich man, poor man, beggarman, thief, doctor, lawyer, merchant, chief."' His dry chuckle was heard, 'Unless you count James J. Martin, Proprietor of Elite Haberdashery, Evanston, Illinois, purveyor of men's furnishings and accessories as the merchant. And that's a laugh. We sell caps to match those knitted covers for the heads of your wooden golf clubs... Big deal.'

Nobody laughed.

For an insignificant man who rarely spoke, Martin could open the floodgates of speech when he got going.

He was off now, partly to divert the people he had taken into his charge, partly because he had been thinking, and in the dark no one could see him. He was just a disembodied voice like the rest of them. 'I'll bet you don't know half who some of the people are we've had on board, outside of the Senator and that Harvard Professor and his family, because he got his name in the papers for discovering something, and that retired ham actor who used to be a matinée idol. I took the trouble to find out. I promised my wife that I'd keep a diary so that I could tell her everything about the trip. Hell!'

He fell silent for a moment while they waited. 'It's down in my cabin along with all the movie film I took to show her when I got back. Oh well.'

The sinking feeling, the hot flushes of guilt and shame were back at him again.

'So who were they?' Rosen asked. 'We met a lot of nice people.'

'Like in the rhyme, "Rich men, poor men... lawyers."' Martin had found his voice again, 'Stockbrokers, a band leader who had been a roller skating champion once; a half-dozen presidents or vice presidents of corporations, English and American and a big German paper manufacturer; there's a feller calls himself Master of Trinity Hall at Cambridge, I guess that's some kind of teacher, a couple of Sirs, a London taxi-driver and his wife, a saw-mill manager, a guy who runs a big hotel in Waukeegan, another who manufactures surgical instruments; the chairman of a football club, or whatever they call it from Leeds, a couple of writers, an illustrator, a bank teller, a guy who owns a hair dryer factory, trained nurses, advertising executives, television producers, salesmen, you name 'em, we've had 'em.'

Martin had brought back something that had seemed to have happened eons ago, the cruise.

They had forgotten that the lazy shipboard days, dances and parties and the novel and exciting shore trips had ever existed, or the people who had participated in them as well as themselves. One couldn't know, meet or cultivate everyone on such a voyage; one formed friendships, little groups or cliques with common interests who went around together, sat in the smoking-room after dinner, played cards, or gossiped and made up their excursions in the same manner.

But it was these last rather than the shipboard life that Martin was calling to mind, because they were always running into other groups formed in the same manner, bar-gaining in shops or street markets, sitting at sidewalk cafés, arguing with taxi-drivers, entering the same night clubs to drink bad whisky and see tatty shows, trying to make themselves understood by natives.

One had a bowing, or greeting acquaintance with all these without ever knowing who they really were, or what they did. But each of the survivors retained snatches of memories of their shore trips: Rock apes in Gibraltar that snatched off the postiche of an animal-loving wife of one of the passengers; the souvenir shops, one next another, in Sierra Leone selling doubtful ivory curios; the very dark officials and policemen uniformed in dazzling white; the open market with Africans chattering like monkeys in the medina outside Dacca and the beautiful textiles and hand-embroidered shawls they had acquired in the Syrian quarters there, and the scrambling for fake African carvings in Monrovia.

They could recall the pounding of the samba and carioca rhythms that was Rio, the dinning of Trinidad's steel bands and the cheap thrill of walking through Recife's red light district with each house or crib showing a madonna or bleeding heart nailed over the door.

They had not got to know one another well but their shapes and sizes had become familiar particularly in that last rout of a shopping spree in Curaçao. The closest they had come to fraternizing was in the all-out Christmas party and dance when the various cliques had broken their perimeters. Now that Martin brought them and the days past to mind, they could remember hardly any of them wholly. They had become relegated to faceless characters, passers-by in the never-ending walkathon around the promenade deck.

Rogo asked, 'So what are you trying to say? Maybe the Professor was doing some good with that discovery, and the Senator was an important man. But who else?'

Martin replied, 'That's just it. Why should just we escape and hundreds of others die?'

Rosen laughed suddenly. 'You want to know why? Because we were all members of The Strong Stummick Club. Remember? We talked about it at lunch that day, and he spoke and thought about "that day" as though it had been years ago and not just torn from the calendar a few hours before. We didn't get seasick and we didn't want to miss our dinners either. This is a reason we should be saved?'

Rogo's flat voice again: 'We ain't out of it yet.'

Miss Kinsale said, 'I think we are all very important.'

They heard Martin's dry chuckle again. 'Will the world stop wagging if we get bumped off? What do I want to get back for? I told you—I want to prepare our new spring line for men. Men! That's a laugh! It's going more and more pansy every day. If I don't make it, I've got a married son in the dry goods line. He'll take over the business; my wife will be looked after and James J. Martin, haberdasher, will have disappeared without a ripple, except that the local undertaker who's got his eye on me will have been done out of a job and preacher Hosey denied the opportunity of telling a lot of lies about me. What about you, Shelby? How indispensable are you?'

Shelby answered, 'Well, I don't know. I was working on the design of a lightweight pick-up truck, using a new alloy, capable of doing the work of some of the heavyweights at cheaper cost.'

'And if you shouldn't happen to be there to finish it?'

Shelby had to think just that much too long before he replied, and then his voice was almost as flat as Rogo's, 'I suppose somebody else will. There's a young kid in my department...'

Whose brains you were picking! Jane thought to herself, and was amazed at the still unplumbed depth of her contempt for her husband. Yet she remembered it had all seemed so normal in those times when her husband had come home from the plant in a good mood, saying, 'That Parkins is a bright boy. We've solved the axle problem that has been worrying me. They'll be tickled when I show them the print.' All reasonable, all right; business going well, clever husband, appreciative superiors and only a faint, hardly perceived niggling, *'We've solved that axle problem.'* Who solved it?

Martin called, 'Muller?'

There was no self-pity in the laugh that echoed through the shaft. Hubie said, 'None of you know me very well, or anything about me. But I can assure you that I am completely useless and unimportant except to myself. I toil not, neither do I spin. There isn't a single soul outside of a handful of mommas who see a rich and eligible bachelor on the loose earmarked for their daughters who gives a damn whether I live or die. Like Martin's undertaker chap, if I vanish, they'll consider I've played them a very dirty trick.'

'I care!' said Nonnie fiercely and loudly.

Martin asked, 'And you, Nonnie?'

She said after a moment's reflection, 'I'm a rotten dancer or I'd have been a star by now, or something. But me mum and dad think the world of me. They'd miss me coming home for the hols. Me dad's a long distance lorry driver but he always manages to get back for Christmas. Mum's a dear. I've got a brother and a sister both working. We have a regular old beano when we get together.'

In the dark, Muller smiled at how easily Nonnie slipped into the speech of her town and class when she spoke of home and wondered whether he would be able ever to cure her of it, or whether he even really wanted to do so.

Jane Shelby spoke out coldly and succinctly, 'I cannot justify myself. I have been true neither to myself nor to others; I have lived not my life but that of somebody else; I have nothing but disgust for myself...'

'Jane!' For once there was a true hurt and agony in Shelby's voice.

'Oh, Dick,' cried Jane Shelby in quite another tone. 'If we're to die I wouldn't want you to think I meant I'd ever been untrue to your bed or your dignity. It's just me I've let down.'

Martin said, 'Sorry. I wasn't meaning to open any cans of peas. For that matter maybe I haven't been that kind of a success either.' The eternally floating blonde hair; the sinking-in delight of the cushiony pink body; the duplicity that would have been needed for that weekly visit to her pad in Chicago...

Susan spoke up for herself. 'I'm a student. I was going to study art and perhaps become a designer. I don't suppose that matters any more, really.'

Her father protested, 'Oh yes it does. Of all of us, Sue, perhaps you're the most important. You should have your chance in life.'

The girl thought; *I wonder if you would be saying that if you knew.*

'As for me,' Manny Rosen put it, 'I could go today, to-morrow, next week, next year. I'm retired. My son is running the business like his father did. Only the best on the market and everything fresh and tasty. So Rosen's Midnight Delicatessen goes on and my relatives don't get any more from me whether I live or die so who cares? Isn't that right, Belle? We've had a good life.'

Belle said, 'Don't bother me with talk. I'm not feeling good.'

Martin asked, 'What about Kemal? What made him quit that other gang and come with us after he'd found out that the way was blocked?'

Rogo said, 'Yeah, where does he come in. A coupla times we wouldn'ta looked so hot without him.'

Muller mused, 'I can't answer what he is thinking or feeling, or how important he is to himself, but one thing I know; of all of us he's the one least concerned with dying, or afraid of it. But I can tell you the kind of village he comes from in Anatolia, because I've driven through them. A cluster of white-washed stone hovels with red tile roofs and a mosque so small the minaret is no bigger than a stovepipe, or so it seems. The muezzin has to climb up a ladder inside.... No electricity, running water, telephones or radios, but a good school and teacher. The women in the fields wear baggy cotton trousers and yellow scarves around their heads. He's probably longing to go back there. And he thinks the greatest man that ever lived was Kemal Ataturk.'

In the darkness the Turk moved and grunted, 'Ataturk hokay, hokay!'

Muller continued, 'The wonderful incongruity is that in his hovel, in this primitive village there will be a picture of Ataturk in full evening dress; opera cloak, silk hat and all, hanging on the wall. As for what made him join up with us, your guess is as good as mine, and mine is for the same reason we went with Scott. Scott may have had a little of Ataturk in him.'

Nonnie whispered, 'I could listen to you talk all day long and all night.'

Muller replied dryly, 'You may have to.'

Martin said, 'Come on, Rogo, it's your turn. Give!'

CHAPTER XXII

'We Were Intimate'

In the dark silence punctuated by some new kind of creaking in the ship, they wondered what would be forthcoming. The detective gave them quite a wait until Muller thought he was probably going to tell Martin what to do with himself, when he began in a curiously mild and explanatory tone:

'With me, see, it could have gone either way, like. I was a tough little East Side wop. My old man had a fruit-stand on the corner of First Avenue and 6th Street. I guess I gave him plenty of trouble, always fighting and stealing. Sure, I stole. We had a gang, the Dirty Walyos. That's another name for Eytalians. We used to fight the Irish on Second Avenue and grab stuff off shop counters and run. I was a real stinker. So there was this parish priest, Father Tamagno in our neighbourhood, and he saw me take on a kid twice my size, just with nothing but left jabs because I'd hurt my right hand. So he put me in the Golden Gloves. I won the 118-pound championship and made the team that went to Chicago to fight in the Inter-city. We beat them 9 to 7. I won by a knockout. They gave me a blue silk bathrobe with my name on the back in gold letters, "MIKE ROGO—GOLDEN GLOVES CHAMPION", and put my picture in the paper. See, I was on the team. So after that I couldn't be a bum any more.'

He trailed off for a moment and Muller was wondering what it was that impelled him suddenly to talk as though in the confessional. He, himself, had been half listening to him and half to the groaning of the ship, and he was certain that he had felt movement in her again. When she went would she upend and spill them all helter-skelter atop one another down the tunnel and into the horrors of the lake that contained Scott and Linda, and God knows how many others before finally extinguishing them? He was more sickened and afraid of that lake than he was of dying.

Rogo took up his narrative again. 'Father Tamagno wouldn't let me turn pro. Maybe I could have made a pile and ended up like the rest of them punch-drunk stumble-bums hanging around The Garden. He made me study and got me into the Police School instead. See, but I coulda been just as easy on the other side. You get me? Just another young punk, pushing narcotics or shaking down pants' pressers and cleaners and dyers for protection for the mob. I've kicked the hell out of so many of them punks, they don't show their face in my district. Well, they got plenty more like me in the Sixteenth Precinct. Johnny Broderick, he's dead now, come from there. And Irish Paddy Mahan, Joe Klopfberger and Frank Myers, tough cops, all of them are still around. Okay, so I'm not there any more. Another jail break, another jewellery store stickup, a couple more junkies dead on the sidewalk. Some other cop gets the *Daily News* hero award. I'm just saying there's a lot of luck in it.'

He trailed off again and they thought that he had done, when he spoke again. 'But you know,' he said, 'you got Linda all wrong. She wasn't like she made out. She'd had a tough time of it from the word go. Anyone else would have gone under.'

'Oh yes,' broke in Jane Shelby, 'I thought so.'

'Yes, ma'am,' Rogo agreed, 'that's what you said. Her stage name was Linda Lane, but her right one was Cosasko. Her old man was a bum and a drunk and her mother worked both sides of the street. They come from Sandusky, Ohio. When she was eleven, her father broke her in. They never had a dime except for what the old woman made on her back. When she was fourteen, the kids on the block dragged her down behind the signboard on a vacant lot and took turns. At sixteen she was put on the street with the old lady pimping for her.' He added, 'You never heard no story like that before, I guess.'

No one said anything. They were thinking of the doll figure with the spear through her heart.

'But she had guts. She wasn't going to be like them. She ran away to L.A. and got a job as a car hop. She was getting real pretty by then. She had the figure and the legs in them short skirts. Some bum gave her the one about getting her in pictures, knocked her up and blew. She was lucky. She miscarried. Then she wasn't so lucky. She got in with a bad bunch around Hollywood and Vine. When they stole some big daddy's Caddie, she was in the car with the thief when they made the collar. She got eighteen months with four off for good behaviour. When she came out she changed her name to Linda Lane, signed up with Central Casting and did some extra work. Then she got a break. Or maybe it wasn't. An assistant director picked her up out of the mob and set her up in an apartment in the Garden of Allah.'

They were remembering Linda now, the pouting lips, the china blue eyes, the ridiculous curls piled up on to her head and the bristling aggressiveness.

Rogo went on, but his voice was again becoming the flat monotone of the police officer giving a charge. 'So this assistant director becomes a director and he makes Linda a starlet, see? They've got all these kids on the lot they use for publicity, or dressing up a scene and they're supposed to become stars someday, but most of 'em wind up in the ash can. So then one day, drunk, driving home by himself to wifey, this director wraps his Thunderbird around a lamppost. Linda moves on to a nuts and bolts manufacturer who's had his eye on her. But now the publicity department has got her fixed up with a fake family and fake home town and Linda Lane is the girl next door. She might have made it maybe if she'd let it go at that, but she was crazy to go on the stage. They'd taught her to sing and dance a little. This nuts and bolts guy buys her into a musical that is being put on on Broadway, called *Hello Sailor*. *Hello Sailor* is the bomb of all time and the critics crucify Linda. The nuts and bolts guy is yellow and takes a powder back to L.A. I'm around to pick up the pieces.'

Manny Rosen corroborated, 'I remember your coming into the store and saying you were crazy about this kid.'

Muller asked, 'Did you know all this about her?'

Rogo's voice became even flatter. He replied, 'See, when somebody from out of town comes into our district, say like in show business, we check up a little on the background in case they got connections and there's any trouble later, or some hood tries to move in and we can put the fire out before it gets going. The L.A. Detective Bureau lets us have a look at the book.'

Martin said, 'Ouch!'

Nonnie said, 'I did hate her, but I wish she was back again with us now.'

Jane asserted, 'But you never let her know that you knew, did you?'

Rogo replied, 'What for? It made her happy to think I didn't. It wasn't easy for her at any time, always afraid she'd run into someone from the coast who'd know she'd been in stir. It puts a chip on your shoulder, don't it?'

The question remained hanging in the stifling air. Susan Shelby was reviewing in her mind: Incest, rape, whoring, thieving, failure and death. Was that what life was like outside the boundaries within which she had been sheltered? And how secure were these now, since her mother had opened the closet door? She saw Linda impaled again and thought that in a way, too, a spear had been driven through her own person. She still did not want to die.

It was growing hotter. Drawing a full breath no longer seemed to satisfy the lungs. And from one of them there in the dark, breathing was audibly laboured. Martin turned on his lantern for an instant. It was Belle Rosen. Her husband was sitting with his back against the side of the tunnel with her head pillowed in his lap. Even by the yellowish rays of the fading battery he could see that her skin had turned the shade of clay. He thought she looked like one of those grotesque modern sculptures one kept seeing in the papers. He shut off the light and speculated upon how much time had passed since they had reached the top. He wondered, too, about the air supply. There was no way of knowing whether what they were breathing was part of the whole that was keeping the ship from sinking, or whether they were in a little pocket trapped in the stern, which was on the verge of giving out.

No one seemed disposed to further talk when Rogo had finished. Martin felt he ought to keep them going by distracting them down to the last moment. He began, 'You said you thought we were all very important, Miss Kinsale, what about you?'

They heard movement from the quarter where she had settled herself close to Jane Shelby. 'Oh,' came her reply, 'I meant all of *you*. I'm not at all important.' And after a moment's hesitation, 'Though actually, ours is a very good family. My mother's sister married a Brigadier on Alexander's staff. He was one of the famous Desert Rats in Cyprus, Brigadier Catesby. I'm sure you've heard of him. He was one of the Lincolnshire Catesbys.'

Muller thought to himself: *I hope Rogo is impressed*, and then wondered why she had placed the redoubtable Brigadier in Cyprus if he had been a Desert Rat, instead of with Montgomery at Alamein.

'But our side come from Norfolk,' Miss Kinsale continued, 'near Thetford. Such a beautiful property. I remember it from my childhood, the gardens and the servants and our old nanny. She must be almost eighty now. There were two iron stags on the gateposts and our head gardener used to make up stories about them. Oh, and then the pheasants. So beautiful. The Earl of Waldringham, who lived near by, used to have permission to shoot over our property.'

'Oh,' said Muller, 'I know it. That must have been Telford House. Bumbles Waldringham was at Harvard with me and I went to stay with them at Greatgreys whenever I was in England. I remember the iron stags because I passed the place in the car on the way to Bumble's.'

They could hear Miss Kinsale's long drawn out exhalation before she spoke again. 'I think Norfolk is such a beautiful county, though Lincolnshire is lovely too; the Brigadier would often ask us there. Dahlias were his hobby...'

Something niggled at Muller's mind and he spoke before he thought, 'Why, then you must be a Cokington.'

Miss Kinsale said, 'A what?'

'One of the Cokingtons of Norfolk. Old family. Telford House was one of their places in the county.'

Then he wished he had never opened his mouth. What was a Cokington doing clerking in a bank in a suburb like Camberley? The wait for her reply seemed endless. He tried to think of some way to change the subject.

Miss Kinsale finally spoke, 'Well, you know; *relations.*' Then she added, 'Of course, things change so. Death duties, and things. But I'm quite happy in my little—in our little property in Frimley and from my window I can see a corner of Sandhurst—to keep my memory of Gerald alive. He was my fiancé.'

Muller had a compulsive feeling of *déjà vu.* With people like Miss Kinsale there was always that young dream fiancé killed in the war. It was either at the very beginning or just in the last days before peace was declared.

The lines followed almost as he might have imagined them:

'Gerald passed out from there. Graduated, I suppose you Americans would say, and was killed at Nijmegen. We used to go walking together down to Frimley and back in the evenings.'

Nonnie said, 'Oh dear, I'm so sorry.'

The spinster sighed, 'First Gerald and now Frank. It's almost too much to bear.'

It was only in Muller that the coupling of the two names set up a faint alarm bell. What on earth could she have meant by it? A Gerald was possible, but Frank Scott? And what was all that hocus-pocus about Telford House? Of course, she *might* have been one of those distant cousins who sometimes arrive for a few days' visit and then are never seen there again.

Rosen asked suddenly, 'What kind of a minister was this fellow anyway? First he prays and then he curses God, like in the New Testament Christ gives it to the fig tree.'

Martin said, 'Well, for one thing he believed in action.'

'But did he really believe in God?' Muller queried and then added, 'Does anybody? Actually?'

'Oh yes,' breathed Miss Kinsale, 'I do. With my heart and soul. There is God watching over us. He sent Dr Scott to give his life so that we might be saved.'

Muller thought he felt the ship quiver beneath him again and added to himself, 'Or so that He might amuse Himself playing cat and mouse until He got ready to swallow us.'

Rogo said bitterly, 'What did Linda give her life for? What kind of a life and death did she get?'

Miss Kinsale reprimanded, 'Oh, Mr Rogo! Aren't you a Catholic? Don't you go to Mass?'

'Yeah. I was brought up one. But it don't answer about Linda or what was done to her. What if Scott was sent to get her knocked off? If we hadn't followed him, she'd be alive still.'

'Or we'd all be dead,' Muller concluded.

Nonnie said, 'I don't know what I believe, but I say my prayers every night.'

Susan added, 'I do, too.' But her mother said, 'I haven't said mine in years.'

Muller declared, 'I'm an agnostic. You're a good Baptist, Martin, what exactly do *you* believe?'

Martin cleared his dry throat. He was glad that they had hit upon a subject that seemed to get them all going again. He replied, 'Not a good Baptist, just a scared one. All my old man and our preachers ever put into me was the fear of God. Now my son's never been to church in his life. I never made him and he never went. He's all right. I never scared him like my folks scared me.'

'*You're* a churchgoer, aren't you, Mrs Shelby?' said Miss Kinsale.

'Yes,' Jane replied, 'we go regularly when we're at home. But I'm afraid it's strictly social.'

Shelby said, 'Jane, how can you?'

She turned on him, 'You know it's so! I'm afraid I'm on Mr Rogo's side: Why? Why? Why?'

Caught up in their own fears, fatigue and discomforts they had forgotten that her son was missing. She savaged her husband with, 'What goes on inside *you* when you sit up straight and sanctimonious on the snob side of the aisle in St Matthews? What do you expect when you say, "My God" or "God help me"? A breakdown service?'

Shelby's answer was so lame that Muller felt a sudden compassion for him. He was little-boy-lost. 'I don't know. I guess maybe I never thought about it.'

Manny Rosen said, 'If there wasn't our God, there wouldn't be a Jew alive today.'

Martin wanted to say, 'If there is, he sure managed to thin you out a lot,' but refrained. To him the Jewish God was a policeman quite different from the Baptist God, with a different set of rules for punishing. Rosen's God was as remote to him as the Manitou of a Red Indian, or the Allah of the Arabs. He, himself, was going to catch it in the neck for adultery and no mistake. But Rosen would hear the roll of thunder if he ate a ham sandwich. Anyway, in these days, God was not the Jew's problem any more. It was their capacity to irritate people.

'Papa,' Belle Rosen said, 'hold my hand. I ain't feeling so good.'

Rogo's angry voice burst out of his angry thoughts. 'Your God, my God, what's He got against us; what's He got against me? What have I done? Why doesn't He act like God? Sure I was a louse when I was a kid, but I took plenty punishment. We went to Mass and confession, Linda and me, regular. Okay, I killed some guys, but they were rats. What about all the guys who get killed in wars? The fellers that killed them come home with medals and are heroes. What did He have to trun down Linda like that for to die like an animal? She never done nothing to anybody, but He had it in for her from the word go.'

Muller thought to himself: *Why can't people think clearly when they get God on the brain? If Linda hadn't disobeyed Scott, she'd still be with us and bitching at him. But if I told Rogo that, he'd hit me.* Aloud he said, 'What I would like to know is which God image was in Scott's mind: Gran'daddy in the sky? Or a sort of glorified coach sending him out on to the field to win the big game?'

When no one replied he continued, 'I am amongst the mystified. When I call myself an agnostic, I merely mean that unlike most Christians I do not consider myself the centre of a Universe conducted on wholly inexplicable lines, by a Father and Son. The animistic Gods who dwelt in trees, stones, brooks and deep places in the forest were much more attractive as were the Pagan Gods of the Greeks or the politically practical Gods of the Romans. When modern man finally settled upon a Creator made into his own image, he endowed Him with most of his own worst characteristics: vain, vengeful, cruel, capricious, capable either of being bribed with trinkets or conned by flattery. There must be something somewhat more impressive behind the galaxies.'

'How unhappy you must be, Mr Muller,' Miss Kinsale said.

Muller gave way to a momentary flash of irritation. He said, 'The stars don't know their names and I doubt very much whether God even knows what He is like.'

Miss Kinsale looked shocked and Nonnie bewildered. The latter said, 'But the stars *have* names, haven't they?'

Muller did not reply and left Nonnie vaguely disturbed. *Her* God happened to like being sung to loudly on Sundays, but there was nothing wrong in that, and perhaps when she introduced Muller to Him in their little church at Fareham Cross just outside Bristol, he might come to feel as comfortable as she. This was followed by a moment of panic. Muller, man of the world, gent, standing outside Fareham Cross Parish Church with Mum and Dad, being patronized by Mr Stopworth, the Vicar. Mr Stopworth *was* patronizing. Even Dad said so. Why was this man wanting to marry her? Would she be able to keep him happy? In a moment's agony of doubt she wished that the ship had gone down while they were coupled as one.

Muller felt the slight shudder that had run through her and pulled her closer to his side and placed an arm about her shoulder. He said, 'If you ask me, Scott had his head turned by all that yelling and cheering and publicity.'

'If you ask me,' Rogo said, 'Scott was a faggot.'

'A what?' The query was torn simultaneously from Shelby and Martin.

'A panzola! Queer as a coot. Linda tried to kid herself he had a letch for her, but when she went for his pants in the dark, he yelled bloody murder. Look, nobody's kiddin' anybody any more. Don't you think I know what went on down there in that engine room, when he threatened to break her arm. He didn't like dames. Scared stiff of them. He could hide out behind that turned-around collar and nobody would ever suspect, would they? A lot of those tough, bust 'em-up guys, whether they're hoods, or football players are half-ass panzolas only they don't know it. The more scared they are of women the more they throw their weight around and make with the hairy chest. Scott was one of 'em.'

'Oh no!' The exclamation came from Miss Kinsale, but breathed with such horror that for a moment it seemed to them that another person had spoken. 'Oh no!' she repeated. 'You mustn't say such a thing, Mr Rogo. He wasn't at all like that. Not at all.'

They were all stunned to silence by the intensity of her denial until Rogo said, 'Excuse me, ma'am, I wasn't meaning to give any offence. I was only saying...'

'Anyway, he couldn't have been,' Miss Kinsale then continued as though he had not spoken. 'You see, I *know*. I... we were going to be married. He was going to send for me to come over to the United States.'

The shock waves sent out by her statement reacted differently upon all of them. Martin controlled a sudden desire to laugh until he remembered the animal howl of pain that had come from the mousy little spinster at Scott's suicide. Shelby thought: *God, have I been floating upside-down throughout this whole voyage? Maybe all my life?*

Miss Kinsale had been sitting up close to the Shelbys. Now she leaned down to whisper to Jane. She said, 'Since we are going to die, I can tell you.' Her sibilation dropped lower, 'We were intimate during the voyage.'

Muller heard it and was moved once more to compassion as was Jane, but her emotion was mingled with anger.

'Oh, my dear,' she said and could bring herself to do no more than repeat it and Miss Kinsale was not asking for pity. Inwardly she was raging against the dead clergyman: how dared he amuse himself during the voyage with this poor, cast-off-by-life and passed-by woman? What was he accomplishing by making an outrageous offer of marriage to a woman old enough to be his mother? Was that it then, that he was the little games-playing boy who never grew up and wanted his mummy? Did he think it was a gesture of charity to let her once warm her cold hands at the fires of love? Or had he been one of those monstrous psychopaths who under the guise of religion sneak under a woman's skirts like an incubus to bring them personalized contact with the Deity or the Devil? She was glad Miss Kinsale could not see her disgust.

'Oh, Hubie,' Nonnie whispered, 'how awful for her, the poor thing. They were going to be married and she saw him throw himself away.'

'Hush!' he said to her and held her still closer to himself, as though this was the last good, clean, sane person left in the world to cling to. For him it was the final pathetic fantasy. Perhaps there really was that Brigadier from Lincolnshire; the Miss Kinsales of life usually managed to have one in the family. But thereafter Telford House, the Cokingtons, Gerald and all the rest were dreams.

And now Scott. Safe to tell; he was dead. No doubt she had been in love with him from a distance. Her despair at the suicide had emanated from a stricken woman. But Scott—with Miss Kinsale—what would she confess to next? Pregnancy?

But Rogo's eyes and fists were squeezed shut, his teeth bared and he was shaking from head to foot in blind, insensate rage. His throat was choked with the killer's urge to batter and destroy. And the object of his fury was no longer there. Had he been wrong all along about Scott? Was he one of these horny bastards who hides behind a clerical collar? Had he been having a bang at Linda during the voyage? And was the incident by the side of Hell Lake nothing but an elaborate cover? If he did lay Miss Kinsale, he could also have taken care of Linda and he knew that she had been hot for him. And she was dead and he had followed her. He felt he would explode in a madman's yell or strike out at anyone when from Belle Rosen came a long-drawn-out wail of pain, 'Oh, my God!'

Rosen panicked. 'Mamma! Mamma! What's the matter? For God's sakes, make a light, somebody.'

'Lights on!' commanded Martin.

They shone upon a Belle Rosen whose lips had turned dark black in the dim rays and whose great breasts were heaving as she tried to draw in breath in short gasps, while crying, 'Oh, my God.... The pain...'

Lord, thought Muller, who had once seen a victim before, *she's having a heart attack.*

From somewhere came the sound of a metallic clang, a thump and a scraping. Muller thought, *Here we go!* and held on more tightly to Nonnie. But Martin cried sharply, 'What was that?' and Kemal was staring up at the dark space above his head.

Rosen groaned, 'Don't talk about noises. Can't you see my wife is sick. What shall I do? What shall I do?'

Muller said, 'Keep her quiet. It's the only thing to do until...'

Miss Kinsale said, 'I will pray.'

'My God, my God! Oh, my God!' moaned Belle.

'Mamma, Mamma, I'm here.'

Shelby cried, 'Air! There's no air. That's why she can't breathe. I can't either.'

They all heard the scraping and bumping then and after that a twang like the parting of a cable, repeated twice more.

Muller gasped, 'They've come! They've come! That was from over our heads. Quick! While we've still got the strength, tap back to let them know.'

Martin cried, 'Hey—Kemal! Get up there. Take the axe. Where's the axe?'

In the remaining light of their fading batteries they looked about them and then at one another. It was impossible any longer to achieve a full deep breath. They were gasping and gulping like netted fish. Yet they managed to roll their bodies away from where they had been sitting or lying in case the axe was there.

Rogo said to Shelby, 'You had it last.'

'I didn't. I thought Martin had it.'

Muller said, 'We've got to tap back. Where is it? Where is it?'

Miss Kinsale said, 'Dr Scott has it.'

'What? Scott is dead!'

'He took it with him.' They stared at Miss Kinsale. 'It was tied around his waist. I saw the light flash from it as he left us.'

Rogo croaked, 'The dirty bastard! So he's killed us after all.'

CHAPTER XXIII

Everything Goes in Threes

James Martin, the least muscular and athletic of the group still had something left in his spare frame. Holding one of the hand torches, he pulled himself laboriously up through and over the crosspieces leading to the hull, hauled back and struck with all the remaining force that he could muster. But there was only the shattering of glass against the steel and a faint plink that could not possibly have penetrated if there was anyone outside. Martin wondered if in their last struggle to live they had not mistaken those ever-present noises of the ship, herself fighting to the last to remain above the surface.

Martin jumped down again, or rather fell. He rasped, 'I guess that's it.'

Muller said, 'Nonnie—it's such a pity. I'd have been good to you.'

'It doesn't matter, Hubie. Are we going to die now?'

'I think so.'

'I love you.'

'Yes, Nonnie. Stay close.'

Rogo repeated, 'That stupid bastard!'

A weird metallic voice that had no resemblance to anything human reverberated through the stifling space, 'Is there anyone there?'

'My God!' whispered Muller. 'They're talking to us. But how can they?'

The voice was like the flat, strangulated, vibrating sounds emanating from radiophonic head sets. It continued 'Is there anybody down there? This is Commander Thorpe of the U.S. Air-Sea Rescue destroyer escort *Monroe*. I am using an electronic amplifier. If you speak we will be able to hear you.'

Martin struggled with the fetid air for the last measure of oxygen. 'Yes, yes! We're down here.'

'Okay! We hear you. How many are you?'

'Eleven. Six men and five women. But we're dying. There's no air any more. Can't you get us out?'

'Yes. Be patient. We can't cut you out yet. We'd burn up the remainder of your oxygen.'

Rogo suddenly lost control, 'Patience my ass. What the hell do you think we climbed up here for, to choke to death? Get us out you bastard!'

The impersonal metal voice that could not carry any inflection of sympathy replied. 'We must get air to you first. They're bringing over a drill, pump and sleeve we use on submarines. Don't panic. You probably have more air than you think you have. Don't move. Don't talk unnecessarily. Try to take half breaths slowly.'

Rosen raised his eyes to the roof, 'My wife. She's terribly sick.'

Muller said, 'It looks to me like a heart attack.'

The voice replied, 'We have a doctor here with us. He will speak to you.' A pause. 'This is Lieutenant Worden. I am a doctor. What are the symptoms?'

It was strange, how when told there was more air than they had thought, there seemed to be such. Muller was able to reply, 'I saw a heart attack once. Pain. Lips blue.

Worse off than us, fighting for breath.'

'Keep her quiet. Loosen her clothing. We'll get to her shortly.'

'If we don't sink first,' Shelby muttered. The sensitive microphone they were using picked him up.

'We don't think she'll sink—yet.'

'Loosen her clothes, he says.' It was Rosen speaking. 'What clothes?'

Muller suggested, 'Undo her bra.'

'In front of everybody? She wouldn't like that.'

'Oh for Chrissakes, Manny,' Rogo said.

Jane Shelby leaned over, got her hand beneath Belle's back and unhooked her. She said, 'This is no time to be fussy.' The huge breasts flopped.

'Papa, Papa, help me,' Belle moaned.

'Just stay quiet, Mamma. They're coming in a minute.'

'You see,' whispered Miss Kinsale, 'it didn't really matter about the axe. Dr Scott knew what he was doing all the time.'

They waited in the smothering airless heat, using the remainder of their batteries for the comfort of seeing one another on the brink of rescue, or equally the edge of eternity. Muller had no doubts but that the ship would give way before they could be effectively reached. The ironies of their toilsome ascent to the summit had been too consistent. There were more bumpings and scrapings and metallic sounds from overhead.

The voice said, 'The equipment has arrived. It was used to free sailors imprisoned in the capsized *Oklahoma* at Pearl Harbor. It has since been refined. A hole will be drilled via an airtight sleeve and air will be pumped in to you. You'll be able to breathe properly. We'll continue to pump it while we cut away the plates. Where are you situated? Not directly in contact with the hull?'

Martin was able to reply. 'No. We are in the propeller shaft tunnel. The hull is about ten feet above our heads.'

'Good. Stay where you are and hang on a few minutes longer.'

Shelby wondered how much more death those few minutes could contain. What if the *Poseidon* should lurch to the bottom and carry their rescuers with them? He felt suddenly beyond caring. What would life be like thereafter if they were pulled out of this trap?

Jane thought how her son would have gloried in the fulfilment of his prediction that they would be found, that the elaborate machinery set up to salvage downed astronauts from their steel capsule shell was functioning. Her stricken heart cried out silently, 'Robin, Robin, where are you?' She knew then and there that she would never see him again.

Susan thought: *We are going to be saved. What will I be like? Must I tell my secret? Will it always be a shadow over me?*

Martin felt drained of everything but that last spark of life that he refused to concede.

From overhead came a sudden machine-gun rat-tat-tat, which stuttered, halted, started again, stopped once more and then settled down to a steady whining clatter.

Muller said, 'They're drilling, Nonnie.' And then he added, 'If God is the jokester I think He is, this would be the moment to pull the rug out from under our feet for His big laugh. Maybe Scott called the turn.'

Miss Kinsale whispered once more, 'He died to save us all,' and this time Rogo did not comment.

From the metal voice: 'We are through the outer plates. Are you still all right?'

Rosen croaked, 'For God's sake, hurry. Mamma's hand is so cold.'

Belle suddenly said clearly, 'You wanted I should go on so I could see Irving and Stella, Simon and little Hy and Myra. Well, I did it, didn't I?'

'Yes, Mamma, you did. You were great. Just great,' and he looked around at them again for confirmation. 'Maybe she's getting better again.'

No one said anything. The drill suddenly gave a loud, screeching whine and bit through the inner shell above their heads, and they saw the gleam of its inch-wide diameter as for a moment it rattled against the sides of the hole. With it came the first oily whiff which could be drawn into tortured lungs. The drill was withdrawn and a moment later, a black tube was thrust through the hole to come to rest a foot or so below the inside of the hull. Then as a steady thumping was heard from above and outside, the first stream of fresh, cool air flowed over them, resuscitated and revitalized them so that they were able to raise first a feeble cheer and then, as the oxygen began to make them a little drunk, laugh and cry.

But simultaneously as though the pin-prick in her skin had touched a nerve, the ship began to groan and creak again, to cry out in her joints and distant parts. There was a moment's movement and from the direction of the engine room a piece of loose steel clanged like a bell. Beneath them the floor quivered uneasily. From overhead came sounds of scurrying feet and rattling gear and a voice that said, 'Stand by to...'

'Jesus!' said Muller. 'It's the Big Laugh after all. She's going.'

Rogo cried, 'The sons-of-bitches have let all the air out!' And he yelled up, 'Okay, you rats, run out on us before you get your feet wet!'

The voices and the scrabbling continued but they could not hear what was being said. The fresh air continued to blow in upon them and the noises of the pumping never stopped.

Then the Commander spoke directly to them. He said, 'We're not leaving you. We think she'll stay up long enough for us to get you out. It won't be long now.'

Muller said, 'They've got guts. If we go, we take them along with us.'

The voice calmed them again. It said, 'The doctor wants to have another word with you.'

After a moment's pause they heard, 'This is Lieutenant Worden speaking now. How is the sick lady?'

Rosen groaned. 'How can I tell? She's better with the air.'

Lieutenant Worden said, 'Good. I'm going to pass down a hypodermic through the tube. Does any of you know how to administer a hypodermic?'

'I do,' said Rogo and they stared at him in astonishment. He added, 'A cop also got to know how to deliver a kid.'

Muller said, 'Good man,' and did not hear what Rogo said between his teeth.

They heard a slight clinking sound. A syringe emerged from the tube, butt end first attached to a thread. Rogo reached up and plucked it forth. 'I've got it,' he said. 'Where?'

'The left arm. Intramuscular.'

Rogo approached her holding the needle. He said, 'This won't hurt you at all, Belle. You'll be okay. Smart guy that doc.'

Rosen said, 'See, Mamma, now you'll be all right. Today a heart attack is nothing any more. Look at your uncle Ben, he had one when he was sixty and he lived to be seventy-five. Even Presidents of the United States, who got terrible worries. So today they don't like the way your heart is—they change it. Just lie still. You got nothing to worry about.'

Belle Rosen opened her eyes and said, 'That's good,' and then died without further ado. Her eyes remained open and staring.

Rogo the expert on death muttered to himself, 'Oh Christ, no!' and in desperation jabbed home the needle into the flesh of her left arm, just below the shoulder. The staring eyes had already begun to glaze but Rosen was not yet aware.

He said, 'Mamma, you heard me? Everything's going to be all right.' Then in sudden alarm he cried, 'Mamma! Mamma! Why you looking so?'

Muller never would have imagined that Rogo could have so much tenderness in him as he put his arm gently about his shoulder and said, 'Manny, I'm sorry. She can't hear you. It's all over. She ain't with us any more.'

Rosen became a frightened little man, not quite able to understand. He cried, 'What? What? But she was getting better. She only spoke to me a minute ago. You gave her the injection. Why does she look so? Is she really sick? For God's sakes, then, get the doctor!'

The others were frozen into immobility by pity, by horror and even anger at this last cruel irony. And Miss Kinsale prayed aloud, unconsciously paraphrasing the late Reverend Scott, saying, 'Dear God, if you want any more of us, take me.'

Rogo shouted up in the direction of the pierced hull, 'Doc! Are you there, Doc?'

'Yes, I'm here.'

'This is Detective Rogo speaking. I gave the injection, but I'm afraid it was too late. I'm afraid she's gone. How long will it be before you get through?'

'They're going to begin cutting now. Do you know how to massage a heart?'

Rogo looked doubtfully at the mountain of clay that had once been Belle Rosen and said, 'I could try.' The massive breast was in the way and beneath it were layers of fat covering the ribs encasing the silent heart. He tried to push the huge mammary aside to get at the area.

Rosen screamed, 'What are you doing? Keep your hands off her! Leave her alone!'

Shelby said, 'Rosen, control yourself. It's first-aid. The doctor told him to.'

Martin cried, 'Oughtn't we close her eyes? She's looking as though we'd all let her down. I wish we'd sink, right now—the lot of us.'

Muller offered to Rogo, 'If you'll show me what to do, I'll try to help you.'

The detective nodded and said, 'Get on the other side. Try to lift the rib cage up and down if you can manage. Like this; slowly—one two, one two.'

The two men bent to their work. Nonnie was crying. Rosen, still bewildered, kept asking, 'What are they doing? Why are they touching Mamma? Why doesn't the doctor come?'

Jane Shelby said, 'It isn't an indignity, Mr Rosen. Don't you understand! They're trying to make her heart go again.'

In the dim light Manny Rosen's round face looked almost babyish in its total bewilderment, 'Her heart go again? But why? Did it stop?'

Jane said, 'Yes, I'm afraid it did.' She wondered how she could be so cool and matter-of-fact in the face of this further tragedy, this additional wanton stealing of life from a good and innocent person, until she realized that she had been immunized. Never again in life would anything ever shock or hurt her.

Martin repeated, 'Can't you close her eyes?' It was one thing to be haunted only by a picture in his mind of Wilma Lewis in her cabin—*their* cabin, and another to be locked in a chamber with a dead woman. Were Wilma's eyes open too, and staring through the murky waters?

Rogo said, 'It ain't working. We'd better wait 'til the Doc gets here.'

From overhead came a tapping and the metallic voice, 'Keep away from this area now, everyone. We're going to burn through.'

The pace of the thumping from above increased and was followed by a roaring, ripping sound. In the black roof of the hull, in the vicinity from which the sound had come, there appeared a glow, a thin, orange-coloured line. They smelled burning metal and felt the heat.

Shelby advised, 'Be calm, Mr Rosen. They're cutting through to us now. The doctor will be here in a moment.'

Almost with resentment Martin watched the orange line turn a corner and then another on its way to forming a square some three feet in diameter, almost with resentment. Ten minutes earlier, five even, might they have saved Belle Rosen?

The molten square was complete now and he wondered why the cut-out section did not tumble down inside, until he realized that they would have made the cut on the bias so that this could not happen. He heard the clink of steel levers prying at the burned away edges of the hole. It lifted a crack and then suddenly the whole segment came away, letting in a flood of pearly morning light that dimmed the last of their ebbing torches. Two dungareed legs appeared, followed by a leather-jacketed torso and a blond young man with short-cropped hair and bright blue eyes dropped through. He said, 'I'm Lieutenant Worden. Where's the heart case?'

Muller and Rogo made room for him and he knelt by her side and made his examination. Then he closed the lids of her eyes.

When he had finished he asked, 'Which is the husband?'

They pointed out the frightened Rosen whose lips were now trembling like those of an infant and his limbs shaking as well. The doctor said, 'I'm sorry, sir, to have to tell you she's gone. There's nothing more we can do.'

'You mean she's dead? Mrs Rosen is dead?'

'Yes, I'm afraid so.'

Rosen fell to his knees beside his wife and began to rock back and forth, crying, 'Mamma! Mamma!' and then, 'Mamma, why did you have to go just when we were getting saved?'

Another pair of legs, leather jacket, cropped head, another young man, this time followed by a ladder, was let down, and then braced firmly against one of the steel crossbeams. The young man said, 'Lieutenant Jackson. Who's in charge here?'

Martin said, 'Well, I suppose I am, or was. But you take over, son, I've not got much left.'

'Commander Thorpe wants all of you out of here as fast as you can. There are blankets up topside. Will those of you who are able, go up the ladder as quickly as possible, where you'll be looked after. If anyone can't, we'll send men down to bring you up.'

Martin said, 'I guess we all can, except for...' and he nodded in the direction of Belle Rosen.

The young man looked and said, 'She sick?' And then added, 'Oh, I'm sorry. We'll have her out after the rest of you. Can the women go first, please?'

Two sailors dropped down. They saw the seamed face of an older officer topped by the gold-braided, white cap of a Commander in the opening calling, 'All right, Tom, get them started.'

Martin said, 'It's all over. They want us out. The women first.'

And now that their release was at hand, each one of them felt the strangest reluctance at moving, as though they were wishing to tempt Fate by not hurrying, almost as though they were afraid to climb up one more set of steps to face a world where things were rightside up.

'Please,' urged Lieutenant Jackson.

Martin said, 'Miss Kinsale, will you go first?'

All through their climb it seemed that after Scott, Miss Kinsale had been first. She looked both bewildered and embarrassed. During the last stages of their ordeal her nudity had not worried her. She had not seemed even to be aware of it. But now with strangers about she became conscious of it again and she said, 'Must I?'

A sailor said, 'There's a blanket up there for you, lady. Can I help you?'

Miss Kinsale said, 'I really oughtn't to be the first. There are others who...'

The sailor coaxed, 'Lady, let me give you a hand.'

She said, 'No, thank you, I'm quite all right,' and marched up the ladder steadily.

They heard the voice of the Commander with its note of urgency, 'Come along the others, please. What's the delay, Jackson? Do you want more men? Do they need help?'

Muller thought: *He must be afraid she's going down.* Aloud he said to Nonnie, 'Get up there quickly.'

Nonnie said, 'I don't want to leave you.'

Muller snapped, 'Do as I say.' Frightened by his tone she went. He ordered, 'Susan... Jane...' The three women crawled up the ladder and vanished from view.

Shelby watched them go. Even in this last moment he had failed to be decisive.

Martin said, 'Okay, Rosen, Shelby, Muller, Rogo, Kemal. I'll go last.'

Rogo said, 'Nix! I go last. I've sucked hind tit all the way up. I might as well stick to it. Maybe if I have any luck, this can will go down before I make it.'

Rosen said, 'I don't go without... her.'

Shelby had a moment of panic mixed with anger. Always the Rosens, the cause of frustrations and delays. What if the steamer were to take her final plunge before he had got up that ladder? Those damn.... But even his own mind balked at adding the word 'Jews', and he felt a flush of shame, as he looked at that obese, inert figure and thought of her brave and miraculous swim.

Martin said, 'Okay, Shelby, get up there. Muller, Kemal...'

Rogo said to Rosen, 'I'll stick with you, Manny, 'til we get her out of here. Go ahead, Martin, beat it!'

Rogo and Rosen were left alone as a sailor called up, 'Send down more blankets and some line!' The stuff came hurtling down.

Rogo advised, 'Don't look, Manny. They'll do the best they can for her. Anyway, whatever happens, she's out of it.'

The sailors wrapped the body in the blanket and made a sling for it.

Rosen asked, 'Why did this have to happen to her? She was so great, so wonderful and I always laughed when she said she had a heart. Even in the last minute I didn't really believe it.' And then he added once more, 'She was great, wasn't she?'

Rogo replied, 'Yeah, she was great, Manny. Right from the beginning she was a champ.'

Rosen suddenly looked at Rogo and said, 'Oh my God, Mike, I shouldn't be talking! You had it happen to you, too.'

Rogo said, 'Yeah, that's right.'

A sailor called up through the opening, 'Okay!' and the body of Belle Rosen began its upward journey. When it reached the aperture the feet were lowered and the head raised, so that she would pass through and then she was gone.

Rogo said, 'Okay, Manny, now you can go.'

His limbs were still shaking so that the two sailors had to hold and help him. Half-way up he turned and looked anxiously at Rogo who was standing, surrounded by the now burned-out lamps and flashlights. 'You coming, aren't you, Mike?'

In his mind Rogo had been travelling back along the shaft tunnel to the platform of the catwalk, across the upside-down engine room to recall the figure of his wife impaled. But he remembered it was no longer there.

In that last moment of retrospection he knew that he was not the kind to take his own life. He had been hoping that the ship would take it, as it had so many others and do it for him. But the ceiling was still beneath his feet. He replied reluctantly, 'Yeah, I guess so.' He climbed the ladder and out into the blinding early sunshine where a blanket was thrown over his shoulders and he stared dazed and with amazement, as were the others, at the right-side up world and flotilla that surrounded them.

CHAPTER XXIV

'Say Goodbye'

In addition to the lean, grey American destroyer escort standing off only some few hundred yards in the flat calm sea, there were two other ships. One was a modern liner of some twenty-four thousand tons with a streamlined red and blue funnel, British, the R.M.S. *London Tower* of the Antilles-Tower Line, half a mile away, its railings black with passengers. The second was a rusty German tramp freighter of twelve thousand tons, the *Helgoland.*

One motorized lifeboat from the *London Tower* was standing by close to the stern, another had made fast beneath the bow of the *Poseidon*. All about was a mass of flotsam that had not yet drifted away from the whaleback hull in the windless sea. There were empty life-rafts, unsinkable lifeboats wrenched loose from their davits at the capsizing, deck-chairs, caps, odd bits of clothing. Four U.S. Air Rescue planes cruised overhead.

The *Helgoland* had a lifeboat out as well, sloppily rowed by seamen and was messing about by the stern, until the Commander picked up a megaphone and shouted, 'What the hell are you fellows trying to do.'

A man in khaki pants and white singlet, but wearing an officer's cap, arose and trumpeted back in a thick German accent, 'We vant to get a line on her. Salvage!'

'Sheer off!' The Commander bawled irritably. 'Can't you see we're trying to get these people out of here? After that I don't care what you do.'

The German spoke an order and the rowers gave way. They sat there watching.

The Commander called down through the breach in the hull, 'Anybody else down there?'

'No sir!'

'Check again and hurry. She's not going to last much longer.' He turned to the group and said, 'All of you here? Anyone missing of your party?'

Jane Shelby said, 'I've lost my son Robin. He was ten.'

The Commander repeated, 'Your boy? Where was he? Was he just with you?'

Jane said, 'No. Much farther down, much earlier. I can't remember which deck—we climbed so many. It was when the lights went out and there was a rush.'

The Commander said, 'We've only picked up three sailors in a life-raft,' and then added, 'but we're taking some people off from the bow. He may have got into that group. I'll ask. What was his full name?'

'Robin Shelby.'

A radio man was standing by with a walkie-talkie. The Commander said, 'Check on the bow and ask if there's a ten-year-old boy named Robin Shelby.'

For the first time the party became aware of the activity at the other end of the *Poseidon*, two city blocks away.

It was too far off to recognize faces, but there were passengers and sailors and Muller noticed in the bright, semi-tropical, morning light several black dinner-jackets of the men passengers stood out incongruously. He was conscious of a strange resentment and he wondered whether Shelby and Martin felt the same, for he saw them shielding their eyes and staring down in that direction.

All through the harrowing climb under Scott's leadership he had thought of the rescue of himself and the others, if achieved, as an exclusivity limited to them as a reward for their courage and effort. They had fought and overcome insuperable odds, had suffered horror, fear and death and had won through. He was aware even that he had been thinking of the newspaper stories beginning, 'The sole survivors of the *Poseidon* disaster were...'

There they were in the stern, ten scarecrows, bruised, filthy, naked, shocked and exhausted and at the far end were others being lifted from a similar hole, some apparently still fully clothed.

What had happened? How had they managed? Had there been some easy way of access to the bow? Had they simply climbed or walked there without travail or trouble, and waited for rescue? Or had they, too, been through some terrible adventure and by what right? Who had led them? Had they, also, left dead behind them on the way?

Muller was haunted by speculation as to what would have happened to them if instead of following Scott they had waited with the others in the dining-room. Would they have managed just as well and perhaps without losing so many members of their party? The sight of those others emerging aroused a sense of bitter loss and deprivation in him and increased his self-loathing so that he could not rejoice that others, too, had made their way to safety. Then he thought that if he had remained in the dining-room he never would have met Nonnie...

All of them were staring at the continuing operation at the bow. Shelby was thinking; *Oh God, please let Robin be there!* And then he thought of himself as asking this favour of whom and what? And he knew that he had lost his last security. Along with his marriage belief in the God Service to which one could apply for help had been destroyed.

And yet, kneeling close by the red-painted keel, blanketed like an Indian, Miss Kinsale quite alone and unconcerned was offering up her final prayer of gratitude, 'I thank Thee, Lord, that Thou hast seen fit to spare us.'

Shelby's mind went back to his feeling of embarrassment that moment so long ago when Scott had gone down upon his knees. He felt confused, choked and close to breakdown.

Martin was thinking that he, too, used the name of God and he was both frightened and ashamed. The thought went:

My God, what if Wilma Lewis were to be amongst them? He again saw his whole way of life threatened.

Kemal, the Turk, had no shame. He was shading his eyes trying to identify crew members who were being brought up from the hole in the bow. He was hoping that none of them would be from the group he had abandoned. He wanted to be the only one clever enough to have saved himself by joining on with the mad priest and his friends.

The radio man, who had been muttering into his walkie-talkie, now said, 'Sir!'

The Commander replied, 'Yes, Harper?'

'There's no ten-year-old boy, Robin Shelby, up forward, sir.'

'Is that every one now?'

'Yes sir. Thirty-two passengers; twelve crew.'

The Commander said, 'I'm sorry, ma'am, there's no child with those people.'

Jane thanked the Commander and then asked, 'Will you be able to look any further? Is there any possible hope?'

'Ma'am, between here and up there it's all double bottom. We might try a cut, but...'

The hull beneath their feet shuddered and from deep within the ship came a rumbling. A great belching bubble arose from her port side, throwing up oil in a geyser-like eruption that disturbed the flat calm of the sea on that beautiful morning. The body of a man in sailor's dungarees came up with it.

The Commander ordered, 'Call in that lifeboat! Get these people off at once.'

The radio man talked rapidly into his walkie-talkie; other sailors signalled and the lifeboat with the legend 'LONDON TOWER' on her bow, closed in and made fast to the lines festooning the twenty-five-foot high side of the bottom-up hull. The two gigantic port-side propellers and the slab of the forty-ton rudder dwarfed everything and everyone. More of a forward tilt had developed.

'Come along! Come along!' the Commander ordered impatiently. 'Quickly with these women. The men will follow. You first, ma'am. We'll get you squared away afterwards. We've too much gear in our own boats.'

A seaman from the London Tower grasped the bottom of the Jacob's ladder which members of the *Monroe* crew had slung from the keel to the waterline.

The Commander looked at Jane keenly and asked, 'Can you manage? Will you be able to climb down?'

'Yes,' she replied and was struck by the irony that the last climb to safety should be down.

'You'll have to take off your blanket for the moment', the Commander said. 'But they have others in the lifeboat. There'll be a man to help you.' Then he repeated, 'We'll sort out where you come from when we get you away.'

So once again Jane exposed herself, still too close to the familiar nudity of the adventure to think of what she might look like, but suddenly bitterly resentful as half-way down the ladder, with a seaman preceding her and another following, she turned her head to see a photographer rise up in the stern of the lifeboat and aim a camera at her. It was the first time she had thought of a civilization to which they had succeeded against all odds in returning, and it made her feel sick.

She was followed in quick succession by her daughter, Miss Kinsale and Nonnie, then her husband and Muller, Martin and Kemal.

There seemed to be some argument going on between the Commander, the detective and Rosen, but she could not hear what was being said. Finally they, too, came down the ladder and were helped into the lifeboat by the young Third Officer in charge.

Rogo was saying, 'Don't you worry, Manny. They promised they'd bring her.' Manny must have been refusing to leave without Belle's remains.

The Commander called down, 'Okay. Thank you, that's all!'

The officer said, 'Right, sir,' and then gave the order, 'Cast off!'

The coxswain aft and the leading seaman forward let go the lines and the lifeboat fell away from the hulk as her engine stuttered into action. The ten survivors sat huddled close together, a tight little group that threw an aura of isolation about themselves from the crew of the lifeboat which included a nurse who draped blankets over them, made them comfortable and fussed about them until she became aware that they neither really needed nor wanted these ministrations, but seemed to wish to be left alone for whatever reason. She retired to the stern.

The men from the *Monroe* quickly lowered their equipment into their two motor launches, in one of which the body of Belle Rosen had already been deposited and then with their officers scrambled down themselves into the boats and stood away. The lifeboat from the German freighter now approached directly beneath the stern and a crewman managed to fling a rope around the rudder post of the *Poseidon*. They picked up the end and began to row back with it to where their ship was lying a quarter of a mile off, evidently with the intention of passing a cable through and taking the hulk in tow.

The Commander megaphoned to them angrily, 'You goddam fools, you haven't got a chance! Do you want to get sucked under? Cut loose!'

The man wearing an officer's cap replied, 'Keep your advice to yourself! We know what we're doing. There was a capsized ore carrier last year that floated for forty days. They finally had to sink her with explosives.' He laughed and then said, 'I'll call you as my witness that we were the first to get a line aboard. We've already radioed for two of our big salvage tugs.'

The exchange penetrated to the ears of the survivors. Would their ship have remained thus for forty days and forty nights? Had the whole desperate adventure then been for nothing?

Rogo said, between his teeth, 'Go on, you bitch, sink! I don't like Krauts.'

Already the tremendous effort made by the group and their triumph seemed somehow to have been diminished. All they had suffered had begun to fade into the back-ground as in one way or another they were realizing they would have to get used to the idea of living again. Muller, looking over to Martin, thought he seemed to have shrunk even more in size, almost disappearing into his blanket. He had lost his command and was no longer needed.

And still the *Poseidon* hung there, looming motionless, tall and solid as a building, the sun reflecting redly from the anti-fouling paint on her bottom.

The lifeboat began to turn in a wide circle. To the survivors the sights and sounds, the three ships stationed near by, the buzzing of the engines from cutters and launches, the wreckage strewn upon the sea and above all the implacable wall of the capsized ship seemed to come to them as though heard and seen under glass. The nerves that brought sight and sound to their brains were not yet fully functioning. They felt themselves floating between two worlds, ready for neither and for a moment Jane Shelby found herself almost wishing to be back inside the darkness, struggling upwards, reaching for a goal. Here it was achieved and she was neither prepared for it nor glad.

Susan reached out a hand from her blanket to touch her and ask, 'Are you all right, Mother?' And then she added, 'I feel so funny.'

Jane said, 'Yes, I do, too.'

The second lifeboat from the *London Tower* which had taken off the survivors from the bow section of the liner crossed their course as they were completing the circle. It was crowded and their eyes took them in but did not yet interpret what they saw:

lifeboat, crew, survivors from the *Poseidon*, sailors, several stewards still in their white jackets, women huddled under blankets, all floating upon that glassy sea, not yet ruffled by so much as a breeze. Too incongruous; too unbelievable.

Muller suddenly cried, 'My God!' and Nonnie said, 'What?' in alarm.

No more than a dozen yards separated the two lifeboats. 'It's The Beamer and his girl.' Muller shouted over, 'Hoi, there! Bates! Pamela!'

The Beamer looked up. He was still wearing his dinner-jacket, his shirt open at the neck. The girl was wrapped in a blanket and he had his arm about her. His face was quite red, and as he recognized the others, he broke into a broad grin. Both he and the girl waved. In one of The Beamer's hands was a bottle. The great and potent deity, Bacchus, had looked after his own again.

A sudden rush of tears came to Nonnie's eyes, 'I'm so happy they made it. All the time I've been thinking of them lost down there in the dark, and her staying behind to look after him.'

Miss Kinsale's thin, white arm emerged from her covering after some trouble with her long hair, to wave. She said, 'I do hope he'll take care of that child, after all she's done for him,' and then added in a curiously matter-of-fact-voice, 'But I don't suppose he will.'

Susan cried, 'Oh, but he couldn't leave her now. And didn't you see, he was holding her.'

'...and a bottle too,' Miss Kinsale concluded severely. 'He was drunk and so was she. He'll leave her, of course. I know men like him.'

Muller said, 'Actually something much worse is very likely to happen. He'll marry her and on the way back from the Register Office, she'll start to try to reform him.'

Susan thought: *How very odd to be sitting here in this boat this way, engaged in such a conversation.*

The other lifeboat finished its crossing and made for the liner.

Jane Shelby had already hungrily ransacked it with her eyes as it went by. Now she was aware that her husband's gaze was intent upon the white wake from its stern. He was shaking his head from side to side, unconscious of being observed. 'He wasn't there,' he said. He looked utterly miserable and forlorn.

Jane Shelby felt a pang at her heart and she thought: *What are we all doing here? Where have all these ships come from? Who are these people? What have they to do with us? Why have we lost my Robin? How dare we still be living? For what purpose! It's all so meaningless.*

And out of this came yet another, but this one was firm and clear. *I must repair the damage I have done. To destroy this man and all that is left, is just as senseless as everything that's happened to us all. Somewhere it must stop.*

Aloud she said, 'Richard, give me your hand. I need it.'

He looked at her in astonishment for a moment, unsure of himself and her and then took the hand she extended.

Jane said, 'We shall be needing one another to grieve together,' and then added, 'I didn't mean any of the things I said down... down there,' and she glanced up at the wall of the *Poseidon*, but already the 'down there' was beginning to dim as something that had been dreamed rather than lived through. 'I was out of my head; out of my mind with grief and worry about Robin. I didn't know what I was saying. It wasn't true, any of it. I was simply lashing out blindly. Dick… we've lost our son!'

Shelby looked at his wife in amazement, moved with emotion and yet simultaneously filled with elation, as much of the self-confidence of which he had been deprived flooded back into him again. Now that she was admitting that she had not meant them, he could not even remember any more the things she had said that had so destroyed him. They did not matter; they were not true; he had been rendered whole again. He reached for her, pulled her close to him and held her. He whispered, 'I'll try to make it up to you somehow.'

Jane covered the inward shudder she could not suppress at the cliché, by moving closer inside her husband's arms.

Susan regarded her mother with admiration and grew a little older.

Despite the tropical sun now climbing into the sky, Muller felt suddenly depressed and chilled. Intuitively without wholly hearing he had picked up Jane's gesture and everything about him was in rebellion against the wantonness of the taking of the life of a child under circumstances of the utmost cruelty. For the rest of her days this mother must be tortured as to how he had perished and to what extent she herself had been to blame for his loss. How could one both rejoice that the drunken Englishman and the poor, besotted lump of a girl who had attached herself to him were safe and at the same time mourn for the death of Belle Rosen? What was one to think of the futility of the other lives in their party snuffed out? The brave and lunatic Scott; the stuff of which saints were made? The much-sinned-against Linda? And for what great purpose had the Turk Kemal been preserved—to return to his country and thereafter to find another job —four hours on and four hours off, tending the lubrication of yet another piece of machinery? And would Rogo be any good thereafter, without his woman to torment him?

And why had he himself survived? For Nonnie whose life and person henceforth had been given over into his hands? And into what category did Nonnie fall? Reward? Punishment? Delight, or a millstone around his neck? For even now as he held her close to him, his thoughts turned to his friends and he asked himself: 'What on earth will they all say?'

Martin's head had emerged like a turtle's from his carapace of blanket and his eyes behind their gold-rimmed spectacles, too, had quested over the rescued in that other lifeboat. He half-feared, half-hoped he would see a figure, or catch a glimpse of thick, burnished hair or a flash from those eyes in which he had so often lost himself. But Mrs Wilma Lewis was not amongst them.

Martin thought to himself: *So, I am to be let off scot free, after all. Saved and maybe even a hero when the papers get the story. And I'm nothing but a rotten little runt who spent his holiday servicing a randy widow. And nobody will ever know; no punishment, no trouble. Adultery on the house.*

There was no need even to tell his wife and make her miserable. Mingled with his relief there was still that faint sense of disappointment. Somehow in some way he *ought* to have been made to suffer.

Muller turned to the officer and asked, 'Where are we? What ship are you from? Where are you going?'

'Royal Antilles Line, sir. R.M.S. *London Tower*. Veracruz, Havana, Bermuda and London. We're homeward boundnow. We'll soon have you and your friends comfortable. You've been very lucky, if I may say so, sir.'

'Yes, I know,' put in Shelby. 'Have you any idea what happened?'

The young two-striper replied, 'Seaquake, sir. We were well to the north-west of it and didn't even feel the shock. Two other ships in the area are still unreported. They may have gone down with all hands. You were luckier. The Air Force people pitched in after the news of the quake and one of their radar planes picked you up just after midnight and dropped flares that told them the story. We received a message from the shipping Computer Centre on Governor's Island at two o'clock this morning to proceed to this area to search for survivors along with the German freighter. The *Monroe* was only two hundred miles north of you on a recovery exercise for an unmanned space capsule launched from Cape Kennedy. I expect you'll learn about all of it when we get aboard, sir.'

Shelby felt his heart contract. It was as though his son had been speaking, Robin who had known about all such things as moon shots, computer centres and recovery exercises; Robin who had never had his chance to take the pathway to the stars. The stab of pain reminded him that for Jane it must be perpetual. Men simply had different mechanisms for caring about their children. It would be agony when at home he picked up the football with no one to whom to throw it. And he saw himself again on his lawn with the ball spiralling through the air, Robin racing down field and at his call, 'Look up!' turning over his shoulder and pulling it down.

His attention was recaptured by something the officer had mentioned. 'London?' Shelby said. 'But we're Americans, we don't live there.' It was almost as though he had felt all along that at the end of the climb and if he ever broke through the skin of the *Poseidon*, he would find himself back home in Detroit.

'I suppose some arrangements will be made about that, sir.'

Martin said, 'I want to get a message back to my wife in Chicago.'

The officer nodded and said, 'You'll be able to do that, I'm sure.'

Shrouded in his blanket to the crown of his head, Manny Rosen shivered and was heard to say, 'Mamma! Mamma!'

Nonnie wanted to comfort Rosen. She moved and the blanket slipped from her body, revealing the twisted pink breech clout, the strip tied around her breasts and the dead white skin streaked with oil. The engineman of the lifeboat gawped at her and somehow beneath the grime divined her as one of his own. He said, 'Coo, where was you at when it 'appened? A fancy dress ball?'

Nonnie's face suddenly went smaller and her mouth pinched and mean. She turned on him and spat out, 'Nark it!' In her voice Muller heard everything he both feared and loved: her vulgarity, her vulnerability, all the years of struggling and fending for herself and being at the mercy of anyone who wanted to make a joke or a pass.

He pulled the blanket around her shoulders again with one hand and with the other tilted up her small face and looked into it. The intemperate streak, the shadow of her commonness was still at the corners of her too-small mouth, yet he felt touched again.

Whether it was that her sharp instincts had picked up his emanation, or now that it was all over and promises made under duress of death in her mind were not meant to be kept, she whispered, 'You don't have to marry me, Hubie. And I'd never leave you. I'd stay with you as long as you wanted me to.'

He was being given his freedom and against every counsel of sanity and intelligence, he struggled against it. She would be content to be his mistress until he cast her off. It was the expedient and sensible thing to do. Every instinct told him so. They would have great fun for a while and then well, the two pieces of their different worlds that they might have tried to paste together would have come unstuck. And yet he did not wish her to have the chance to leave him, to be the first to say, 'Let's call it quits, chum.' Never!

He used again the phrase he had in the bowels of the *Poseidon* when he had tried to comfort her, 'Hush, Nonnie! It's so impractical when you're travelling.' He felt her tense body relax and was satisfied, and yet the echoes of her class would not die away entirely and holding tightly to his decision and all his desires embodied in her, he heard his inner self querying: 'What *am* I going to do? What on earth am I going to do with this girl? What will they all say? What will my life be like from now on?'

From within the *Poseidon* a muffled explosion sounded and there was another bubbling eruption of water in the vicinity of the inclined bow section. An officer's cap stiff with gold braid came up with it. Muller muttered, 'So when they renamed you *Poseidon*, they offended the god of earthquakes.'

Nonnie asked, 'What did you say, dear?'

Muller conquered the impulse to say, 'You mustn't call me "dear",' and merely replied, 'Nothing, Nonnie. Say goodbye to the ship.'

Nonnie began to cry again and because her cheeks were covered with oil, her teats retained their shape and slid whole, one after the other, down her tiny face. 'And all my chums.'

'I'm afraid so, Nonnie.' She buried her face in the folds of Muller's blanket. He loved her greatly.

CHAPTER XXV

L'Envoi

The cutter from the *Monroe* drew alongside the lifeboat and reduced its speed until the two craft were sailing parallel to one another, a few yards apart. The Commander called over, 'Is the gentleman who...' he hesitated and then added, 'Whose wife...'

Rogo shook Rosen gently by the shoulder and said, 'Manny, I think he wants to talk to you.'

Rosen's head emerged from his blanket. He blinked his wet eyes in the bright light, looking around to orient himself.

The Commander said, 'I'm sorry to bring this up in this way, sir. I haven't had the chance to learn your name yet. Your... Your wife's body has gone in our other cutter. She's being taken aboard our ship.'

Somehow even with his thinning hair stuck together and standing up from his skull and the vitality and roundness drained from his face, the little man managed to muster the most astonishing amount of dignity. He said, 'My name is Emmanuel Rosen. Please, can I be with her? I would like to be with her. Can't you take me?'

'Yes,' the Commander replied, 'we will. It won't be long now.' Then he asked, 'How many Americans are there amongst you?'

Martin, his leadership relinquished, seemed no longer interested. Muller replied for him, 'Six. Mr and Mrs and Miss Shelby, Mr Martin, Mr Rogo and myself.'

'British?'

Muller said, 'Two. Miss Kinsale here, and...' he hesitated for only the briefest moment, 'Miss Parry. Miss Kinsale was a passenger. Miss Parry was on the entertainment staff.'

The Commander asked, 'And the other?'

'He's an oiler from the engine room,' Muller explained. 'He joined our party led by...' He stopped, astonished at how completely the Reverend Frank Scott had gone out of his mind. Well, it was too long to go into now and he concluded, 'He's Turkish. His name's Kemal. He only speaks Turkish, Greek and very few words of English.'

Kemal grinned and waved a hand when he heard his name.

The Commander said, 'He'll be better off for repatriation in London then, I imagine. They can send him home from there.' He raised his voice so as to include the entire group of survivors, 'I have been in communication with the Captain of the *London Tower*. He will take all British and Europeans. There are some Belgians, Greeks and a French couple along with some more British members of the crew in the other boat. We have had our instructions from Washington. We'll take you Americans aboard the *Monroe* and put you ashore at Miami, where arrangements will have been made to get you home.'

'Oh dear,' said Miss Kinsale, 'I suppose we shall have to be saying goodbye to one another, then.' She spoke as though it might have been the last day of the voyage with luggage stacked up all about and farewells being made on the promenade deck. The others were startled. They had not yet thought to the point that they might be separated, that their odd but valiant company would be broken up. The trials they had suffered ought to have linked them together somehow for ever.

But no one knew exactly what to say to her: 'So nice to have known you,' simply would not do. Neither did expressions of sympathy at the loss of Scott appear to be in order. As far as outward appearances were concerned, Miss Kinsale seemed either to have recovered from this tragedy, or mastered her emotions. And thinking these thoughts, they were reminded themselves of how strangely and completely the Reverend Dr Frank Scott had been elided from their minds. How could someone who had played such an important part in their survival, have so wholly escaped them now that they were saved? He was simply gone, the mystery of him as yet unsolved. Had he ever really existed?

Jane Shelby came to the rescue with, 'Oh, how awful. We must write to one another.'

'Oh yes, indeed we must,' replied Miss Kinsale and made a curious little movement with her hands and then laughed self consciously saying, 'How stupid of me! Of course I haven't my handbag any more. Browne's Bank, Camberley will reach me. It's easy to remember.'

Jane said, 'A letter addressed to my husband care of the Cranborne Motors Company, Detroit, will find us.'

They were already approaching the flank of the *London Tower*. She was painted white from waterline to top deck. They could hear the splashing sound of the bilge water running from her sides, and see the massed banks of the faces of the passengers high up on the promenade and boat decks. Here and there the sun splintered sharply from the lenses of cameras pointed downwards.

The Commander said, 'Third, after you've dropped the two English ladies and the engine-room hand, will you bring the Americans over to the *Monroe*? She'll be moving in closer.'

The Third Officer replied, 'Of course, sir.'

The *Poseidon* was now farther down by the head, so that the upturned keel slanted perceptibly. Only the indomitable Germans still held connection with her. Their lifeboat towing the strand of rope, now doubled, had reached the side of the freighter and was being taken aboard. There was something ridiculous yet courageous about that absurd line snubbing her sternpost.

The sight only irritated Rogo who said, 'I hope she takes 'em all with her when she goes. They murdered my buddy at Bastogne.'

And then they were under the sheer dazzling side of the steamer. Two iron doors had been opened and a set of steps let down. The lifeboat made fast. With the proximity of those faces staring at them, Muller and Nonnie had moved apart. The bowman stepped on to the narrow landing platform and the Third Officer said, 'The British passengers, please,' and went over to Miss Kinsale. He said, 'You'd better take my arm. We'll have you in some clothes and comfortable in a moment.'

The nurse said, 'Let me help you, dear,' and put a motherly arm about Nonnie who had instinctively risen to her feet at the call for the British. She turned half helplessly to Muller and said, 'I'm British. I ought to go, oughtn't I?'

He had been so wholly unprepared for this sudden turn of events, that caught off his guard, he heard himself say, 'I suppose... Perhaps...' He looked vaguely about and made not one single, solitary movement to stop her.

The nurse was shepherding Nonnie, 'You poor thing, what you must have suffered! A cup of tea and bed for you and you'll be right as rain.'

Miss Kinsale was already on the platform steadied by a sailor. The Third Officer pulled Nonnie up alongside, followed by the nurse and Kemal. The coxswain gave an order and suddenly with that mysterious, unfelt movement that characterizes boats there were yards of open water between the lifeboat and the steamer.

Muller was standing up, a puzzled expression on his face. He cried, 'Nonnie! You'll be all right, they'll look after you.' And then almost as an afterthought he added, 'I'll come for you.'

Jane Shelby waved. 'Goodbye, Miss Kinsale! Good luck! We'll write.'

The gap widened. Rogo, Martin, the Shelbys and even Rosen were waving and calling, 'Goodbye, Miss Kinsale! 'Bye-bye, Nonnie! So long, Kemal!' It was all happening so quickly and antiseptically that Nonnie had not even time for tears.

Muller's voice carried to her, 'What was that name of your town?'

'Fareham Cross, outside Bristol. Avon Terrace,' she shouted, her voice shrill to make itself heard above the farewells, 'Number twenty-seven. They all know me mum and dad, there.' And then as what was happening at last began to dawn upon her, came a wail, 'Oh, Hubie!'

As distance diminished the tiny face into a speck punctuated only by two eyes, Muller cupped his hands and shouted again across the ever-widening strip of water, 'I'll come for you, Nonnie!'

He was still in the grip of the paralysis that had caused him to let her go and at that moment, too, was registered the certainty that he would never see her again. A feeling of desolation and emptiness seized him. What had happened? Why had he let her go? What had made him do it? Even as he saw her figure and that of Miss Kinsale vanish inside the flank of the steamer he thought of shouting to the man in charge of the boat to turn around and go back, to let him off to join her. But he did not do so. He was unable to say the words and the farther away they drew from the liner, the more impossible it all became.

His conscience was already beginning to resolve exactly how and why it had happened. It was of course the devilish coincidence that the London Tower should have been a British vessel homeward bound. Or, if Nonnie had only said, 'Do you want me to go,' instead of 'I ought to go, oughtn't I?' he would have continued to reply from his heart, 'No, no! I never want you to go.'

In the feeling of emptiness and misery that gripped him he felt he was now one with Rogo, Rosen, the Shelbys and perhaps even poor Miss Kinsale. A thought of reprieve came to him: *You have still a chance. You don't have to board the American ship. The lifeboat will be going back to the* London Tower. *You can go with it, and where she is, slip up behind her and put your hands over her eyes and she'll be in your arms again.* The picture lifted up his spirits again.

Martin was struggling desperately to wrench his mind away from that cabin buried beneath the sea in the huge hulk. He might indeed have got off scot free, but as long as the *Poseidon* was still there he could think only of Mrs Lewis. Would her eyes be open or closed?

In an effort to distract himself and wipe out the picture from his mind, he turned to the detective who was watching the operation of the German freighter trying to put a steel hawser aboard the capsized liner. She had launched another boat besides the one still attached to the stern of the *Poseidon* by the thin filament of rope.

Martin said, 'Come on, Rogo. Now that it's all over, who were you really after on our ship?' And then he added, as an idea suddenly struck him out of the blue, 'Say, look here, would it have been Scott?'

With great deliberation Rogo turned his blanketed figure towards Martin and gave him his cold, policeman's stare, the small piggy eyes peering out from a face so begrimed he looked like a minstrel man. His lips hardly moved as he replied succinctly, 'For Christ's sweet sake, why don't you leave me alone? What difference does it make now, whether I was or I wasn't? The son of a bitch is dead, isn't he? And so is my wife.' And then he added with a sudden chilly viciousness, 'And so is that big, blonde broad you were shacking up with.' Then he turned his back on Martin again.

Strangely Martin was not even startled. If anything he felt almost a curious sense of relief.

He said, 'So you knew?'

Rogo swivelled his head, 'Yeah,' he replied, 'I knew.'

For only an instant Martin wondered how Rogo had found out, before he came to the consideration of what did it matter? He had not got away with it as he had thought. Perhaps there were others as well who had known. And with this somehow his world seemed to click into place again.

Muller, who had been sitting next to Martin had heard. *Why, you little bastard!* he thought to himself. *So you're the one who got it made with her,* and he could not keep his mind from wondering how it had been and what the grey, dry, little man had looked like, sporting with the big, voluptuous woman.

And what about Rogo and Scott, Muller was wondering now? And how many things would remain unanswered from this fatal adventure?

There was a hail and the sound of a rope slapping on to the foredeck of the lifeboat. They had approached the grey steel flank of the *Monroe*, lying low in the water, her deck dotted with sailors and officers in their tropical whites.

Muller saw that her superstructure was a mass of electronic gear and antennae. Both her cutters were tied up alongside. The Commander who had organized the rescue was already on board, looking down from the rail. Two sailors manned a landing companionway.

Scott and Rogo; Rogo and Scott! 'What difference does it make, now, whether I was or whether I wasn't. The son-of-a-bitch is dead, isn't he?' The detective's answer repeated itself through Muller's mind and sent him searching back for clues in their relationship during their struggle. Rogo had hated the Minister. But then Rogo had hated everyone.

The lifeboat had been made fast and the Shelbys were being helped aboard. Rosen followed, stumbling as he went, for he had eyes only for what lay wrapped like a large package towards the stern. Muller followed with Martin and Rogo, as usual, bringing up the rear. Was there something, then, more sinister in the relationship between Linda, Scott and Rogo? Or was Rogo merely once and for all, fed up with the endless queries as to what he had been doing on the boat and had given a snotty answer? Muller again asked himself the question heard at the beginning of the voyage, Why shouldn't a policeman take a holiday cruise like anyone else? And then: how would a man like Scott become involved in anything that would call for pursuit by the tough guy of the Broadway squad? It was too absurd.

The steel deck of the *Monroe* was hot under Muller's bare feet. The Commander noticed it and said, 'We'll have you fixed up in a minute.' And then as Martin and Rogo were assisted on board, called down, 'Thank you, coxswain. Cast off!' He turned to the survivors and said, 'We have cabins and clothing ready for you.'

The names were still going around in Muller's head: Rogo; Linda; Scott. The water at the stern of the lifeboat churned white as the propeller thrashed and the boat moved off. Muller thought: *Linda dead; Scott dead; what did the two men have to say to one another when they both went down to the poor creature impaled upon that sliver of iron? And was it only petulance because he thought his God was going to spoil his achievement in bringing the party up from the depths of the overturned ship that had caused Scott to throw himself to his death? Or, had some words been slipped to him out of the side of the policeman's mouth which had made Scott determine that it was better to die than to live? No, it made no sense, but then neither did the minister's cursing of all the old biblical Gods before finishing himself off.* It was obvious there was no further information to be had from that smooth, bland, expressionless face of Rogo and never would be.

Muller looked out across the water at the diminishing stern of the lifeboat; now several hundred yards away on its last trip back to the *London Tower* lying gleaming in the ever-mounting sun, and felt an icy pang at his bowels. Nonnie! His resolve to go to her! Absorbed with his thoughts of Scott, he had blindly and like a sheep followed them all on board and let the boat get away.

Involuntarily he raised his arm in a gesture that was the beginning of a wave to try to summon them back, even as he realized its futility. They would neither see it nor, if he were to shout, hear.

He was aware suddenly of Rogo's cold eyes on him and the sneering orifice forming at the side of his mouth from which the words emerged, 'So you let her go.'

Muller did not reply. There was nothing he could say, for it was true.

But Rogo was not yet through. The flat monotone of his voice never changed as he said, 'I always knew you was a prick.' Nor was there anything that Muller could say to that evaluation either. And Rogo added finally, 'I'd say it was a break for the kid at that. Guys like you are poison for anybody with a heart.' And with this he turned his back upon Muller.

The doctor had joined the Commander and said, 'I think, sir, we had best get these people to rest and some treatment. They've been pretty badly shaken up,' when there was a stir that ran all through the men aboard the destroyer escort and sudden shouts and cries of, 'There she goes! She's going!'

There was a rush to the rail. The Commander, the doctor and the seven Americans remained fixed and staring, watching frozen as half a mile away, the bow of the gigantic black whale-back suddenly dipped beneath the glaze with which the sun had varnished the surface of the sea and inevitably began to slide forward.

There was another startled shout from the men on the frigate. The seaman at the bow of one of the German freighter's boats which had been attached to the hulk by a line, was not smart enough with his axe to cut loose, and in a split second before the line parted, the craft had been overturned, spilling the men into the sea. Aboard the *Monroe*, Mike Rogo threw back his head and laughed chillingly, 'Drown, you Kraut bastards!' he shouted.

The stem of the *Poseidon*, her quadruple screws looking like giant electric fans, lifted high into the air and it seemed that she was about to go to eternity silently, when with a suddenness that made Muller jump, the three ships standing by tied down their whistle chords, sirens and hooters in a last mourning cry and salute to the one-time queen of the sea.

For a moment yet she hung there and then with dignity and a grave despairing finality, slid beneath the surface. Where she had once been there was now nothing but a mass of oil slick and floating debris, through which the second lifeboat from the German freighter picked its way to the other members of its crew floundering in the water.

James Martin thought: *So I'm not to be let off scot free after all; there is to be punishment. Maybe old Hell-Fire Hosey had something.* Martin told himself that Rogo was a tough little monkey and a cop. He might not be above blackmail. And had Muller overheard as well? Martin knew that in the end when he got home, he would tell.

Emmanuel Rosen had slipped unnoticed from the group and had seated himself, head in his hands, by the wrapped figure on the hot steel deck.

When the shouting arose and the sirens roared, he looked up in time to see the last of the *Poseidon* and murmured, 'Mamma, Mamma, I wish I was on it still. I wish we both were.'

Jane and Richard Shelby were standing shoulder to shoulder, Susan by herself some little distance away. Shelby's mind was racing to the beginning of the catastrophe and he was asking himself, 'Ought I not have followed Scott? Was the man some kind of a lunatic? A screw loose from being hit on the head by football players? Were those taken off from the bow the people who had remained quietly in the dining-room, waiting for an officer to come and tell them what to do? And if he had done so, would his son still be alive? How could a man know? What could a man do? And now they would never know what had happened to the boy. But he thought to himself: *Jane has forgiven me whatever*, and slid his arm about her waist and from somewhere she summoned the strength not to pull away from him.

It was a terrible moment for her to be hoping and praying that her son was already dead, that the piece of her flesh that was being torn from her side was no longer animate or conscious and that he need not suffer a second death, that what she was witnessing was only his burial.

She bore no grudges, blamed no one but herself and the lie she had lived for this tragedy. And she now bade a silent farewell not only to her son, but to that other self that had emerged for so brief a moment, too late and was now gone, to be buried as deeply and finally as the unhappy ship.

Susan Shelby was gripping the rail hard and letting the tears flow for all the losses she had sustained on this fatal voyage: her brother, her youth, her image of her father and of her home.... But there was yet for her another reason to weep.

The eyes from which the tears fell too had strained as the lifeboat from the *London*

Tower carrying the rescued crew members had passed. She had been looking for a baby face, light-blue eyes and pink cheeks beneath sandy hair, a head that she had held close to her breast. It was not there. This boy, hardly older than herself, whose random encounter with her would for ever change her life, had been snuffed out like all the rest. She was unable in her mind to see him in his death, wherever it had overtaken him, but only knew that it was unfair for him not to have had his chance.

And then with a curious, surging desperation that rose from some depth inside her came the wish, the hope and thereafter even a prayer that she might be pregnant by him; that he had not died wholly, that a part of him had been left behind to live the life that he had lost. And she saw and felt that if it were so, the birth would be one of the most momentous joy for her.

It would be a child like himself, with the beautifully formed mouth, a button nose and rosy cheeks and she would take it one day to—where was it? Her mind reverted for an instant to that dark and terrifying moment, but it seemed dark and terrifying no longer, but only a happening. Hull, that was it! He had said he had come from Hull, and his mum and dad had a fish and chip shop there. It should not be so difficult to find the parents of a young sailor who had gone down in the *Poseidon* catastrophe and place the child in their arms and say, 'Herbert didn't die really, all of him. This is a part of him.' And at the picture she smiled to herself and whispered, 'Please, God, let it be so.'

www.ingramcontent.com/pod-product-compliance
Lightning Source LLC
LaVergne TN
LVHW090034270225
804405LV00003B/47